THE SPARK

THE SPARK

BOOK ONE *of the* GEMMA CHRONICLES

J. A. SAUNDERS

Visit J. A. Saunders' website at www.jasaundersbooks.com or contact J. A. at jasaundersbooks@protonmail.com

The Spark

First Edition.

ISBN: 979-8-9870926-0-6

Library of Congress Control Number: 2022918752

Cover art by: Natasha Nicole - www.natashanicoleartistry.com

Printed in the United States of America

For Mom and Dad

Without your love and support, this book never would have seen the light of day. Especially you, Mom. Thank you for being my sounding board. Thank you both for giving me the courage to jump.

Kings Hills
The Veil Forest
Binthrell Forest
Kapür
Millisthia Lake
Tyreen Bridge
Eidärien Lake
Mountain Rise
Tyreen
Dano
The Cattaway
Seakvia Lake
The Verlasian Lands
N
W   E
S

EIGHTEEN YEARS AGO

It was a cool country night in an evergreen forest clearing. A small log house nestled next to a quiet flowing brook. The house contained a happy family of five. Warm firelight flickered, scattering dancing shadows across the trees. Singing, often interrupted by the high-pitched laughter of children, floated through the air, tickling the ears of the surrounding forest life.

Dean picked up his six-year-old daughter, Serania, tossing her in the air, triggering squeals of excitement. The middle child, Andrea, joined in the laughter as she was spun around by her mother, Thalia. The youngest sister, baby Gemma, giggled, pumped her arms, and kicked her legs, infected by her family's joy and delighted by her parents' singing.

"In the dark of night shines a great light.
Not without, but within resides your might!
Let go, let go, no longer control.
Let go, let go, in tune with your soul.
Let go and remember to allow full surrender.

No walls, and no tether, can hold back the power.
Let go, let go, see not with your eyes.
Let go, let go, the shell is a disguise!"

Dean fell to the floor, Serania landing in a laughing heap on his belly.

"Sing it again, sing it again!" she pleaded, lisping her s's because of her missing front teeth.

Dean laughed. "I wish I had an ounce of your energy, my little caterpillar!" He tickled her sides and was rewarded with even higher squeals.

Andrea wriggled free from her mother's arms, going to her elder sister's defense. "No more tickling!" she demanded, her fists on her hips, ready to fight.

"Ah, my little soldier, come to save your sister from the tickle monster!" Dean's eyes twinkled with mischief while Andrea worked to pry his fingers from Serania. Soon both girls piled on top of their father, giggling while they held him down.

Thalia laughed and shook her head as she picked up Gemma, who had rolled over onto her tummy and was trying to crawl toward her siblings. "Oh no, you don't. You're too young to join in that, my love."

The baby looked up at her mother, confused and angry to be told no, then looked back to the happy scene in front of her. She leaned forward, reaching out her arms to her father, hoping he would let her join.

The front door opened with a loud bang as it hit the wall behind it, making all five family members jump and the youngest cry. Their friend, Bruce, rushed into the house, looking pale and winded. "Dean! They've found you! They're on the way here; you need to run!" he doubled over, gasping for breath, his hands shaking on his thighs.

Thalia shared a knowing look with her husband. They had discussed the chance this might happen but hoped this day would never come. She subtly shook her head, not wanting to believe what she was hearing, and pulled Gemma closer, holding her protectively against her chest.

Dean took Andrea's hand and placed it in Serania's, then knelt so he was eye to eye with them. "Serania, my love, I need you to be brave. I need you to take care of your sister. Can you do that for me?"

Serania nodded, her eyes wide and her face white. She sniffed as tears spilled down her cheeks.

Dean gently wiped the tears away. "Never let go of your sister's hand. Stay with your mother, but do not let go of Andrea's hand, okay?"

Serania nodded again. "Yes, Daddy," she whispered, trying to put on a brave face.

"That's my girl!" Dean wiped another tear from her eye.

"Dean, we don't know how much time we have; you must go now!" Bruce urged.

Dean tenderly touched Andrea's face. "Be strong my little soldier." He stood and turned to face his wife.

Thalia's muscles tightened, her stomach squeezing into a tight knot, while Gemma's crying escalated, feeling the tension in her mother's body.

Dean took his wife's face into his hands, holding her gaze, the look in his eyes as strong as steel. "Thalia, take the girls out the back door and run. Do not stop. Do not look back. And no matter what, do not come back for me."

Thalia shook her head, refusing to accept what she heard. How could she leave the man she had loved for what felt like her entire life? "I won't leave you. I'll fight by your side! We're better together!" Her voice came out tight, fighting back the tears burning at the back of her eyes.

Bruce turned from looking out the window. "Dean!"

They were out of time.

Dean kissed Thalia tenderly. "I love you, Thalia." He gently caressed his youngest daughter's blond hair, giving her a light kiss on her forehead. Turning to his older daughters, he gave each a kiss as well. "And I love all three of you girls."

Thalia could see the struggle in his eyes, trying to be brave for his wife and daughters, while at the same time holding back the pain of saying goodbye. A lifetime of memories flashed before her eyes. Memories she thought she'd have years more to add to.

Dean looked once again into Thalia's blue eyes. "I can't fight well if I'm worried about protecting you four. Take the girls, keep them safe. You're the only chance they have." He grabbed a sword he had hidden in a cupboard. "Now go. We'll buy you as much time as we can." He and Bruce both nodded grimly to each other.

Thalia knew by their faces that both men accepted they wouldn't live through this night. With her final glimpse into the face of the only man she had or ever would love, Thalia grabbed a child's blanket from nearby and used it to secure her youngest daughter to her. She took Serania's hand, and fled out the back door, willing herself not to look back. Her breathing came in ragged, short breaths as she fought the pain of her heart ripping in two. She ran as fast as possible with Serania half-holding, half-dragging Andrea. To Andrea's credit, she didn't cry, but with her mouth clenched tightly, did her best to keep up with her mother and older sister.

They were only seconds from the house when the sound of shouting and metal against metal reached Thalia's ears. Her chest tightened painfully, knowing the chances of her husband living for more than a few minutes were slim. She forced her legs to keep going, picking Andrea up every few steps when she stumbled while tears ran freely down her face. Gemma's cries grew into loud wails. Thalia tried to calm her while they ran, but nothing would assuage her youngest daughter's fear.

Thalia's steps faltered as the cacophony far behind her ceased. Her husband and Bruce were dead, and now they would be coming after her and the girls. She pulled Serania in front of her, kneeling. She was about to do the hardest thing she had ever had to do. Her voice shook as she tried to be strong for her girls. "Serania, take Andrea, go as fast and as far as you can into the forest. Go to our secret place, okay? Can you do that for Mommy?"

Serania nodded, wiping her eyes and nose with the back of her hand.

Thalia smiled through her tears, pulling Serania into a tight hug. "You are such a brave, strong girl." She released Serania from the hug, holding her at arm's length, and her voice broke as her chin quivered. "Wait until morning in our place, then start working your way to Bracken's house. He will help you. Can you remember how to get there?"

Serania nodded again before her eyes pinched tightly, and she swung her arms around Thalia's neck, holding tight. "I don't want to go, Mommy! Please don't make me go!"

Thalia squeezed her daughter firmly, unable to tell who was shaking worse; she or her daughter. Reluctantly she peeled her daughter from her neck, forcing her back. "I'm so sorry, my love, but I need you to go. I can't go with you this time." She brushed tears from Serania's cheeks, but more replaced them as fast as she wiped them, making the gesture useless. "You need to be strong for your sister. She needs you to keep her safe. Can you be brave for me, sweetheart?"

"Y-yes, Mommy." Serania's voice was nearly inaudible through the saliva and tears mingling in her mouth, but she pulled her shoulders back, holding her head higher, accepting the responsibility.

Thalia knew it was a lot to ask of her, but it was the only chance she could give them. She took a necklace from her pocket and put it on Serania's neck with shaking fingers. "Take this. Keep it hidden." She tucked the necklace under the collar of Serania's dress. "Never lose it, never let it out of your sight, and don't wear it unless you have to."

Thalia turned and studied her middle daughter's face. Even in the chaos and all the fear, the little four-year-old's face was stern, looking like she was ready to fight. Andrea had never been afraid of much; she was born to be a protector. "Andrea, you must stay with your sister. You two need to protect each other, okay?"

Andrea gave a grave nod. Thalia hugged them both one more time and sent them off. She felt the last tendrils of her heart tear into a million pieces as she watched her two daughters slowly disappear into the darkness. Andrea looked back with wide tearless eyes. Her tiny face was white, and she looked like she was about to pull away from Serania before the darkness took them both. Thalia's resolve almost broke. She considered running after her daughters and going with them, but she knew they would never stand a chance with Gemma crying as she was.

With a soft anguished cry, Thalia ran in the opposite direction of her two girls. She knew the men who had killed her husband would find her; they would follow her baby's crying. Once they did, they would kill her, too, when they found out she didn't have what they were looking for.

Thalia stopped as soon as she was far enough away from where she had parted from her two daughters, falling hard to her knees. She fumbled with the knot tied in the blanket that held her child to her snugly, but soon had it undone, and gently placed the crying baby in the bushes. Leaning over her, she pushed the hair from her daughter's face. "I love you so much, my dear Gemma." She kissed her forehead, her tears mixing with her daughter's. Sitting up, she took another necklace from her pocket. "Do you know why we called you Gemma?" She waved her hand over a part of the blanket, and a pocket opened. "Because you are more precious than any gem in the world." A sob poured from her throat as she placed the necklace in the pocket, waving her hand over the opening to seal it shut again. "I'm so sorry, sweetheart. I won't be here for you and your sisters as you grow up."

She said a silent prayer to the Creator for her daughters as she stood, praying the men would not bother Gemma once they had dealt with her, and if so, someone would come along and find her. Many hunted in these woods, there was a good chance someone would eventually come along.

But what if they don't come soon enough? The thought of her daughter slowly dying, abandoned in the forest, weakened her knees. The thought of the men tracking her other two daughters and slaughtering them without remorse was too much to comprehend.

She gazed down at her daughter one last time. "I will always love you," she whispered, her voice barely audible due to the tightness of her throat. Then, squaring her shoulders and standing to her full height, she doubled back, pushing her legs to the brink; Gemma's cries growing fainter behind her.

The sound of breaking branches and men running drew closer. Thalia stopped, slowly lowering to her knees on the forest floor. She spoke to the wind, her eyes looking straight ahead. "I'll be joining you soon, my love."

The shadow of a man emerged from behind a tree into her line of vision, followed shortly by another man with a torch. By the torchlight, Thalia could make out the last man she would ever see. A sneer distorted his handsome face, the firelight reflecting off many silver-capped teeth. His hair was worked into long dreads pulled back by a leather tie behind his neck.

"Thalia, Thalia...did you have to make us chase you into this revolting forest?" He chopped a few branches out of his way with his sword. "You knew you could never outrun us. Why couldn't you make it easy on us as your husband did?"

At the mention of Dean, Thalia's muscles tightened, and some of the fear fell away. She lifted her chin. "You will never find what you're looking for, Fovos."

Fovos' sneer turned into a scowl. "Now see, that's what Dean said before I put my blade through his gut." He waved his sword in front of her face. "He's not dead yet. I decided to let him slowly bleed out. Do you know how long it can take to die from a gut wound? It can take days sometimes." His eyes glinted in the firelight. "Especially if you know exactly where to pierce them through."

Heat rushed to Thalia's cheeks as her anger grew, but she refused to give him the satisfaction of any more of a reaction.

His face darkened and his jaw shook, enraged by her silence. "Where are they?" He slapped her hard across the face, knocking her to the ground.

Blood filled her mouth, and a tooth moved loosely. Her pulse pounded in her ears. She smiled in satisfaction as she looked him in the eyes. "You lose again! You will always lose!"

Fovos yelled as he raised his sword over his head. But before he could swing, the man holding the torch grabbed his arm. "We can't kill her! We need to keep her alive to find them."

Fovos yanked his arm free. "No amount of torture will work on this one. We'll have to find them without her."

"We can't go back empty-handed. You know what he'll do to us—"

Fovos swung around; his sword tip held at the torchbearer's throat. "Undermine me again, and I will add your rotting corpse to the ones back in the house."

The torchbearer put his hands up and backed away. "I'm not taking the blame for this if we can't find them."

Fovos spit in the torchbearer's direction and turned back to Thalia. "Looks like you lose." He plunged the sword into her abdomen. Pulling it free, he bent down and slowly drew the sword across her throat, watching with a slight grin as the light faded from her eyes. Standing, he wiped the sword on his pants, pausing as he heard a faint cry from deeper within the forest. "Search her," he indicated the woman with a sharp jerk of his chin.

As the torchbearer reluctantly searched the woman's bloody body, Fovos stomped to the source of the crying. He came to a small moving bundle lying on the forest floor. Squatting down, he used the tip of his sword to move the blanket aside and roughly searched around the child. Coming up empty, he punched the ground, cursing, making the baby scream even louder.

The torchbearer came up behind him. "The mother doesn't have them, sir."

Fovos stood with a guttural shout. "She must have sent them with the other two brats." He grabbed the torchbearer's tunic, making the man flinch as he pulled him close to his face, "Find them, search every part of this forest. Tear the whole thing down or set it on fire if you must! We're not leaving here empty-handed!" He shoved the man back.

The torchbearer straightened his tunic, keeping his eyes low, and dipped his head, "Yes, sir!" He glanced at the crying baby. "What about that one?"

Fovos flicked his gaze down, his lips lifting with disgust. "Kill this one. It's of no use to us."

The torchbearer flinched as Fovos brushed past him back into the forest. His insides tightened as he stared down at the screaming baby. Pulling his sword free, he stepped over to the child, but seeing her defenseless form, he couldn't bring himself to kill her. He sold his sword, not his soul. Bending, he wrapped the blanket around her, tucking in the sides to keep out the cold night air and covering her head as much as he dared. "I'm sorry I'm such a coward, little one. I know it might be better to kill you and get it over with. Put you out of your misery, but I can't. Maybe someone will find you."

Standing, he shook his shoulders, trying to ignore the chill working its way down his back. It felt akin to someone pouring icy water over him; he knew he'd be cursed for this. He moved away quickly, leaving the child's cries to haunt the uncaring forest.

Thomas rolled his head from side to side, trying to relieve the ache that had set in. It had been a long day at the market. He was made to work with his hands, not stand all day talking people into buying his fare. That's why, when he married Mariah, they started a farm together so he could be outside, work the land, and keep moving. He never anticipated how much he would dread every market day.

Once every week, he would go to the market and sell any extra produce they had to help buy the tools and feed needed to keep the farm running. But standing still, trying to shout louder than the other vendors, trying to get people's attention, was never something he wanted to do. To make matters worse, his mare was close to giving birth and required rest at home, forcing him to walk back in the dark, pulling a heavy and uncooperative cart behind him.

As he walked along the road, something in the air seemed off. He shivered, pausing to pull his cloak tighter and rub some blood flow into his bad leg. Thirty-six years ago, shortly after he and Mariah were married, a wagon fell on top of him and his leg had never been the same. The long day of standing, mixed with the travel to and from the market, was taking a toll on his aging body. All he wanted to do was get home as fast as he could.

He took note of a faint path off the road, which headed through the forest; it was one he'd taken on many occasions. If he took the path, he could shave off a lot of time, but it would be dark, and he had never traversed it with a cart before. He took a step forward but stopped again. Looking into the forest, he felt drawn, like the forest was beckoning him in. The wind blew through the trees, sounding like voices whispering in anticipation. He knew it was probably his tired mind playing tricks on him, but he couldn't shake the feeling that he needed to go that way. With a short sigh, he shook his head and headed toward the forest path.

Trudging deeper and deeper into the forest, Thomas grumbled to himself about the roots that made it hard to pull the cart along. "Brilliant idea Thomas, going on a path not designed for carts in the dark." He spoke out loud, the noise helping dispel the night's gloomy feel.

The density of the canopy above made the temperature drop a few degrees, reminding him that winter was coming, and it was coming fast. Soon his only trips to town would be once a month for supplies or to sell livestock. Faint sounds in the distance made him halt. He thought he heard shouting, and maybe even screaming, though he couldn't be sure. He strained his ears to pinpoint what direction they were coming from, but in the dry air, the sound carried far, making it impossible. He shook his head and hastened on, hearing what sounded like the occasional shout, until the night sounds faded back to nothing more than the crickets and small wildlife flitting from tree to tree.

As the night sounds steadied, his mind wandered. This night was different, as if something breathed into his soul to be ready. Ready for what, he didn't know, but he had long ago learned to pay attention to the nudging of the unseen.

A flash of movement in the corner of his vision made him jump and drop the cart handles, pulling his hands up to cover his startled heart. He turned, half expecting to see only a shadow, and calmed as a small fluffy creature, the likes of which he'd never seen before, moved into the light.

"Well, hello there! You scared me half to death, little fellow." His heart rate slowly calmed.

The animal was about the size of a man's closed fist, and not a large one, at that. It had big round ears and a long bushy tail. A strip of dark grey fur encircled ice blue eyes that held an intelligent stare. The rest of its body was covered in snow-white fur that gleamed in the lantern light. It rose to its hind legs and held one squirrel-like forefoot up, pointing into the forest, its head swiveling from Thomas to the direction it was pointing and back again.

Thomas followed the critter's pointing with his eyes. "You want me to go in there?" He didn't know why he asked the animal the question. It wasn't like an animal could understand him.

The creature squeaked and ran with the occasional hop toward the direction it had been pointing. For one moment, Thomas thought better of following an unknown animal, albeit a cute one, into the dark forest. What sane person would do that? But as he debated, the tug returned to his soul with a single word: *Trust.*

Shaking his head, he took the lantern from the cart and followed where the creature had gone, praying he wasn't making a mistake.

They walked for some time. The fluffy animal would occasionally pause, turning around as if to make sure Thomas was still following, then proceed on. More than once, it lifted one foreleg, making a gesture like it wanted Thomas to hurry up. Soon the animal stopped and spun in circles, squeaking emphatically and jumping up and down. Next to it, a small bundle lay on the cold ground, wriggling intermittently.

Thomas slowly set the lantern down and knelt by the bundle. He saw that it was a blanket of some sort and opened it to check what was inside. "Oh, my! What in Elefrisia are you doing out here?"

The little girl was dangerously cold to the touch, and Thomas could tell by her eyes that she had been crying for quite some time. Her little fingers and lips looked blue in the lamplight. When he picked her up, she whimpered, too exhausted to cry. "Shhh, it's okay; I'm not going to hurt you," he said, holding her close to do his best to provide her warmth.

He scanned the surrounding area. "How did you come to be here? Who do you belong to?"

Squeaking at his feet drew his eyes down. The fluffy animal scurried deeper into the forest, looking back and squeaking.

Thomas picked up the lantern, following the animal until it stopped, pointing once again. Thomas stepped closer, going cold with what he saw. A young woman lay on the forest floor, the dirt looking black from the blood that soaked into it. She was a beautiful woman. Her waist-length brown hair fanned out around her, and blue eyes stared unseeing at the forest ceiling. Even in death, he could see kindness etched onto the woman's face. He knew this woman must have been the baby's mother. His heart broke for the little one he held in his arms as he tried to imagine what must have transpired to lead to this gruesome outcome. The light from his lantern seemed to dim as if the world itself was mourning for the woman, now lifeless on the ground.

Thomas sighed and shook his head as he turned to the furry animal. "There's no shortage of cruelty in this world, is there, my little friend?"

The animal's ears and tail drooped as it nodded in agreement.

Thomas refused to leave the woman lying there like that. He took the child to the cart and laid her gently in it. She whimpered quietly, and he feared she might be too close to death to save. The animal hopped onto the baby's stomach, curling up and trying to provide warmth with its tiny body.

Thomas smiled grimly, "Watch over her for a moment for me, would you?" The animal dipped its head solemnly as Thomas headed back for the woman.

He struggled to carry the woman back to his cart, often stopping to catch his breath and give his bad leg a rest, but soon he had her loaded. He tied the baby in her blanket around him, hoping his body warmth would keep her alive while they traveled. The fluffy animal worked its way down into the blanket to be as close to the baby as possible.

Thomas glanced back toward the forest and thought he saw a glint of light, but it was gone fast enough to make him wonder if his mind was playing tricks on him. He gently patted the baby's back before picking up the cart handles to finish the journey home.

Many thoughts played through his mind as he limped along the path. He had planned to have Jim, one of his workmen, go to market today for him. He wondered what would have happened to the child if Jim had gone. He wouldn't have needed to take the shortcut through the woods. Would the child have been left to freeze to death in the night? The cold night air pierced his nostrils, reminding him to pull faster for the baby's sake. Not for the first time, he cursed having a bad leg. If he could run and didn't have to pull the wagon, he could make it home from this point in less than thirty minutes. As it was, it took him the better part of an hour before he saw the fence marking his property.

At long last, he could see the warm lights of his house breaking through the pitch-black night. Mariah must have been watching for him, for light came flooding out as she opened the door.

"Thomas!" She called with a strained voice, "What took you so long? I was beginning to worry…" Her voice slowly trailed away as she saw the bundle tied to her husband.

Thomas couldn't see her face with the light behind her, but he had been married to her long enough to guess the look of confusion that must be written there.

"I had a bit of a detour today, my love."

He set the cart down and walked up to his wife, untying the blanket as he entered the house. Mariah looked at him quizzically, her face filling with wonder as soon as she laid eyes on the contents of the bundle.

"What is this, Thomas?" she asked as she reached for the baby, carefully picking her up and holding her close.

"I'm not sure of the story, but I am sure it must be a sad one. This baby was in the forest along with a dead woman, who I assume must have been her mother," he said wearily, his shoulders slumped with exhaustion.

"What?" Mariah looked down at the child with tears forming in her eyes. "They killed the mother and left the baby to die in the cold? Who would be that cruel?"

"I don't know, but I was led to them by that little guy," he said, pointing to the animal that had jumped down upon entering the house and was now standing on their table, staring intently at the baby.

Mariah smiled. "So, you were sent to watch over her, were you?" She stroked the creature's small fluffy head. It leaned into her hand while a soft purring sound vibrated from its throat.

Thomas looked at her, puzzled. "What do you mean?"

She lifted her head in surprise. "Sometimes I forget that you and I grew up in two distinctly different parts of Elefrisia." She held her free hand out, and the animal hopped into it. "This little guy is a Scruff, Tom. They're intelligent creatures, though rarely seen in these parts. They're not too fond of many people and choose carefully who to befriend. You don't ever want to be on the bad side of a Scruff." She lowered the Scruff back to the table. "They're known to be mischievous toward those they don't like. No one knows why, but sometimes they choose a person they want to protect. There's speculation there must be a Scruff king who gives them the order to watch specific people. Some history even suggests they used to watch over the royals."

"Well, that one's decided that the baby is his. He rode in the blanket, keeping an eye on her the whole way home," Thomas said as he walked back to the door.

"Where are you going?" Mariah set the child on the couch near the fireplace as she warmed up some goat milk.

He sighed heavily. "Someone needs to bury the mother. I don't know who she was, but she deserves a proper burial."

Mariah nodded sadly. "I'll take care of the child. You do what you must."

He took one more long look at the small infant, then walked outside, preparing himself for the unhappy task ahead.

Mariah prepared a bottle of milk. She only had the bottles they used to feed the kid goats since she and Thomas were never able to have children of their own, but she made do with what she had. The baby cried, not liking the taste of the goat's milk or the foreignness of the bottle, but soon instinct took over, and she was drinking her fill.

Mariah's muscles relaxed, and she said a silent prayer of thanks that the baby took to the bottle so quickly. "Don't worry, little one. No one will hurt you here."

She hummed to the baby while she ate. Soon the little girl's body was warm, her stomach full, and she fell fast asleep.

Mariah made a makeshift bed for the baby by rolling up blankets and forming a box on the ground so she couldn't roll out. Once the child was settled, she picked up the blanket that had been with the girl to lay it over her but paused as she took in the blood stains. "No, this won't do until I have it cleaned up." Something on the corner of the blanket caught her eye, and she laid it flat on the floor to see. There were letters stitched into the corner, a date, and a name.

"Aren't we in luck! This must be your birth date and your name," she whispered as she pulled it closer. "Gemma. That's a beautiful name." Her lips curled up in a pleasant smile, thinking of how fitting the name was. For years she had prayed for a child. Now she finally had a daughter, something that was worth more than any gem in the world.

Something else caught her eye as she was looking at the stitching, a small tear directly above the name. It looked like someone had sewn a secret pocket into the blanket. She tried prying it open with her fingers but made minimal progress. Setting the blanket down, she found a knife and returned, using the knife to cut the rest of the stitches. Reaching in, she pulled out a necklace. The leather cord that formed the body of the necklace was unremarkable, but the jewel that hung at the end shone as if someone had captured a star. The light lasted for a moment, then it disappeared, leaving the jewel looking like plain, clear glass.

She gasped. There was no way to tell what had caused the glow, but she knew she was holding something precious. Whispers of a song came from the jewel when it was shining, and she felt a longing rise in her soul.

Her gaze remained mesmerized by the jewel for a moment longer. "But this isn't mine to keep," she whispered, looking at the sleeping baby.

Finding a fresh blanket, she laid it over Gemma and tied the necklace gently around her wrist. "Something is special about you, little one," she said, brushing her soft cheek. The Scruff came over, sniffing the necklace curiously. He crawled onto the baby's stomach and turned three times before curling into a little ball.

Mariah chuckled. "I guess you get to be little Gemma's protector."

The Scruff stared at her with large, knowing eyes.

"You'll make sure she doesn't try to eat the necklace then?"

The Scruff gave an offended look with a sharp squeak, making Mariah laugh softly.

"Hmmm...every good protector needs a name," she tapped her chin, looking at the ceiling. "What do you think about Theo?"

The Scruff tilted its head, looking much like he was contemplating the name, then he squeaked and gave a swift nod.

"Then Theo it is. Baby Gemma and her protector, Theo." She brushed Gemma's hair gently. "I don't know why the Creator brought you to us, but I promise, you will always be loved. I wonder what the Creator has in store for you?"

CHAPTER ONE

"Gemma! Come down for breakfast, or you'll be late again." Mariah's voice drifted up to Gemma's room.

"Coming, Mom!" Gemma ran her hands down her shirt, sighing. The lantern light showed how thin and worn her tan shirt and black pants were, but she hadn't washed her better work clothes yet, and she didn't have anything else suitable for work. With a shrug of resignation, she threw on her favorite belt, which held a pouch containing most of her treasured possessions, and a small sheathed knife her father had given her on her tenth birthday. Shoving her feet into a pair of black boots that came up to just below her knees, she laced them quickly, grabbed a black vest adorned with pockets sewn haphazardly across the front, and threw it on.

Her grey eyes scanned her room while she absentmindedly played with the jewel on her necklace. There were clothes and books strewn across her bed and the floor; she would have to clean that up when she got home. Swiftly braiding her wavy, dark-blond hair, she smiled as the braid made a satisfying thump on her low back. She'd started growing it out when she was fourteen. Now at eighteen, it was finally the length she wanted, at least for now. It never quite seemed long enough.

With one more glance, she turned and walked to the hatch in the floor, extinguishing the lantern before descending the familiar ladder to the main level of the house.

She loved their home. It wasn't large; to most, it would seem tiny. To her, it was cozy, filled with items full of memories. The living room, dining room, and kitchen were all one large room. Three chairs sat around a circular table topped with a hand-painted vase of wildflowers. She noticed the flowers were starting to wilt and made a mental note to replace them soon. It wouldn't be much longer before winter would claim all the flowers, and she dreaded the lack of color that came with it.

In front of the cheery fireplace sat two rocking chairs and a small couch, her mother's hand-knitted throw draped across the back. The only other room in the house, other than the attic that served as Gemma's room, was her parents' bedroom which was only big enough for their bed and a chest of drawers.

Mariah stood in front of the stove, covered with flour from making her famous buttermilk biscuits. She had won the Dano biscuit-baking contest five years running. Of course, that was back when Dano had celebrations. Now, everyone was too poor to care or celebrate.

Gemma came up beside Mariah and kissed her on the cheek. "Good morning! And how are you on this fine morning?"

Mariah smiled, chuckling lightly. "Fine." She put a plate of biscuits in the middle of the table, moving the vase of flowers to the counter. "What has you so happy today?"

"Oh, you know me and sunshine, Mom. It's a beautiful sunny day! How can I help but be happy?" Gemma grabbed a plate from the cupboard and sat at the table, piling a couple of biscuits onto it.

"The sun isn't even up yet!"

"But I can tell it's *going* to be a sunny day today! I can feel it." Gemma said brightly. "Where's Dad?"

"He had to help old Joe with a wagon wheel this morning. He has a lot more to do for other people since we don't have as much to take care of around here anymore."

Gemma knew her mother was trying to sound lighthearted, but she could hear the pain in her voice. She remembered how much bigger their farm had been when she was little. To her, it felt like there was no end to the fields and animals. She used to wander around helping the different farmhands with whatever the day had called for, but life was getting harder in the country, and they could not sell as much at the market. It wasn't long before they sold bits of land and some animals to pay for what they needed.

She had cried saying goodbye to so many farmhand friends as her father had to let them go. Now they were left with a small parcel of land that only housed a few animals and a small vegetable garden. It gave the family more than enough food, but her dad had to pick up more and more side jobs to earn the coin they desperately needed.

Gemma worked some shifts at the local tavern, a job she despised but was willing to grin and bear. It wasn't much pay, but it helped her parents, and it kept her busy between that and helping her dad with the upkeep of the farm.

A white ball of fur plopped onto the table and snatched the biscuit from Gemma's hand as she was about to take a bite.

"Hey, Theo, get your own biscuit!" she said, trying to snatch the biscuit back. "Where have you been this morning? What trouble have you gotten into before the sun's even up?"

Gemma laughed as he filled his cheeks with the biscuit, not at all apologetic for stealing it. She knew it was useless to try to get the stolen food back from him, but she never stopped trying. He squeaked, telling her a story with his mouth full.

She listened intently to Theo's series of squeaks and watched his forefeet move around dramatically. Theo didn't like Luke, a boy who was a little too interested in Gemma for his comfort. He made it his life goal to make the boy as miserable as possible so he would leave her alone. She didn't waste time trying to convince Theo that she didn't mind. Luke wasn't a bad guy, but she wasn't interested in him for more than friendship. She was only eighteen; she had plenty of time to think about boys later.

Mariah sat at the table, sliding a couple of eggs onto Gemma's plate. "I'm still bewildered how you can understand him like you do, Gemma. I can hardly ever figure out what he's trying to tell me." She used her finger to rub under Theo's chin. "I guess maybe that's a good thing. If I knew all the tricks he was playing on people in town, I would have to try to stop them before they happened. As it is, I'm able to use the excuse of ignorance. But I daresay the whole town would have been happier not knowing Scruffs existed." She shook her head with a glint in her eyes.

Gemma grinned, remembering the incident with grouchy old Gretchen involving Theo, a swarm of bees, and a rather angry skunk. "Ah, you know Theo makes this town a better place. How else would they have something to gossip about every week?"

Mother and daughter shared a laugh as Theo stuffed his cheeks with yet another biscuit. Gemma slapped his forefoot away from her eggs as she started in on them with her fork.

Mariah gently shook her head. "I swear, I have never seen such a tiny thing eat so much!"

"He has to keep up his energy for all the mischief he has to do." Gemma gulped down the last bite off her plate and stood to rinse off her dish in the bucket of water sitting on the counter.

"So, what was Theo so emphatic about this morning?" Mariah asked, biting into a biscuit.

Gemma looked over her shoulder and smiled at Theo. "He thinks I should do my best to avoid Luke in the future."

"Luke? Oh, but he is such a nice boy! He's kind, and his family has always been good to us."

"Yes, but Theo doesn't like the thought of anyone coming before him in my life." She picked up a towel to dry her plate. "Not that he needs to worry. I don't think any man could catch my eye right now. I have too much to think of here at home."

The moment the words left her mouth, she wished she could take them back, seeing the pain that played across her mother's face. "Besides that," she said brightly, "how would we have any time for mother-daughter things if I were out being courted by some guy?" She put her plate away. Walking to her mother, she wrapped her arms around her and kissed the top of her grey head.

"Someday, someone will catch your eye, my dear, and then I'll have to say goodbye." Mariah's voice cracked on the last word.

With one last squeeze, Gemma headed to the door. Turning back, she told her mother, "Even *if* I get married someday, I'm staying in Dano. We won't have to say goodbye, but for a night." She smiled wide, holding out her hand for Theo to jump on board. He hesitated a moment, eyeing the biscuits and making smacking noises with his mouth. With a resigned squeak, he abandoned the plate of biscuits, hopping onto her outstretched hand and scuttling up to her shoulder. "I'm working a double shift again today; Mary is still out sick. I'll be back late."

Mariah's face fell. She'd made it known how much she hated her daughter having to work so much to help keep things going. "Okay, dear, but if you're going to be too late, maybe you should stay at someone's house, so you're not walking home in the dark. If you do that, make sure you send a note with Theo to let me know, okay?"

"Yes, ma'am, love you!" Gemma said as she headed out the door. She heard her mom's voice call out, "Love you, too!"

She ensured that all the animals were fed and watered, a chore she insisted she take care of to ease her dad's workload. By the time she finished, the sky was greying with the approaching dawn, urging her quickly down the path to the forest shortcut heading to town. She breathed in the cool, crisp morning air, delighting in the birds twittering as they welcomed the day.

It was hard having only one horse between her and her father. She made sure to walk so her father could ride. It was harder for him to get around these days, and life hadn't been kind to his body. But she loved her walks. It was a good two-hour walk to work if she took the road the whole way. Using the forest shortcut, she saved time, but it was still no small trek to do twice a day.

Theo did all he could to keep her spirits up as they walked, especially trudging home after a long work day. He would sit on her shoulder and point out things he found interesting along the way. Most days, it was a welcome relief from the monotony of the trail, but it made her late to work on more than one occasion.

Gemma smiled as the morning light slowly shone through the trees, and she breathed in another huge lungful of fresh pine-scented air.

If she had her way, she would always be outside, a trait she shared with her dad, but the tavern was the only place she could find work, so she dealt with being stuck indoors all day. The work was only a couple of days a week, but even so, her mind always wandered, wishing she could be outside exploring the forest or swimming in the lake or down a stream. Theo was none too happy with the arrangement either. He was forced to stay out of the way all day while she worked. As a result, he often got himself into trouble due to his constant need to get into stuff. The town liked it better when Theo was occupied elsewhere, as he was less likely to cause trouble that way.

The sun was starting to burn away the morning fog when the outskirts of town became visible. Coming into town was her least favorite part of the day. Vacated buildings sat ghostly, whispering of better times and depressing her spirit. The streets on the outskirts of town were empty, making the place feel abandoned even though many still lived there. Only a few years ago, she would have been dodging carts and horses as people bustled about their business. Now she ambled down the center of the street, watching the breeze blow through broken windows. It was a relief when she made it to the Anvil even though she hated it there. Being the only tavern for miles, there was always a steady stream of people coming and going. Those signs of life lifted her spirits.

She walked into work and jumped into the flow of things, saying the usual good mornings to the other workers while Theo hopped off her shoulder, disappearing farther into the building. She watched him go, hoping he didn't do anything too crazy today.

The morning passed uneventfully, quickly transitioning into the busy lunch rush. Even as the town slowly died, travelers came through every day on their way to or from Tyreen, the bustling trader's village to the north, though even their numbers were dwindling.

As the day dragged on, Theo scurried under tables, snatching scraps that fell on the floor. Thankfully, he was sticking to leftovers after the last time Gemma had her pay withheld to make up for the food he'd eaten while she worked.

A little while later, Theo decided to make a game of seeing how many chicken bones he could stack onto one customer's pile of hair. Her white hair was pulled high on her head, now with chicken bones sticking out, making it look like some creepy many-armed snowman.

Gemma tried not to laugh and hoped her boss wouldn't see what was happening. The last thing she needed was for Theo to get her in trouble again. She was already in trouble for an incident involving rocks and soup a couple of weeks back; one more significant blow-up, and she might lose her job, but she couldn't tell him to stop. It wasn't his fault that being stuck indoors made him antsy. She felt the same way. Honestly, his little shenanigans throughout the day were the only things that made work bearable for her. Without him the walls would feel like a prison.

Later in the afternoon, Caitlin, the only other girl in town around Gemma's age, came in to work the even busier dinner rush. Gemma took turns with Caitlin waiting tables and washing dishes, though she let Caitlin do more of the waiting while Gemma stayed hidden doing the washing.

Caitlin was the kind of girl who could talk to anyone. She had brown curly hair that bounced every time she moved her head. She knew how to use her crystal blue eyes and luscious curves to reel in any poor sucker who looked her way.

Gemma was sometimes jealous of her. Caitlin could walk into a room, and all eyes were on her instantly; she didn't even have to say a word. Gemma could fall through the roof, land smack dab in the middle of a group of people, and they would keep going about their day, oblivious to her presence.

It wasn't all bad. Being someone who faded into the background allowed her to go many places unnoticed, and with Theo as her companion, she discovered some intriguing things about the town. Like a series of underground tunnels, though they weren't the safest to explore. Unfortunately, her "invisibility" couldn't always hide her; she was caught more than once due to her clumsiness.

She didn't always mind being the unnoticed one. She never thought herself ugly, but she knew her slim frame wasn't alluringly beautiful either, more plain than anything. Sometimes she wished she could trade her dark blond hair and grey eyes for Caitlin's beauty queen looks. But the constant trail of men following Caitlin around reminded Gemma it wasn't always bad not being noticed.

Gemma hummed as she dried a mug while Theo scrubbed a plate next to her. The boss once tried to run Theo out when he helped with the dishes, saying it wasn't sanitary to have a rodent cleaning. Gemma had to hold Theo back as he shook his tiny forefoot, trying to give her boss a piece of his mind. She explained that Theo was a supremely clean Scruff, not a rodent, and he would never do anything to compromise the cleanliness of the Anvil. She didn't know if her boss agreed because of what she said or because he could tell Theo was contemplating making his night a long, miserable one if he didn't let Theo stay and help. Theo's reputation was well known in town, after all. Her boss conceded to let Theo help, on the condition none of the customers ever saw him.

Caitlin swept in with her usual exuberance. "There is the cutest guy *ever* out there, Gemma! You have to come and see!" She took Gemma's arm, pulling her out to the front room before Gemma could set down the towel and mug.

"You're not trying to set me up with your brother again, are you?" Gemma grumbled.

"What? No! This guy is so much cuter! Besides, my brother wouldn't risk trying to talk to you after what Theo put him through last time." She tugged Gemma harder still, followed by the pitter-patter of Theo's feet.

Caitlin swung her around, pointing and bouncing on the balls of her feet, not caring in the least if the man saw her pointing at him. "See, isn't he the most handsome thing you've ever seen this side of the Cattaway?"

Gemma followed her finger and saw a young man sitting in a booth, reading a book. He was handsome; she had to give Caitlin that. His dark brown hair looked exactly right, even though it was messy. His body was well toned with a chiseled face, and his skin was tanned from the sun, telling of a life spent mostly outdoors. As she studied him, he looked up as if he could tell someone was watching, and his eyes locked with Gemma's. His eyes were dark brown, the kind that seemed like endless pools, but there was something about his look that raised the hair on the back of her neck. He didn't break the gaze but looked on intently until Gemma blinked and looked away.

Caitlin squealed beside her, making Gemma jump.

"Ooh, he is so darn cute! And did you see that? He couldn't take his eyes off you! You have to wait on him!"

"Why don't you wait on him if you like him so much?" There was no way she was going to go anywhere near that guy. Even the thought of it made her hands tremble.

"Oh, come on, Gemma! I have a boyfriend, and you don't." She pulled Gemma's arm but was unable to budge her.

"I don't want a boyfriend. Besides, you might not have a boyfriend by next week." She glared at Caitlin. "You know they hardly ever make it a month with you."

Caitlin laughed, shrugging her shoulders, and moved behind Gemma to push her forward. "Well, if you fail, I'll take a turn!"

"I told you, I don't want a boyfriend," she protested, bracing against Caitlin's pushing.

Before she had time to react, Caitlin snatched the mug and towel out of her hands, disappearing back into the kitchen. Gemma pursed her lips before shuffling forward. She stumbled as she walked to his table and had a horrifying image of herself falling flat on her face in front of him. A furtive glance told her he hadn't noticed her misstep, being entirely engrossed in whatever he was reading. She breathed deep, steeling her nerves, and ignoring Theo's small growl of protest behind her.

Stop being such a coward! she scolded herself. *He probably won't notice you, like all the other guys who come through here. He most likely has some amazing lady waiting for him somewhere.*

As she neared his table, he set his book down, and looked up.

Gemma put on as good a smile as she could muster. "What may I get you today, sir?"

"Sir? I didn't think I looked that old." His voice was deep and smooth. He smiled, but the smile didn't quite reach his eyes.

Gemma's cheeks burned, and her hands fluttered to her braid, pulling on it nervously. She found herself unable to look him in the eye. "I'm sorry...m-my parents trained me too well, I guess,"

He held a hand up. "I'm kidding. My parents brought me up well, too." He gave her a half-smile.

Gemma relaxed, her smile becoming genuine. *He seems nice. Maybe I'm overthinking things.* "Would you like anything?"

"I'll take some onomay and some water."

Gemma nodded. The drink was one of Elefrisia's specialties: warmed milk with honey and clove. It was an acquired taste, but it was one of her favorites.

"Anything else?" She was trying her best to act as naturally as possible, but her skin tingled and she didn't know what to do with her hands.

"That's it for sustenance."

She nodded. "That'll be two scaifin."

As he handed her the coins, he asked, "I'm new to town; is there anything interesting to see or do here?"

She glanced at the book he had been reading, noticing it was in another language, not anything she recognized. "Not unless you like walking by vacant buildings."

"What do you like to do?" He looked at her expectantly, once again not looking away from her eyes, as if he was trying to see into her soul.

She cleared her throat to shake off her nerves; something about the way he looked at her made her feel exposed. "I-I like to spend most of my time in the forest. There are a lot of places to explore, neat animals everywhere, and a lake with some of the best swimming spots around..." She stopped when she realized she was rambling, but he looked at her curiously with that same half-smile.

"There's something about being outside that nothing else can compare to, huh?" His smile finally reached his eyes.

Theo jumped up to the table, giving the man a wary look. He hunched down, his hindquarter wriggling and a growl building. Gemma scooped him up quickly while he shook his tiny forefoot at the man. "I'm sorry, he doesn't take too kindly to strangers."

"It's no problem; he's just doing his job," the man said nonchalantly.

Something about his statement sounded an alarm in the back of her mind, but she didn't have time to wonder about it when a group of loud men came in demanding beer. Muttering a quick apology, she went to get his drink so she could wait on the new group, dropping his order off quickly while avoiding eye contact.

She was still feeling unbalanced by her encounter with the handsome stranger as she took mugs of beer to the group, but thankfully none of the newcomers paid attention to her.

For the rest of her shift, she didn't get a chance to talk to him again; she was too busy running around between the tables and keeping the beer-drinking group's mugs full. She often glanced to see if his drink needed refilling as an excuse to talk to him again, but he was the slowest drinker in the world.

Theo had placed himself where he could keep an eye on the handsome man; he looked deep in thought as he stared at him.

It was long past time for Gemma to head home, and even though the place was packed, she couldn't wait any longer, so she headed to the back to say goodbye to Caitlin. "Sorry to leave you with this whole mess, but I promised mom I wouldn't be home too late. She won't like that I'm walking home in the dark as it is."

Caitlin shrugged. "No problem!" she said brightly.

Gemma couldn't help feeling inferior to Caitlin's ability to handle anything. She was the kind of person who could handle two full bars single-handed and probably juggle mugs of beer simultaneously. *Does this girl ever run out of energy?*

Caitlin hugged her. "You've been here all day, and hey, it's not the worst I've ever seen! Besides, I get to keep looking at that cute guy until he leaves." She winked and patted Gemma's shoulder as she walked by.

Gemma shook her head. Caitlin was never shy about anything, but she and Gemma had been friends since childhood, and Gemma had long-since become accustomed to her quirks. "Come on, Theo, time to go home."

He looked up from the plate of desserts Caitlin had set before him, the only thing that had been able to steal his focus from the young man. He wiped his mouth delicately, trying to muster more of his dignity.

Gemma giggled as he jumped up to his favorite perch on her shoulder. "Don't worry. I won't let anyone know about your weakness for sweets."

He squeaked in protest, letting her know he could easily pass up a dessert; he didn't want to offend Caitlin by turning down her generous gift.

She raised an eyebrow. "You keep telling yourself that."

He harumphed, crossing his forelegs across his chest.

"You know I'm right. And you love me for being honest."

He looked away for a moment, then turned and licked her cheek.

She chuckled, then stole one last glance at the young man who was too engrossed in his book to notice as she left. A slight twinge of sadness bloomed in her chest, but she scolded herself for wishing he'd been looking for her. After all, she was nothing more than a waitress in a small, dying town; why should he pay any attention to her? Then again, she wasn't sure she even wanted his attention. The way he had looked at her was unnerving. Something in his eyes made her unsure if he was someone she could trust. Since he was a stranger, most likely passing through, it wasn't something she even needed to worry about.

The night air caused goosebumps on her arms as she stepped out into the street. "They named the Anvil appropriately, Theo. I feel like I've been in a furnace and hammered out all day."

Theo patted her cheek, squeaking, reminding her she was lucky she didn't have to work in a fur coat all day.

"Make me feel worse, why don't you?"

He smiled, then rubbed his head against her neck.

She scratched between his ears. "I guess it could be worse, huh?"

He agreed, and the two started the long journey home.

Peace settled over Gemma at the sound of crickets quietly chirping, little unseen musicians of the night. She wasn't fond of walking home in the dark, but with Theo on her shoulder, they would often make games along the way. About a year ago, they had started a game of Gemma walking with her eyes closed while Theo sat atop her head, making noises and tugging on her hair to direct her. She would laugh as he pretended to be a captain on a ship, steering her around obstacles and under branches. Tonight, however, she was more tired than usual, and Theo was agitated. He kept looking behind him and scurrying from shoulder to shoulder. His nervousness was setting off the alarms in her mind again, but the long day made it hard for her to focus on it.

The moon glowed full in the sky, providing enough light through the forest canopy for her to see decently, but she still stumbled on a small vine worming its way across the path and froze as a loud snap rang out from behind her.

Theo's ears turned back, and his nose wiggled as he stood on his hind legs to sniff the air.

The snap seemed too loud to be one of the usual woodland creatures she came across, but she didn't know much about the forest at night. She always tried to be home before the sun went down. She hated the dark, and something about being in the woods after sunset unnerved her. For reasons unknown to her, she kept picturing a dark shape with a sword sneering at her, ready to strike.

As she looked around, her imagination made each tree morph into a sinister shape, ready to attack at the slightest notice. Her heart sped up as her mind conjured up the worst reasons for the noise she had heard. Theo's tenseness was making her even more on edge. Maybe her wild imagination wasn't far off if he was on guard.

Looking over her shoulder, she thought she caught a glimpse of movement out of the corner of her eye. But nothing was out of the ordinary when she turned her full attention behind her. Every sense in her body screamed that something wasn't right.

She turned her gaze, using her peripheral vision. Her father taught her that movement at night could be seen better by the periphery rather than a direct stare. Theo jumped from her shoulder to a nearby branch, softly making his way deeper into the trees.

"Wait!" she whispered, but he didn't answer.

A moment later, Theo's squeal pierced the quiet.

"Theo!" She ran toward the noise, pulling her small knife from her belt. She didn't know what she would do, but the thought of Theo being in trouble pushed most of her common sense out the window. Fear had a lousy way of making it hard to think straight.

She held her knife up in front of her as she ran. Her parents insisted she never go without some form of defense when walking home alone, but she'd never put her knife to use before.

Theo jumped out of the branches onto her shoulder and tugged her ear to pull her the other way. She took the hint. If Theo thought it unsafe, she knew she had to listen to him.

As she turned to run, something slammed into her from behind, knocking her face down to the ground, making her come close to cutting herself with her knife. She screamed and struggled, kicking her legs backward, trying to free herself as strong arms pinned her down. The fall had knocked the wind from her, and she couldn't catch a full breath with the assailant's weight on top of her. She scanned around, hoping for a sign of Theo, but he was nowhere in sight. Her assailant spat out a string of curses, and Gemma hoped it was due to Theo causing as much trouble as he could.

"Get off me!" she screamed. Panic rose, threatening to take over when one of her elbows finally landed, and the man groaned, loosening his grip enough for her to turn onto her back.

Theo's white fur gleamed in the moonlight while he dashed up and down the man's arms, trying to target his face, biting the man anywhere he could. Finally, he found the man's nose and bit down hard.

Gemma cringed as droplets of blood splattered her face. The man yelled and grabbed at Theo, providing the opening she needed. While he was distracted, she slashed at the man, her knife tip skimmed across his neck, causing him to scramble back.

She'd learned from Caitlin's brother, who was known for getting into trouble, that in a fight with someone stronger than yourself, it was best to keep as much distance as possible between yourself and the assailant. With that in mind, Gemma stood up, sheathed her knife, and ran. "Come on, Theo!"

Theo scrambled behind her, catching her pant leg, and working his way up to her shoulder. Glancing back, she saw another shape come out of the trees and attack the first. She didn't stop to see who it was or why the person attacked the other man; all she could think of was getting home. Her parents would hold her and reassure her that she was safe and had nothing to fear.

Theo squeaked urgently in her ear and held on as she ran.

She was a fast runner. Years of walking to work and gallivanting in the woods with Theo helped her fly, but tonight she ran faster than ever, adrenaline pushing her legs beyond anything she knew possible. Her heart pounded in her chest, and her lungs started to burn as she gulped in large breaths of air, but she pushed on. Her ankle caught on a root, and she fell to the ground hard, managing to get her hands beneath her before her face hit the ground. Theo flew forward, landing on his feet. A slight pain burned in her ankle, and her forearms had scraped the ground hard. Blood flowed down to her wrist, and she tried to get her bearings so she could move on again.

Before she could get her feet under her, a hand grabbed her by the hair and pulled her to her knees, causing her to cry out. Theo jumped on the man, making him release his hold on her hair. She swung around with an elbow to his groin, and the man went down hard. Footsteps pounded up the path from where she was first attacked, and she moved to stand, her legs shaking underneath her.

"Gemma!"

Hearing her name froze her; the voice sounded familiar, but she couldn't place it in her panicked state.

Her mind screamed at her to run. The voice came from around a bend in the path, and there was no telling who had called. If it was a friend, she could be found at home. If it was not, she would have a head start toward home, but the familiarity of the voice and the absence of malice in it made her unable to decide a course of action. A man rounded the corner but wasn't close enough to make out his features.

Theo crouched, tensing in case he was needed again.

The man slowed, taking in the scene before him, with Gemma in a half-crouch, ready to run, and her assailant lying on the ground, moaning. The new man came up to her, and he was finally close enough for her to recognize. It was the young man from the Anvil. She couldn't remember if she had told him her name or not. *Is he here to harm me?* He hadn't looked to be a man of ill intent, but he didn't come off as all that warm either.

The man used the pommel of his sword to hit Gemma's assailant over the head, causing him to fall unconscious to the ground, then sheathed the sword and took her by the arm. "We need to get you out of here, now!"

She was too confused to think coherently. A part of her felt she should run and take her chances on her own—he was a stranger after all—but another part felt safer not being alone. Making a quick decision to trust the man who may have saved her life, she pulled her arm back, scooping down to pick up Theo, and ran toward home. "What are you doing here? I don't remember telling you my name, so how do you know it? How am I supposed to know if I can trust you? Who are you?"

The man kept a steady pace beside her, making furtive glances over his shoulder from time to time. "Not exactly the best time for fifty questions! For now, all you need to know is that our parents were friends long ago, and I'm your best shot to stay alive."

Gemma tried to concentrate on breathing. "Our parents?" She paused for a breath. "My parents never mentioned any old friends."

He was in good shape, his breathing coming easily as if this was not the first time he had been running full out through a forest. "Not Thomas and Mariah, Dean and Thalia."

Gemma skidded to a stop, tripping with the shock of those words, forgetting for a moment that her life might be in danger. "How do you know Thomas and Mariah aren't my real parents? And how do you know those names?"

He took her arm again, looking at her intently. "Listen, I will tell you everything when I can, but right now, we need to keep moving."

Gemma didn't move, unsure of what to do.

The stranger breathed out heavily, "I know you have no reason to trust me, but that man back there was most likely not alone, and I don't know how long he'll be unconscious. We need to put as much distance as possible between him and us right now. I'll explain when I can, but right now, we need to go!"

She was afraid and uncertain, but she knew he had a point. Theo gave her a small nod; he knew they weren't safe out in the open. With a quick puff of air, she ran again with her rescuer—a stranger who knew more about her life than even her closest friends—running beside her.

CHAPTER TWO

Thomas sat across from his wife, deep in conversation. There was so much to figure out. They could only stay afloat for so long. People were moving to the bigger towns, leaving small places like Dano behind to die. It was hard times across Elefrisia ever since the uprising and the fall of the monarchy twenty years ago. Now the land was split in two. Those west of the Cattaway River believed in the old ways and served Travis Stillwater, the man who had taken up leadership when the royal family was murdered. He'd pushed Skotadi—the tyrant responsible for the deaths of the royals—and his men back across the river. Those east of the river were forced to serve Skotadi, who wasn't satisfied with half of Elefrisia. He wanted all of it under his control, but thankfully, there was still enough resistance to keep him at bay.

Thomas had done everything he could to keep their lives as comfortable as possible, but now his shoulders sagged, weighed down by the pressures of the task. "I don't think we can make it another year, Mariah. I've had to work for free, taking jobs on promises of payment. This town won't last much longer. We might have to consider selling and starting over."

Mariah shook her head. "Who will buy this place, Tom? You said yourself the town is dying. No one will want a small plot of farmland in a place going nowhere. Who would be able to buy anything in times like these, anyway?"

Thomas sighed. "I know." He took a drink from his cup. "That's why I think we'll have to pack everything up and start over somewhere else. Somewhere fresh."

Mariah leaned back; eyebrows raised. "Just walk away?" She stood and started pacing. "This is our home, Tom! It has been for going on fifty years! You can't expect us to walk away from all that."

Thomas stood and walked to his wife, reaching out and holding her still from her pacing. "I know it's a lot to ask. I don't want to say goodbye to this place any more than you do, but we must think about what's the best thing to do. Yes, it's scary to walk away from all we know and start again with basically nothing. These are uncertain times, but I believe we have no other choice. We've fought hard, but we can't keep fighting anymore. Neither of us is as young as we once were."

Mariah looked him in the eye. "What about Gemma? This is the only home she's ever known. We can't uproot her like that. It would be too cruel, Tom! She's already been through enough, even if she doesn't remember it."

He pulled her into his arms, rubbing her back comfortingly. "Gemma is strong. One of the strongest people I know. She's certainly the sweetest girl I have ever had the pleasure of knowing. She won't complain, no matter what we decide. You know she will support any decision we make."

Mariah sniffled as a shudder ran through her body. "I know. We don't deserve such an amazing girl, but I'm afraid it will break her heart. And, knowing her, she'll suffer in silence. She won't want us to feel guilty for the decision to move her." She pulled back enough to see his face and sighed, her shoulders drooping. "I'm with you in whatever decision you make. I decided to follow you for the rest of my life when I vowed to be your wife. I trust you, Tom, and I know you will do what's best for the family."

Thomas kissed her lightly on the lips. "I think you have more faith in me than I do."

Mariah smiled and leaned her head on his shoulder.

The peaceful moment was interrupted by pounding footsteps drawing closer to the house. The door flew open, and two breathless figures spilled inside, slamming the door behind them. Mariah rushed to Gemma, her eyes skittering over the blood splatters on Gemma's face and the multiple scratches across her arms. "What's going on?"

"I was attacked!" Gemma exclaimed breathlessly. Theo jumped off her shoulder, watching out the nearest window while Gemma paced to calm her breathing.

Mariah's face blanched and her hand shot to her mouth.

Thomas stepped forward, looking from Gemma to the young man with her. "Explain."

The man looked Thomas directly in the eye, confident despite Thomas' fierce look. "Your daughter is in danger. I have reason to believe the man who attacked her is connected to the people who killed her parents eighteen years ago—"

Gemma whipped around to face the stranger, the blood draining from her face as she grasped one of Mariah's hands to steady herself. Fear shone in equal measure on both of their faces.

Brayden glanced Gemma's way but continued. "Gemma must have something they want. Unfortunately, they're the kind of people who will stop at nothing to find it."

"And who are you to know so much about my daughter's past?" Thomas' eyes bore into the man like daggers.

"My name is Brayden Levine. My father was David Levine; I know you met him once."

Thomas nodded gravely. A part of him always knew this day would come, though he prayed he would be wrong. That night in the forest had never left his nightmares, and he knew the cruelty that had started there would sooner or later spill back into their lives.

He would never forget the deep sorrow on David's bloodstained face when he stumbled to Thomas' front door. Nor would he forget the words David spoke. David's last warning was burned as deeply into Thomas' mind as any brand into skin.

"Keep constant vigil, for the evil that began this night is relentless. Should it find the girl survived, her life may be forfeit. I fear there may be no safe haven for her in all of Elefrisia."

Thomas never saw David again, but ever since that day, he'd been prepared for something to come and shatter the comfort Gemma had known.

Thomas entered the bedroom and came out with a loaded pack and canteen. "I've been preparing for this for eighteen years, though I prayed this pack would never be needed," he said heavily, handing the pack to Gemma. She took it and the canteen without a word, but she couldn't hide the terror shining from her eyes.

Thomas continued. "I always expected someone would come and try to finish what started the night we found you," he shook his head, "After so many years, I hoped I was wrong, that the evil ended that night. I never wanted this day to come, but I am so grateful for all the years of having you safe with us. We had the privilege of watching you grow into such a strong young woman."

Gemma's eyes swiveled from her dad to Brayden and back again. "What are you saying?"

Thomas faced his daughter, his eyes misting over. "I'm saying your mom and I are too old to be on the run with you, and you're no longer safe here. You need to go."

Gemma's mind buzzed and it felt like someone had swiped the floor out from under her. "No, Dad—"

Thomas drew forward, placing a hand on either side of his daughter's arms. "Go with Brayden and stay safe." He let her go, his mouth in a flat line as he turned toward Brayden. "I don't know you, but I know your father was a good man. Theo hasn't run you off yet, which means he senses good in you, too." Theo puffed up with pride. "I'm trusting you to keep her safe because I'm left with no other choice." He reached out his right arm.

Brayden clasped Thomas' forearm solemnly as Thomas spoke. "Promise me you will do everything within your power to protect her and, when possible, to bring her back home to us."

Brayden straightened, lifting his chin. "I promise."

Thomas held his gaze for a moment longer, then nodded, satisfied.

Gemma ran into her father's arms, squeezing him tightly. "I don't want to leave you both. I wasn't supposed to have to say goodbye!" She didn't try to fight the tears falling down her face.

Her mother came over, and hugged her from behind, then turned her to kiss her forehead. "We *will* find each other again." Her voice shook, and her cheeks were wet with tears. "I promise we will find each other in this life or the next."

Gemma shook her head, her gaze going from her mother to her father. She knew they weren't her birth parents; they had told her the truth about her origins right from the start. They had always told her the truth.

Once she had asked them why they didn't pretend to be her birth parents, and Thomas responded, "The truth is like a bubble of air in water; no matter how hard you try to hold it down, it will always find its way to the surface."

Remembering back, she realized how amazing her parents were. They took in a stranger's child and raised her as their own. They buried her mother, and always taught her to love her birth parents, even though they hadn't known who they were. They had poured so much love and kindness into her life that she'd never known true sadness. Her heart was not breaking; it was shattering, having to leave the two strong pillars in her life. "I'm not saying goodbye because we will see each other again." She hugged them both one last time before pulling the pack onto her back. Slinging the canteen across her body, she stepped to the door. Theo jumped back up to his perch, clutching her shoulder firmly, trying to reassure her.

"Take good care of our girl, Theo," Mariah called out.

Theo squeaked with a solemn salute.

Gemma looked over her shoulder. She took in the cozy home that she had grown up in. A thousand memories flashed before her eyes. Learning the stove was hot, then being comforted by her mother as she held her burning fingers. Losing her first tooth, and her father proudly putting it on display. She remembered being embarrassed about it, but now she would give anything to return to those happy times.

Brayden told Thomas as they stepped out the door. "I promise I'll do everything in my power to bring her back safe and sound."

Gemma had one last glimpse of the beloved faces of her parents before the door to the only life she had ever known was shut, and she turned to face a future that felt equivalent to jumping off a cliff into darkness. It was hard to take that first unknown step. She looked at Theo, who returned her gaze with such strength that it eased her fears by a small margin. Facing Brayden, she said, "I sure hope you turn out to be someone trustworthy. And I hope you know what you're doing."

He met her gaze. "Whether or not I'm trustworthy will be proven to you soon. As for the other, I sure hope I do, too."

CHAPTER THREE

The crispness of winter's approach cooled Gemma's skin as she followed Brayden off the road and into the trees. A part of her questioned having such blind faith in a stranger. Her father and Theo trusted him, but she didn't understand why.

A horrible thought sprang to the front of her mind. "How do we know they won't go looking for me at my house?" She pictured them torturing her parents to find her.

Brayden peeked over his shoulder, never slowing his pace. "They don't care about anyone but you. They're good trackers; they'll know we didn't stay there."

Those words caused conflicting emotions; half happy her parents would be left alone, half terrified someone would jump out of the trees at any moment to grab her. "But you're sure they won't hurt my parents?" A branch slapped across her cheek, making her wince as she ducked to miss another one.

A beat passed before he answered. "No. I'm sorry, I can't be sure."

She was grateful for his honesty, but the truth weighed like a stone in her heart. She entertained the idea of running back to the house to make sure her parents were safe but pushed the thought away. Her presence would only add to their danger, and she knew worrying about them wouldn't help anyone. With a silent prayer for her parent's protection, she focused on keeping up with Brayden.

They stopped shortly for Brayden to grab a pack he had stashed in a cluster of trees. He took a small swig from his canteen, and Gemma took the chance to cool her own throat. "You seem oddly prepared for this."

His face remained expressionless as he answered. "It's best if we stay silent for now. There's no telling who might be around."

She ground her teeth. *I'm not an idiot. I know we aren't out of danger yet.* She wanted to learn more about the man she was trusting with her life. Digging her nails into her palms, she forced herself to remain quiet as they started running again.

After what seemed like hours, Gemma's conditioned legs were protesting, and she was breathing in quick hard gasps. Her shoulders ached from the pack, and her ankle throbbed. Scratches crossed every exposed part of her skin from branches, and she pressed a hand to her side, trying to quiet a twinge. She tried to hide her weariness but soon stumbled every few steps as if the forest floor had grown extra roots in her path to trip her.

She fell hard, throwing Theo off her shoulder. Brayden helped her up, then started forward, keeping his pace to a brisk walk. He spoke over his shoulder, "We can catch our breath for a while,"

Gemma nodded even though Brayden wasn't looking; she didn't have the breath to speak. Theo returned to her shoulder, slumping down, also grateful for the change in pace. He was tired from hanging on, keeping alert for any sounds of pursuit, and ducking many wayward branches.

Gemma breathed in deep as they moved on, thankful for the chance to slow her racing heart.

Brayden glanced her way. "I know you're tired, but we can't stop. We'll walk for a while, but we should pick up the pace when you're ready."

Gemma grimaced. The thought of going on made her want to cry. The farther they went, the more distance grew between her and her home. She had never been away from Dano; the farm could never be left alone. If her father needed something from a neighboring town, he would wait for the traveling market to make its way to Dano. There had never been any reason to travel.

She watched Brayden's back as he forged ahead with determination; he wasn't planning on stopping any time soon. Pursing her lips, she reluctantly kept on.

The night dragged on like an endless nightmare, running until they couldn't, walking until they could run some more, stopping only long enough to drink water and catch their breath. Gemma couldn't figure out how Brayden made his way in the dark so efficiently. He walked and ran as if it was daytime. Whenever she worked up the courage to ask if they could stop for the night, a distant sound or a flicker of light far off in the forest would press them on again.

What seemed like an eternity later, the air grew steadily warmer, and grey light diffused the dark of night. Birds chirped as they prepared to begin another day. Gemma envied their bliss. Grogginess descended on her like a heavy blanket trying to pull her eyes closed. Her throat was raw and dry after hours of gasping in the cold night air. Even Theo's squeaks of encouragement fell on deaf ears.

Brayden finally stopped, noticing Gemma's bone-tired appearance. "We can take a break and refresh, but don't sit down. You'll find it even harder to stand up again."

Gemma gratefully fell against the nearest tree, trying to take as much weight off her legs as possible. Her hands trembled as she opened her canteen, and spots danced in her vision. Brayden didn't look much better. His face was drawn, and his hair slicked down with sweat. Even so, he stood on the balls of his feet, ready to bolt at a moment's notice. Gemma was sure, however, that she would trip over her feet if she tried.

Theo had firmly planted himself between Gemma's neck and her pack, choosing to be squished by her pack rather than endure the constant barrage of branches. His small movements tickled Gemma's neck as he wriggled to find a more comfortable position. Not for the first time, she wished she could trade places with him and let him carry her for a while.

She sipped her water, trying to conserve it and keep from overtaxing her stomach. That was something she'd learned the hard way earlier in the night.

As her breathing eased, she asked the question that had been burning in her mind all night. "My dad trusted you when he heard your name, but he never mentioned a David Levine to me. So why was he willing to trust you so quickly?"

Brayden's jaw worked as he contemplated answering. "It's—"

The three were jolted to alertness when a shout carried across the breeze. Theo scurried from behind her neck, securing his perch on her shoulder once more. The sound of snapping branches drew closer at an alarming rate.

Gemma and Brayden bolted in unison. A crash behind them drew Gemma's eyes. A man burst from a clump of trees, dreads flying about his head. Theo squeaked with rage, though she had no time to wonder at his reaction as she focused on nothing more than staying upright.

Adrenaline shot through her veins, spurring her forward. They broke out of the tree line like an arrow from a bow. The ground sloped upward, showing nothing but the sky beyond.

At the top of the slope, they skidded to a stop. Gemma's stomach did a somersault as her momentum nearly pushed her off a forty-foot drop that ended in a wide frothing river.

Brayden searched around, his eyes growing wide, uncertainty flashing across them for the first time. He peeked over the cliff in front of them. "We're going to have to jump!"

Gemma's heart sped like a galloping horse, ready to explode. She peered over the cliff, her eyes going wide as they zeroed in on the many boulders and jagged rocks.

Theo's tiny claws dug into her shoulder and hair, preparing for the jump. She didn't have time to question Brayden's decision. He grabbed her arm, tugging her off the cliff as he jumped, a guttural shout echoing close behind them.

Her stomach dropped, and she couldn't get more than a shallow gulp of air as she fell, her arms flapping in a subconscious effort to slow her fall. Her feet slammed into ice-cold water, which shot up her nose as she plummeted below the surface. A moment later, she surfaced, coughing and cringing from the pain that made it feel as if her brain was on fire. She tried to get a breath but soon found herself under water again, turning and churning like she was a toy in a child's pail of water. Her pack tore off, drifting away. Theo and Brayden were nowhere in sight. Internally she prayed Theo wouldn't be swept too far from her. A memory of her dad teaching her to relax and let the current take her came to mind, but before she could put any plan into action, she felt a sharp pain on the side of her head. Darkness crept in; then, she couldn't feel anything at all.

"*G*emma, *you are more precious than any gem in the world...I will always love you...*"

The comforting voice faded as something soft tickled Gemma's nose. The left side of her body tingled from warmth, and she slowly cracked her eyes open. Wiping the collected crust from her eyes, she looked around, grimacing at the dry, cottony feel inside her mouth. Theo's small pink nose shot toward her face, followed by his tongue, overjoyed she was awake. Her lips cracked as they turned up in a slight smile. "Well, hello, Theo." The words came out hoarse and cracked.

Theo squeaked, pressing his head against her cheek and neck.

Gemma chuckled softly and scratched Theo's head. He leaned into her hand, making soft purrs. Wincing, she sat up stiffly, as every muscle in her body protested the movement. Her vision faded around the edges, and the world spun, but the dizziness slowly receded, leaving a high-pitched ringing in her ears. Her head pounded as though a group of miners had taken up residence, and she could hear the blood rushing through her veins with every beat. Lightly brushing the side of her head, her fingers found a small lump protruding. "Ugh," she groaned.

Theo rubbed his side against her, his eyes large with sympathy.

She shuddered, her bladder not so gently begging for her attention, but she ignored it, taking in her surroundings. She was on a cot in a one-room wooden cabin. All the furniture was of sturdy cedar. Open windows let the fall breeze blow gently in while rays of light reflected off dust particles floating slowly to the floor. One small table with a few chairs dominated the middle of the room. An ancient stove sat unused, topped with a teakettle in the farthest corner; a few small cabinets were fastened on the adjacent wall. Everything had a thick layer of dust and a hint of rodent odor.

Examining her arms, she noticed the scrapes and the cut on her wrist were clean. Her canteen leaned next to the cot, and she was surprised to see her pack leaning against the wall next to Brayden's; she thought she'd lost her pack forever. "I missed a lot while I was out, didn't I?"

Theo nodded, and she grabbed her canteen, relief washing over her as she felt its weight; it was filled to the brim. The water stung her dry lips, but washed smoothly over her dehydrated tongue. Forcing herself to take slow sips, she fought the urge to gulp it down and once again told her bladder to hush.

When her throat was soothed, she set her canteen down and slowly stood, yelping as her legs seized with pain. She pushed herself to move, hobbling around the room like an old woman to get her blood flowing.

The cabin's quiet was surreal after the mad dash of the night.

Theo scurried around the room, sniffing everything.

Gemma shook her head. "I'm sure you've already found any scraps of food that might have been lying around."

Theo squeaked indignantly, going into a rant she knew all too well. He always justified his love of food somehow.

She reached out, and he hopped into her hand. "I know, I know, it takes lots of energy to be my protector, so you need all the food you can get." Her face tightened. "Especially now, huh?"

He nodded with a slight puff of air.

Gemma rubbed his ears with her thumb. "Where is our mysterious rescuer?"

Theo mimicked casting out a fishing line.

"I see."

Rather than searching for Brayden, she snuck out, finding a suitably secluded spot to answer her insistent bladder. Returning, she walked around the room, glancing at various items strewn about. The cabinets held a few dishes and silverware, but nothing more. She found a drawing of a family portrait on a windowsill but couldn't make out much, for it was too faded by the sun. A few fishing items and a couple of animal traps cluttered one corner. The stove squeaked sharply as she opened the door. She slammed it shut as the rodent odor poured out making her gag and hold her nose. As she looked around, she absentmindedly reached for her necklace. Her heart leaped to her throat, and her veins turned to ice when her fingers met only skin.

Rushing back to the cot, she searched through the sheets and under the cot. Theo squeaked at her and tugged on her shirt, but she hardly noticed in her panicked state. Tears pricked the back of her eyes. That necklace was the only thing she had of her birth parents. Behind her, the door creaked open, and she pulled her knife from her belt, whipping around.

Brayden threw his hands up; a couple of fish tied to a line in his hand swayed wildly, sending water splattering. "Whoa, it's me!" He lowered his arms. "I'm glad you're not a knife thrower—that could have been a disaster." One corner of his mouth tipped up.

Gemma sheathed the knife, taking calming breaths and ignoring the sarcasm in his voice. "Can you blame me for being jumpy?" Her throat tightened. "I can't find my necklace. I guess I must have lost it in the river."

Brayden set the fish on the table, withdrawing her necklace from one of his pockets. "I took it off you," he held it out to her. "For now, you need to make sure you don't wear it."

Her muscles relaxed as her fingers closed around her precious possession, and she hugged it close to her chest.

Theo squeaked and glared at her with his best *I was trying to tell you* face.

She glowered at Theo before asking Brayden, "Why shouldn't I wear it?"

Brayden pulled a knife from his belt, grabbed a bucket of water from outside, and proceeded to clean the fish with expert movements. "I'll get to that. It's a lot to explain."

"Okay, so explain," she demanded, looking at him expectantly.

He lifted an eyebrow, his jaw tightening. "I don't have to tell you, you know. I could tell you to trust me and not give you any explanations."

Gemma pursed her lips, knowing she was being impatient, but that didn't excuse his snapping remark.

She snatched up Theo mid-stride as he stomped toward Brayden with a warning growl. She set Theo on a chair, giving him a silent command to stay and behave. He harumphed, plopping onto his butt and crossing his forelegs across his chest.

Gemma shook her head, turning her attention back to Brayden. She opened her mouth to give him a piece of her mind when he held up a hand to stop her.

"I'm sorry, that was uncalled for." His face remained tight despite his words. "Look, we've both been through a lot in the last twenty-four hours. How about we get some food in us before we delve into everything?"

Gemma didn't care for this plan, but she didn't want a fight either. Closing her eyes, she took a calming breath and then nodded.

Brayden continued working on the fish in silence.

Gemma noticed how confidently he worked, as if he had been doing that his whole life. She blinked as she realized she was staring at his arms, at how strong they looked, and the few wide scars that ran across them. Many of the scars looked like they came from burns, but it was hard to tell. "What happened after I blacked out?" She didn't care if he wasn't in a chatty mood; the silence made her uncomfortable.

Brayden's work on the fish never slowed as he answered. "I grabbed you, and we floated down the river until we came to a break in the cliffs and I pulled you to shore. We were lucky we weren't in a wider part, otherwise we might have been stuck floating for hours. Your little furry friend—"

"Theo," Gemma offered.

"Theo...he's the one who spotted your pack caught on a log. Thankfully, it didn't take long to find this cabin; we were fortunate we weren't washed any farther downstream. The farther south we go, the fewer signs of civilization and the wider the river becomes."

She winced. Thinking of all Brayden had been through to get her to safety, she scolded herself for having been so focused on her own soreness. "You carried me and two packs all the way here?"

He shrugged. "As I said, finding the cabin didn't take long."

"Still, I'm sorry I wasn't able to help." She bit her lip, and her anger toward him dimmed. "How long was I out?"

"All yesterday and through the night."

Her jaw dropped. Living on the farm, you got up early to do chores and didn't go to bed until they were finished. Never in her life had she slept that much or even dreamed about trying to. "What about the people after us? Won't they catch up since we've been here so long?"

"They shouldn't. The cliff on that side stretches for miles in both directions. They'll have to run along the cliff until it drops down to the river. It should take them a few days. And Theo and I have been taking shifts keeping watch."

She wondered why Brayden wasn't dead on his feet. He couldn't have been able to get much rest while she was unconscious. "What's to keep them from scaling down the cliff? Or jumping in as we did?"

"I don't know if you forgot, but it was a miracle we missed all the rocks. Not to mention, that part of the Cattaway is the fastest and most dangerous part for miles. They'll have to travel a long way to find a place they can safely cross. I thought you explored a bunch during your free time?"

She crossed her arms, shifting her weight to one hip, not appreciating his condescending tone. "I never explored that far from home. In case you didn't know, I don't make a habit of dashing through the forest all night." She fought the urge to stick her tongue out at him. "Where are we anyway?"

"There's no way to tell how far we drifted, but we're on the east side of the Cattaway."

"The east side?" She dropped her arms, her stomach tightening. "Isn't that placing us in more danger?"

He rolled his head from side to side. "Yes and no. They'll be looking for us on the west side, which should buy us some time, but yes; we need to be cautious on this side. Especially considering how far south we are. I didn't plan on us having to jump into the river. I misjudged how close we were." He frowned. "I apologize for the need to jump from the cliff."

She opened and closed her mouth a few times, not sure what to say. His apology took her off guard. He was snapping at her one moment, then apologizing in the next; though the apology sounded like it irked him to say. She didn't know what to make of this man. "Are you ever going to explain why my dad was so quick to trust you?"

His jaw clenched, and he gave her a sideways glance. "Food first." Then he took the fish outside.

Gemma threw her hands up, then let them fall and slap her legs. She had the mind to sic Theo on Brayden, but she feared he'd never answer her questions if she did that. There was no choice but to wait for him to decide he was ready to tell her everything. She stomped outside, joining him by a small fire, and did what she could to help him with the meal.

They worked in silence, each stewing over their own frustrations. Gemma frequently glanced at Brayden as they worked. Every movement he made was swift and confident, never straying from his task. Again, she found herself noting how strong he was. His life must have been one of physical labor. He didn't seem unkind. That became abundantly clear in how he took care of her scrapes, but he was guarded and on edge with her. She wondered if he was an introvert or if something about her was making him act closed off. Her gaze kept drawing back to his face, being pulled in by his handsome features. Heat rushed to her cheeks when he caught her staring, and she jerked her eyes down, thankful he continued working without comment.

Theo's constant chatter helped her mood a bit. He was back to his usual happy self, running around and sniffing the cooking fish with relish. Food always livened him up.

After the fish was cooked, Gemma and Theo brought it in while Brayden piled dirt on the fire pit. Gemma placed a couple of plates and forks on the table and sat down, her stomach rumbling loudly.

Theo didn't wait for her; he was already digging into a fish head before Gemma had picked up her fork.

She grimaced while he slurped and crunched. Fish was not her ideal breakfast. Mariah always made the best breakfasts, with eggs, bacon, and biscuits. But her trepidation fled as she put the first bite in her mouth. She made a small moan as the fish melted on her tongue. Her mouth slowed mid-chew as she realized she'd never known hunger, not like this. Even with how hard things had become in recent years, her father kept plenty of food on the table. With the realization, guilt washed over her. She said a prayer of thanks for everything she'd taken for granted and promised to thank her parents for all they did the moment she had the chance.

Brayden soon joined them, sitting without a glance at either of them and digging into the fish.

Gemma finished first, leaning back, and fidgeting with the end of her braid while she waited for Brayden to finish. She wriggled in her seat, anxious to hear what he had to tell her. It appeared as if he was taking enjoyment in drawing out the meal. She scolded herself for being so quick to judge. For all she knew, he was mulling over the best place to start.

After he finished, he stood and rinsed off his dish. Gemma rolled her eyes as she followed suit. *He's definitely drawing it out on purpose!*

As they resumed their seats at the table, Brayden finally spoke. "Okay, I'll explain. But know that I might not have all the answers you're hoping for."

"Finally!" She exclaimed before snapping her mouth shut. The word came out angrier than she meant it to.

He narrowed his eyes, leaning back and crossing his arms across his chest.

Gemma sighed, closing her eyes. "I'm sorry." Opening her eyes, she did her best to explain. "My life was simple. Normal, even, for eighteen years. Then, out of nowhere, I'm attacked, saved by some guy who knows things no one should know, forced to leave my parents, and chased all night!" She couldn't stop her voice from rising. "Oh, and came close to dying. Don't forget that part."

He took a few slow breaths before relaxing his arms. "Okay, you're right. I imagine this all must be scary and confusing for you. I'll tell you what I know if you can set aside your impatience."

Gemma bit the inside of her cheek. This man confounded her. He had risked his life to save her, but he acted like he begrudged that decision. He'd been short and curt anytime he'd talked to her so far, but he'd taken the time to clean her wounds when she was unconscious. She wasn't sure if she could trust anything he told her, but she needed to know what he knew. Forcing her body to relax, she gave him the go-ahead.

"Okay. First, as I said, my parents and your birth parents were best friends. Close enough that my mother even named one of my sisters after your mother, Thalia."

That name did strange things to Gemma's insides, but she fought to hold her tongue.

He continued. "Our parents were Keepers; people chosen to keep and protect jewels of power. My dad told me the jewels are called song jewels. All I know is that the people who have them tend to be able to do things others can't, but my dad never elaborated on what that meant. I remember him mentioning something about the jewels longing to be together, but unfortunately, I don't know what he meant by that either."

Gemma couldn't stop herself from asking, "If your dad knows so much about all this, why didn't he come with us?"

Brayden's eyes darkened, and he took a deep breath.

Gemma wasn't sure if he was mad that she interrupted or if she had struck a nerve.

He was silent long enough for her to regret having opened her mouth, then he answered, "He passed away when I was thirteen."

"Oh. I'm so sorry." She wanted to kick herself for being so thoughtless in her questioning. She hadn't considered that he might not have both parents living any longer. Thinking back on what he'd said so far, she remembered he'd talked about his father in the past tense. *Way to go, Gemma.*

He shrugged, acting nonchalant, but he couldn't hide the pain in his eyes. "It's okay; it's been a long time. The problem is he didn't get the chance to give me as much information as I should have had. You see, the Keepers pass their knowledge down from one generation to the next. Training is supposed to start at twelve, but my circumstances were different. I don't remember a lot of it, but I'll tell you all I can.

"From what I know, each jewel standing alone has power—what that power is, I couldn't say. But if you combine all the jewels, it's believed the one wielding them would be almost invincible. After seven years, the jewels bond to the person wearing them. Unfortunately, I don't know the significance of the bonding."

Gemma leaned in. "You said, jewels. How many are we talking about?"

"My dad was convinced there were a total of seven jewels, but only six of the jewels show up in recorded history. The seventh one was, as far as anyone knew, merely legend. No written evidence can be found. It's only known by folklore, having been passed down through stories. Even most of the Keepers didn't believe a seventh jewel existed, but my dad firmly believed in seven jewels. He said that seven was the number of the Creator, and it made sense that there would be seven jewels since he believed the Creator Himself made them. I never knew what to believe, but since you're being doggedly pursued, it must be because you have the seventh jewel."

Gemma pulled her necklace out of her pouch. She held it up to the light, watching as the clear jewel swayed side to side without reflecting much light. "How could this be the seventh jewel?"

"May I?" He held out his hand. Gemma handed him the necklace, and he studied it closely, reciting, "As black as night, as orange as firelight, always changing yet ever the same, greener than life at the core of its name, red as blood, blue as a flood. Black, orange, multicolored, green, red, blue." He stared at the necklace, lost in thought for a moment. "Dad made me memorize that," he said softly, handing her back the necklace.

"But that's only six colors. I still don't understand what my necklace has to do with all that or how anyone knew I had it." She rubbed her temples. Nothing made sense, and with each bit of information she received, more questions formed in her mind.

"My dad told me the legendary seventh jewel was colorless. He called it the Cornerstone jewel. Believe me, I wish I knew more than that, but all I know is that the Cornerstone is important, maybe even more important than the rest. That must be the Cornerstone. It *has* to be. There's no other explanation for why you were attacked, and they didn't let up. The only reason I can think of is they're after your jewel."

Gemma held it up once more. "But you can see it's only glass!"

She placed the necklace on the table with a frustrated grunt. It was clear the necklace was nothing more than a cheap trinket. The only value it held was the sentimental connection to her birth parents.

Brayden leaned in; his eyes alight. "Your parents were Keepers, Gemma. It seems probable your mother must have hidden the necklace on you before she died. That's the reason they're after you now. They couldn't care less about some girl who didn't die like she was supposed to eighteen years ago. The only thing that ties this all together is that you have something they desperately want. Something they'll do anything for. Somehow, they must have figured out what you have."

"Why now? Why did it take eighteen years for them to figure out I had it?"

"I don't know. Unfortunately, I didn't get to complete my training. There was so much I was supposed to be taught, but I only know a few facts. I wish I could answer all your questions. I have as many questions as you do, but I can only tell you as much as I know." He leaned back with a heavy sigh.

Gemma couldn't sit still any longer. Standing up, she paced the short length of the cabin despite the protest from her muscles. She mulled over the information, willing it to make sense. Theo didn't offer any input; he was too busy munching on the fish heads again, making her stomach turn. "Okay, I'll accept that you don't know a lot, but you told me not to wear my necklace. Why?"

"It was something I remember my dad saying, something about a connection the jewels created when worn, but, again, I don't know exactly why." He looked as upset as she was.

They both fell into silence. Grabbing the necklace, she returned it to her belt pouch. There were so many unanswered questions. She tried not to be angry at Brayden. He could only tell her as much as he knew, but she hated that he didn't know more, and she couldn't shake the feeling that he was holding a lot back. So many questions bounced around in her mind, all piling up together, overwhelming her and making her head hurt. How did her enemies miss the jewel when she was a baby? The necklace had been with her since she could remember, which meant someone had found it. She'd never thought to ask about it.

Her mind reeled faster and faster. Who were her birth parents, really? Why didn't Brayden's dad contact her? He died when Brayden was thirteen; she'd never asked his age, but he couldn't be but a few years older than her, so why leave her in the dark? Why did all this happen to someone as invisible and insignificant as she?

Resentment toward her birth parents rose within her. She knew it was unfair to blame them for anything, but she couldn't help it. They had died without leaving her any information, not even a note explaining all this. She was left to stumble blindfolded around an obstacle course with nothing to guide her. If it had been so dangerous to be a Keeper, shouldn't they have left something, anything, explaining all this in case something happened to them? Did they think they would somehow be spared any danger?

She moved to the window. The grassy valley looked so peaceful. The river gurgled along playfully. A doe and her fawn strolled down by the river, stopping every couple of feet to eat or drink. The calm and peace of the scene mocked her, reminding her she might never have that kind of peace again.

So many times, she wished for her life to have more meaning. There was a time when she longed for adventure. She figured most people did if they were honest. Now she was living an adventure of a lifetime, and all she wanted was to have her dull, ordinary life back. Ironically, she was sure that if she had her old life back, it wouldn't be long before she longed for adventure again. "So, this is what my parents died for. They were killed keeping the jewel from those who are now after me?"

"They gave their lives to keep the jewel out of evil hands." Brayden sat up taller, his voice laced with pride.

Gemma stared at the fawn with its mother. She imagined the doe would most likely sacrifice her life if a predator attacked. Even some birds were known to protect their young from fire, burning to death themselves to keep their little ones safe. Her mother had done that for her, laying her life down to protect her daughter.

Some of her resentment ebbed away. They died doing what was right, protecting countless others, but they still died, and the evil that prematurely snuffed out their lives was alive and well in the world. She had always tried to see the best in the world and others, but sometimes fighting for good felt hopeless; evil seemed to win more times than not. Evil had no rules, no one to tell it to stop. It did whatever it desired, not caring about the lives it crushed. Once it squeezed every ounce of life out of an area, it would move on to destroy the next beautiful thing. Stopping evil was like trying to hold back a landslide—impossible and hopeless.

She remembered being five years old, having climbed a tree and then becoming too scared to figure out how to climb back down. Back then, she'd called for her dad. He hadn't hesitated. He came out and convinced her to jump into his arms. She trusted him completely, jumping without a doubt that he would catch her. Now there was no one to call, no one to come and catch her. This time, she was being asked to jump without knowing if anyone was below. She was inadequate. Why was she the one given the necklace? She was nobody. Why didn't her mother find someone older and wiser to give the jewel to? All the questions slammed into one another, piling up like sand to bury her.

"That's how you knew my name. Your dad told you about me, didn't he?" Gemma asked, not looking away from the window.

He answered slowly, hesitantly. "The night your parents were murdered, my dad went to help them, but he was too late. Our house was a hard day's ride from yours, and he had to take it on foot. By the time he got to your house, Dean, your father, was already…gone."

Despite his annoyance with her earlier, he was trying to tell her in the gentlest way possible. Whatever misgivings she had about him, she was now convinced he must be a decent man. She pressed her lips together, determined not to cry.

Brayden continued when she didn't say anything. "My dad followed the trail left by the men through the forest, hoping to have the chance to save your mother, but all he found was an empty patch of ground stained with blood. He followed cart tracks, and they led him to a house. He was met by your father and he inquired about your mother. Your father informed my dad that he'd already buried your mother. My dad asked if your father had seen any children with her—"

Gemma spun around. "Children? Plural?" Her heart had jumped like a rabbit at the sound of the word.

"I'm sorry. I thought they would have told you. You have—or had—two older sisters, but I don't know what happened to them." He let that sink in for a moment. "When Thomas told my dad he'd found you and your mother's body but no other children, my dad assumed you didn't have the jewel. He figured you would likely be safe, so he decided to leave you with Thomas and his wife.

"He tried to find your sisters, but they vanished. He decided it would be best to let Thomas and Mariah raise you, but with no leads on your sisters and no direction to search for the jewels, he chose to stay close and check on you as you grew up. My dad watched you grow, taking time to try and find any trace of your sisters and the jewels through his contacts, but nothing ever surfaced."

There was a hint of bitterness in his voice as he talked about his dad, stopping Gemma from asking the questions she wanted to ask. Why did his dad never once talk to her? He'd been in Dano but remained hidden from her life. She didn't know how to feel about the news that someone had been watching without her knowledge. Knowing he was an ally made it a little better, but it was unsettling. She rejoined Brayden at the table.

Brayden studied her face, his voice growing quieter. "I met you a few times before that awful night." At her wide eyes, he explained, "I was five, so I don't remember much, but that's the truth of how I knew your name. After my dad died, I took his place watching out for you. I promised him I would."

Gemma's face burned like someone lit a stove next to her. It was worse knowing *he* had been watching her. Her pulse spiked at the thought that he could have been there at any given moment of her life, and she wondered how she'd never noticed him before. He couldn't have been hidden every day. It unnerved her to think how good he must be at blending in that she never once noticed him over the years.

She wondered how Theo could have missed him. Theo never missed anything. She narrowed her eyes at him.

Theo must have known the conclusion she'd come to. He glanced up quickly with a short squeak. This was something they would have to discuss later.

Gemma glared at him. His ears pulled down behind him, and he wrung his forefeet nervously. She shook her head but didn't press him; there were more important matters to discuss. Theo relaxed, grateful for the reprieve, and timidly returned to his eating.

Brayden watched the silent exchange, his face awash with confusion. With a shake of his head, he plowed on. "My dad always ingrained it in me to ensure we watched from a distance. I don't know why, but he was convinced you would be safer if we didn't involve ourselves in your everyday life.

"I did. For so long, I did. But I wanted to meet you, meet the person my dad had spent so much time worrying about. That's why I was at the tavern the other night. I wanted to see what you were like face-to-face. I know this won't make any sense to you, but I had questions that needed answering, and meeting you was the best way to answer them." He leaned back, a corner of his mouth lifting. "It's a good thing I was there, though. Who knows what might have happened to you if I hadn't been?"

Gemma chewed on her cheek while she thought. What kind of questions did he have that could only be answered by meeting her? Something wasn't adding up, but she couldn't figure out what. She returned to the window, leaning against the windowsill, more comfortable with the extra space between her and Brayden. That comfort vanished when he joined her a moment later.

Exhaustion washed over her as her mind tried to grapple with the new information. Her life would never be the same. There would be no returning to normal. From here on out, it would be one uncertainty after another. Her life had gone from order to chaos at breakneck speed.

Theo climbed to her shoulder, curling his tail around her neck protectively. He growled a little toward Brayden. Sensing her unease; he would always take her side. She put her hand on him to let him know it was okay. "So, there's no way to know how they found me in the first place. Which means we won't know how to hide."

"Unfortunately, yes. Why it took this long for them to find you, why they didn't kill you eighteen years ago, all of that I can't answer. They weren't the type of people to show mercy." He spat out the last words as though they were acid.

Gemma analyzed Brayden while he looked intently out the window. She wished she could read his mind. How much was he not saying? Did he know more about her parents than he said? Was she sure she should trust him as much as she did? She wasn't sure if she should ask, but she decided to risk it. "What about your mother?"

He turned to her, his eyes dark with anger. "That's not a discussion for right now." He returned to the table, sitting down heavily.

She wanted to demand an answer. How was she supposed to trust him if he kept everything hidden? If Mariah were there, she would remind Gemma that the surface of a lake didn't reveal what's underneath; one would have to dive in to discover what lay beneath the calm surface. That's exactly what she wanted to do, dive in, and drag the answers out of him, but she feared she'd already pushed more than she should for one day. She swallowed any further questions about his past. He probably trusted her as little as she trusted him, after all.

Gazing out the window once more, she noticed the doe and fawn were gone without a trace. Everything Brayden said played through her mind. It was all too much and not enough. She'd had two older sisters, a mother, and a father who loved her, and all of them were ripped from her. And for what? A mystery jewel that most were convinced didn't exist? "What do we do now?" The question came out near a whisper.

"Honestly, I have no idea. We shouldn't stay in one place too long. We should keep moving. I don't know how quickly they'll find us."

"And what, just keep running? We can't run for the rest of our lives!"

"I know. I'm not saying run forever, but until we have a better plan, we have to keep on the move. We'll start heading north. Being this far south will put us in more danger."

Gemma remembered how often her parents had talked about the Nahastian Army that lived around Skotadi's castle in the Verlasian Lands, east of the Cattaway and deep in the south. The farther south one traveled, the more danger they placed themselves in.

Brayden's voice cut into her thoughts. "We should get prepared to leave. Going north will make our progress harder as winter sets in, but nothing about this will be easy, and it's the only heading we have for now."

"I guess I have no choice but to follow you then." She looked him in the eye. "Theo trusts you—well, he's willing to tolerate you—so I'll do my best to trust you, too."

Brayden dipped his head. "I'll do everything I can to keep you safe, Gemma. I promised Thomas, and I never break a promise."

Gemma knew he would follow through with what he said. She still wasn't sure she liked him, but she had no choice but to trust him for the foreseeable future. He had more answers, and she needed those answers so she could make sense of everything that was happening. He might be stern and guarded, but he was genuine in his role of protecting her. Sticking with him would give her the time to pry more answers from him, and maybe figure out why he kept himself aloof. "I'll hold you to that promise as well. And I'll never let you forget it."

He smiled for the first time since the tavern. "I guess we'll have to hold each other accountable then." He held out his arm. "Deal?"

"Deal," she said, clasping his arm. A small ember of hope sparked within her. The journey ahead was going to be arduous, but maybe they would be able to find some common ground along the way.

CHAPTER FOUR

Fovos cracked his knuckles with harsh jerking movements, imagining each subsequent pop as a bone breaking in the blond wench's body. Growling, he pounded his fist into the ground. She was just out of reach. Her pack had brushed his fingertips before she fell out of sight. He'd gathered the men and followed along the cliff until nightfall, but the landscape refused to provide a way to scale down safely, and there was no sight of one coming soon. The vile river moved at the speed of a frantic horse; there was no telling how far the wench had been carried. Fovos knew they would be searching on through the night; there would be no rest until his prey was found.

A slight twinge started at the base of his skull, demanding his attention and forcing him to stop. With a howl of rage, he ran his sword through one of the men to expel his pent-up irritation. Skotadi couldn't have summoned him at a worse time, but Fovos knew if he ignored the summoning, he'd feel a lot more than a twinge. He sucked his teeth, then spit forcefully to the side before closing his eyes. This way of communicating irked him. The feel of someone else controlling his mind was enough to make his stomach turn, but it came in handy when out in the field.

Skotadi was the only one Fovos knew who could enter people's minds. No one knew where he learned the skill, but it made him a powerful adversary. Fovos took pride in knowing that Skotadi couldn't control his mind without his permission; he could only control the minds of those too weak or ignorant to resist. But he could make Fovos' life a living nightmare if ignored.

Fovos rolled his shoulders and cracked his neck before opening his mind. The black in his vision slowly morphed into a dim room. He stood in a two-hundred-square foot room. As he held his hands up, they were misty, like looking through a dense fog, but he could feel the stone under his feet and smell the stale, musty air. In the back of his mind, he was aware of his physical self, with closed eyes, standing on the cliff, but this mental version of himself felt more real. He scanned the room. The walls, ceiling, and floor were made from dark grey stones, adorned with nothing more than a few torches. The chill air of the windowless room made the space as welcoming as a tomb. The room was empty except for a stone throne at the far end, which was currently unoccupied. He cursed under his breath. This was something he should have expected; an urgent call just to tarry.

Under Skotadi's control, Fovos was rooted in place, barred from moving. Crackling from the torches drew his eyes—their feeble light tried and failed to fill the entirety of the room. He grumbled to himself about electric lights, a new invention of the Efevretites that worked much better than the crude torches and lanterns. Only the wealthy could afford them, which meant, of all people, Skotadi should have been the first to have them. However, Fovos was smart enough never to question Skotadi's reasons for keeping to the old ways. To question Skotadi was to risk forfeiting one's life, and Fovos had too much love for his own life to risk it in such a foolish manner.

A chill ran down his back in the same instant Skotadi materialized from a deep shadow along the wall. Fovos flinched inwardly, thankful his discipline was enough that his face didn't show it. Skotadi often arrived in such a manner, preferring to take people off-guard. Fovos examined the darkness along the wall, but the shadows were too deep; there was no telling if there was a door there or not. Rumors abounded amongst those of the Nahastian Army that Skotadi was able to travel through shadows as one would travel through a doorway. No one could prove one way or another, but Fovos wouldn't be surprised if Skotadi had such a command of darkness.

Skotadi strolled to the throne without a glance toward Fovos. He eased his lean, six-foot frame down, leaning back and resting an elbow on the arm of the throne. The pale white skin on his shaved head gleamed in the meager torchlight, and he ran his index finger and thumb across his full, black mustache and beard. He regarded Fovos with half-lidded eyes. His eyes were like pools of oil, and the whites of his eyes appeared red from a distance due to the many red veins.

Fovos swallowed, but his throat was dry, causing the swallow to scratch and irritate, and he coughed. The last time he'd failed to bring back the jewel, Skotadi made Fovos watch while he poured liquid metal down the throats of the other men of the search party. There hadn't been any need to touch Fovos; the gurgled screams of the men being the only warning he'd needed. Not that the men dying bothered him—death was something he found fascinating to watch—but he had seen the message in Skotadi's eyes; he was running out of patience, and the thought of Fovos' own death wasn't as thrilling. That was eighteen years ago; there was no telling what Skotadi would do now.

The minutes stretched as Skotadi sat quietly, staring at Fovos.

Fovos' blood ran cold, and every hair on his body stood on end. He breathed deeply, hating his body for showing any signs of weakness. It wasn't Skotadi's stare that caused this visceral reaction. Those black eyes were enough to cause anyone to be unnerved, but what made Fovos' palms sweat was Skotadi's mere presence. The man radiated a wave of terror as though his body was producing an invisible cloud of misery and fear to envelop everything around it.

The light from the torches dimmed, or maybe it was just Fovos' hatred toward the man on the throne making the room darken; he couldn't say. He knelt stiffly, his eyes dropping to the floor. "My lord."

Skotadi leaned forward. "I see you have failed again, Fovos."

Fovos winced involuntarily. Skotadi's voice, like honey to the weak-willed, jabbed like ice into Fovos' brain. "There were...unexpected circumstances, my lord. One of the men decided to advance on his own. And she had help that we were unaware of."

Skotadi stood up slowly. "So, you bring me excuses again instead of what I sent you for." His voice remained casual as he spoke.

"We're still tracking her; she won't get far, and now we know what to prepare for. If I could have kept on the move, I would be drawing closer to her as we speak…"

Skotadi sauntered forward, drawing out each step. "You say I'm wrong for calling on you?"

Beads of sweat started to work their way down the temples of Fovos' physical body. "Of course not, my lord, only that I would serve you better continuing the search. I know I will not fail again—"

His head snapped to the left from Skotadi's backhanded blow. Fovos' physical self mirrored his mental self's movements. Blood trickled down his physical nose, but he couldn't wipe it away while absent from his body; only Skotadi could affect both selves at once. Fovos shook his head; abuse was nothing new to him.

Skotadi knelt, leaning in. "You have been searching and failing for years, Fovos. Only once did you ever retrieve anything useful."

Fovos' head snapped the other direction; his physical body copying again. His world darkened and then turned red, either from pain or rage, he didn't know, but the blood pounded louder in his ears. He desired nothing more than to see Skotadi dead. Twenty years ago, he'd had the chance. Skotadi had been vulnerable for the first time, but Fovos hadn't realized how much he would eventually hate this master. Skotadi had grown more insufferable with each consecutive year. He was still vulnerable, but his power had grown significantly over the years. For now, Fovos had to be patient.

The doors behind Fovos clicked open. He groaned as he looked back.

Kalami Telfer sashayed slowly into the room, her chin tilted down and her hand on the hilt of her sword. She was breathtaking to behold. Standing a head taller than Skotadi, her elegantly muscled frame exuded femininity without hiding the warrior beneath. Her dark olive skin was complemented by hair as dark as a shadow that swept back into a long ponytail hanging to her waist. High cheekbones and perfectly formed eyebrows accentuated dark brown almond-shaped eyes. Around her neck, she wore a leather choker with a blood-red jewel dangling perfectly between her collar bones and drawing attention to the low cut of her shirt. She sported her usual attire: black pants and a blood-red leather corset over a black sleeveless shirt. Every article of clothing accentuated each curve. She knew how to be alluring to men, not only in how she dressed but in every movement she made.

A wave of desire rose unbidden within Fovos' chest. He lifted his upper lip and would have spit if he could. The weakness of his flesh sickened him. "Kalami." He spoke between his teeth, grinding them together hard enough that pain shot through his jaw.

Her eyes flicked toward Fovos, but she gave no other acknowledgment. Stopping before Skotadi, she bowed low, a hint of a smile playing on her lips as she saw the hunger on both men's faces. "My lord?" Her voice rang crystal clear in the cold chamber, beautiful and deadly as a viper.

Skotadi held his hand out to her. "My Kalami." He gestured toward Fovos with a flick of his hand. "This fool has failed me again."

Kalami smirked. "As we knew he would."

"Yes, but I'm a generous man. I give people more chances than they deserve." Skotadi shrugged.

Fovos narrowed his eyes. He would have used many words to describe Skotadi, but generous wasn't one of them.

"I'm placing you in charge now, Kalami," Skotadi said. "You will go and do what Fovos has failed to accomplish."

She dipped her head slowly, drawing out the movement. "Yes, my lord."

Fovos blanched. Never had Skotadi risked sending his precious Henathian into the field. He balled his fists, standing to his full height, ignoring Kalami's quiet snort. "Am I expected to take orders from her?"

Skotadi tilted his head. "I was told I should have you killed for your failures." He said it as calmly as one deciding which shirt to wear.

Fovos eyes snapped to Kalami. She didn't attempt to hide the glint in her eyes.

Skotadi waved a hand. "However, you have served me for so many years. I've grown fond of you, like a stray dog who becomes part of the family." He smiled coldly. "I will come up with another plan for you, Fovos." He faced Kalami. "Take as many men as you deem needed."

She bowed and started for the door.

"And Kalami." Skotadi's voice reverberated off the walls.

She stopped mid-stride, turning.

"You will not fail me." He smiled, showing all his teeth, but the words hung in the air.

Fovos grinned darkly as Kalami paled a shade, though his glee was cut short when her mouth curled into a wry smile, any hint of fear washing from her face as quickly as it had come.

"Of course, my lord. You will receive exactly what you're asking for." She bowed again, glancing briefly at Fovos with unmasked disgust, then she was gone, leaving Fovos alone with Skotadi.

Fovos' blood once again turned to ice.

Skotadi returned to the throne. He pulled on his beard with one hand, the corners of his mouth lifting while his quiet stare made Fovos squirm.

Fovos' hatred swelled like a black monster in his chest, sinking its teeth deep into his heart. Someday, if he lived long enough, he would watch the life drain from Skotadi's eyes. He didn't even care if he was the one responsible. He was tired of this master. But he knew how to be patient; he knew how to bide his time. He could be the lion stalking its prey, slowly, inch by inch. And if another beast took out his prey for him, that only meant less work for him. For now, he bowed. "What are your orders, my lord?"

CHAPTER FIVE

Gemma, Theo, and Brayden made their way steadily north. Gemma's heart longed for the chance to soak in the beauty of the land around her. She'd never seen such magnificence before. Long mountain ranges rose on either side, the Cattaway snaking between them. The mountains and the valley were blanketed with deciduous trees, their leaves a collage of flaming oranges, vivid reds, and cheerful yellows, making any paintings Gemma had seen pale in comparison. In Dano, a few trees had their leaves change in the winter, but she'd never seen so many at once, and the sight took her breath away. However, despite no sign of pursuit, Brayden maintained a grueling pace, driving them from sunup to sundown with few breaks along the way, causing her to keep her gaze mostly glued to the ground to retain her footing. Gemma struggled to adapt to the constant demand on her body, often causing her to jog to catch up with Brayden while he stood, arms crossed, waiting for her. His attitude toward her became exceedingly short as the days went on.

The evenings were the worst. The first night after they left the cabin, Brayden picked a secluded spot hidden in a cluster of trees to stop for the night. Gemma helped him gather brush and branches to make lean-tos. She didn't mind that part in the least, but when Brayden told her to get a small fire ready, she looked around, hands fidgeting at her sides.

"Gemma, what are you doing? You can make a fire over there." He pointed to a spot over his shoulder, not pausing from his work on the shelters.

Theo tugged her hair, squeaking a few short squeaks.

"Right. How hard can a small fire be?" She gave Theo a tight smile, then set to work, finding some twigs and branches.

After a couple of minutes, she had a nice pile of small twigs, bigger branches, and a circle of stones beside them. She sat back on her heels, her eyes boring into the empty circle. Absently she reached up and petted Theo's head. "How do I get it started with nothing to start a fire, Theo?" she whispered, furtively glancing toward Brayden.

Theo squeaked, shrugging his small shoulders.

"What do you mean you don't know? You always brag about how smart Scruffs are."

He squeaked, rubbing his forefeet down his fluffy fur.

"I know you have fur, but you've watched people make fires before."

He crossed his forelegs, squeaking louder.

"I did watch Mom make fires, but she always had that piece of iron and flint she used. I didn't see any of that in my pack!" Her voice rose as she forgot to whisper. "Why would Dad forget to pack something so important—"

"What's the problem over here?" Brayden asked, now standing directly behind Gemma, making her jump.

She cleared her throat, clasping her hands together. "I, um...well, I don't exactly know how to...start the fire." She scratched her neck, scrunching her lips to the side.

Brayden's mouth flattened to a straight line. "Eighteen years and no one taught you how to start a fire?"

Gemma crossed her arms over her chest. "I know how to start one with an iron and flint, but I don't have any of that at my disposal."

"For a girl who grew up outside of town, you sure sound like a city girl." He stepped away, scanning the ground.

She stood up and followed, straightening her arms and balling her fists. "There is a lot I know how to do. The fact that I don't know how to start a fire without tools doesn't make me a city girl!"

He grabbed a stone off the ground. Jerking his knife from his belt, he struck the stone, producing a quick spark. "The tools are all around you. You just need to be observant."

Gemma turned her face away.

"This is simple stuff; how did your parents never teach you this?"

Her gaze remained locked on the ground while she blinked back hot tears. It wasn't lost on her that she probably knew less about survival than the average person. She knew how sheltered her upbringing had been. Her parents went above and beyond to make her life a happy one.

Theo growled at Brayden, scooting closer to Gemma's cheek.

Brayden sighed heavily. "Okay, let's try this again." He held the stone out to her. "I'll teach you." His voice remained tight.

Gemma reluctantly took the stone, not looking him in the eye. "Now what?"

Theo offered his little squeaks of encouragement, patting her gently on the shoulder, but they didn't ease the tightness in her stomach. She quietly listened as Brayden pointed out how to recognize the type of stone that would produce a spark when struck.

He strode back to the circle of stones and began chucking some of them away. "Never use these stones for a fire." He held up one of the stones, then replaced them with new ones. "They explode, and you'll be dodging fragments." Lastly, he shook his head at Gemma's wood pile, tossing aside most. "You can't burn the branches that are so green. They smoke too much. Make sure you don't get leaves in the fire either; we don't want to signal where we are."

Gemma pulled her arms in tighter and tighter as he spoke. *I didn't do anything right.*

"Okay, grab some of that dry grass over there." Brayden pointed over his shoulder, his eyes fixed on the new circle of stones.

Gemma did as he asked, handing him the grass and kneeling beside him. She didn't want to be that close to him, but she knew if she didn't pay attention, it would only exasperate him more. Theo leaned out curiously, stretching his neck, his nose twitching up and down as he watched.

Brayden quickly bunched the grass into a bird's nest, then set it in the middle of the circle. Holding the rock above the grass, he struck knife against stone. A spark fell into the grass and caught, springing the fire to life. He bent down and blew until flames ate at the grass, then he leaned back, his hands outstretched toward the fire. "It's as easy as that."

Gemma eyed him sideways. With a frown fixed on her face, she copied what he showed, making her own bird's nest. Holding the rock in her left hand, she struck it with her knife but instantly dropped the stone as the blade missed her thumb by a hair.

Brayden snatched the stone off the ground before she could protest and lit the bird's nest for her. "Blow on it quickly."

Gemma leaned forward, blowing, but smoke wafted into her lungs as she inhaled. Theo jumped off her shoulder as her body convulsed with hard coughs.

"Maybe you should let me do the fire building from here on out." Brayden's lips twitched, and the corners of his eyes pinched.

Gemma shot to her feet, still coughing, and stomped away. She plopped down on a tree stump and hugged her arms around herself. Brayden had his back to her, but his shoulders shook, and she knew he was laughing at her. Glaring at his back, she dug her nails into her palms. *Of all people, why'd I have to get stuck with him?*

Theo joined her on the stump. His lips turned up in a smile, and he exhaled short puffs of air.

She swiped a tear off her cheek. "You're not supposed to be laughing at me either. You should be taking my side and go poke Brayden with something sharp."

Theo tapped her leg kindly, squeaking.

"What do you mean you have a plan?"

His eyebrows wiggled up and down, and he rubbed his forefeet together with a small purr.

That night, as Brayden sat down next to the fire, he shot to his feet with a muffled yell, rubbing his backside. He whirled around, snatching up a small Needlevine that occupied his seat.

Theo puffed out his small laugh, and Gemma tucked her chin, pulling her lips between her teeth as Brayden shot her a glare. She expected a scolding, but he threw the vine away and dropped to his seat without a word.

In the morning, he woke to his bootlaces tied together and his pockets full of worms. He stomped over to Theo, kneeling. "Okay, you and I need to have a serious talk." He tramped off, indicating with his head for Theo to follow. When Gemma started to rise, he held up a hand. "This is between him and me."

"But you won't understand—"

Theo squeaked that it was okay and hopped toward Brayden.

Gemma watched them disappear behind some trees. She paced while she waited, her gaze flicking toward the trees every few seconds. Biting her lip, she played with the end of her braid. With a forceful exhale, she stepped in their direction but paused as Brayden came out from behind the trees, Theo sitting on his shoulder.

As Brayden brushed past her, Theo hopped to her shoulder.

"You gonna tell me what you two talked about?" she asked Theo.

Theo yawned, stretching his hindquarters back, and shook his head.

Gemma growled, crossing her arms, but she knew better than to press. Trying to pry information from Theo was impossible until he was darn well ready. She rolled her eyes and tried to put the matter out of her mind.

Later that day, Theo jumped off Gemma's shoulder and made his way to Brayden, riding with him for a while. Over the next week, he started splitting his time between Gemma and Brayden, much to Gemma's dismay and befuddlement. How could one talk make such a difference to Theo? But the Scruff didn't offer any explanation, and Gemma gave up trying to ask.

Every evening was filled with near arguments between her and Brayden as she struggled with the many tasks he tried to teach her. He showed her how to make snares, but she often set the snares off by accident as she set them up. She'd never had to trap animals before. Growing up on a farm, all the animals were kept in easily accessible pens. She longed to be home with her parents and their encouragement. It didn't help matters that Brayden never passed up an opportunity to point out her many failings, and Theo refused to take her side; instead, he squeaked advice for her to calm down and not worry so much.

One thing that lifted her spirits minutely was when Brayden showed her plants to watch out for, some edible, some poisonous, and others medicinal. For once, she didn't struggle, but that was partly because of Theo helping her remember which was which.

She conversed with Theo often, his encouragement and stories helping to take her mind off her growing annoyance toward Brayden.

Once, as she talked to Theo, Brayden asked her how she understood what he said.

"I don't know. I just do." She shrugged one shoulder.

"'I just do' isn't an answer."

She threw her hands up. "I don't know what else to say. I've always been able to understand him."

Theo squeaked quickly before Brayden could prepare a comeback.

Gemma blinked. "Huh. Why didn't you tell me that years ago?" She looked at Theo.

"What?" Brayden's voice rose a couple of decibels.

"He says the Scruffs speak a language anyone can learn if they take the time. Apparently, I can talk to him because I grew up with him talking to me. My brain just learned it as I grew."

Brayden shifted his weight back. "So, anyone can learn it?"

Theo squeaked and nodded.

Brayden studied Theo for a moment, then turned on his heel and marched on.

Gemma watched him go. She lifted her hands, then dropped them with a slap. "I hate it when he walks off without saying anything."

Theo rubbed his head against her cheek, then scurried to the ground, quickly catching up with Brayden.

"Great. Now they're both just walking off." She dug her thumbs under the straps of her pack and trudged ahead.

Days turned into weeks as they journeyed on; eventually making a wide berth around the Tyreen Bridge. Gemma wanted to cross back to the west side, but Brayden informed her that crossing the bridge would leave them far too exposed. Each day, Gemma expected some new danger to catch up to them, but thus far, the worst part of their travels was the constant bickering between her and Brayden.

As the days passed, she became increasingly uncomfortable. Her clothes were torn and caked with dirt, and her head itched from the lack of washing. She tried cleaning in the river, but the water was ice cold, and without soap, her efforts were fruitless.

Her thoughts often turned to home, longing for her mother's homemade goat milk soap and regretting never having learned how to make soap of any kind. The idea of asking Brayden if he knew how flitted through her mind, but she pushed it away. There was no way she would ask him for any kind of help. In any case, she imagined she smelled like a stray dog. The knowledge that Brayden smelled the same helped, but she wondered if she looked as bad as she felt, then scolded herself for worrying about it. Brayden was the only human around, and she figured he didn't care how mangy she looked. *It's not like I care what he thinks anyway.*

After so many days of nothing but staring at the ground as she plodded along, her mind became numb to the details around her, making it easy to become lost in thought. Today was no exception, mind occupied and eyes glazed while she kept up with Brayden's constant march. She didn't know what drew her attention to the lack of Theo's squeaks, but he wasn't with her or Brayden, and she didn't see any sign of him in the surrounding trees. "Hey, wasn't Theo just with you?"

Brayden didn't look back as he answered, "He took off ahead. I think he saw something he wanted to check out."

"Why didn't either of you tell me?"

"I didn't know I needed to." His shoulders straightened, and he picked up the pace.

Gemma sped up. "Well, how long has he been gone?"

He glanced over his shoulder, his face tight. "I honestly didn't keep track. Don't worry; he can take care of himself."

"Thanks, but I know that better than you do. I *have* known him my entire life, after all."

"Okay, I'm sorry I said anything." He shoved a branch out of the way with more force than was necessary.

"It's not what you said; it's how you said it."

"And how was that exactly?"

"With a patronizing tone of voice."

He laughed without humor. "It's not my fault you take everything personally."

Gemma stopped in her tracks. "Why do you keep doing that? It's like you're always angry at me, but I can't figure out why. Are you mad because you've had to teach me so much? Am I too slow for your liking? Do you just like riling me up?"

He stopped, putting his fists on his hips, and looking up with a shake of his head. "Let's just forget it and move on." He started marching again.

Gemma slipped her pack off her back and dropped it to the ground, crossing her arms. "No." She shifted her weight to one hip. "I'm not going anywhere until you finally talk to me."

Brayden stomped over, picking her pack up and shoving it toward her. "We don't have time to stand around and chat. There's still a lot of ground to cover while it's light."

She narrowed her eyes. "No."

He glared at her, his breathing accelerating.

Gemma matched his glare, her jaw set.

He threw her pack to the ground. "Fine. You want to talk, let's talk." Pulling his pack off, he let it drop with a loud thud on the ground. "First, you were a disaster at making a fire. Then you knew nothing about hunting or general survival. If you weren't so slow, we could've made it twice the distance. And let's not forget the time you mistook stinkweed for a seasoning." He wrinkled his nose. "Stinkweed! Couldn't you smell how bad it was when you were picking it? You're as ignorant as a child, and I have to do everything for you. It's like you've never had to lift a finger in your life!"

Gemma dropped her arms. "Seriously? That's what has you so mad at me all the time? Just because I never had to survive in the wild, you've decided I'm awful?"

He paced. "You forget I watched you from afar. I saw how your parents coddled you. You lived a life of ease, and you act like being on the run only affects you."

"I know it doesn't only affect me! But I'm trying to do my best." Her eyes pricked with the warning of tears again, but she swallowed them down, refusing to let him see her cry. "You didn't have to stick with me. You're the one who told my dad you'd keep me safe. Being here with me is your choice."

He stepped up to her. "I have to follow through."

She held his gaze, her heart thudding like a bull ready to charge. "Why? Why is it so important to stick with someone you obviously can't stand?"

He balled his fists and then raised a finger at her. "You're not the only one who lost family eighteen years ago, but you act like the world centers around you. My parents were gone when it happened. Men stormed through our house, killing my sisters and my brother. I only survived because I was knocked unconscious, and they must have assumed I was dead. When I came to, my father was holding me, and my mother clung to the lifeless bodies of my sisters, shrieking like she was being skinned alive. No one could console her. And you know what my mom did after that?"

He took a step forward, forcing Gemma to stumble back. "She spent nearly every moment of every day asking about you. 'How was Gemma today?', 'Gemma learned how to dance!', 'How tall is she now?'. The questions and comments never ended. It was like she had decided she'd lost all her children that day and lived vicariously through the stories of your upbringing.

"I watched as she slowly faded away, refusing to take care of herself. I did everything I could to get her attention, to bring life back to her. *I* was her son; she should have seen me! I would sit at her feet and talk to her, and she would never respond! I even went as far as to promise her I would watch out for you when Dad couldn't, but nothing worked. Whenever Dad would bring home news of you, she would light up and be the mother I remembered again. I could see love in her eyes, but it was never for me; it was for you. For *you*!" He jabbed the finger in her direction, continuing his advance, his voice growing louder with each step. "The girl who lived in bliss, never knowing the tragedy of that day. The girl who had two loving parents who made sure she never felt unwanted. You were her reason to live!" His nostrils flared, and his chest heaved. "But even you weren't enough for her to cling to life, and she died, leaving my dad and me behind!"

Gemma held her arms out in front of her, face white and eyes wide. Her muscles tensed, ready to bolt. She searched the trees for any sign of Theo. He would jump on Brayden and give her a head start.

Brayden glowered at her, his eyes flitting over her face. Slowly his face fell, and he closed his eyes. His shoulders slumped as he stepped back, hanging his head low.

Despite the softening in his demeanor, Gemma stood like a statue, not daring to make any sudden movements.

Brayden put his hands on his hips. After a few deep, shaky breaths, he said, "I'm sorry. The last thing I wanted to do was scare you." He rubbed his hand through his hair. "You didn't deserve that." When she didn't immediately drop her hands, he softened his voice. "I wouldn't hurt you, Gemma."

Tears rolled down Gemma's cheeks, from fear or empathy, she didn't know. She sniffed, rubbing her nose as she struggled to make her muscles relax. "I'm sorry you had to go through all that. I..." Her arms dropped to her side. What could she possibly say?

He shook his head. "I shouldn't have exploded on you like that. I have no excuse for my actions."

"No, I deserved it. I pushed too hard, and I'm sorry. And I've been nagging at you for weeks. I didn't know how much you've been through." She bit her lip, watching the pain play across Brayden's face.

He leaned his back against a tree. "I know. I haven't been the best company either." His gaze met hers, his eyes glassy. "I know none of it was your fault. You were a kid; you didn't even know my family existed. But I watched you live your carefree life, and I..." He swallowed hard. "Again, I'm sorry."

Ever since Gemma was little, she hated when anyone was in pain. If someone near her cried, she'd cry along with them, even if she didn't know them. Watching Brayden standing there, looking like a weight was crushing his shoulders, she couldn't fight the flood of compassion that washed over her. She edged over to him. When he showed no more aggression, she slowly wrapped her arms around his neck.

He stood stock still for a few breaths, then hesitantly wrapped his shaking arms around her.

Gemma whispered. "I truly am sorry you went through all that. I wish someone had been there for you."

Brayden's arms tightened in a quick squeeze before he pulled away. He blinked rapidly, scratching the back of his head and clearing his throat. "I guess we should get on the move. We don't want to lose too much daylight." He looked around. "And we need to figure out where Theo ran off to."

Gemma gave him a faint smile. "He probably found another stonebird's nest to ransack. I can't get over him eating those raw eggs. It's so gross!"

The side of Brayden's mouth tipped up. "It is nasty, isn't it?"

They shared a small chuckle.

An object flashed through the air, slamming into the back of Brayden's head before he took a step.

He dropped like a stone.

CHAPTER SIX

Gemma stared blankly as Brayden fell hard to the ground. She lifted her foot to step toward him when a crunching of leaves sounded behind her, and a strong arm wrapped around her waist. The feel of sharp steel pressed against her throat accelerating her heart and making her muscles stiffen.

Brayden moaned, slowly pushing up from the ground. He stood unsteadily, one hand on the back of his head, the other pulling his sword free.

The man holding Gemma hissed. "Stop moving, boy, or I'll slit the girl's throat!"

Gemma gagged at the foul smell of his breath against her cheek.

Three other men emerged from the forest, one behind Brayden and one on either side. They were all dressed in dappled grey and brown cotton that had allowed them to blend into the forest colors unseen. The one to Brayden's right held a crossbow aimed at his chest. The one to his left held a cutlass, and the one behind him picked up the curved piece of wood that had bashed Brayden in the back of the head.

"You two were making enough ruckus for all of Elefrisia to hear."

"Okay," Brayden said, holding a hand up. "We don't want any trouble. You can take anything you want without a fight if you let her go."

Gemma stiffened, pulling her head back as the knife slipped against her throat. A slight trickle of blood slid down her skin.

Brayden's face hardened. "Let. Her. Go." His grip tightened on his sword.

The man held Gemma tighter as he laughed. "You aren't in any position to make demands, boy! Now drop your sword!"

Gemma racked her brain for a way of freeing herself from the man's grip. She could reach the knife on her belt, but the steel against her throat threatened to cut deeper with each movement she made. If she stabbed the man, would her throat be slit in the process? Even as the thought passed through her mind, the blade against her throat burned as it bit deeper, drawing tears from her eyes. Again, she scanned the trees, but Theo was nowhere in sight. What if these men had somehow captured Theo, or worse, killed him? Why else would he not be here, trying to tear this man's eyes out? Her heart hammered in her chest, making it harder to stand still as her breathing quickened.

Brayden furtively glanced at the two men on either side, shifting his weight from side to side.

Gemma hoped he was thinking of a way to win this fight, but the bite of the knife warned her how slim their chances were.

The man holding Gemma moved his grip from her waist to her hair, pulling her chin higher to expose more of her neck. "If you don't want your little girlfriend here to lose her head, I suggest you stop moving!"

"What do you want?" Brayden lowered his arms.

The man tightened his grip on Gemma's hair, making her gasp. "Now that's a question that's hard to answer. There are so many things we want. Ain't that right, boys?"

His comrades chuckled in response.

"I want to get out of these cursed lands, but seeing as that's not happening any time soon, I'll settle for something more immediate." He leaned in, so his lips were brushing Gemma's ear. "I'm sure two travelers like you must have a few fin on you." He breathed in deeply. "Also, my men and I haven't had any female company for quite some time. If you don't struggle, we might have a fun time together. Don't worry; I'll make sure we all share."

The blood drained from Gemma's face, and she found it hard to take a full breath.

Brayden's face turned red, and his eyes darkened. "I swear I'll kill you."

The man laughed. "Are you thick in the head, boy? I have your girl's life in my hands. One small flick of my wrist," he slipped the knife downward, drawing more blood. "And she's gone. That'd be a waste of something so pretty, now, wouldn't it?"

Gemma locked eyes with Brayden. She wanted him to stay, to fight for her, but there was no reason for both of them to die. If he ran, at least he would live. "Just go, Brayden—"

"Don't be ridiculous, Gemma. I'm not going anywhere."

Never before had she been so grateful for her stoic rescuer, but she worried they would both be dead before sunset.

A woman's voice came from behind Gemma. "If you know what's good for you, you'll do what the gentleman said and let the girl go."

The man holding Gemma whipped around, pulling her with him and cutting deeper into her throat in the process.

A young woman stood a few paces away, aiming a loaded bow. She was shorter than Gemma, her frame lean and strong. A sword was strapped to her waist over a green thigh-length tunic that was split on either side to show her black traveling pants. She had a leather arm guard on her left arm and a leather glove on her right hand. Her long brown hair flowed loosely around her shoulders, and her blue eyes stared unwaveringly. The way she held herself and the stern look on her face gave off a regal essence, but what caught Gemma's attention was little Theo sitting comfortably on the woman's shoulder.

The woman eyed the man holding Gemma. "I said, let the girl go." She spoke each word slowly as if she were talking to a child.

"There's four of us, missy. I think I like our odds."

Another woman's voice came from behind them, causing the man to turn and shuffle back once again. "Aw, that's adorable! You think you hold the advantage. I'd pat you on the head, but I rather abhor lice."

The newcomer was even shorter than the first. She had a hood pulled up over her head, masking her face. Her pants, knee-high boots, long-sleeved shirt, and leather vest were all black. In her hands, she twirled two short swords. She pulled the hood back, revealing short-cropped blond hair and blue eyes. Her face, small and round, was as beautiful as the first woman, though her wolfish smile was enough to give Gemma chills.

Spittle splashed the side of Gemma's cheek as the man holding her spoke. "If you think holding those swords scares me, think again. Why don't you go back to your mommy, little one?"

The blond woman's mouth flattened, her shoulders pulling tight.

"Ugh." The brunette shook her head. "You had to bring up size, didn't you?"

The blond woman's eyes narrowed, her hands white-knuckled on her short swords. "Who are you calling little, ugly?" Her eyes shifted to the other woman. "I know what I promised, but I'm going to kill them."

The brunette sighed heavily. "We have to give them the chance to surrender."

"Nah! Criminals in these parts are wanted dead or alive." She twirled one short sword. "I'm thinking dead."

"Cool down. It's only right that we give them a chance to surrender." The brunette directed her attention to the men. "Let the girl go, and we'll let you live. We'll take you in to get a fair trial."

The man holding the crossbow spoke up for the first time. "No one holds fair trials anymore. We're not going anywhere with you!"

The woman lowered her bow with a sad shake of her head. "Have it your way then." She nodded to the other woman.

The blond woman pulled her lips up into a smile that looked like it should be on a cat about to pounce on its prey. "Thank you for being uncooperative. I needed a good warm-up today."

In the next breath, she threw her short swords like throwing knives. They planted simultaneously into the man with the crossbow and the one with the curved wood. Before the bodies had even hit the ground, she ran forward, pulling her sword from the man closest to her, and threw it through the man with the cutlass. In the same flow of movement, she pulled a dagger from her belt, throwing it at the man holding Gemma. It landed with a sickening thud into his right eye.

Gemma pushed the man's knife away from her throat as he fell to the ground. Her stomach turned as she watched his body twitch before slowing to a stop. She pressed her hand against her burning throat as she stared at the dagger protruding from the man's eye. The world tilted, and she breathed shallow breaths through her mouth. Everything had occurred so fast that her mind couldn't make sense of what she was seeing.

"Are you okay?" Brayden took a step toward her, lightly touching her elbow when she didn't respond. "Hey, how bad is it?"

"I..." She stepped away from the dead body, unable to tear her gaze away from his blank, staring eye. She'd never seen a dead person before.

Brayden stepped in front of her, blocking her view of the dead man. "Look at me." His eyes scanned her face and neck.

She pressed her hand harder against her neck, trying to conceal it from his prying eyes. The wound screamed at her with every move she made, but she didn't want to worry him, not after he'd made it known how useless she was. "I don't think it's as deep as it feels." Without thinking, she reached behind his head with her free hand. "What about you?"

Brayden brushed her hand away, stepping back. "I'm fine."

Theo jumped to Gemma's shoulder, bringing a margin of comfort with his slight weight. "Where have you been? I was so worried about you!" Her hand shook as she hugged him to her cheek, needing the feel of his soft, warm fur. Her heart continued to pound like it wanted to escape her chest.

"He came to get us," the brunette woman said. "He's a smart little guy."

Gemma scratched his head. "Yes, he is." She looked at the two women before her. "But why was he getting you? Who are you?"

A rustle sounded behind her, and Brayden's eyes went wide. Turning, Gemma saw the man with the crossbow lying on the ground. Blood gurgled from his lips as he aimed the crossbow directly at her with an angry scowl on his face, then he squeezed the trigger.

She watched the bolt fly directly toward her heart. The certainty that she was about to die washed down her spine. Warmth sparked in her chest, and pressure grew around her like water building behind a dam. The pressure expanded and then exploded outward with a deafening bang. A high-pitched ring, singing, shouts, and Theo's squeaks filled her ears simultaneously. The melody sung sounded oddly familiar, but it sounded like someone trying to sing to her through water, and she couldn't make out the song's words. Heaviness, like being buried under hundreds of feet of dirt, weighed down on her. The last thing she saw before darkness overtook her was the bolt shattering into dust.

CHAPTER SEVEN

Brayden lay on his back, staring at the sky above him, noting the distinct lack of tree cover. His ears rang loudly, his head throbbed, and his eyes couldn't focus. Whatever force had emanated from Gemma threw him back, knocking him unconscious for a moment. A little way away, he could hear the two women's voices, but his hearing was too muffled to make out what they were saying. Sitting up slowly, he gingerly investigated the extent of the damage on the back of his head, grimacing as he brushed a long gash. His fingers came away covered in blood, but he'd survive.

He stood on unsteady legs and paused with his hands on his knees until the world stopped spinning. Once he could move without fear of passing out, he glanced around. Uprooted trees and the remains of bushes littered the ground like a tornado had torn through the place. His gaze skipped around the debris, then froze as he zeroed in on Gemma lying unmoving in the center of the devastation. He staggered her way as quickly as he could while he struggled to remember to breathe. If she was dead, his promise was broken, and years of his life were wasted.

Theo stood on her chest, staring at her face and squeaking while he tapped her with his forefeet.

Dropping hard to his knees beside her, Brayden took her face in his hands. "Gemma! You better not be dead." He lowered his ear to her nose. His muscles turned to jelly, and he finally took a deep breath when he heard the small rush of air pull into her nose. "Thank the Creator!"

Theo squeaked, looking up at Brayden and then back at Gemma, wringing his forefeet together.

"She's alive, buddy."

Theo sniffed the blood on her neck, looking back at Brayden with another worried squeak.

Brayden brushed wisps of Gemma's hair out of the way and peeled pieces of grass and debris from her wound. Blood stained her pale neck, and the flow hadn't yet stopped. Thankfully, his canteen was still strapped across his body, and even though it was badly dented, it hadn't lost its contents. He unscrewed the top, pouring water over Gemma's wound and wiping it with his shirt sleeve. She'd hidden how severe her wound was. Anger rose in his chest. Why would she hide something so important? In the back of his mind, he knew everything occurred too fast for anything to be done about her wound, but it didn't excuse her actions. "How am I supposed to protect you when you keep things like this hidden, you stubborn woman?" The bleeding refused to stop, and he grew more worried by the second.

"What the Mathana was that?" The blond woman made her way toward Brayden, rubbing her shoulder, the other woman following close behind.

The brunette knelt to study Gemma's face. "Is she all right?"

"I don't know." He cursed under his breath. If he didn't get control of the bleeding, she wouldn't be okay.

"Hey, you going to answer what in Elefrisia just happened?" The blond woman snapped her fingers in front of his face.

He ground his teeth, forcing himself to remain calm. "I don't know what happened; I saw the same thing you did."

The brunette's eyes scanned the surrounding trees. "We shouldn't linger here. These woods aren't safe, and that...disturbance is sure to attract unwanted attention."

"I'm well aware of that, thank you." He applied pressure to Gemma's wound, glancing around. "I need something to stop the bleeding. I had what I needed in my pack, but I have no idea where it ended up."

The blond woman gestured over her shoulder with her thumb. "I hate to break it to you, but I'm pretty sure I saw your packs back there, and let me tell ya, you won't be getting much use out of them anymore."

The brunette placed her hand on Gemma's neck, next to Brayden's hand. "I'll watch over her while you gather what you need."

Brayden hesitated. These women had stepped in to save his and Gemma's lives, but that didn't mean he was ready to trust them.

The brunette held his gaze. "I won't harm her; you have my word."

When he remained in place, the blond woman put her hands on her hips. "Or you could just stay here and let her bleed out."

"I don't know either of you and as you said, these woods aren't safe—"

"If we wanted you dead, we would've waited for the crooks to finish the job."

Even though he knew she had a point, trusting anyone, let alone this loud-spoken blond woman wasn't easy.

Theo squeaked, moving his forefeet in wild gestures.

Brayden watched him, his face blank. "I'm sorry, Theo. I have no clue what you're saying."

Theo blew out a puff of air, plopping down onto his butt. He pointed to his eyes, then at Gemma, then crossed his forefeet in front of him, lifting one fur-covered brow.

It still didn't sit well with Brayden, but he knew every minute wasted on debate was putting Gemma's life at risk. "Just keep pressure on her neck for me, please."

The brunette did as he asked while he jogged toward the tattered remains of his and Gemma's packs, his own pain momentarily forgotten. The blond was correct; there wasn't much left. Everything not made from sturdy material was ripped and torn, and the tougher items were warped and broken enough to be rendered useless. To make matters worse, his coin pouch was nowhere in sight. Grabbing what few scraps of usable cloth he could find, he hustled back to Gemma and pressed the swaths of material against her neck.

"I'm Serania, by the way," the brunette said, then gestured to the blond. "And this is Andrea."

Narrowing her eyes toward Serania, the blond added, "I'm Drea, thank you very much."

He eyed them but kept his mouth closed in a hard line while he finished his temporary patch on Gemma's neck.

Serania waited, watching him work. After a minute of silence, she shook her head and stood. "Since you lost your possessions, you're welcome to share what we have."

"Speak for yourself!" Andrea crossed her arms, then at Serania's withering look, she added, "Fine. I'll share my food. But don't even think about asking for fin. You're not getting a single scaifin from me."

"Thanks, but I don't want your fin, and we don't need your help." Brayden picked Gemma up while Theo remained firmly attached near her collar bone.

"See, this is what I keep saying," Andrea jerked her arms wide, focusing on Serania. "Why do we bother helping people when this is the kind of thanks we get?"

"Because it's the right thing to do, Drea."

Brayden glanced at the two women. If it had only been Serania, he might have been tempted to stay and let her help, despite her being a stranger. She seemed kind and genuine. But Andrea's attitude marred any gentleness from Serania, making him desire nothing more than to get away as fast as he could. "Thank you for the assistance, but I've got it from here." He quickly strode away.

Andrea called out, "You're welcome, you ungrateful—"

"Wait!" Serania rushed to his side. "I know you don't know us, but the sun will set in a few hours. I've heard rumors that this part of the forest is hazardous after dark. There's a cave nearby that we've been sheltering in, and we have healing supplies there."

Her offer was tempting, but his mind recoiled at the thought of putting their lives in the hands of people he knew nothing about. "I have it handled."

Serania kept pace with him. "We only want to help—"

"Yeah, she didn't mean "we"," Andrea interrupted as she jogged to catch up.

Serania shot Andrea a scolding look. "I do mean we." She grabbed Brayden's arm, gently pulling him to a stop. "There's safety in numbers. And, as you've seen, we can be helpful in a fight. If you go on, you'll only be risking both of your lives, especially with the condition she's in. You can trust us."

Brayden swallowed. Everything in him screamed to keep away from anyone he didn't know, especially this side of the Cattaway. Andrea had moved faster than anyone he'd ever seen before, killing the bandits within the span of a couple of blinks. He wasn't too proud to admit that his chances of winning a fight against her were slim. Besides, her abrasive manner felt like a cheese grater on his nerves.

He could decline their offer, take Gemma and Theo, and figure out a place to keep them safe for the night, but if Serania was telling the truth, he could be risking all their lives. On the other hand, if he trusted them and they turned out to be of evil intent, their lives might still be forfeited.

His arms tightened under Gemma, and he looked at her pale face. The makeshift bandages he'd placed on her wound darkened as her blood seeped through. She needed more help than he could give without his possessions.

All his life, he'd prided himself on focusing on the things he could control and moving on from the rest. Making the promise to watch out for Gemma hadn't been the wisest decision. She was a walking catastrophe waiting to happen. But he'd made the promise; there was no changing that now.

Theo worked his way into Brayden's line of vision, then hopped over to Serania's shoulder, squeaking and staring at Brayden with soft eyes. There was no need to speak the language to understand; Theo was asking him to trust these women.

He pursed his lips, exhaling heavily through his nose. "Lead the way." The words left a bitter taste in his mouth.

"Maybe you do have some brains in your head after all!" Andrea smiled, skipping away without a backward glance.

Brayden stared at her back. He swore a long time ago he'd never hurt a woman unless out of self-defense, but breaking that rule was starting to look enticing.

Serania strode ahead, nodding for Brayden to follow. "We should hurry. There's no telling who or what might be heading this way."

He watched the two women walk quickly away. If Theo was wrong, they might all be imprisoned or dead soon, but with no better options, he had little choice. Being backed into a corner made his skin crawl, but he forced his feet to move.

They soon arrived at the base of a mountain. The cave entrance was mainly concealed with strategically placed vines and branches. Serania held the vines to the side for Brayden to duck inside. The temperature dropped a few degrees as he entered, and the scuffle of their feet echoed loudly off the walls.

Light flared as Andrea built a fire, illuminating the small space while the smoke from the fire drifted farther back into the cave. The ceiling was tall enough for Brayden to stand and have room to spare. A couple of bedrolls lined one wall, with various travel bags sitting adjacent. On the opposite side sat a crudely made shelf with a pot, a couple of dishes, some cutlery, and a few cups. Above the shelf, herbs hung on a line to dry.

"You can set your friend over here." Serania gestured to one of the bedrolls. She lifted the blanket looking expectantly at Brayden.

With tight muscles, he made his way over to the bedroll, gently setting Gemma down.

Theo squirmed his way to her side, pushing her arm so he could curl up between her ribs and the crook of her elbow. He laid his head on her arm and released a long heavy breath.

Serania draped the blanket over them, tucking in the sides; Theo remained glued to his spot despite being fully covered by the blanket. "I hope your companion is all right. Was she the cause of that blast?"

She rummaged through a bag, then handed Brayden some scraps of clean cloth and a bottle of ointment.

He accepted the cloth and ointment with a quick nod of thanks. His eyebrows raised as he read **Sifa** written in bold letters on the label. Sifa ointment was made from the rare Sifalian herb, known for its powerful antiseptic and healing properties. It was an expensive ointment, not a healing supply found on the typical traveler.

"I have no idea what exactly happened." He peeled off the crude bandage, wet a clean new cloth with the ointment, and then gently cleaned the wound. "I've never seen anything like it." He had no doubt Gemma carried the Cornerstone jewel. What happened earlier only reinforced what he already knew, but he'd never expected that amount of devastation. In all the books he'd found that even hinted at the special jewel, none mentioned what it was capable of, only that it held immense power.

"Hmmm...well, for now, you all are welcome to stay as long as you need." She smiled warmly. "Though it would be nice to know who we're hosting."

Andrea looked up from the fire. "Yeah, I need something better to call you than dumb a—"

Serania whipped around, her eyes hard. "Drea, watch your tongue."

"So touchy." Andrea rolled her eyes, leaning her shoulder against the cave wall and crossing her arms. "Well, what's it to be? Gonna give us a name, or should I make one up for you?" Her lips turned up in a sly smile. "I've got some pretty good ones picked out."

Brayden debated giving them a false name, but with his luck, Gemma would wake up and blurt out his name without any thought, unmasking his dishonesty. "It's Brayden."

"It's nice to meet you, Brayden. As I said, you're welcome to stay." Serania leaned closer to Gemma and winced. "That wound's going to need to be sewn." She started rummaging through the same bag as before.

Brayden watched her looking through the bag, his frown deepening. "You're rather prepared for wound care."

Andrea laughed. "Serania's collection of medicinal items is ridiculous! She probably lugs more around than your average healer."

Serania abandoned the first bag and searched in another one. "It never hurts to be prepared."

"What you are is paranoid," Andrea mumbled while she sat and tossed a few sticks onto the fire.

"Something you conveniently never complain about when I'm mending your many wounds," Serania shot back, her eyes focused on the bag.

Andrea mimicked talking with her hands and rolled her eyes dramatically while she shook her head.

Serania let out a puff of air, moving to another bag. She glanced over her shoulder and gave Brayden an apologetic look, then looked at Gemma and asked, "Is she your wife?"

"No, definitely not." He inwardly cringed. The words came out harsher than he'd meant them to.

"Oh." Her eyes fluttered to his, then back to the bag. "You just act like she means a lot to you. A dear friend then?"

He stared at Gemma, the innocent question sending his mind reeling. So much had happened in the last twenty-four hours. If she had asked him the question yesterday, he would have laughed in her face; the thought of ever being friends with Gemma was ridiculous. But he couldn't stop thinking about the look on her face after he yelled at her. Her face was awash with sadness, but it wasn't for herself; it was for him. Even after he'd scared her half to death, she'd felt compassion for him and risked comforting him. "She's...my charge." It would have to do.

"Finally!" Serania pulled a small leather case from the third bag she'd searched. She unwound a leather tie from around it and handed Brayden a curved needle and some thread. "I'm sorry, I haven't organized my bags in a while." She sat back on her heels, indicating toward Gemma with her chin. "What's her name?"

Brayden eyed her, then pointedly looked around the cave. "Looks like you two have been here quite a while. Why are you hanging out here if this area is as dangerous as you say?" He prepared the needle and thread, then leaned over Gemma. His muscles froze. He'd stitched up his fair share of wounds on himself, but his hand faintly shook. The image of her jerking awake because of the pain and making her wound worse shot through his mind.

Serania's warm hand covered his, and he met her eyes. Her mouth tipped into a kind smile, and she gently took the needle from him. "Let me. You should rest a bit and tend to your wound."

By the time he thought better of letting a stranger care for Gemma, she was already at work, her hands showing the confidence of experience. He leaned back heavily on his heels, inhaling a shaky breath. It didn't make sense why he couldn't do something as trivial as stitch a wound. His only answer was the hard hit to his head; it must have been worse than he initially thought. Serania was right; he needed rest. Now that the urgency to take care of Gemma was wearing off, his own pains were making a comeback with a vengeance. Every muscle in his body screamed like it had been stretched to the limit, and it felt like a flock of woodpeckers had taken residence in his head.

He scooted back and leaned against the cave wall. Dousing another scrap of cloth with the Sifa ointment, he held it to the back of his head, sucking in a breath at the sting. "So, will you tell me what brings you both here?"

"Are you going to tell me the name of your charge?" Serania countered gently, one eyebrow arched.

He matched her arched brow. "You both hold the advantage. We're at your mercy. And I'd like to know who I trust with our lives."

"Wouldn't it be easier if we wait for your charge to wake up? I'm not a fan of repeating everything."

"I'd rather you just answer my questions and prove you can be trusted as you claim." His voice was rising again, but he didn't care.

"Calm down, lover boy." Andrea rested her hands comfortably on the hilts of her swords. "If we decided to kill you, it would be swift; you wouldn't feel a thing."

"Andrea!" Serania jerked her gaze toward the other woman. "I swear if you don't start behaving—"

Andrea waved her hand toward Serania, cutting her off. "Yeah, yeah, you'll never let me hear the end of it."

What have I gotten us into? Brayden avoided looking in Andrea's direction, speaking instead to Serania. "The moment she awakens, we'll take our leave."

Serania finished Gemma's stitches, then cleaned the needle and moved to Brayden. "Both of you need rest and time to heal. You should stay until you're steady on your feet."

Theo's muffled squeak sounded from underneath the blanket.

Once again, Brayden had no idea what the Scruff was truly saying, but he'd heard enough of Theo's squeaks over the weeks to guess; Theo was content to stay for a while. "The moment she's awake, I expect answers." He tried to brush Serania's hands away, but she grabbed his wrist with a surprisingly firm grip.

She held his gaze, her face a perfect picture of calm. "I'm stitching up your wound whether you like it or not."

Brayden narrowed his eyes. He didn't like relinquishing his care to another, but the wound was in an inconvenient spot, and he needed to be healthy for the continued journey. Slowly, he leaned forward, turning for Serania to work.

"You have my word. Once she's awake, I'll answer any questions you have," she said as she started stitching his wound.

Brayden examined Gemma's still form. Her skin appeared even paler in the shadows of the cave, and her breathing remained shallow.

Anger that she'd hidden the wound from him rose once again. He was tempted to give her a harsh scolding the moment she woke up, but the memory of her eyes wide with compassion as she stared at him wouldn't leave him. With a resigned sigh, he forced his muscles to relax, grinding his teeth against the sharpness of the needle puncturing his skin. "I'll hold you to that." He laced his words with as much warning as he could muster. He might not win a fight with Andrea, but he wouldn't go down easily either. One way or another, he would get answers from these women.

CHAPTER EIGHT

*"**G**emma. It's time to wake up, my beautiful girl…"*

Gemma jolted awake, sitting up with a gasp. She looked around, her forehead furrowing. Rich pine walls decorated with intricate paintings of tropical forests, waterfalls, and various animals greeted her. Her legs shook as she slowly stood and took in her new surroundings. The scent of cinnamon filled the room, and she breathed in deeply, her muscles relaxing as she looked around. Flickering light from a fireplace danced across a brown loveseat with end tables on either side, each topped with a vase of flowers. Large wooden beams ran across the ceiling, and a thick, soft rug covered most of the wooden floor. A painting above the mantel drew her attention, and she slowly edged forward, glancing around as she neared the painting. Two adults—a woman and a man—smiled, eyes shining brightly enough to appear real. The woman held a baby in her arms, and the man's hands rested on the shoulders of two little girls who grinned wide.

Backing away from the picture, she looked around the room again. "Where am I?" There was no sign of Theo or Brayden. She wondered briefly if Brayden had found another cabin to hole up in while she recovered from whatever knocked her out, but everything in the room looked to be in pristine condition; not a speck of dust to be found. The matching colors and tasteful decorations told the story of a woman's touch, and whoever the woman was, she obviously still lived here.

A loud bird call caught her attention, pulling her gaze to an open window at the room's far end. Bright sunlight spilled in, and white curtains gently rustled in a soft breeze. She padded to the window, her feet sinking into the thick rug.

She leaned her hands on the windowsill as she looked out upon the scene before her. Rolling green hills led to the edge of a sapphire blue lake, smooth as glass. Willow trees graced the sides of the lake, their drooping branches swaying in the slight breeze while birds sang among them. Flowers of every hue and color dotted the ground, butterflies fluttering lazily between them.

Gemma inhaled, briefly closing her eyes as the cinnamon from inside mixed with a sweet scent of vanilla and the smells one would expect of a warm summer day. Glancing over her shoulder, she eyed the dancing fire. The small room should have been stifling, but the temperature was comfortable and welcoming. Her muscles relaxed, and a small smile tugged at her lips.

A door behind her quietly clicked open, and a woman entered. Gemma blinked, glancing at the painting on the mantle and then back to the woman before her—they were the same.

The woman's long brown hair hung loose to her waist, and her blue eyes sparkled with delight. "Gemma, sweetheart, I'm so happy you're here!" The woman smiled warmly. "Here. Take a seat." She led Gemma to the loveseat, sitting down slowly with her.

Gemma gaped at the woman. A memory nagged at the back of her mind, but she couldn't quite grab hold of it. "I know you, don't I? I don't know from where, but...I do know you."

The woman's smile brightened, her eyes crinkling at the sides. "Yes and no." She took one of Gemma's hands in hers. "I'm your mother, Thalia. Well, your birth mother, I guess I should say."

The nagging memory snapped into clarity. A night in the forest, and a beautiful woman leaning over her. *"Gemma, you are more precious than any gem in the world..."* Her heart jumped in her chest like a trapped grasshopper. There was no way she could remember that. She'd been a baby, barely six months old at the time. "But—how, you can't be...I—am I dead?"

Thalia laughed a sweet, soft laugh. "No, my dear. You are very much alive."

This has to be a dream.

Thalia brushed a strand of Gemma's hair behind her ear, resting her hand on her cheek. "You look so much like your father." Her eyes misted, but her smile remained. "I know. Things are a bit confusing for you, and I'm so sorry for that. I would be right there with you if I could, protecting you. But this is your journey now. It's your turn to take up the call, not mine."

Tears welled up in Gemma's eyes. This was the best dream she'd ever had if it was a dream. All her life, she'd wanted just one chance to talk to the mother she'd never known. There were so many questions and so many things she wanted to say. *Since this is a dream, it doesn't matter what I say.* She let everything gush out as fast as it came to mind. "I'm so scared, Mom! I don't think I'm strong enough. I keep messing up. I can't do anything right. Brayden is perfect at everything, and boy does he like to rub it in. I know he must hate being stuck with a bumbling person like me. And I keep saying the wrong things to him. We hardly get along.

"Why, Mom? Why did you and Dad have to die? What am I supposed to do? I can't do this!" Her shoulders slumped forward, and she stared at her lap. "It's all too much."

Thalia drew her into a strong hug. "I'm so sorry I'm not able to bear this burden for you, my dear, but you are so much stronger than you give yourself credit for. You can't expect to do everything perfectly the first time. No one is born an expert at anything; we all must learn. I stumbled around at first until I got the hang of things." She held Gemma at arm's length. Using a knuckle, she nudged Gemma's chin up and leaned in. "Not even Brayden started out great at everything. He had to learn like anyone else, but he's had more practice than you. You'll get there."

The words washed over Gemma like a spring breeze, warming her inside and out. Such simple words, but they held a world of meaning for her. She stared into her mother's eyes, wishing she could stay there forever, looking into those eyes, studying that face. Her mother was gorgeous with her heart-shaped face, perfectly straight nose, full lips, and brilliant blue eyes. Joy emanated from her.

Thalia took Gemma's hands in both of hers and then held them out, scanning Gemma from head to toe. "Look at you! You've grown into such a stunning woman, my Gemma." She stared for a moment before lowering her arms. "As for your other questions, I wish I could answer them all. I have so much I want to tell you, but I don't know how much time we have. I'll answer as much as I can right now. The rest you will figure out as you go."

Gemma didn't know what questions to ask first. *Not like it matters since this is all in my head.* She brushed the thought away, biting her lip. "I wish I could have known you and Dad."

Thalia's smile wilted slightly. "I do too, my love. I have a feeling you would've been a daddy's girl." They shared a quiet laugh. "But life takes turns that only the Creator could expect. Someday, we will get the chance to know one another. For now, you have some great friends to take care of you." She squeezed Gemma's hands, her nose wrinkling. "Theo is quite the troublemaker, isn't he?"

Gemma chuckled, pulling one hand away to wipe her nose. "Yes, he is, but he's also my best friend. I don't know what I would have done without him. He's one of the best parts of my life, even when his antics get me in trouble."

Thalia's eyes twinkled with playfulness. "We all need a little bit of chaos in our lives. Keeps life interesting." She arched an eyebrow and lowered her chin. "What about Brayden? He's a lovely young man, and he's done such a good job keeping you safe."

Gemma groaned, leaning back. "He's only keeping me safe because he feels obligated. And he's so confusing! One moment, he almost smiles; the next, he's scowling at me like he can't stand me. The first real thing I learned about him was that he practically hates me for things his parents did that I had no control of! He drives me nuts!"

Thalia nodded; her mouth grew serious, but her eyes remained soft. "Don't judge him too harshly, my dear. He's traveled a hard journey and hasn't learned how to see past what his eyes tell him, but I think he's on his way. Be patient with him."

"I've tried to be patient. The number of things I haven't said in order to keep the peace could fill a book!" Gemma crossed her arms, jerking one leg over the other. "I get that he's had it hard. His life has been awful, and I wish none of it had ever happened to him, but that doesn't give him the right to blame me. How was I supposed to know how much his mom focused on me? And if I did know, how was I supposed to stop her from doing it? I was a kid; I couldn't have done anything."

"I know, my love, but pain is a powerful thing. It can blind us to the truth. Sometimes it makes us think the lies *are* the truth. Everyone has their own journey to take, and some of us take longer to work through things than others." She pulled one long tress of Gemma's hair through her fingers, slowly brushing it behind Gemma's shoulder. "Again, be patient with him while he works through his own mind. The past can be hard to let go of, especially one filled with so much trauma. Don't give up on him yet."

Gemma squirmed uncomfortably. This dream wasn't going as she wanted. If her subconscious was controlling this, she needed to have a stern discussion with herself.

Thalia's mouth flattened into a hard line. "You want my permission to keep on disliking him."

Gemma leaned forward, throwing her arms wide. "He's being impossible! This whole trust thing goes both ways, you know. He could work on being kinder to me."

Thalia sighed. "Everyone wants change, but no one wants to be the one to make the first step. Try to see it from his perspective. He was a child himself, and his mother didn't give him the attention and love every child craves. If I'm correct, you both recently made some headway toward civility with each other."

"Yeah. Well, sort of. He blew up at me and, like an idiot, I hugged him." Heat washed over her face, and she picked at some dirt under a fingernail. She couldn't believe she'd hugged him, especially after how mad he'd been. *Why do I act without thinking all the time?* "He must think I'm just a silly girl."

Thalia placed a hand on Gemma's knee. "How did he react when you hugged him?"

Gemma stared harder at her hands. "I think I freaked him out at first, but then he hugged me back."

"See? These things take time. You can't expect him to be an open book at day one. He has years of resentment built up inside."

Gemma exhaled harshly through her nose, letting her hands fall limply in her lap. She knew that her mother was right, and it irritated her. After all, Brayden could have shoved her away and yelled at her to keep her distance. For all she knew, hugging him could have been the trigger to set him off again, but he'd apologized and looked devastated for blowing up in the first place. She bit her lip, lowering her head.

For the first time, the gleam in Thalia's eyes dimmed. "I wish...but it is useless to wish for what should have been. The past is the past, and nothing can change what's already happened." She squared her shoulders, sitting up to her full height. "We have important things to discuss."

"Like why in Elefrisia you gave me the necklace you did. Is it really what Brayden thinks it is?"

"Yes, my dear. I wish I could tell you it's not, and you'll be able to return to your normal life, but I can't. You have a long road ahead of you, and things will likely keep getting harder."

"Why would you give something so precious to a baby? What if I'd lost it? What if I decided to give it away?"

Thalia looked up at the ceiling for a moment, taking a few breaths before returning her attention to Gemma. "I can't explain my decisions right now." She held up a hand to stall Gemma's protest. "Believe me, I want to tell you everything, but there are powers at work that you can't understand—"

Thalia snapped her mouth closed as the light in the house darkened like a cloud passing over the sun. What sounded like hundreds of voices whispering filled the room, and a pressure built around the two women, making the air feel thick and heavy.

Thalia's eyes darted around the room, her face drawing tight. "This is too soon! I hoped to have more time!" She turned her focus to her daughter. "I wish I could tell you what is to come, what challenges you'll face, but I'm no seer." Her words came out in a rush as the whispering grew louder. "I can only tell you that I love you. I know you'll have the strength needed to make it through what lies ahead. You have more friends than you know. It'll be hard at first, but you'll need to trust those the Creator places in your path." The room shook, rattling the paintings on the walls. Thalia shot to her feet, pulling Gemma up with her.

The place shook again like a giant was trying to pound it into the ground. Gemma watched as the paintings on the walls rattled, threatening to fall with each new shake. "What's happening?"

"I'm sorry, my dear. I wish we had more time, but I risked too much already. Listen to me, Gemma. You need to find the other jewels. Find them quickly and keep them safe."

"What? How am I supposed to do that?"

Thalia grabbed Gemma's shoulders in a vice-like grip. "The jewel will show you—"

"What do you mean? Can't I stay here with you?"

"I'm sorry, my dear, I truly am. I know it doesn't make sense to you yet, but you need to remember this, it's important; the jewel will show you when it's time." She pulled Gemma into another bone-crushing hug. "I will always love you," she whispered.

An invisible force wrapped around Gemma's waist and pulled with enough strength to rip her from her mother's arms. She screamed as the force threw her from the room and into darkness.

CHAPTER NINE

The scent of campfire smoke filled Gemma's nostrils as she woke with a start. Every nerve in her body tingled, and her heart raced like a galloping horse. Her gaze skittered around the darkness before settling on a small fire a few paces away. The two women from the forest sat on the far side, their faces turned up toward Brayden, who paced on the other side of the fire. They talked in hushed tones, low enough that she couldn't catch what they were saying.

The hammering of her heart slowly receded as she realized the room, her mother, and even the shaking and darkness had been nothing more than a dream. Laying her head back down, she bit her lip. It was cold despite the blanket on top of her, and she shivered, pulling the blanket tighter. Throbbing pain in her neck made her wince, and she investigated it with her fingers, finding a long line of rough sutures. Realizing how close she'd been to dying made her mouth dry.

Theo's warm, familiar body jerked at her side, followed by a soft barking squeak.

She peeked under the blanket. Theo's eyes fluttered behind closed lids, and his lips occasionally pulled back in a growl. His forefeet, resting on Gemma's arm, intermittently twitched like he was chasing something.

Gemma smiled before lowering the blanket and turning her gaze back to the group around the fire. She knew she should join them, but her muscles felt heavy, the way they do while returning to shore after a long swim.

It wasn't comfortable lying on the ground, and something hard pressed painfully into her shoulder blade, but it was peaceful. As long as the others thought her asleep, they wouldn't bother her, and she wouldn't have to face them. Closing her eyes, she willed herself to go back to sleep. Maybe, if she were lucky, she'd go back to the cabin and be able to hug her mother once more. Even though it was just a dream, it had been a beautiful dream up until the end, and she wasn't ready to let it go. But as she concentrated, her body hummed with wakefulness, and her bladder chose that moment to remind her it needed emptying. She sighed heavily, opening her eyes again, all hope of more dreams dashing away. Sitting up on one elbow, she pulled the blanket off Theo's sleeping form, gently rubbed him, and whispered, "Hey, buddy. It's time to wake up."

Theo jerked awake, blinking rapidly. His eyes settled on Gemma, and he leaped toward her face with a loud, ecstatic squeak.

Gemma chuckled as Theo attacked her face with his tongue. "Okay, yes. I'm glad I'm safe, too!"

Theo's squeaks and Gemma's movements alerted the others, and Brayden moved quickly to her side. "Hey, how are you feeling?"

She sat up the rest of the way, continuing to rub Theo as he pushed into the non-injured side of her neck. "I'm okay, all things considered." Taking the hand Brayden offered, she stood up. "How long was I out this time?"

"Maybe five or six hours."

The brunette spoke up, still sitting by the fire. "What do you mean 'this time'? Do you make a habit of being rendered unconscious?"

"Never before, but apparently I do now." Gemma pulled her arms close, rubbing them while she walked toward the fire. "Who exactly are you two anyway?"

Brayden gestured toward the women, "This is Serania and Andrea, but—"

"It's Drea; just Drea." Andrea lifted her chin, her eyes narrowing at Brayden, who returned her glare in kind.

Gemma gave the women a small wave. "I guess it's nice to meet you."

Brayden sat across from the two women and stared directly at Serania. "As you can see, she's awake. Now you can start answering questions."

Andrea's forehead wrinkled as she raised her eyebrows high. "I think you two should be the ones answering questions. After all, you're the ones who went all 'BAM! I can shatter a bolt in midair and knock down every tree in a thirty-foot radius!'" She made an explosive sound with her mouth and mimicked it with her hands.

"Wait, what?" Gemma's insides squeezed, and she looked at Brayden, who gave a faint shake of his head. She breathed in deep. *I couldn't have done all that!* Her mother from her dream told her she did indeed have the Cornerstone jewel, but that was just a dream.

Serania shot Andrea a scolding look, the likes of which Gemma had only ever seen on a mother's face, before turning to Gemma. "You should have something to eat. You must be starving."

What's with everybody always wanting to eat before they explain things? Gemma thought, but at the same time, her stomach rumbled. "I am hungry, but...give me a second." She stepped toward the entrance of the cave.

Brayden moved to follow. "Where are you going?"

She froze mid-step, heat rushing to her cheeks. Her bladder continued to yell at her, but she didn't want to blurt out in front of everyone that she desperately needed to pee.

Andrea's voice rang out loudly in the small cave. "She's been out for hours. Bodies weren't made to hold everything in for so long." She didn't look in Gemma's direction while she grabbed a piece of meat and popped the whole thing in her mouth.

Thanks a lot for blurting that out. Gemma stared at the ground. "Yeah, I'll be right back." For the first time in her life, she missed being invisible. Although every part of her wanted to dash outside as fast as possible, she forced herself to take normal-paced steps.

Brayden called as she exited the cave, "Make it quick. We have a lot we need to discuss."

As soon as she was out of view, she picked up the pace. "Theo, next time create a distraction for me so I don't die of embarrassment."

Theo placed a fisted forefoot across his heart with a solemn squeak.

"Good. I'm holding you to that."

He grinned, then hopped to a tree branch, turning his back to Gemma to give her privacy.

After she finished, she rubbed his head. "It would make it worse if I stayed out here for a while, huh?"

He nodded and squeaked.

"Yeah, that's what I thought." Steeling her nerves, she headed back into the cave. To her relief, none of the three occupants paid her much mind, and the tightness in her stomach eased a little. She joined them at the fire, sitting between Brayden and Serania and keeping her gaze locked to the ground.

Serania held out a chunk of dried meat. "It's not much, but it's good."

"Yeah, this time, she managed to make it edible," Andrea said around a mouthful of meat.

Gemma took the food, her mouth watering as the aroma met her nose. She couldn't remember precisely when she'd eaten last, but by the rumble in her stomach, it must have been a while.

Theo leaned around Gemma's neck, his forefoot slowly inching toward the piece of meat. She smiled, tearing off a portion and handing it to him. This time she couldn't have been more thankful for his reassuring familiarity.

Serania pulled another piece of meat out and nibbled on it. "Now. We know Brayden, and you know our names; it would be nice to know yours as well."

Brayden held up a hand. "I think you two owe us some answers first."

Serania tucked her feet to the side, leaning on one hand. "Is it really so much to ask for a name?"

"Yes, it is. And you gave me your word that you would talk as soon as she was awake." His eyes remained hard. "So, talk."

Serania relaxed into her arm. "I guess I can't fault you for keeping things close to the chest. Let's just try to have a civil conversation." On the word "civil", she pointedly looked between Brayden and Andrea.

"Why? Civility is so boring." Andrea took a loud swig from her canteen, a hint of a smile around her lips.

Serania shook her head. "I must apologize for my sister. I promise wolves didn't raise us, no matter the evidence to the contrary."

Gemma pulled her knees to her chest, wrapping her arms around her legs. "You're sisters? What's it like traveling with someone so close?"

"Oh, it's great." Andrea's eyelids drooped. "I get to be pestered every five minutes when she decides I'm not acting as I should."

"Well, someone needs to uphold a better standard," Serania said.

"Come on! Everyone tiptoes around, afraid they might offend someone. I'm just the fresh air of honesty they all desperately need."

"Your 'fresh air' has gotten us into more scrapes than anything else. Like when you had the entire Creston Crew after us because you asked the leader's son if he ran into too many walls as a child."

Andrea giggled. "I've never seen a face so smooshed. It was an honest question!"

Serania shifted so she sat on her heels, turning toward her sister, clearly growing more agitated. "You'd be rotting in prison or dead if not for me smoothing things over on more than one occasion."

"Ha! Like anyone could catch me to throw me in prison. None of them even came close."

"Because I negotiated for you."

"Because I have mad skills, and they—"

Gemma held up her hands. "Okay, okay. I'm sorry I asked."

Serania pursed her lips, returned to sitting on one hip, and smoothed out invisible wrinkles on her tunic, while Andrea stuck her tongue out at her sister, her lips turned up slightly, looking like she was having fun with the tense situation.

Brayden shook his head, looking up at the ceiling as he mumbled, "Give me patience."

Gemma pulled her lips between her teeth, suppressing a grin. At least his patience was being tested by someone else for a change.

Serania spoke, her voice tight. "I'm sorry. It's not good conduct to bicker with my sister in front of you."

Theo squeaked a string of high, quick squeaks while hopping to the ground to search for more food, eliciting a giggle from Gemma.

"What did he say?" Serania asked, watching Theo dive into a travel bag, his tail the only thing still visible.

"He said—wait," Gemma's gaze snapped to Serania. "You know he's speaking when he squeaks?"

"He is a Scruff, isn't he?"

Gemma's mouth fell open, and she stared at Serania. Growing up in Dano, no one, other than her mother, knew of the existence of Scruffs. It made sense others wouldn't be so ignorant, but it was still a shock.

"Yes, he is. I've never met anyone else who knew that. Have you met many Scruffs before?"

Serania shook her head, glancing back toward the bag Theo had now entirely disappeared into. "No, but I've read about them. Some books had illustrations, and he's exactly how they were depicted."

"That leads to one of my first questions," Brayden cut in, pulling his shoulders back and sitting up straighter. "Before, you said Theo came to get you. Why would he do that? And for that matter, how did he know you were close enough to find?"

Gemma jolted to attention. "That's right! I forgot about that."

Theo's head popped out of the travel bag, a large piece of dried fruit hanging from his mouth and another in his forefeet.

Gemma caught his gaze and narrowed her eyes at him. He squeaked in the back of his throat, slowly lowering back into the bag. *You and I will have to have a long talk, my mischievous little friend.*

Serania shrugged. "I don't know how he knew we were there. We were just walking along when he jumped in our path, squeaking emphatically and gesturing for us to follow."

Andrea interrupted, "Which we did, then saved your sorry as—butts." She grinned at Serania. "Then the thanks we get is a forceful flight into the nearest tree, nearly killing us."

"You were almost killed?" Gemma knew her face must have whitened at least three shades. She swiftly looked to Brayden. "Did I—"

"No one came close to dying, just a few bruises, nothing more." Brayden lifted his eyebrows, boring his eyes into her with another slight shake of his head.

She snapped her mouth shut at his look. He knew she almost slipped about the jewel, and she scolded herself for forgetting there were strangers present.

"Just a few bruises, my foot," Andrea mumbled, rubbing her shoulder.

At Gemma's worried look, Brayden brushed a hand through the air. "I don't know about you two, but I've taken worse beatings than that."

"I nearly bit my tongue off!" Andrea protested, but her lips turned up at the corners. "It was awesome, though. You've got to teach me how you did that."

"She didn't *do* anything." Brayden leaned forward, his muscles tensing.

"I have eyes. I know what I saw."

He glared at Andrea. "We were all standing there. For all I know, one of you two caused it."

"She was the one lying in the middle of it all, not us." Andrea sat up to her full height, bringing the top of her head barely level with Brayden's shoulders. "Why would I try to blow myself up? That makes no sense!"

"I don't know, maybe whatever you did went wrong? She's not a magic user; she couldn't do something like that."

"How are we supposed to know? You haven't told us anything about her. We don't even know her name!"

Out of the corner of her eye, Gemma saw Theo's head pop out of the bag. His eyes swiveled back and forth between Andrea and Brayden while he popped food in his mouth.

"You two were the ones reluctant to answer my questions." Brayden's hands balled into fists, and his knuckles started to whiten.

Andrea flung her arms, her face hardening for the first time. "Look in the mirror, bud, because you've been just as tight-lipped."

Gemma glanced at Serania, hoping she would step in and stop this, but she held her mouth tight, leaning her head into her hands and rubbing her temples.

Brayden moved to rise, and Gemma caught his arm, squeezing tightly. "Please, stop!" She tugged Brayden's arm. "Please."

Brayden dropped back onto his seat, jerking his arm from her grasp, and turned his gaze toward the cave entrance.

Gemma watched the muscles in his temple flex and knew he wouldn't calm down any time soon. Gently tapping him on the arm to get his attention, she indicated to the back of the cave. "Can I talk to you for a minute?" She stood and headed toward the darkness, thankful he followed without protest.

He started speaking in a harsh whisper as soon as they were far enough away. "I don't trust them, Gemma."

"I know, but they saved our lives." She did her best to keep her voice neutral, trying to assuage his anger.

His eyes narrowed. "It was too convenient that they stepped in when they did."

"Convenient or not, they helped us when we needed it the most."

Leaning in closer, he lowered his voice enough that Gemma had to strain to hear. "That's part of the reason I don't trust them. How do we know they weren't watching us for some time before then?"

She paused. The thought hadn't occurred to her, but she brushed it away. "Theo was with them. He wouldn't trust them if they'd been stalking us."

He crossed his arms, leaning back. "You've been out for hours, and they refused to answer my questions until you were awake. Not exactly the actions of someone trustworthy."

She stepped closer to him. "From what I can tell, you weren't exactly an open book yourself." Hesitantly, she placed a hand on his forearm. "And how long did it take you to finally talk to me when we first met? I trusted you when you were a stranger who had done nothing more than save my life, just like them."

His shoulders dropped an inch, and his eyes hardened. "That was different, and you know it."

"That's just it. I didn't know it at the time. All I knew was some guy I didn't know saved me, and then I trusted him without knowing anything more than his name." She let that sink in before pressing on. "I know you saw Theo on Serania's shoulder when they first showed up. I'll admit, I'm not always the best judge of character, but Theo is. Why do you think I was so quick to trust you?" At his raised eyebrow, she added, "Mostly trust you." She smiled gently. "Theo wouldn't have been with her if he didn't have a good reason to trust her."

He kept his mouth flat, the muscles in his neck strung tight. "Just be careful what information you give them. There are a lot of wicked people, especially on this side of the Cattaway." He leaned in so his face was inches from hers. "One wrong move or word on their part, and I make no promises what I will or won't do."

She nodded; it wasn't great, but it would have to do. "I'm going to tell them my name."

He turned away from her, placing his hands on his hips and looking up at the ceiling with a shake of his head.

She waited, worry working into her as she watched him stand there, his back muscles straight as a board.

Finally, he turned back to her. "I don't know how much information the people after you have. For all I know, they don't know your name, so it might not matter. But if they have your name, and you let it slip to the wrong person, I might not be able to protect you."

"That's a risk I'm going to have to take."

He held her gaze, then closed his eyes and took a deep breath before opening them again. "I'm just trying to protect you."

She dipped her head. "I know, and I trust you, but I need you to trust me as well."

He nodded. "Just...be careful." And with that, he walked back to the fire, dropping to his seat and staring into the flames.

She bit the inside of her cheek, praying she didn't just lose the minuscule amount of ground she'd recently gained with him, and slowly joined them at the fire. As she sat down, she met Serania's stare. "My name is Gemma."

"Gemma?" Serania's eyes faintly widened but quickly relaxed. "That's a nice name."

"Thank you." As an afterthought, Gemma nodded her head in Theo's direction. "And if you didn't catch it, that's Theo."

Theo's head popped out from the bag, and he squeaked around a mouthful of food.

Serania nodded, her eyes focused down as she picked at a string on her tunic. "So, where are you two from?"

"That's the question you start with?" Andrea looked from Serania to Gemma, then back again. "Not 'are you maybe some powerful magician that's going to turn me into dust if I offend you'?"

Brayden opened his mouth, but Gemma interrupted. "We're from Dano, a small town south of Tyreen." Glancing at Brayden, she saw his mouth pull into a tight line, and he shook his head. She was definitely straining his trust, but something about these women made her want to trust them. At least, she wanted to trust Serania; her mannerisms reminded Gemma a bit of her mother, Mariah. Andrea, however, was a bit scary, but she didn't seem evil either.

When she said "Dano", Serania and Andrea both froze, but Gemma didn't have time to wonder at their reaction before Brayden interjected. "Now return the favor and tell us where you're from."

"We're from a few places, but we've spent most of our lives around Gadenthy," Serania answered quickly. "So, you're from Dano? Were you born and raised there?"

Theo snuck back into Gemma's lap, pushing his way under her hand, and she rubbed him absently, sending an apologetic look to Brayden before answering. "I was raised there, yes. I'm not sure where I was born. I was adopted."

Andrea pulled out a dagger and sharpening stone and started drawing the blade across it. Her eyes remained glued to her work, and her mouth pulled tight, but she leaned in toward the conversation.

Serania's eyes flitted to Andrea, then back to Gemma. "I see. Do you know who your birth parents were?"

Gemma squirmed. These questions were bordering on a little too personal. She looked to Brayden, expecting him to jump in and force the line of questioning to stop, but he was staring at the two women, his eyes narrowing and an unreadable look dawning on his face. "Um, their names were Dean and Thalia Tamim."

Andrea dropped the rock she was working with as her head snapped up, her eyes wide.

Serania's eyes instantly misted, tears spilling freely toward her upturned mouth.

Gemma looked between the two women. "What?" She turned to Brayden, but he was still staring at the two women.

Theo remained silent, eyes large and a wide goofy smile on his face.

Gemma pulled her braid in front and fidgeted with the end. "You're creeping me out. Why are you both looking at me like that?"

Andrea bent down, picking up the stone she had dropped, slowly putting both stone and knife away, all humor and orneriness gone.

Serania wiped the tears from her face, finding her voice. "I'm sorry. I know we must seem like a couple of lunatics." She chuckled, wiping tears from her cheeks. "Really, I'm sorry; I imagined this going a lot differently in my head." Her smile widened. "Gemma, we're your sisters."

CHAPTER TEN

Brayden made a sound like someone punched him in the gut. "Serania and Andrea. How did I not make the connection? Serania, you look just like how I remember Thalia."

"It's okay, Brayden. I didn't remember you until just now either. Your name seemed familiar, but we were both so young the last time we saw each other," Serania said.

Gemma stared blankly at the two women, a faint buzzing sound ringing in her ears. "What did you just say?"

Serania scooted closer. "I know it's a lot to take in, but our parents were Dean and Thalia Tamim, too." She reached out toward Gemma's hand, then stopped, lowering her hand to her lap. "I always dreamed of finding you someday but never believed it could be."

Gemma couldn't take a full breath. It seemed impossible that these two women were her long-lost sisters. Of all the people in Elefrisia, how was it they were the ones to rescue her and Brayden? Theo rubbed against her arm with reassuring squeaks, but she hardly felt him.

Once, when she was little, she fell down a steep hill. It started slow, but as she rolled and slid, she picked up more and more speed, unable to grasp anything to stop her descent. She felt the same now, her stomach churning like she was rolling down another hill. Her mind reeled from the information, and all she wanted was to grasp something to steady her. Deep down, she thought she should be happy. After all, she now had the siblings she'd always wanted, but it was too much added to the rest of the chaos of her life.

Theo worked his way up to her shoulder and squeaked in her ear, reminding her to breathe.

"You're my sisters." She said it more to herself than to them.

Serania still smiled, more tears streaming down her cheeks. "We are."

Andrea stared at Gemma, her eyes alight, but she looked more like someone who had received a gift and didn't know what to do with it.

Gemma wondered if she should hug her sisters or smile—show them she was happy to be reunited with them—but at the same time, these women were still strangers to her. Blood didn't make someone automatically family. Thomas and Mariah weren't Gemma's blood parents, but to imagine not having them was like trying to picture a color she'd never seen before. They were her parents and always would be. But here sat two blood-related women, and she knew next to nothing about them.

An image of another world flashed through her mind. One where her parents weren't murdered, and she had grown up playing and fighting with her sisters. She could picture the three of them laughing with the kind of familiarity that comes from years of shared experiences. Her heart broke with longing for things that would never be, while at the same time, parts of her were pulled into place like a shattered mirror being sucked back into its frame.

Theo's small squeaks drew her attention, and she eyed him. "You knew they were my sisters. That's why you went to get them."

He smiled, but his smile vanished when Gemma narrowed her eyes at him.

"We need to have a long discussion soon." She sighed as Theo's ears drooped, and she gave him a comforting pat before turning her attention back to Serania. Leaning back, she pulled her arms closer. "Well, I guess you found me."

Serania wiped away the rest of her tears, straightening her shoulders. "I don't expect you to accept us right away, Gemma. I was old enough the night we were separated to remember you. I used to hold you while Mom sang you to sleep. You used to hold onto the end of my hair while you fell asleep." Another laugh bubbled forth. "Once, I found you stuck in the corner, screaming your head off. It was before you learned to crawl. I thought you had rolled yourself there and couldn't figure out how to get out. Your little face was beet red. It turns out Drea had rolled you there. She was trying to get you to play pirates with her, and she wasn't happy that you weren't cooperating. Putting you in the corner was your punishment for not following your captain's orders."

"See! I always knew I was meant to be a leader," Andrea said with a satisfied grin.

Serania's face beamed, and she bounced on her seat. "It took me forever to calm you down after that one. I used to take you everywhere. Mom always told me that if I kept holding you so much, I would spoil you, but from the day you were born, I decided I would make sure you were always loved and always safe. I've felt like a part of me has been missing all these years." She leaned forward, holding Gemma's gaze. "I know we can't get back all the years we lost, but if you're willing, I hope we can start getting to know each other and maybe become friends."

Gemma forced down the hot tears that threatened to flow. "I've been in Dano this whole time. Why didn't you ever come looking for me?"

Serania's smile faltered. "We thought you were dead. We heard that both our parents had been killed. You were six months old; I knew there was no way you could have lived if our mother was dead." Her eyes brimmed with fresh tears. "I'm so sorry, Gemma! Had I known you were alive, we would have come for you years ago." She rounded her shoulders, looking at the ground. "In all honesty, I was afraid. Dano was filled with so many painful memories; I couldn't face going back there."

Gemma inhaled slowly, examining the two women across from her. Andrea sat, leaning back, her arms crossed and an ornery glint in her eye. Serania leaned forward, her countenance steady and inviting. The two women were like night and day. Gemma imagined Serania to be a shoulder to cry on and share secrets with. Andrea felt more like the one who would beat someone up for Gemma and then excitedly reenact the entire event. There were, however, subtle similarities. The blue eyes that looked straight into the soul, the curve of their mouths when they smiled, and the general structure of their faces. Looking at them now, Gemma knew the same similarities were written on her own face, except for her eyes. "I have grey eyes," she whispered, not meaning to say it aloud.

"You got those from Dad," Serania answered.

Gemma's eyebrows drew together, and her heart sped up slightly. The mother in her dream had said she looked so much like her father. She didn't know anything about her parents, and Brayden never mentioned the color of their eyes. It didn't make sense how her subconscious could conjure that information.

As she mulled over everything, a small twinge tugged at the pit of her stomach, and she focused on it. It was unlike anything she'd ever felt, like someone had tied a string to her stomach and pulled. Following the direction of the pull with her eyes, her view settled on Serania. Whispers stirred in her soul. "You have a jewel, don't you?" She didn't know where the question came from. It felt like it hadn't come from her so much as *through* her.

Serania tilted her head. "What makes you say that?"

"I have no idea," Gemma answered honestly with a shrug.

Serania tapped a finger on her thigh, then looked at Andrea.

Andrea held her hands up in front of her. "Don't look at me; Mom gave it to you."

Serania hesitated, then pulled a small bag up from under the collar of her tunic. She opened the bag and drew out a necklace. The chain was plain silver, and a single blue jewel hung from it. Like Gemma's, this necklace was unremarkable, but as Serania held it up, Gemma felt the string tug harder in her gut, beckoning her. Her hand itched to reach out and hold the necklace.

"Mom gave this to me the night we fled. She told me to keep it safe." Serania slid the necklace back into her bag and tucked it once more under her collar.

"You know not to wear it," Brayden noted, his eyes shining.

"Yeah. Mom told me not to wear it unless I had to. I didn't listen at first; I didn't have anything else to remember her by, but something changed on the seventh anniversary of Mom's death. I don't know how to describe it." She looked up and to the right. "It felt like I was exposed. You know that feeling you get when you know someone's watching you? It felt like that. I don't know how I knew it was the jewel, but I did. So, I took it off, and the moment I did, the feeling was gone. I've never put it on since."

"What's so special about the necklace anyway?" Andrea asked.

Brayden sat forward. "It's not the necklace, just the jewel attached. They have a lot of power. More than anyone knows. I only know a few things my dad taught me. Unfortunately, most of what we need to know died with him. A lot of what I know is speculation from what research I've been able to do."

Andrea arched an eyebrow. "So...how much power are we talking about?"

Serania groaned. "Honestly, Drea, like you need any more help in the fighting business."

"Hey! You never know when you might need a boost, especially with our lifestyle."

"What do you mean with your lifestyle?" Brayden eyed them both.

Andrea opened her mouth to answer, but Serania cut her off. "Traveling in these dangerous times. You never know what type of people you'll meet on the road." She shot a warning look toward her sister.

Frustration pooled in Gemma's chest. She'd been nothing but honest with Serania, answering questions she had no reason to answer, and now Serania was keeping something from her. For a moment, she debated pressing them for answers, but she didn't know either of them well enough to know how they would react. For now, she'd let it go.

Brayden scowled as well. He looked at Gemma, the muscles in his jaw working.

"It's okay," Gemma said before he could start off on the two women. The last thing they needed was another argument. A shiver ran down her spine, and she stared at the cave entrance.

Brayden followed her gaze, his body tensing. "What is it?"

"I don't know; I just had a bad feeling."

Theo lowered the front of his body, his eyes boring into the cave entrance as the silence stretched long.

Andrea shifted forward, whispering loudly, "What are we all looking at?"

Gemma tore her eyes away, looking at Andrea. "I'm not sure how safe we are here. What if someone finds the entrance?"

Andrea relaxed, leaning back. "No one's going to see this as a cave."

"But what if someone does?" Gemma pulled her knees to her chest, hugging them tightly. "We were already assaulted by bandits once. What if someone worse comes to find us?"

Andrea blew air through her relaxed lips, her nose scrunching. "In case you've forgotten, those bandits are now deader than firewood. Anyone or anything else will meet the same fate." She smiled wryly, her hand moving to the hilt of one of her short swords.

Brayden eyed Gemma, and she shook her head. She couldn't explain the sudden foreboding feeling any more than she could explain how she knew Serania had a jewel.

He crossed his legs in front of him, resting his elbows on his thighs, and turned his attention to Serania. "I need to know how it was that you two just happened to be in the same area as us. What brought you to this part of Elefrisia?"

"Some crazy old Efevrie," Andrea mumbled.

At Gemma's and Brayden's confused looks, Serania jumped in. "We were asked to look for something by an elderly Efevrie gentleman. He said it was something precious that desperately needed to be found." She paused, looking at Andrea. "Come to think of it; he never said exactly what the precious thing was, only that we would know it when we saw it."

"You know, I did mention that before you decided to drag us halfway across Elefrisia," Andrea answered.

Serania rolled her eyes. "You didn't mind because you thought it would be something valuable."

"He said it was precious beyond measure!" Andrea crossed her arms. "What a load of drim that was."

Serania ground her teeth at her sister before her eyes went wide, and she whipped her gaze back to Gemma. "It *was* priceless! He must have been talking about you."

Brayden leaned forward. "How could some Efevrie know where to send you to find Gemma? Something doesn't add up."

Serania shrugged. "I'm telling you the truth, and we don't know any more than that."

The group settled into silence. Gemma continued to rub Theo as he turned from side to side, leaning into her hand. So many things weren't making sense. As Brayden said, how could an Efevrie know where to send her sisters? She'd met a few Efevretites over the years as they came through the Anvil, but none of them had been the talkative type. Mainly they chose tables in the corner and remained quiet with their noses stuck in books. Even if one of them had known about Gemma being Serania and Andrea's sister, how could they have possibly known she'd be on this side of the Cattaway now?

Andrea's voice jolted Gemma from her pondering. "So, we answered why we're here. What about you two? What the Mathana brought you to these parts?"

Gemma looked to Brayden. He breathed out hard through his nose as he swallowed, then his shoulders relaxed, and he met her gaze with softened eyes. "It's up to you."

She looked at him in surprise. *Maybe he's finally learning to trust me a bit.* With that in mind, she pulled her necklace from her pouch, holding it up for her sisters to see. "We accidentally ended up on this side of the Cattaway. I was attacked a few weeks back by people presumably looking for this jewel."

Andrea stared at the jewel. "Ah, so that's how you nearly killed us. That makes so much more sense."

Gemma put the jewel back into her pouch. "I guess that must have been me, though I honestly have no idea how I did that."

Andrea narrowed her eyes, drumming her fingers on her thigh, and then looked at Serania. "How come you've never blown anything up?"

"I didn't know the jewels held any power." Serania shrugged. "Even if I'd known, I wouldn't have had a clue how to use it."

"Trust me, I don't have a clue either," Gemma said with a small laugh. "Hence the nearly killing you part."

Andrea nodded her chin toward Brayden. "So, there are more jewels out there?"

"Yes," Brayden answered. "Seven in total."

Andrea whistled, her eyebrows once again working their way up her forehead. "Then it's obvious, isn't it? We should find the jewels before anyone else does. If one jewel has the power that Gemma displayed, just imagine what all seven could do." She rubbed her hands together, her mouth turning up into a grin. "I have a list of people to have some fun with if we get our hands on that kind of powe—ouch!" She rubbed her arm where Serania had just punched her hard. "What? I can't be the only one thinking about the benefits here."

Brayden's voice held a hint of annoyance as he said, "Even if we started looking for the jewels, it wouldn't stop people from pursuing us. And if the wrong people figure out what we're doing, they might come after us even harder. We don't know how many are after us. It could be only one person or a whole army. And in case you didn't know, none of us has a clue where any more jewels are."

Gemma spoke up timidly. "But she's right; we have to find the jewels."

Theo butted in, squeaking his agreement.

Brayden held Gemma's gaze, his face growing stern. "Even *if* we knew where to start looking for the next jewel, you have no idea how dangerous searching would be. The jewels are scattered across Elefrisia. There's no telling how far apart they are; for all we know, some of them could be thousands of miles from here. It could take years to track them all down, and that's *if* everything went right."

"Okay, it sounds like a stupid idea when you put it like that." Gemma pulled her legs closer, looking at the ground. The idea to tell them about her dream passed through her thoughts, but she swept it away; they would only chalk it up to her imagination.

Andrea stood, pulling a long dagger from her belt. "Well, if anything else, Gemma, you need to have a way to defend yourself." She held the dagger by the blade so Gemma could take the handle.

"But I already have a weapon."

"You, dear, have a toothpick. This is a weapon."

"Gemma!" A voice shouted, making Gemma jump. She looked over her shoulder, but no one was there. The voice was the same as the mother in her dream, but it sounded like the woman had shouted directly into her ear.

Theo gave her a quick glance, then jumped off her shoulder, placing himself in the shadows of the cave.

"You alright?" Andrea asked, watching her warily.

"I'm fine; I just thought I heard something." She held the dagger up awkwardly. "What exactly am I supposed to do with this?" She had practiced with her small knife, but her only opponents had been trees and bushes that never fought back. Even then, she'd been smacked by more than one branch bouncing back at her.

"For now, just hang onto it. Training starts tomorrow." Andrea's eyes lit with excitement, and she handed Gemma a sheath for the dagger before returning to her seat.

Gemma strapped the sheath to her belt and slid the dagger into it. "Thanks, Drea, but I don't know if I'll be much help in a fight."

"I'll teach you; it's easy." Andrea leaned back. "Not like you need it. You'll probably just disintegrate any attacker."

Gemma groaned. Andrea wasn't going to let that go any time soon.

"You'll learn quickly," Brayden said. "Defense isn't as hard as you think."

Gemma raised an eyebrow at him. *This, coming from the man who spent weeks watching me fumble about?*

"Come to think of it, why haven't you taught her anything yet?" Andrea crossed her arms with an accusing glare. "I'm pretty sure you've been traveling together for a while now."

"We haven't exactly had time—" Brayden started, his voice growing tighter.

"It was my fault," Gemma interrupted. "Poor Brayden was stuck teaching me basic skills like hunting and fire-starting." She gave him a small smile. "He didn't have much time for more advanced training."

"Do you even know how to fight?" Andrea asked him, sounding skeptical.

Gemma once more jumped to his defense. "He saved my life when I was attacked."

"But he didn't lift a finger when those bandits had you all surrounded."

"You didn't give him a chance! I'm sure he would have fought them just fine." Even though she and Brayden hadn't always been on the best of terms, she didn't like how Andrea talked to him.

Brayden tapped Gemma's arm to settle her. "I can fight. So, between the two of us, we'll have Gemma trained in no time."

"Between the three of us," Serania added. "I know Drea stole all the glory with the bandits, but I'm quite adept at combat as well."

"Then I have four teachers to help me," Gemma informed them.

Andrea's eyebrows scrunched. "Four?"

Theo squeaked from the shadows, jumping up and down ecstatically.

"Oh." A loud laugh burst from Andrea, her eyes squinting nearly shut.

Theo squeaked, then growled as he dashed from his hiding spot in the shadows and jumped on Andrea. He scurried up her arm and started tugging on her hair.

Andrea laughed louder, whipping her head back and forth and swatting at Theo.

"Theo, come on." Gemma stood to rescue her sister from Theo. A part of her wanted to let him drive Andrea crazy after the way she'd talked to Brayden, but it wouldn't be right.

"Gemma, I tried to warn you..." Dream Thalia's voice whispered inside Gemma's mind before another woman's voice stopped Gemma in her tracks. "Well, isn't this a quaint little picture?"

Gemma whirled around to see a tall woman with olive skin sauntering into the cave, followed by five men wearing black hoods, their faces hidden in shadow.

CHAPTER ELEVEN

Theo squeaked loudly and ran to Gemma, climbing atop her shoulder while growling at the newcomers. Brayden and Andrea leaped to their feet, swords in hand. Serania stood, swiftly nocking an arrow.

Andrea stepped closer to the newcomer, the top of her head level with the olive-skinned woman's ribcage, making her appear like a child standing before the tall woman.

Gemma caught her breath at the sight of the red jewel hanging from the tall woman's black choker. Streams of sadness emitted from the jewel like a living thing pleading for help. The sadness intensified as if the jewel could feel her gaze, and her knees became shaky.

The tall woman's lips curled in a satisfied smile. "Honestly, when Skotadi sent me after you, I thought it might be difficult. Fovos failed so many times to bring the jewel back. I thought I might finally have a challenge on my hands. But this?" She snorted. "I feel like this is a waste of my talents."

Gemma forgot to breathe. All this time, she hoped that the first attack was merely a random act by a few people who happened to recognize the jewel. That the one responsible could be the leader of the Nahastian Army had never occurred to her.

Glancing around the cave, her heart skipped a beat as she realized the tall woman and her entourage blocked the only obvious exit. They had only two options; fight or flee into the cave, hoping there was another way out. She followed the line of smoke drifting back into the darkness. There had to be an opening back there, but for all she knew, it was nothing more than a small hole.

Brayden's knuckles whitened on the handle of his sword. He grabbed Gemma's arm and pulled her to stand behind him, his eyes locked on the danger ahead.

Andrea twirled her short swords, matching the tall woman's smile. "Maybe you should reconsider what you find easy. It's been a while since I've had a good fight. I would love a challenge if you think you're up for it."

The woman laughed derisively, looking down at Andrea. "You? Challenge me? Why don't you sit down and let the grown-ups talk?"

Andrea's smile vanished, and she lowered her chin. "I once read that giants used to exist, but they all died off—too stupid to distinguish rocks from bread. I don't know how you slipped through, but I'll make sure I remedy that."

The woman's eyes flashed with anger. "I am Kalami Telfer, daughter of High Chieftain Sokem Telfer of the Henathians."

Andrea paled a shade and took a small step back.

Kalami stood taller as she continued. "We Henathians live, eat, and breath war. I have been fighting since I was old enough to hold a blade, and you think you can stand against me?"

Andrea's grin slid back into place. "Ooh, a Henathian! I thought all of you were taken out years ago." She laughed as Kalami's smile turned into a scowl. "On second glance, you're much shorter than I thought you'd be. I've always wanted to fight one of you; this should be fun!" Lowering her stance, she twirled her blades, her grin growing wider.

Gemma couldn't stop the shiver that worked down her arms as she looked at Andrea's face. For the first time since meeting her sister, she wondered if the fierce woman might just be a sociopath. Whatever she was, Gemma said a silent prayer of thanks that Andrea was on her side.

Kalami's eyes narrowed as she slowly drew her sword, the steel singing as it exited the sheath.

Gemma swallowed hard as she stared at the blade. It was nearly as long as Andrea was tall, starting thinner at the hilt and flaring out a quarter of the way up. One side was straight and looked sharp enough to slice cleanly through bone. The opposite side was jagged like a saw blade with a gut hook near the tip. She was sure the sword's weight alone could cleave a man in two. Andrea's short swords looked like playthings in comparison.

Kalami widened her stance. "I have a rule against killing children, but I think today I'll make an exception."

Andrea ground her teeth. Anger and delight playing across her face in equal measure.

Serania eyed Gemma sideways as she slowly drew back her bowstring. "Just stay behind us."

Gemma started as she realized she hadn't drawn her weapons. Pulling out her knife and dagger, she held them up in front of her. She attempted to mimic the others' posture, widening her feet and softening her knees, but her stomach constricted. *I might as well be holding sticks considering how well I can use these.* If Kalami and her men made it past the other three, she'd be dead within seconds.

Theo growled deep in his throat, and his claws extended, pricking Gemma's shoulder.

In a flash, chaos ensued. Andrea and Kalami clashed with shouts and growls like two rabid dogs intent on tearing the other apart. Brayden took on two of the men at once. Serania shot the farthest man with an arrow to his gut, then swung her bow over her shoulder, quickly unsheathing her sword as another man rushed at her. The last man skirted past Brayden, advancing on Gemma. He smirked as he took in Gemma's meager defenses.

"Why don't you just give me those before you hurt yourself?" He held out a hand as he continued to advance.

Theo leaped from Gemma's shoulder, landing gracefully on the advancing man's sword hand. With a loud squeak, he bit down on the man's thumb, clenching his jaw tight while growling deep in his throat.

The man yelped in pain and dropped his sword. He whipped his hand violently, throwing Theo off.

Unfazed, Theo climbed up the man's leg, biting through the man's clothing, his razor-sharp teeth leaving bloody stains with every bite.

Gemma remained rooted to the floor, watching helplessly as her life-long friend defended her. If she tried to harm the man, she might hit Theo or even hurt herself. The rest of the group battled on, filling the cave with a cacophony of shouts and steel clashing against steel, but she had no idea how to offer assistance.

The man swatted at Theo as he retrieved his sword. With another harsh smack, Theo was sent sailing to the floor. The man swung his sword at Theo.

Gemma gasped and rocked backward as the tip of the sword flashed inches from her face. Another swing made her stumble back a few steps. Her foot caught on an uneven part of the ground, and she fell hard on her butt, ducking as the sword swung over her head. The man's eyes remained fixed on the tiny Scruff; Gemma completely forgotten in his annoyance.

Remembering the dagger in her hand, Gemma stabbed at the man when he stepped close enough. Her stomach lurched as the blade sank into the man's calf, and she gagged.

The man cried out in pain and swung his sword around.

She let go of the dagger, snatching her hand away seconds before the man's sword swung past where her wrist had been.

The man turned to her; his eyes narrowed to slits, and his nostrils flared. "You'll pay for that, you little wrach!"

Gemma crab-walked backward as fast as she could while the man roared, raising his sword.

Brayden stepped to her side and roughly heaved her to her feet with one hand while blocking the man's swing with the other. "Move,

move, move!" He grabbed Gemma's hand, tugging her along as he ran deeper into the cave.

"Theo!" Gemma shouted as she hurried toward the darkness. Slight tugging at her pant leg told her Theo was with her. Once he was on her shoulder, she breathed a small sigh of relief. "Stay in my sight, okay? I need you to be safe!"

He squeaked his promise, looking back at their pursuers, ready to defend her again if necessary.

"Drea!" Serania's stern shout echoed off the walls as she pushed Gemma with one hand, urging her to move faster. "Let this one go; let's move!"

The light faded as they ran deeper into the darkness. The walls pressed in on either side, forcing them to continue in single file. They slowed to a blind shuffle as the last of the light vanished. Gemma couldn't see even a few inches in front of her, and she held her hands up as they moved deeper into the lightless world. Kalami's angry shout echoed from far behind. "Get torches. Now!"

"None of them were dying." Brayden's voice drifted from the front of the line. "I nearly severed one man's neck, and he kept fighting!"

"I know," Serania answered. "Some sort of magic was at work."

Andrea's growl of disappointment sounded from the back of the group. "All I needed to do was cut off their limbs. It's not like they can fight without arms."

"Maybe you might have accomplished that, but we have someone who needs protecting," Serania reminded her.

Gemma knew she was the only one in the group who needed protecting, and it ate at her how useless she'd been in the fight. She'd stood there like a statue, watching everyone else fight. The only hit she'd made was because the man was too distracted by Theo to remember she was there.

Brayden jerked to a stop, and Gemma bumped into his back. She grunted as someone slammed into her back, sandwiching her in the middle.

Shouts and the faint flicker of torchlight came from far behind.

Brayden cursed. "It's a dead end. We need to search for another opening."

Gemma blindly felt along the cavern wall, noticing the area had opened into a more expansive cavern. Scuffling sounds around her told her the others were doing the same.

"Here," Serania said in a quiet voice, near Gemma's right.

Brayden's voice echoed close to Gemma's left. "Where are you, Gemma?"

Gemma found his shoulder. "I'm here."

He took her hand, pulling her toward Serania's voice. "Stay with me."

Andrea grunted in irritation as she brushed past Gemma. "We abandoned a glorious fight for a stupid escape through the dark."

As they shuffled along, Gemma kept her hand in front of her face, expecting to crash into a wall or bang her head on a low part of the ceiling at any moment.

Shocked cries sounded ahead, followed by Brayden's surprised shout, and his hand tore from Gemma's, throwing her off balance. She took a step to steady herself and gasped as her foot met only air, sending her body into freefall. A small scream ripped from her throat, mingling with Theo's loud, startled squeak.

When she and Brayden had jumped off the cliff into the river, watching the river rush closer, knowing at any second, they would meet it while not knowing what lay beneath, that had been only a little unsettling compared to this. Falling into the dark abyss with no reference for how far they were falling or how soon the ground would meet them, was terrifying. She pulled her arms into her chest and braced for the inevitable jolt at the bottom.

The fall only lasted a second, but the breath was knocked from her lungs as she hit the ground hard and started rolling and sliding for what felt like hundreds of feet. Her head smacked the ground with a loud thud as she came to a sudden stop. A scream tore from her throat as a searing pain shot up from her shin.

Serania's tense voice rang out in the darkness. "Who's hurt?"

"Ugh." Andrea groaned close to Gemma's right side. "It wasn't me, though I would have been happier if a giant hadn't landed on top of me."

"It's not like I had control of my landing." Brayden's voice came from the same direction as Andrea's.

Gemma opened her mouth to speak, but a fresh wave of pain shot up her leg, and all she managed was a strangled cry. She swallowed, fighting the surge of nausea that threatened to empty the contents of her stomach.

"Gemma, are you okay?" Serania asked.

"Sure she is," Andrea answered. "She just likes to scream in pain for no reason occasionally to keep us on our toes."

"I'm pretty sure my leg's broken," Gemma managed between gritted teeth. "Theo, where are you, bud?" He hadn't made a sound since the fall, and a picture of him being flattened beneath her during the slide made her heart skip a beat. Finding him in this darkness would be impossible if he was hurt somewhere. Even his white fur would be no match for the lack of light.

She was beginning to hyperventilate when his small squeak reached her ears and his soft fur brushed against her hand. A loud sob burst from her throat as she picked him up, hugging him gently to her chest.

Someone shuffled closer to her, and a hand hit her injured leg, causing her to yelp in pain again and nearly crush poor Theo in her hands. "Yeah, that's the broken one."

"I'm sorry." Brayden's voice echoed next to her ear. He found her arm, then gently moved his hands down her leg. "This blasted dark! I can't tell how severe the injury is if I can't see it!" He navigated her leg as cautiously as possible, but each contact made her wince. "I'm sorry, Gemma. I can't do anything to help if I can't see what I'm doing."

"I understand," she mumbled between gritted teeth.

Theo whimpered in her ear, and he brushed against her cheek. She could tell it also bothered him that he couldn't help her; he always hated when she was in pain.

"What's that glowing?" Serania asked.

Gemma looked around before noticing a slight glow emanating from under the flap of her pouch. With shaking fingers, she withdrew her necklace. The cavern instantly flooded with light, causing the group to snap their eyes closed.

"Gees! A little warning next time," Andrea said, holding an arm over her eyes.

"Sorry, I didn't know it did that." Gemma held the jewel farther out, squinting until her eyes adjusted enough to look at it more closely. Wisps of light floated from the jewel and drifted to the ground before fading like smoke from incense. She stared, entranced. The last vestiges of doubt about her jewel disappeared like a drop of water evaporating on a sunny day.

A pulse of pain drew her back to the problem at hand, and she looked down at her leg with a groan.

Serania and Andrea scooted to her side, every exposed part of their skin covered with scratches and gashes from the fall.

Brayden bled from a deep cut on his forehead. He smeared the blood away from his eyes with the back of his hand while he looked closely at Gemma's leg. "I need to cut your pant leg to see what we're dealing with." His face fell as he looked around. "I lost my sword in the fall."

"Here." Andrea handed him one of her short swords. "Not even a fall into Mathana could tear these bad boys from me."

Brayden took it with a quick thanks, then looked Gemma in the eye. "I'll work as carefully as I can."

Gemma nodded, pulling her arms closer. She could see everyone's breath in the jewel's light, and goosebumps rose on her bare arms. Her body shook, partly from cold and partly from pain, but she did her best to still her muscles.

Serania rummaged through a small traveling bag she still had slung across her body. "Thankfully, I always have a few things on me." She pulled out a small clean cloth and leaned closer to Brayden. He brushed her hands away, but she grabbed his chin. "You're about to use a blade to cut near my baby sister's leg. I want you to be able to see properly."

Brayden relented, letting her wipe away the blood. She pulled out a small bag of powder and pressed it into the wound until the bleeding slowed.

"Not perfect, but it will have to do." Serania threw the soiled cloth away with a satisfied nod.

Brayden shook his head, then carefully cut Gemma's pant leg. He sucked in a breath at the sight of the deep purple bruising spreading along her shin. "I don't see any blood; that's a good sign." He felt Gemma's leg with both hands.

Gemma pursed her lips and dug her fingers into the ground as his work sent shafts of pain shooting up to the top of her leg.

He gave her an apologetic look. "I think it's a clean break." He scanned the surrounding area. "It needs to be stabilized, but I don't see anything down here we can use for a splint."

The cavern's ceiling rose high enough that it faded into darkness. The walls and floor, like the cave above, were nothing more than rock and more rock. He was right; there was nothing useful for a splint anywhere in sight. A flash of movement at the edge of the jewel's light caught Gemma's eye, but as she focused, nothing stirred, and she shook her head.

Serania gazed up. "No sign of pursuit yet, but who knows how long that'll last. I can't make out where we fell from. We couldn't have fallen that far. Otherwise, none of us would be walking at this point. That means the hole is most likely hidden. We can only hope that if we can't see out, our pursuers might not be able to see in." Bending down, she gently placed a hand on Gemma's leg. "I wish I had something to help, but all our supplies are back at camp. I might have been able to use some arrows, but I only have one left. The only other thing I have is this." She pulled her bow up from the ground, now broken in two. "I landed on it a few times on the way down, but the wood is too curved to help."

"Well, great," Andrea grumbled. "We don't have to worry about dying in a heroic battle. Now we get to slowly starve to death in a freezing dark cavern." She pulled her arms closer to her body. "Why is it so finting cold down here anyway?"

Theo's tail wrapped around Gemma's neck with a gentle squeeze. He squeaked in discomfort. Even with his fur coat, cold was one thing he absolutely hated.

Serania glared at Andrea. "I don't know why it's so cold, but no one's starving to death. We'll find a way out."

Andrea looked around the cave, scrunching her chin. "Right...I'm sure we'll have no problems at all finding an exit from a cavern, in the middle of a mountain, in the middle of nowhere, with an injured person in tow."

Brayden frowned at her. "Either we find a way out, or we die trying. I, for one, would like to start moving. The longer we stay here, the more difficult things will get."

"Well then, lead the way!" Andrea stepped aside, sweeping one arm out. "Looks like we get to have some quality family time. Nothing like certain death in a deep, dark cave to bring us closer together." She grinned, clapping her hands together.

Serania threw a pebble at Andrea. "Seriously, you need to cut it out, Andrea!"

Andrea easily dodged the pebble, her smile growing wider. "Ooh, using my full name. I must be in big trouble!" At Serania's withering look, Andrea rolled her eyes. "Ah, come on. I'm helping to lighten the mood."

"Oh yes, and the phrase *'certain death'* is the perfect mood lightener," Serania countered, her voice growing louder.

"You always have to be so serious all the time—"

"Somebody has to since cracking jokes is what you enjoy most in life!"

"Somebody needs to enjoy something! You spend all your time brooding about our family. It's always, 'If only this; if only that.' You live in the past—"

"Hey!" Brayden hissed loudly before lowering his voice. "We're all beat up. We're in a cave that, for all we know, could go on for miles, and Gemma has a broken leg." He eyed Andrea. "It's obvious you both have some things you need to work out, but right now, we need to work together, *as a team*, and find a way out of here. You two can argue all you want later, when we're somewhere safer."

Serania frowned. "You're right. I'm sorry, Gemma, it was thoughtless of us to start an argument at a time like this."

"It's okay." Gemma didn't care one way or the other about the argument. Her thoughts were consumed with pain and the idea of traversing the cave with a broken leg. Grimacing, she sat up straighter. "I guess we need to start moving. I'm just going to need some help getting up."

"Hang on." Serania pointed. "Brayden, something's glinting over there. Is that your sword?"

Brayden jogged over and came back, sword in hand. "Looks like it survived...mostly." He held it up to the light, showing the tip broken off and multiple chips along the blade. "It'll have to do until I can replace it."

"Didn't anyone ever teach you two to take better care of your weapons?" Andrea twirled her short swords, showing them to be in perfect repair.

A wave of sadness washed over Gemma, and she fought the tears pricking her eyes. "I lost my knife. The one Dad gave me when I turned ten." As an afterthought, she added, "And I lost the dagger you gave me, Drea. I'm sorry."

"Ah, man! That was my favorite dagger." Andrea winked. "I guess I'll just have to steal another one."

Serania groaned. "Let's just get moving."

Brayden put his arm around Gemma's waist, giving her a boost, and she yelped, doubling over as she accidentally put weight on her broken leg.

Serania rushed in, supporting Gemma on the other side. "What I wouldn't give for a crutch right now. You'll have to lean on us as we go."

Gemma wanted to protest. She hated being a burden on them, but as she straightened, the blood drained down to her toes; her heart pounded so hard in her chest that she could see the vibration with each beat. For a moment, she feared she would pass out as her ears rang and her vision narrowed to a pinpoint. Pulling her lips tight, she told herself to remain conscious, fighting the waves of nausea and exhaustion that made her head feel like it weighed fifty pounds. She held her necklace out to Andrea. "I can't hold onto Brayden, Serania, and this at the same time."

Andrea took the necklace, gazing at it for a moment, then laughed in surprise. "I half-expected this thing not to work for me. Neat!"

Theo squeaked quietly, and Gemma nodded. "Go ahead, I understand."

After one more squeeze, he made his way to Andrea's shoulder so he could ride point.

Andrea glanced around the cavern. "Soooo...which way? Should I flip a coin?"

"Just walk; we'll figure it out as we go," Serania ordered.

"Aye, aye, captain," Andrea mumbled with a sarcastic salute.

They moved slowly, a procession of wounded and weary travelers. Andrea remained in front, holding the necklace out in front of her, the light dancing with each step. In her free hand, she kept one short sword prepared for any surprises. Brayden and Serania moved joltingly with Gemma hopping on her good leg between them.

Every muscle in Gemma's body shook from cold and the effort to keep moving. Her jaw ached from her teeth chattering nonstop, and her world shrank down to nothing, but using every ounce of will to take the next hop, each one causing slicing pain.

As they continued deeper into the darkness, the ground slowly sloped downward. The temperature dropped, and the darkness pressed down on them like it was trying to smother the light that dared invade its solitude.

After a while, Andrea looked back at the trio. "Drim, Gemma, you look like death warmed over." She sucked a quick breath between her teeth. "Maybe not even warmed over."

"Thanks, Drea. That's just the look I was going for," Gemma mumbled through her teeth.

"She's right; we should let you take a break," Brayden said as he and Serania gently lowered Gemma to the ground

Theo hopped over to her, rubbing himself against her hands, trying to give her some of his warmth.

She put both hands around him gratefully, noting the goosebumps visible on the rest of her companions. If they didn't get out of this cave soon, they wouldn't have to worry about starving; they would freeze to death first.

Brayden pulled a handkerchief from his back pocket and gently wiped Gemma's face. "You look like you picked a fight with a pounce of Roich Cats."

"You keep a hanky in your pocket?" Gemma's words came out in stuttering jolts as she shook with cold.

He paused. "Are you making fun of me for being a gentleman?"

"I would never do a thing like that." She faintly smiled.

He studied her for a moment before returning her smile, but his smile faded as he watched her body shaking. "We need to get you warmed up, but my coat was in my pack."

Gemma met his eyes. Fear darkened his features, and she knew the fear was for her safety, not his. Her heart warmed in her chest. "I'm sure we'll get out of here soon. I'll be fine."

He swallowed hard. "I hope you're right."

"I am," she said with more confidence than she felt.

Serania put a hand on Gemma's arm. "Gemma's right. We'll make it out of here, no worse for wear. Drea and I have been in worse scrapes than this."

"Whatever," Andrea spit out. "I have never been stuck in a freezing cave with no end in sight before."

"Andrea!"

"I know. I know. You're lying to make her feel better." She grinned maliciously. "But there is a bright side; we'll all go together!"

"Andrea, I swear—"

Andrea held up her hand, softening her face. "Just saying, we can keep each other company." She averted her eyes, her smile becoming more genuine. "You must admit that part is nice. It's better not to die alone."

Gemma caught the tiny amount of vulnerability that snuck past Andrea's mask of humor. Somewhere, under all that sarcasm and fierceness, was a young woman Gemma hoped to get to know. However, finding her wasn't going to be easy. "You must have had an interesting life if you've had worse scrapes than this." It didn't matter if they were lying to make her feel better; she jumped at the opportunity to learn even a small detail about their lives.

"Oh, we have many stories. We'll tell you all about them when we get out of here. Right now, however, our only focus is getting out and finding somewhere warm." Serania bent down to help Gemma stand.

Out of the corner of her eye, Gemma caught another flash of movement. "Did you guys see that?"

Theo stiffened, sniffing the air. His head swiveled from left to right, and he hunched down with a low growl.

Brayden and Serania halted and looked around.

"No. What did you see?" Brayden asked.

"I don't know. Something moved over there." Gemma pointed toward her left.

Brayden and Serania unsheathed their swords, staring out into the darkness.

Andrea handed Gemma the necklace and drew her second sword, moving slowly forward as her eyes scanned around.

Gemma strained her ears, listening for any signs of movement, but apart from the sounds the group was making, nothing else seemed out of the ordinary. She began to worry the flash was nothing more than her imagination playing tricks, and she caused everyone to be on guard for no reason when a cold presence pressed in beside her. She bit down a scream as her gaze settled on a pair of wide, black eyes.

CHAPTER TWELVE

The eyes stared at Gemma. At least, she was fairly sure they stared at her. They were entirely black, and with no pupil or whites of the eye, it was hard to tell which direction the creature looked. It resembled a lizard but stood about two feet tall; much larger than any lizard she'd ever seen. Its face was shaped like most lizards, wider in the back and coming to a point at its nose. It stood on its hind legs, with its front legs held up, giving her a perfect view of its razor-sharp talons. Its skin was pale green, like the color of rotten cabbage, and was nearly translucent, showing dark veins running underneath.

Gemma shuddered when she noticed its black eyes didn't reflect a hint of light. But what made her want to scream was its mouth. The mouth tipped up like it was smiling, but the smile was all wrong; like a grin on a corpse, it didn't belong there. Sharp jagged teeth jutted out around its mouth, and it made a low humming noise deep in its throat.

Slowly reaching out with shaking fingers, Gemma tapped Brayden's leg without breaking eye contact with the lizard. He jerked around and inhaled sharply.

More lizards slinked out of the darkness, forming a circle around the group.

Gemma tried counting them, but there were too many, and they faded into the darkness. She imagined there must be hundreds waiting to get closer to the wayward travelers, each with the same unnatural smile and eyes void of light. Her breaths came in short quick bursts; she had never been more terrified.

Theo's claws extended, and he leaned toward the lizard closest to Gemma, growling a warning for it to back off.

Brayden, Serania, and Andrea pivoted around, eyeing the mass of lizards before them.

"Right. I'll take the couple hundred to the right; you guys can get the couple hundred round the left," Andrea said, rolling her shoulders and softening her knees.

Serania eyed the lizards around the circle. "Hold. They may not be here to harm us. It could be they're only curious."

Andrea snorted. "Sure. Curious if we taste like chicken or pork."

The one in front of Gemma hissed, and she whispered, "I agree with Drea. I don't think they're friendly." She slowly reached for her dagger, and her heart jolted as she remembered she no longer had a means of defense.

Theo continued to growl, moving down to Gemma's lap, his eyes glued on the lizard. He lowered his head and shoulders, wiggling his hindquarters in preparation. The lizard mimicked his movements, both ready to pounce.

With lightning speed, the lizard closest to Gemma lunged forward, mouth widening, aimed straight at her face, while the other lizards pounced toward her friends, moving like they shared one mind.

Thankfully, Theo was faster than the lizard. He jumped onto its face, clamping his mouth down on its scaly nose, his slight weight enough to drag the lizard's head toward the ground. It made a screeching sound that sounded like metal dragging over metal, and it backed up, using its front talons to scratch at Theo.

Theo clamped down harder, growling louder, as the creature whipped its head back and forth to dislodge him.

Another lizard came behind Gemma, making light contact before Brayden slashed off its front leg.

Andrea shouted for Brayden's attention. "Give this to Gemma!" She tossed him another dagger. "Gemma, try not to lose this one; it's the last spare I've got!"

Brayden handed the dagger to Gemma while he beheaded another lizard. Quickly, she slashed at a lizard sneaking up on Theo from behind. Her seated position didn't provide much ease of movement, and every time she jerked with the dagger, it caused more pain in her leg, but she kept swinging, doing her best to keep herself and Theo safe. Anger bubbled in her chest as her blade passed in front of the lizards without making contact. Her frozen limbs were too slow, and the lizards jumped out of the way with little effort. Again, she was the useless one, providing no help for her comrades. A lump formed in her throat as she tried to injure at least one of the lizards.

Out of the corner of her eye, she could see her comrades killing lizards right and left while she continued to slash only air with her dagger. Brayden lopped off the heads of two lizards as they leaped toward him. Andrea laughed as she slashed with both her swords in opposite directions, plowing through the lizards as easily as one would plow through a wheat field. But for each one she killed, two more took their place. Serania handled her sword gracefully, looking more as if she was dancing than fighting, cutting down lizards left and right.

I might as well be a spectator for all the good I'm doing! Gemma had not made any contact, her efforts doing little more than startling the closest lizards. Burning pain made her yelp as a lizard snapped a chunk of skin off her leg. She grabbed a stone from her side and threw it with all her strength at the lizard, hitting it directly in the eye. It screamed and scurried into the darkness.

"Their eyes! Focus on their eyes!" She called out to no one in particular.

Theo heard her and turned his focus on their eyes, jumping from one to another, scratching with his razor-sharp claws. He was making progress now, but with all their progress, more lizards poured out of the darkness, climbing over the rising pile of their fallen. The ring of dead lizards grew to the point where the others found themselves stumbling over dead bodies as they continued to fight.

Brayden growled as he ripped a lizard from his leg, throwing it back into the darkness. "I don't think there's going to be an end to them any time soon! We need to break out and make a run for it!"

"Drea! You remember that time in Farensvir?" Serania shouted over the din of the fight.

"What? We never fought any lizards in Farensvir!" Andrea sliced through a line of lizards, glancing over her shoulder at her sister.

"Andrea! You know what I'm talking about! I have one left, and now is the perfect time to use it."

"Ugh, fine, destroy all my fun." Andrea shuffled back until she was side by side with Serania.

Serania took a small clay pendant from around her neck. "Brayden, you'll need to carry Gemma as soon as I give the signal!"

Theo moved his fighting closer to Gemma, backing up, so he was pressed against her side.

"Gemma," Brayden said between strikes. "Brace yourself! This isn't going to feel good."

Gemma bit down, preparing for whatever pain was to come. Maybe if she were lucky, she would finally pass out. Not that losing more time was appealing, but at least she wouldn't feel the pain.

"Now!" Serania shouted as she broke the clay pendant. The moment the pendant broke, a swirling wind gathered around the group.

Theo jumped back onto Gemma, clinging hard.

In one swift movement, Brayden sheathed his sword, grabbed the necklace from Gemma, picked her up, and swung her over his shoulder so she was dangling with her head at his back. She cried out, clenching her hands until her knuckles whitened, the handle of the dagger digging into her palm.

Serania swirled her sword around her head, and the wind picked speed with each pass.

Andrea sliced her way to the head of the group, making a path through the mass of lizards while the wind whipped faster and faster, picking lizards up and throwing them into the dark.

Serania shouted over the din, "This won't last long. Move!" Even as she spoke, the wind lost some of its power.

The group bolted, Andrea in front, continuing to clear a path, and Serania swirling her sword to keep the wind blowing. As soon as they broke past the last of the ring of lizards, they picked up speed. Serania dropped her arm, silencing the last of the wind. With every step Brayden took, Gemma prayed to pass out, but her mind stubbornly clung to consciousness. Her legs jostled as he ran, and the broken ends of her bone ground together with each movement. The queasiness in her stomach returned with a vengeance, and she squeezed her eyes shut, pulling shallow breaths between her teeth. The last thing she wanted was to throw up all over Brayden's back, but she feared she would lose the battle if they didn't stop running soon.

Gemma lifted her head and watched as Serania glanced over her shoulder. "Run faster!"

"Short legs up here!" Andrea shouted back, but the group picked up speed.

They ran on, taking random turns with no direction, down twisting tunnels. There was no way to tell how long they ran. Eventually, the ground steadily ascended, slowing the group's progress, and Gemma saw a line of lizards nipping at Serania's heels.

Brayden's breathing grew heavier, and sweat darkened his shirt as his muscles strained under his and Gemma's combined weight.

"There's light ahead!" Andrea called excitedly.

As the group burst out into fresh air and brilliant sunlight, Gemma felt a strange popping sensation in her chest, followed by a low thrumming reverberating through her bones.

"Oh, thank the Creator! They're not following." Serania huffed as she slowed to a stop, resting her hands on her knees. "Did anyone else feel that? It's like my bones were turned into tuning forks."

Brayden fell to his knees, his arms shaking as he lowered Gemma to the ground before falling to his seat next to her, taking in large gulps of air. "Yeah, I felt the same thing."

Gemma nodded in answer as she peered back toward the tunnel. There, in the line where the sunlight stopped and the dark began, she could make out light skin and black eyes staring with a look that could only be described as hatred. The lizards hissed in unison, sounding like a rushing wind, but they didn't step beyond the dark.

"That's right! You don't like the sunlight, do you?" Andrea mocked as she threw various items at the line of lizards, making them recede farther into the darkness. "Yeah, not so tough now, are you?" She threw a large stone, hitting one lizard's hindquarters as it ran into the dark.

Gemma noticed her hand was still clenched around the dagger, and she sheathed it before leaning her head back against the boulder, eyeing Serania. "You didn't tell me you were a magic user."

Serania's cheeks reddened, and she averted her gaze. "I'm not. That was just an enchanted talisman. The last one I had, too."

Brayden stared at Serania. "Talismans are dangerous. You never know if they have any secret enchantments attached to them."

"Which is why I hadn't used that one up until now." She swallowed. "Thankfully, it only did as I was told it would."

"Still, you risked a lot," Brayden pressed.

Serania lowered her head. "I know. I'm not proud about using such items, but it was the only option we had."

Brayden studied her for a moment before relaxing. "It did save our lives."

Serania peeked at him timidly. "I promise I don't have anymore. I won't dabble with those kinds of magic in the future."

Brayden dipped his head, and Serania relaxed, closing her eyes with a small sigh.

They settled into quiet, each catching their breath, except for Andrea, who continued to throw any object she could find and shout into the darkness despite the lack of visible lizards.

Gemma still shuddered from the cold even though the sun's warmth tingled her skin.

Theo jumped to the ground, sniffing her worriedly.

"I'm okay, bud," she said through chattering teeth.

Brayden frowned. "I'm sorry. With everything that happened, I forgot you were freezing." He rubbed her arms to speed up her thawing.

A tear of pain slid down her cheek, but she gave him a half-smile. "You mean to tell me you aren't perfect? I guess I'll have to exchange you for a new protector. I can't be running for my life with just anyone."

Brayden chuckled. "At least your sense of humor is still intact." He shook his head as he sat back. "You're making it increasingly difficult to take care of you. After this, try not to break anything else, okay?"

Gemma laughed painfully, "I'll make sure to put that on my list."

He gave her a half-smile before leaning his head back and closing his eyes, basking in the warmth.

The throbbing in Gemma's leg increased as her blood warmed and flowed more freely. Gritting her teeth, she studied their surroundings to give her mind something else to think about. The tunnel they exited sat at the bottom of a vast cliff. She couldn't see the top, and with the surrounding vegetation, there was no way of telling how far it stretched from right to left. It would be impossible for them to climb the cliff, and they would never willingly go back into the caves. The only choice they had was to keep moving forward.

Tall shrubs covered the ground leading out of the caves, slowly fading into taller and larger trees. Leafy vines hung haphazardly through the trees. Colorful birds danced between the branches, their songs filling the air with a soft chorus. The green leaves on the trees were bigger than any she'd ever seen in her life. They looked big enough to wrap around Brayden with room to spare. A small purple fruit she didn't recognize hung on every branch.

Andrea finally abandoned her barrage against the darkness and joined them.

Gemma breathed in deeply. The scent of sweet flowers mingled with the musty odor of humid ground. "That's weird."

Brayden's eyes snapped open, his muscles tensing. "What's weird?"

"The leaves. Look at the leaves."

Each looked around them before Serania asked, "What are we supposed to be seeing?"

Gemma pointed. "They're green. It's fall. They should be turning for winter, but they're not."

Brayden pulled his shoulders back. "You're right. Especially with how far north we've traveled. They should be nearly gone by now."

Andrea furtively looked around. "Why do I get the feeling we just jumped out of the frying pan?"

Brayden furrowed his brow, turning to Andrea. "I thought that would make you happy. The worse the circumstances, the more you thrive."

Andrea kept her eyes locked on the trees. "I'm smart enough to be wary of enchantments. And when forests stay green when they have no right to, that sounds like something eerie is going on."

Silence stretched as each person examined the trees, lost in thought. The light suggested the sun was about to set. *Were we running through the caves that long?* It was the middle of the night when they fled through the caverns. It couldn't have been the rest of the night and an entire day.

Brayden broke the silence. "Before we worry too much about what predicament we now find ourselves in, let's work on your leg. There should be plenty of good sticks we can use for a splint." He moved to rise.

Serania put her hand on his shoulder. "You rest. I'll find what we need."

Brayden nodded gratefully, slumping down. Carrying Gemma for so long had taken its toll, even with his conditioning.

Theo scampered over to Serania, climbing his way to her shoulder and squeaking to Gemma that he would scout the area for potential dangers as Serania searched for the necessary items.

"You might want to skip any desserts from here on out in case I need to carry you again," Brayden said, stretching his back and neck.

Gemma clicked her tongue and gently smacked his chest with the back of her hand. "I'm not that heavy!"

He smiled, a full genuine smile, making Gemma catch her breath. This was the first time she could remember seeing him smile without any guards up. She wondered if so many near-death experiences were helping him to loosen up around her. "I should eat some extra helpings to help you get even stronger. The heavier I am, the more muscle you gain." She grinned. "You know, you should thank me for the opportunity to grow more."

He chuckled and shook his head. "You are something else. I can honestly say I've never met anyone like you."

"Glad I can keep things interesting."

He leaned his head back against the rock, closing his eyes and breathing deeply before speaking. "That's one way to put it."

Gemma watched him for a few minutes while he relaxed. He looked calm, eyes closed, soaking in the warmth of the sun. They had come such a long way in a short amount of time. Something had changed after the big blow-up, and even though that was less than two days ago, it felt much longer. The warmth in her heart grew as she studied him. This man was slowly becoming a steady pillar for her. She still didn't know what to think about him but decided then and there that she would always be able to trust him even if they never became close friends.

Andrea sat down heavily next to Brayden. "Well, I can now check off 'running from carnivorous lizards in a pitch-black underground maze' off my list of things to do before I die." She dusted off her hands.

"You seriously need to find some new hobbies," Brayden said. "I don't know if I should be impressed or afraid of how much joy you find in near-death experiences."

Andrea smirked. "Those are the best kinds of experiences. What else would I do? Everything else is boring."

"Maybe something that's not dancing with death?" he suggested.

"Ah, where's the fun in that!"

Brayden propped up a knee, his face growing serious. "You guys mentioned Farensvir earlier. What in Elefrisia were you doing there? Only murderers and thieves hang out there."

Andrea shrugged one shoulder. "A girl's got to make a living somehow."

"Make a living...I don't know what you mean. What does that have to do with Farensvir?"

Andrea pulled out one of her swords, polishing it with the sleeve of her shirt. "Criminals are everywhere, and plenty of people will pay a pretty fin to have them caught."

Brayden's eyebrows rose. "You're bounty hunters?"

"Hey, you're smarter than you look!" She ignored his offended look and leaned in, whispering conspiratorially. "Serania wouldn't want me telling you all this, but, eh." She shrugged her shoulders again. "I find it's a noble living. It pays well, keeps bad guys off the streets, and best of all, it's a whole lot of fun." Her lips turned up in a vicious smile.

Somehow the news that Andrea was a bounty hunter didn't surprise Gemma, but Serania didn't seem like the bounty hunter type. "How did two women become bounty hunters?"

"For your information, women make some of the best bounty hunters," Andrea said, switching swords to polish. "No one expects us. That gives us the upper hand. As for how, well, suffice it to say, life threw some punches; we learned to cut off its arms."

A shiver worked down the back of Gemma's neck. She liked Andrea. In a lot of ways, Andrea reminded her of Theo, but sometimes she felt like her sister was a little too keen to pull out her swords, and she worried someday it would get her killed.

Sister. That word still felt foreign to her. She was spared delving deeper into her thoughts when Serania came back into view, holding a few sturdy sticks.

Brayden checked on Gemma's leg and frowned. "After all the jostling, the bones moved out of place. We're going to have to set it before we splint it."

Serania knelt, setting the sticks down. "I've had my fair share of broken bones, but I've never set one before."

Brayden looked up at her in surprise. "Even with your collection of healing items?"

Serania leaned back on her heels. "Everything I had was for open wounds and poisons, not broken bones." Her face fell. "And everything I had is back at camp, which is now impossible to return to."

"I can set it. This is one thing my dad taught me well." He held Gemma's gaze. "It goes without saying that this is going to hurt a lot. I'll do it as fast as I can."

"I trust you."

His look softened, and he patted her shoulder reassuringly, then took off his belt. "Bite down on this. It'll help."

Theo hopped down to Gemma's side, placing a foot on her thigh and looking up at her with wide, sympathetic eyes. He leaned into her as if he could somehow take some of the pain for her.

Gemma put the belt between her teeth, her breathing speeding up. This was her first broken bone. Hundreds of times, she'd fallen hard but never suffered more than the occasional impressive bruise. She worried that the pain of setting the bone would be worse than when it broke, but the anticipation was worse than anything else. With a quick nod, she clenched her fists and squeezed her eyes shut.

Brayden took her leg in both hands, manipulating it to realign the bones.

Gemma threw her head back with a muffled cry, startling a nearby bird so that it took flight. The process couldn't have taken more than a minute, but it was the longest minute of her life. Her stomach churned once more and she fretted that she would throw up, black out from the pain, or both.

Brayden rubbed her arm. "The worst part is over."

Serania worked as gently as she could, aligning the pieces of wood, then fastened them to Gemma's leg with strips of cloth she pulled from her bag. When she finished, she squeezed Gemma's hand. "It's crude, but it will do for now."

Andrea gave Gemma's shoulder a quick squeeze. "You handled that pretty well, all things considered."

Serania smiled kindly. "You *did* handle that well. My first broken bone, I screamed like a Marderwonk at the person who tried to set it."

"Scared the living tar out of the healer," Andrea added with a laugh. "He thought she was possessed. Swore he'd never heard anyone scream that loud in his life."

"In my defense, I was only nine."

The group jumped when an unfamiliar voice sounded from behind them. "Gotta get it right ta win tha prize!"

Andrea shot to her feet, drawing her swords. "Fint! What now?"

Brayden and Serania tensed, their hands moving to the hilts of their weapons.

An older woman's cackling laugh rang through the shrubbery. "Dinner never looked so good."

The source of the voice stood up from a large clump of shrubs, revealing a short, squat, old woman with enough wrinkles that it looked like a strong breeze might make her fall apart. Her white, scraggly hair sat in a bun at the top of her head, and she studied the group with bright grey eyes, mostly hidden by white, bushy eyebrows. She smiled, showing startlingly white, straight teeth. Her cream-colored, long-sleeve dress stopped mid-shin, giving a full view of worn brown shoes. In each hand, she held a dead lizard by the neck.

The woman cackled again. "Not easy ta catch, a bit deadly too if ya not careful, but they some mighty fine eaten if ya want ta join me!"

Gemma glanced at Brayden and saw her own bemusement mirrored on his face. Theo stared at the newcomer, his eyes narrowing and his upper lip curling.

Andrea's face hardened. "I have a better idea of what to do with those lizards—"

"We would be delighted, ma'am." Serania cut in. "Those lizards look...uh...delicious!"

Andrea grabbed her sister's arm, jerking her close and whispering harshly. "I've eaten some pretty questionable things in my time, but there was something downright unnatural about those lizards. Not to mention it's being offered by a creepy old lady in the woods! There are about a thousand reasons why we should say a resounding *No!*"

"I don't want to eat lizard any more than you do, but think about it," Serania whispered back. "She probably has a home nearby, it's about dark, and Gemma looks like she might pass out any moment. We need to get her warmed up and find a place where she can rest." She crossed her arms and arched a brow. "You aren't *scared* of a little old lady, are you?"

Andrea ground her teeth and lowered her shoulders. "I'm not *afraid* of anything. But it doesn't hurt to be cautious."

Serania dropped her hands to her hips. "Really? You, talking to me about caution?" She turned to the old woman. "We would love to join you for dinner, as long as we're not imposing."

The old woman's smile widened. "Ah, so nice! I'll be glad ta have ya! Name's Baiya, by the way."

Brayden's hand tightened on the hilt of his sword. "I don't like this."

Serania covered his hand with hers. "Gemma needs more help than we can provide out here." She stepped in closer, forcing him to meet her gaze. "I know you don't trust strangers, but we need the help. We'll all be on guard and ready to protect her if anything presents itself as a threat."

He eyed the old woman before turning to Gemma. "I guess that means I'm carrying you again."

"I could lean on you again." Gemma tried to put on a brave face, but even as she said it, the thought of trying to hop made her want to cry. Her body was spent, and she barely had the energy to keep her eyes open, but she hated being a burden on anyone.

He shook his head. "It's easier if I carry you."

Gemma wished she had the strength to argue, but her limbs were feeling heavier by the minute. "Fine. I guess you can carry me."

"Yeah," he said while he bent down. "I wasn't asking your permission." He lifted her off the ground. "Put your arm around my neck."

"Well, aren't you pushy?" She did as he commanded.

He smiled, but it was his guarded smile once more. Gemma sighed as she rested her head on his shoulder. Yes, his walls were back up, but they did slip for a moment. That thought gave her hope that maybe they were finally on their way to genuinely trusting each other.

Baiya set off into the strange forest with the group in tow.

Serania and Andrea walked in front of Brayden, having a heated, whispered argument. Gemma caught most of it as it drifted back, and she shook her head.

"We should knock her out, tie her up, and get the Mathana out of here," Andrea said. "How much do you want to bet she's some kind of witch getting ready to do something awful to us?"

"Good grief. She's probably lonely and wants some company. Or maybe she's just an old woman who needs help."

"She eats those lizards. That's not right!"

"If we were all judged by what we eat, you of all people shouldn't be trusted."

"It was one time! How long are you going to hold that against me?"

"Forever. Now, be nice. I don't know about you, but I want a chance to rest. Maybe, if we're lucky, even the chance to clean up."

"Seriously? You're more worried about your hygiene than your life?"

Gemma stopped listening as the argument went round and round. If having siblings meant constant bickering, she wasn't sure how much she wanted them, especially since she'd spent enough time arguing with Brayden. The last thing she needed was more people to argue with.

Theo hopped from one person's shoulders to another, looking at the old woman from different angles and shaking his head. His eyes narrowed, and a puzzled look fixed on his face, but he didn't give Gemma an answer why when she asked about it. In his series of squeaks, he told her that he was trying to figure something out and would tell her if or when he did.

The comfort of Brayden's strong arms, and the warmth slowly spreading through her body finally won the battle against Gemma's consciousness, and she drifted to sleep.

A while later, Theo's light weight dropping onto her chest startled Gemma awake as the group stopped before a small, red brick house. The red brick seemed out of place in the middle of the wild green forest. It was one story and looked small enough to only house one or two people. Vines grew on the mossy sides leading to a roof of red clay shingles.

Gemma rubbed her eyes, blinking rapidly, unsure of what she was seeing.

Windows covered every visible wall of the house, but they weren't easy to see; they faded in and out of view. One moment a window occupied a part of the house; the next, there was nothing but red brick in that same spot. The windows were all of different shapes and sizes, strewn haphazardly at different heights, some being directly on top of another like the builders couldn't decide what window design they liked or where to put them, so they chose to cover all their bases. On the front of the house was a short, dark wooden door with every inch covered in handles and knobs.

Brayden's arms tightened around Gemma, and he stared at the house, swallowing hard. Theo stood as stiff as Brayden, his nose twitching nonstop as he bore a hole in the house with his eyes.

Baiya stopped in front of the door, smiling brightly. "Welcome ta tha Sashaying Turtle." She turned one of the knobs to the right of the center, and the door opened without a sound.

Gemma's tired mind tried to picture a turtle sashaying when her thoughts were interrupted by the view in front of her. Through the small doorway was nothing but a short, tiny room. The ceiling sat directly at Serania's eye level, and the room was only big enough for one person to fit at a time. The walls were solid white, but the floor wasn't visible from her vantage point.

Baiya grinned again, then stepped down into the room and vanished.

"What the…" Andrea took a step back; her hands fixed on the handles of her swords.

"Come on down. Mind your head!" Baiya's voice sounded muffled from beyond the walls of the room, and there was a clearer, richer quality to it.

With one last unsure glance, Serania ducked and stepped down into the room. She, too, vanished.

Andrea's fingers twitched nervously, and her eyes were no more than slits. "When this goes wrong, remember I told you so." She gave

Brayden a quick two-fingered salute and stepped down into the room, short enough to not have to duck, and vanished.

Muffled voices drifted out of the room, but the words were impossible to discern. Brayden caught Gemma's eye. "So? I guess we have no choice but to follow?" He sounded like he would prefer to be anywhere else in Elefrisia.

Gemma stared into the seemingly empty room. "I guess. We all should stick together, right?" She looked at Theo, now standing on Brayden's shoulder.

Theo squeaked, then shrugged.

At Brayden's lifted brow, Gemma translated. "He says the choice is ours, but we should remain on guard."

"Okay." Brayden took a deep breath. "Into the crazy house, we go." He stooped low, awkwardly stepping down through the short doorway.

CHAPTER THIRTEEN

Kalami growled in frustration as her torch sputtered, threatening to extinguish any moment. She shoved it toward the nearest man. "Get me a fresh torch. Now!"

The man jumped as her shout echoed off the close tunnel walls and hurried away.

She snatched a slightly more alive torch from one of the other men and continued down the tunnel. It made no sense how she couldn't find where her prey went. For hours they searched, and the jewel always felt like it was just beyond the next curve or right behind a wall, but she couldn't find an opening to get through.

One man beside her groaned and dropped his torch. He pressed a hand against his stomach while he doubled over and sank to the ground. Skotadi's enchantment finally had worn off, causing the two men with too many injuries to succumb to them. The other two men with Kalami watched, the color draining from their faces, as their comrade's movements slowed, then stopped.

Kalami grabbed the closest man's tunic, pulling him to within an inch of her face. "Stop gawking and keep looking." She shoved him away as she ground her teeth together. He mumbled a pitiful apology while he adjusted his tunic and continued the search; the other man wordlessly following suit.

She stretched her neck from side to side as she continued down the tunnel. What she wouldn't give for her fellow Henathian warriors by her side. Henathians were fierce, hardened by a lifetime of training. Every citizen of Henathia was worth ten of these men. Even a Henathian grandmother could show up the men Kalami had with her.

Memories flooded her mind of her father and his Gaiak, the strongest warriors of all Henathia. He and his men could best an army without help. Though, many of the elder Chieftains considered her father soft for his decisions to change some of the harsher Henathian rituals. But Kalami knew she'd be unstoppable if he were here with her. She'd never seen his mercies as weak; she admired everything he did.

She shook her head to dispel the intrusive memories; now was not the time to be distracted by the past. Looking around, she caught sight of nothing but solid walls of rock. If she didn't know any better, she might think the mountain itself was protecting her prey.

The first man returned with a new torch, and Kalami grabbed it as she trudged along. Until this point, the jewel had been easy for Kalami to track down. It had flared to life a few months ago like someone started a massive bonfire for her to see. She had rushed to Skotadi, informing him of her find, ecstatic she had finally found it, a jewel that would trump the power of all other jewels. It hadn't made sense to her why she'd never seen such a strong jewel before. Something of that power should have been lit up like the sun, but all that mattered was that it was now plainly visible. The jewel was on the west side of the Cattaway; it would be easy to find. Skotadi had scowled instead of the smile she expected when she described the jewel's location, but she was in no place to inquire why. She had begged to be the one to collect the jewel, but of course, Skotadi had sent the buffoon Fovos instead. He said Fovos had to redeem himself, whatever that meant.

Fovos. That name sent a shiver of murderous rage coursing through her body. She remembered that night so many years ago, the unnatural darkness, the screaming, her crying, and then that face...

She tightened her grip on the torch until a crack formed on the shaft. The three men whispered amongst themselves, stealing furtive glances her way, but she ignored them.

For years, she painstakingly pushed down all her childhood memories, locking them away behind a wall as strong as iron; or so she thought. Ever since the jewel had flared to life, it was like someone had chipped a hole in the wall, and the memories were leaking through, no matter how hard she tried to shove them back in. At first, she feared someone had skirted around all her mental defenses, but she brushed the thought away. Guarding the mind was one of the first things every Henathian was taught.

A shudder ran down her spine as the screams of years past echoed in her mind again, trying to pull her into their depths. *Someday, I'll stand over your cold, dead body, Fovos. And after you, I'll find a way to make Skotadi pay.* Until then, she would bide her time and do what she had to do until the time was right. No war was ever won on a whim. It took planning, strategy, and a lot of patience. One had to wait for their enemy to be vulnerable, to make a mistake, or until one was sure they couldn't lose. Skotadi had been vulnerable twenty years ago, but she was too young and ignorant at the time. *I should have snuck into his sleeping chambers and jabbed a knife through his neck.* However, there was no honor in slaying an unconscious foe.

They came to another dead end. Kalami punched the rock wall and let out a guttural yell. "Let's double back." She brushed past the men, not turning to see if they were following. After the first flash of the jewel's appearance, it stayed consistently bright for weeks. Then, suddenly, it dimmed. At first, she thought the wearer had become aware of her searching and taken the jewel off. That had happened before. But this time, the jewel didn't completely vanish. With persistence, she was able to find it. It wasn't easy; it was like following an ember that had blown away from the fire, at times winking out, but she could still follow the trail. However, now the jewel had gone completely dark, any small amount of light snuffed out instantly.

The image of that smug-looking blond child with her two play swords popped unbidden to the front of her mind. The fact that she, the heir to the Henathian throne, had been stalled by a girl half her size was a shame she would never live down until she was able to set it right. She could sense the eyes of the men on her. They didn't show it externally, but she was sure internally they were mocking her for losing the battle. But she didn't lose the battle. No, her prey ran like a coward, something no Henathian would ever stoop to do.

"My lady?" One man's quavering voice caused Kalami to stop in her tracks.

"What?" She stepped close enough that the man had to strain his neck to look into her eyes.

He wrung his hand on his torch. "It's just...well, we've been looking for hours, with no sign...maybe we should send word to Skotadi?"

"Be my guest. Send the message that a group of his soldiers, led by his greatest warrior, not only failed to capture the girl and the jewel but let them disappear completely." She threw a stone, hitting the man squarely between the eyes. "Do you want to sign our death warrants, you idiot? Not a word to Skotadi until we have what we came for."

The man rubbed his forehead, smearing blood across his brow. "Of course not, my lady, but Skotadi—"

"Is not in need of information at present," she hissed coldly.

The man bowed, clearly unsure of her decision but too afraid to challenge it.

"We'll start at the cave entrance again." She brushed off any doubts as she strode through the twisting tunnel. It was a risk, choosing to not inform Skotadi of her failure. He had an uncanny way of knowing things he shouldn't be aware of. If he knew she was deliberately keeping information from him, her punishment would be severe. Although, to inform him that she had failed, as Fovos had, meant there would be no end to the misery she would face. Skotadi wouldn't kill her; he couldn't afford to wait another seven years to prepare another Keeper, and there would be no finding the other jewels without a bonded Keeper. But she knew the three men with her would be put to death, most likely in as painful a way as possible, as a warning not to fail again. She once saw Skotadi execute someone by placing him in a glass box and pouring flesh-eating bugs in with him. It took the man several days to die while he screamed in excruciating pain.

She showed nothing but cold indifference toward the men with her. But she knew that these men, like most of Skotadi's army, felt they had no choice but to serve. It was either serve him or die, and they, like she, had chosen the former. No matter how much she hated working with such useless men, she wished no evil on them. She wasn't a monster, that title belonged to Skotadi.

Another memory came unbidden to the front of her thoughts. She sat on her mother's lap, laughing while her mother told her the story of how her father had vanquished the mightiest rabbit in all the land. Her mother was full of fun stories, making them intriguing and hilarious at the same time. More than half of them were untrue, but Kalami didn't care. She cherished those story times with her mother.

"Your father jumped from side to side to fool the rabbit into thinking he was only an exceptionally large rabbit himself—"

"But Father doesn't have fur or floppy ears!" Kalami giggled.

"Not all rabbits have fur, my love. You should see some of the ugly, furless rabbits of the north. And he held his hands up by his head to make it look as if he had huge, floppy ears," her mother said with a severe expression, putting her own hands up above her ears.

Kalami's face scrunched in disgust. "Furless rabbits, yuck! I would not like to see them."

Her mother laughed sweetly. "Not all things that are ugly on the outside are ugly on the inside. I'll have you know those rabbits are the sweetest, kindest rabbits you'll ever meet."

The memory faded, and she pursed her lips. *Not all things are pretty on the inside that are pretty on the outside either, mother.*

This she had learned all too well. Twenty-two years of nothing but hate and cruelty was enough to make Kalami never trust outward appearances. Skotadi was one of those. Anyone who saw him briefly would think him to be handsome. But on the inside, he was a dark, rotting creature who devoured all things good in its path and whose hunger for power would never be satiated.

"Someday, you will get what you deserve," she vowed again, a habit she had gotten into as her hate for the beast grew. Squaring her shoulders, she lowered her chin. There was no room for error; she had to find the blond girl with the rat. The jewel would be in her grasp soon, no matter what. Gaining that power was the only chance she had.

As they returned to the cave entrance, she pointed to the nearest man. "You. Go set the horses free."

He hesitated. "But, my lady, will we not need them for the return journey..."

Kalami silenced him with a glare. "I don't know how much longer it will take to find where the girl went. We'll either have to travel through the cave or scale up and over the mountain. Either way, we can't bring the horses with us. Set them free."

The man cleared his throat before dipping his head and backing out of the cave.

Kalami inhaled deeply to calm her growing agitation. Setting the horses free was another risk. They would head back to their home. If she and the men were not back before the horses made it, Skotadi would know something wasn't right, but she couldn't risk leaving the horses to die. Every Henathian was taught early on to respect and honor all animals—they were essential to survival in the desert. Horses were honored above most as they were the beasts who carried her people across the unforgiving land. She would rather risk punishment than leave the horses tied to die.

Grabbing a torch from one of the men, she stood to her full height and peered into the darkness. She decided on one more pass down the tunnels, and if nothing presented itself, they would be forced to scale the mountain. She couldn't depend on the pull of the jewel. "Time to track the old-fashioned way."

CHAPTER FOURTEEN

Gemma held her breath as Brayden stepped down into the tiny room. The white walls morphed into a fog-like substance which quickly dissipated to reveal a tall, wide room.

Andrea and Serania held their weapons drawn toward a young woman with raven black hair. The woman stared with wide grey eyes. Her impeccably groomed eyebrows rose high on her forehead. She wore an emerald green gown that flowed down to the floor and shimmered with every move she made. In each of her outstretched hands hung a dead lizard. "I promise I'm telling the truth."

Brayden set Gemma down, pulling his sword free as he joined Serania and Andrea. "What's going on here?"

Andrea lifted the point of her swords higher. "She says she's Baiya. Supposedly, she was using a glamer before. I told you guys we couldn't trust her. She's a witch who'll probably turn us into something slimy the moment we let down our guard."

Theo lowered his body, narrowing his eyes as he locked his gaze on the woman and growled.

The woman turned pleading eyes to Brayden. "Please, let me explain."

Brayden held his sword higher. "You better explain quickly."

Lowering her hands, the woman dipped her head. "I *am* Baiya. The same woman who led you here. I use a glamer when outside of my house. The world is not a safe place, especially for beautiful young women like me. I find that most people will leave me alone if they see me as unsightly and harmless."

Serania straightened, relaxing her sword arm. "That makes sense."

Andrea scoffed. "You're not seriously going to trust her just because of that sorry excuse for an explanation?"

"I don't know many who can create such a strong glamer, but it is a wise thing, especially in these uncertain times," Serania answered. "I would do the same if I had the ability and thought it safer."

Andrea turned to Brayden. "Please tell me you have the sense to not trust some magical woman in an enchanted forest?"

Brayden took a step toward Baiya, pointing the broken tip of his sword at her neck. "I don't trust her in the least." He moved close enough that his sword grazed her skin. "How do we know you aren't going to use an enchantment on us as soon as we drop our guard?"

Baiya blinked a few times, pulling her head away from the sword. "I can only promise you that I won't. You saw the only magic I know, just the glamer. It's safe here, but I have no way of proving it. You're just going to have to trust me." She gestured behind Brayden. "If you don't trust me, the door is right behind you, and you're free to leave."

Gemma glanced to her left, and her eyebrows rose. She was expecting to see a small white room with one door, but instead, three dark wooden walls were lined with doors of every shape and size. Thinking back, she couldn't remember the color or shape of the door they entered, only that it was covered in doorknobs. None of the doors she could see had more than one knob. She scrunched her eyebrows. *Even if we choose to leave, how will we know which door to exit?*

After a silence that stretched to the point of being uncomfortable, Brayden sheathed his sword. "I don't trust you." He made his way back to Gemma and picked her up before turning a stern gaze toward the woman. "If I get even a hint of ill intent from you, I promise you won't make it through the hour."

The woman relaxed, her mouth tipping up into a kind smile. "There will be no need for that." She led them through an archway into another room. "Please take a seat. I'll make some tea." With that said, she traipsed through a small archway to the left, through which Gemma could make out a counter topped with cooking utensils.

Andrea sheathed her sword with obvious reluctance as she mumbled a string of curses under her breath.

Brayden walked stiffly to a cream-colored couch in the middle of the room and set Gemma down before seating himself on the edge, his muscles remaining tense and his eyes scanning the room. "This place puts my teeth on edge."

Gemma only half-heard him as she studied the room, her confusion growing by the second. It was longer than her home in Dano and much taller. Far too large to fit into the tiny brick house she had witnessed outside. The redwood floor was polished to a high shine. Her feet sank into a plush gold-and-red area rug. Two cream reading chairs sat on either side of the couch, forming a "U" around a dark, cherry tea table. Tall, dark bookshelves covered the entirety of every wall, each crammed to capacity with books. But the masterpiece of the room was the ceiling, which was at least fifteen feet high. Decorative gold crown molding bordered the ceiling, which was painted with clouds and birds on a background of brilliant blue sky. A rosette medallion stood out in intricate glory in the center, drawing attention to a sparkling crystal chandelier depending from it.

Gemma gaped as she stared at the light. Instead of the candles she expected, the chandelier was lit with electric glass bulbs; their steady shine filled the room better than any candle. She'd heard of electric lights, but no one in Dano was wealthy enough to have them.

She glanced at the books on the shelf behind her. Many had titles in languages she didn't recognize, and some had nothing but symbols for a title. One symbol stood out to her: a diamond with wings and a crown of flames hovering above. It was a symbol of magic, but that was the extent of her knowledge. She'd seen the symbol once long ago in a book an Efevretite read while he was in the Anvil. As she served him, she'd glanced at the open page and asked him about the various symbols. He'd given her a condescending look and told her it was magic a simpleton like her could never hope to understand.

Serania pulled one book off the shelf. "This book was banned in most cities a few years ago. Too many dangerous enchantments."

Andrea's fingers danced on the hilts of her swords. "I don't like this, not even a little bit."

Serania sat on one of the reading chairs, opening the book and glancing through it. "We'll remain on guard, Drea."

"She says as she casually sits and reads a book," Andrea mumbled.

Serania shut the book with a thud. "We need a place to stop for the night, and this place is as good as any other."

Andrea shifted from foot to foot. "There's no way in Mathana I'll be getting any rest here."

Theo squeaked in agreement while he ran along the back of the couch, stopping every couple of steps to sniff the air.

Andrea pointed at Theo. "See, even the squirrel agrees with me." She ignored Theo's angry growl as she scowled at her sister.

"You don't know he agreed; you're just assuming," Serania huffed.

Gemma leaned back against the couch, fighting to stay awake. "He agrees with Drea. He doesn't want to stay here. And he's a Scruff, not a squirrel."

"I'm with him," Brayden stated. "I know you need to rest, Gemma, but there's something not right here."

"Thank you!" Andrea threw her hands up as she started to pace. "Let's knock out the crazy woman, tie her up, and get out of here."

Serania stood with a groan of frustration. "Are all of you forgetting that Gemma can't walk right now?" She paused as she eyed both Brayden and Andrea. "I know this is a strange place, but unless you want to carry Gemma all night, we don't have any other options."

Theo growled deep in his throat and squeaked a few short squeaks.

Serania looked at Gemma expectantly.

"He says he hates to agree but understands the need for a place to rest," Gemma translated wearily. *I'll have to teach them how to understand Theo so I don't have to keep translating all the time.*

Baiya returned, holding a tray laden with dishes. "I'm cooking up some stew, but in the meantime, have some tea. It's my favorite recipe, handed down to me from my great-great-grandmother." She filled cups and handed them around.

Serania smiled as she took the cup offered her. "Thank you, ma'am, for this kindness. We've had a trying couple of days."

Baiya returned her smile, holding a cup toward Gemma. "You're welcome, dear."

Gemma took the cup as Theo bounded to her shoulder, sniffing the contents. A sweet scent drifted to her nostrils.

Theo scooted back from the cup and crossed his forearms as he squeaked his distrust once again.

Gemma gave him a small smile and rubbed between his ears as she took a sip of tea. She closed her eyes as the sweet taste danced over her tastebuds. A collage of warm vanilla, cinnamon, orange, and a dozen other flavors danced perfectly together. Warmth spread through her body, and her mind surged with a burst of energy.

Serania drank her tea, her eyebrows raising in pleasant surprise.

Andrea watched Gemma and Serania before pulling the cup close to examine it. After staring at it briefly, she shrugged and gulped it down in one shot.

Brayden set his cup down without taking a drink and rubbed his hands together. "So, Baiya, how did you come to live in a place like this?"

Baiya looked around the room affectionately. "It's a long story! One I can't wait to tell you all about! It's been so long since I've had company, but for now, how about I draw up some baths for all of you?"

Brayden's jaw set, but Serania's face lit up. "I don't know about everyone else, but I would love a chance to clean up."

"Perfect!" Baiya clapped her hands together with excitement. "I'll go get those ready for you. But first, you, dear, need some of this." She offered a small yellow wafer to Gemma. "It's made from the honey of a special bee with a few other unique ingredients that will help speed your healing. It looks like a herd of wild horses ran you over!"

Gemma allowed Theo to sniff the wafer, and he gave her a small, uncertain squeak. She mumbled a thank you and proceeded to eat it slowly. With each bite, the warmth inside her grew, centering in the areas she was injured. She didn't know what magical healing felt like, but she imagined it felt like this. Perhaps Baiya was nothing more than a nice woman trying to help a few wayward strangers.

"Now, on to the baths!" Baiya chirped.

"Please, let me help you," Serania moved to stand.

"No, no! You rest. It won't take but a moment." Baiya made a shooing motion with her hand as she danced gracefully through a door at the far end of the room. Theo's white fur flashed at Baiya's heels as he followed her through.

Gemma hadn't noticed the door before; in fact, she was sure when she came in, there were no doors or windows, nothing more than the room they had first entered and the kitchen. But as she focused on the walls, she could see doors and windows fading in and out of focus everywhere. They were hard to discern amongst the books, but if she concentrated, she could make out the shapes of round, oval, square, rectangular, and arched doors all over the room. The bookshelves were attached to them, making it look like a piece of the wall itself pulled in when Baiya opened the door.

The windows were harder to make out. They weren't transparent like windows should be, but they *looked* like windows. They were of various shapes and sizes, but each was hazy, like a mirage. If Gemma squinted her eyes and concentrated hard enough, she thought she could make out other rooms through the foggy books, but her sight grew fuzzy as she tried to focus.

Andrea's voice drew Gemma from her examination. "How could drawing up baths for four people take 'but a moment'?" she asked in a perfect mimic of Baiya's fluttery voice. "That woman is far too perky."

"She might have indoor plumbing," Serania said, leaning back into the chair. "It wouldn't be the first place we've seen that has it."

Andrea set her cup on the short table. "Yeah, well, indoor plumbing or not, I say we get the fint out of this freaky house."

Serania rolled her eyes. "There doesn't seem to be any imminent danger."

"I agree with Drea," Brayden jumped in. "Something is off here; even Theo thinks so. Gemma, I know you don't feel up for more travel, but I don't think we should stay here."

It was Serania who answered next. "Look, there are four of us—"

"Five," Gemma chimed in. "Theo would chew you out for not including him in the count."

"Okay, five of us against one. If she turns out to be someone evil, we can handle her."

Andrea snorted. "She obviously has magic, and unless Gemma can blow her up, we don't have a way to fight magic."

Gemma chewed her lip. In the back of her mind, she knew it was wise to listen to Theo and Brayden, but she was having trouble holding onto any worrisome thoughts. She turned to Brayden. "Can we give it one day?"

He held her gaze before exhaling sharply. "One night. We'll leave in the morning." Standing, he paced to the opposite side of the room, running a finger along the bookshelf as he glanced over the various books.

Andrea ground her teeth. "Just so you know, I'm not saving your sorry as—" At Serania's loud huff, she rolled her eyes. "Your sorry *butt*." She turned to Serania. "Is that better?"

Serania nodded. "We aren't barbarians or sailors to go around cursing as often as you do."

"Yes, Mom." Andrea leaned back against the shelf, crossed her arms, and looked at Brayden. "As I was saying, if anything happens, I'll get me and my sister...sisters out of here, but you, you're on your own."

Brayden shrugged as he stared back. "Fair enough. My only promise is to Gemma. You two have to fend for yourselves."

Baiya swept back into the room a few minutes later. "I have your baths ready. Why don't you follow me?" She gestured toward the open door.

Brayden picked Gemma up once again, and she rested her head on his shoulder as the four of them followed Baiya through the bookshelf doorway. They entered a long hallway, the walls of which were covered in clocks of every shape, size, and style. The loud ding-dongs from grandfather clocks collided with the more muted ticks of small pocket-watch-sized clocks. The resulting cacophony was maddening. Gemma covered her ear with her hand, pressing her other ear harder into Brayden's shoulder. *Why in Elefrisia would anyone want a hallway like this?*

Baiya stopped at the first door on the right. "This one is for you, my dear." She smiled at Andrea.

Brayden stepped closer to the door. "I think we would all prefer to stay together."

"As much as I hate to keep agreeing with the bucket head, I don't think we should split up either," Andrea said.

Baiya sighed. "My dear, I promise I won't hurt any of you by giving you baths. These rooms hold no danger for any of you. Besides, you shouldn't be sharing a room with the ladies."

Brayden's cheeks turned red. "It's not like that—I, we..."

Serania put a hand on Brayden's arm. "We'll be fine splitting up for this."

His jaw tensed, but he didn't argue.

Andrea shook her head and mumbled something low under her breath that drew a scowl from Serania before entering the room without looking back.

They walked a few paces farther before stopping in front of another door.

"This one is for you," she said, pointing at Serania.

"I'll take mine last. I'll help Gemma first."

With a dip of her head, Baiya led them farther down the hall. As they entered another room, Gemma's mouth fell open. Like the book room, this one had shelves on every wall, but instead of holding books, these shelves were covered with rocks and gems of all different shapes, colors, and sizes. Light from another crystal chandelier sparkled off the many stones and gems. Even the ceiling had stones set into it. A king-size canopy bed sat against the wall to the right with matching nightstands on either side. A rose-red love seat sat at the foot of the bed. A neatly folded pile of clean clothes that looked suspiciously like some of Gemma's clothes from home was placed in the middle of the loveseat. Along the wall directly across from the door was a dark wooden vanity covered with glass bottles and trinkets. The same hazy windows faded in and out of view on most of the walls.

Baiya led a reluctant Brayden out of the room while Serania helped Gemma into a bathroom more luxurious than anything she could have imagined. Serania was right. There was indoor plumbing. Even an indoor toilet.

Next to the tub, which was big enough to seat three bathers, was a shelf filled with crystal bottles of various colors. Serania helped Gemma undress and lower herself into the pleasantly warm water in the tub. Gemma sighed in delight as the warmth made her skin tingle. At home, it was a rare thing to have a warm bath. Drawing the water and heating each bucketful over the fire was a laborious task, especially with the added work of bucketing the water out afterward. Most days, she washed her hair with cold water, rushing through the cleaning process as fast as possible.

Theo scurried into the room and worked his way around the bathroom, sniffing everything as he went.

Gemma relaxed deeper into the tub. "Now that Theo's here, you could go clean up and come back." She smiled at Serania. "I know how much you want to feel clean again."

Serania hesitated. "I'll be quick." She rushed out the bathroom door.

"Take your time! I'll be a while anyway," Gemma called out, unsure if Serania heard her or not.

Theo helped Gemma choose a soap that smelled of sweet peppermint before jumping in the water with her. He seemed to forget some of his mistrust as he dove under again and again. Gemma giggled as she watched him play; swimming was one of his favorite pastimes.

By the time Gemma had finished rinsing out the third round of soap from her hair, Serania was back, hair dripping and face glowing. Serania pulled the plug from the drain, and Gemma watched, mesmerized, as the water slurped down the hole. *What I wouldn't give to have indoor plumbing at home.*

Serania handed Gemma a fluffy white towel.

Gemma mumbled a thank you and awkwardly worked the towel around her, tucking in the front so it would stay in place. For the next few minutes, Serania struggled to help Gemma out of the tub.

Serania grunted as she tried to lift Gemma out without hurting her broken leg. "I wish you and Brayden were married. He'd have a lot easier time with this."

Gemma snorted. "There's no way in Elefrisia that would ever happen."

Serania adjusted her hold on Gemma and pulled again. "Why ever not?"

"Trust me when I say he's the last man I'd ever marry. And he'd never want to marry me."

They finally managed to get Gemma out of the tub and worked their way into the bedroom. "But he's exactly what a man should be." Serania lowered Gemma to the loveseat and stepped back with furrowed brows. "He's strong, protective, and caring. Not to mention he's quite handsome."

"I think you forgot to mention stubborn, pushy, and a know-it-all." Gemma couldn't hide the irritation in her voice as she remembered the many times Brayden pointed out her failings.

Serania smiled as she helped Gemma dry off. "He is stubborn to a fault. I'll give you that. But the way he cared for you back in the cave; I can't help but admire him."

Gemma knew she was being too harsh toward Brayden, but she was exhausted and in pain, and the last thing she wanted to do was remember Brayden's redeeming qualities. "Well then, you can marry him."

Serania looked off dreamily. "Any woman would be blessed to have him." She shook her head. "But we have more pressing matters. This splint needs some work."

A few painful minutes later, Gemma was dry, clothed, and sporting clean strips of cloth for the splint.

Serania brushed her hands together with a satisfied nod. "Can I braid your hair?"

Having a big sister braid her hair was something Gemma had always dreamed of, and it filled her heart with warmth. "That would be nice, thank you."

Theo worked his way up to Gemma's lap, forcing his head under her hand so he could be rubbed as well.

Serania's nimble fingers ran through the length of Gemma's hair. "I never get the chance to do this since Drea refuses to grow her hair long."

Gemma scratched Theo's belly, giggling as his tongue flopped out the side of his mouth. "I can't picture her with long hair. It just doesn't suit her attitude."

Serania sighed heavily. "Believe me, I know." She leaned around so she could catch Gemma's eye. "But now I have you." Her eyes shone with the smile that lit up her face.

Gemma returned her smile before closing her eyes while Serania continued to work. Memories surfaced of the many times Mariah had done her hair. She wondered where her mother and father were now.

Were they safe? Were they even alive? The longing to see them, to be in their arms, was strong enough that she couldn't stop the silent tears that worked down her cheeks. She pulled Theo closer, finding comfort in his soft warmth. He leaned into her, his body vibrating as he purred softly under her hands. Serania talked as she worked, telling stories of her and Andrea. Gemma pushed the thoughts of her parents away as she listened. Soon she was laughing as Serania recounted some amusing adventures she'd been on with Andrea.

"There. All done." Serania stood, looking over her handiwork. "Do you want to go eat? I'm sure Baiya has something ready by now."

Gemma pulled the braid over her shoulder and slowly ran her hands down the length of it. "I think I'm just going to call it a night."

"Are you sure? A bit of food might help you recover."

Even though her stomach began to growl, the thought of eating lizard stew wasn't appealing. "I'm sure. I'm just too tired for anything but sleep right now."

Serania squeezed Gemma's hands before bidding her goodnight and exiting the room.

Gemma laid back on the bed with every intention to work her way under the blankets, but as Theo's soft fur brushed against her cheek, her eyelids closed, and she drifted into blissful sleep.

Brayden stood, leaning against the wall with an open book in his hands. No matter how much he hated being here, he couldn't help but be drawn to the mass of information this room held. He spent many hours of his life reading, but finding new books in a small town like Dano wasn't easy. Especially after so many books had been burned in the time of the uprising.

He watched from the corner of his eye as Andrea's hands fidgeted on her sword hilts. She was clean but back in the same clothes she had on before. He'd done the same, not trusting anything offered in a place as magical as this. It chafed at him to find himself agreeing with Andrea, but for once, the two of them were on the same page.

The door leading into the hall opened, allowing the chaotic sounds of the many clocks to drift inside as Serania entered the book room without Gemma. Her hair hung heavy with water down her back, darkening the new blue tunic she wore. For the first time, Brayden noticed just how beautiful she was with her heart-shaped face and intense blue eyes. As she gracefully made her way toward him, he couldn't help but notice the gentle sway of her hips. He knew nothing about her, but it wouldn't surprise him if she'd had a long line of suitors throughout her life. "Do I need to go get Gemma?"

Serania shook her head. "She didn't have enough energy left to come back out here. She's most likely asleep already."

Andrea joined them, her eyes never ceasing their constant scan of the room. "Likely story. She probably didn't want to risk being poisoned by lizard stew."

Brayden set the book back on the shelf and headed toward the hallway door.

Serania's voice made him pause. "She's safe and asleep, Brayden. You don't need to worry."

He glanced over his shoulder. "I'll sleep better if I see it for myself."

Serania's mouth tipped up into a gentle smile. "I guess I shouldn't expect anything less."

He continued toward the door. Andrea's grating snicker halted his hand on the knob, but he squared his shoulders and quickly made his way down the hall to Gemma's room. He knocked and leaned his ear to the door. When no response came, he slowly cracked the door, peeking through before stepping into the room and closing the door quietly behind him.

Gemma lay fast asleep on the king-size bed, her broken leg on the bed and her good leg still dangling off the side. Theo's white fur stood out on the red pillow beside Gemma's head. The Scruff stared at Brayden with tired-looking eyes.

"Hey, bud," Brayden whispered, moving softly to the side of the bed. "Do you want me to bring you some food?"

Theo's nose scrunched, and he shook his head.

"Yeah, I don't trust anything around here either." He gently lifted Gemma's leg and set it on the bed, noticing the sweet scent of peppermint that drifted from her. Finding a blanket nearby, he draped it over Gemma and tugged it until it covered her shoulders. As he watched her sleep, his gaze was drawn to the dark stitches standing in stark contrast against her pale neck. Between all the cuts and her broken leg, it was a miracle she'd stayed alert as long as she had.

He turned to Theo. "She's not making it easy to keep her safe, is she?"

Theo released a small puff of air as he shook his head again.

Brayden chuckled, reaching out and gently rubbing between Theo's ears. "I guess we just have our work cut out for us."

Theo leaned into his hand as he yawned loudly.

"I'll let you get some rest," Brayden said, preparing to stand, but he paused as the peppermint scent reached his nose once more. *Of all the smells, it had to be that one.* Memories of his mother humming while she added peppermint to her homemade soap flashed through his mind, and he pushed them away, gazing down at Gemma's face. A stray strand of hair lay across her cheek and over the corner of her mouth. Hesitantly, he took the hair and moved it off her face. In sleep, she looked small and vulnerable. When he made the promise to protect her, it was more out of duty than anything else, but looking at her now, a fierce protectiveness rose inside, startling him with its suddenness.

Snatching his hand back, he shot to his feet. He gave Theo a quick nod. "I'll trust you to watch over her tonight." He turned on his heel and rushed out of the room.

CHAPTER FIFTEEN

Gemma yawned, stretching her arms over her head as she opened her eyes. The walls and ceiling glittered around her in an unnatural light, and it took her a few moments to remember where she was. A soft blanket she didn't recognize lay on top of her. *Serania must have put this on me after I fell asleep.*

Theo slept, curled up in a ball on the pillow next to her, his nose and eyes tucked under his bushy tail.

Trying not to wake Theo, she sat up and slowly swung her legs over the edge of the bed. The scrapes on her arms caught her eye, and she examined them more closely, noting that the aggressive red from last night had faded into a softer pink. She touched the stitches on her neck, her eyebrows raising as she found the cut a lot less sensitive. Even her leg no longer stabbed with pain; instead, it dully throbbed. An idea came to her, and she stood, gingerly placing a slight amount of weight onto her broken leg. A sharp stab of pain shot up from her shin to her hip, and she yelped as she plopped to her seat on the bed. *Well, that was brilliant.*

Theo groaned, stretched, and made a show of an exaggerated yawn.

Gemma rubbed her leg, gritting her teeth. "Sorry I woke you."

He came to all fours, arching his back as he stretched his front legs, accompanied by more loud yawns. After vigorously shaking his entire body, he made his way under Gemma's hand as he squeaked his good mornings.

Gemma laughed. "Good morning, bud. I take it you slept well?"

She picked him up and gave him a good scratch between his ears and down his neck. He leaned into her hand, purring and turning so she could scratch more spots. He loved his morning rubdowns.

"Shall we go see if anyone else is up?"

He gave her his best puppy-dog eyes, forcing her to rub him for a few more minutes first.

"Okay, okay. We should go see who else is awake."

He grunted as his ears drooped, but he hopped down and headed to the door.

Gemma chuckled as she hopped behind him, this time being careful to keep weight off her bad leg. It was nice to see him relax. It had been too long since the last time he was able to enjoy himself. As soon as she opened the bedroom door, the maddening sound of the hundreds of clocks bombarded her eardrums. "I didn't realize how much the door keeps out the sound. Why in Elefrisia would anyone want a hallway like this? It's ridiculous!"

Theo squeaked in agreement, pulling his ears down with his forefeet as he walked upright on his hind legs.

The two made their way through the hall as fast as Gemma could, then breathed a sigh of relief when they exited. As the hallway door shut behind her, the sound of the clocks instantly cut off. *How do they not let any sound through?*

"It's about time you got up, sleepy head." Andrea stood, leaning her back against a bookshelf and shoving a sweet-looking pastry into her mouth. "I told Serania I couldn't promise to save you any food. You snooze, you lose."

"I made sure there would be plenty for you." Serania sat on the couch, a book laying open in her lap, and held up a plate laden with different pastries. "You look much better this morning. How are you feeling?"

"So much better." Gemma hopped to the couch, sitting beside Serania and taking a blueberry muffin. She eyed Brayden, who sat in one of the reading chairs with his back straight and stiff while he intently read another book.

Theo hopped up beside Gemma, sniffing the plate of pastries. His stomach growled loudly as he picked up a pastry and sniffed it, turning it over in his forefeet.

Gemma watched his internal struggle play across his face. He had a weakness for sweets, and since he didn't eat dinner, she knew her small friend must be starving by now. "None of us have dropped over dead, Theo. I'm sure it's probably safe to eat."

His nose twitched from side to side, but his hunger finally won out, and he bit into the pastry, finishing it in only a few bites. With an excited squeak, he grabbed more pastries, one in each forefoot, and took turns taking bites from one and then the other.

Andrea shoved another pastry into her mouth, speaking around the large bite. "Glad to see you no longer look like something the cat dragged in."

Gemma rolled her eyes. "Seriously, I didn't look that bad."

"Yes, you did." Andrea laughed as Gemma scowled at her.

Serania studied Gemma's face. "You do look a world better. Most of your scrapes look nearly healed."

"So do yours." Gemma examined each of her companions. Their cuts and bruises were already fading, except for Brayden's. "How is it possible we've all healed so much?"

"That would be the work of my special tea." Baiya fluttered into the room, holding a fresh pot of tea, and refilled everyone's cups. The golden gown she wore swished with her every move. She looked ready for a ball at a castle. "How is your leg feeling, dear? I hope my wafers are helping."

"It feels a lot better, thank you. Of course, it still can't bear weight, but it's not overwhelming anymore."

"In that case, here." She handed another wafer to Gemma. "These, combined with the tea, will keep speeding up the healing process."

Gemma took it gratefully, eating it without hesitation.

Baiya frowned at Brayden. "You, dear, should have some tea. Those wounds would heal much faster."

"I'm fine." Brayden closed his book and stood. "Thank you for your generosity, but now that we're all up and nourished, we should be on our way."

Gemma choked on her tea. "Couldn't we stay a little while longer?"

He returned the book to the shelf. "We shouldn't risk it."

"But we're safe here. We have food, a roof over our head, and the ability to heal for a while."

Brayden pursed his lips. "We agreed to stay the night. I told you we'd be leaving in the morning."

"I know, but it wouldn't hurt to wait a little longer; even a few more hours would help."

"We should cover as much ground as possible while it's still light."

Andrea held a hand up. "I second that. We should get on the move."

Theo chimed in his agreement.

"And I—what—hop the whole way? Or worse, Brayden has to carry me again?" The idea of moving on was enough to make Gemma want to cry. It had been weeks since she was able to stop and just be. All she wanted was a little time to recover.

"She does have a point," Serania said. She continued quickly when Brayden's face hardened. "Let's give it a little more time. It's hard enough traveling without an injured person. She needs time for her leg to heal."

Brayden placed his hands on his hips. "I made a promise, Gemma. You know that. The longer we stay, the more we risk me not being able to fulfill that promise."

Baiya cut in. "You're all free to leave whenever you like. I won't keep you here, but it would do dear Gemma a lot of good if she were allowed to heal completely."

Andrea narrowed her eyes at Baiya. "You need to butt out, lady. You're not a part of this group."

Serania groaned. "Drea! She's allowed us to stay in her home and eat her food—"

"It's quite all right, dear," Baiya said with a swish of her hand. "I'm nothing more than a stranger. I don't expect any of you to trust me."

"Thank you for being so gracious," Serania said before turning to Brayden. "I'm not saying we become careless and stay; just give Gemma a little more time."

Brayden dropped back into the reading chair, his face firmly set in a deep scowl. "This was so much easier when it was just me, Gemma, and Theo."

Serania gave him a small smile. "I'm not trying to overstep your leadership, Brayden. We'll leave soon, I promise."

He swallowed hard before dipping his head. "We can stay for a few more hours, nothing more."

Gemma tried to catch his eye, but he returned his attention to his book. Her shoulders drooped. He was going to be mad at her for a while after this, of that she was certain. She leaned back and turned her attention to Baiya. "Since we have some time, I would love to hear your story."

Baiya's face lit up in a wide smile as she launched into her story. She had accidentally stumbled into the lizard-infested caverns. Her parents and grandfather found her, and they fought their way out. Injured and frightened, it was a delight when they stumbled across this house after days of wandering aimlessly through the forest.

"Pretty convenient this house was already empty. What happened to the previous occupant?" Andrea asked.

"And what happened to your parents and grandfather? Why aren't they here with you?" Brayden added.

Baiya's face clouded. "Unfortunately, I wasn't as adept at healing then. My grandfather passed the first night, and my parents shortly after. I have no idea what happened to the previous occupant."

"I'm sorry for your loss," Serania said.

Andrea's eyes narrowed. Gemma imagined she didn't believe any of Baiya's story.

"It's okay; it was a long time ago." Baiya offered another smile before hopping to her feet. "Now, I must go find us some more ingredients for lunch and dinner. That is, if you are planning to stay a while longer." She looked at each of them in turn.

Gemma turned to Brayden, doing her best to keep her tone soft. "Just one more day? Please?"

His eyes hardened, and he looked away. "One more." He stomped away, disappearing into the hall.

Baiya grinned. "Fantastic! Make yourselves at home."

The day passed uneventfully. Serania occupied herself by skimming through different books on the shelf. Andrea explored with Theo in tow, determined to learn more about the magical house. Brayden soon reentered the book room and planted himself in one of the chairs, once more engrossed in a book. He refused to meet Gemma's eyes.

Gemma ate as many wafers as she could, and her leg finally reached the point where she could limp rather than hop. She chose to follow Andrea. It bothered her that the doors faded in and out of view, and she pictured Andrea going through one, just to get stuck when it disappeared. Also, sticking with her sister meant Gemma didn't have to be in the same room as Brayden and his ever-darkening mood.

The first room held shelves of candles. Gemma had no clue why anyone would need so many candles in a house with electric lights, but there were enough candles in the room to supply all of Dano for a month. The next room held nothing but cups and other dishes. The next was full of hats. Finally, as Andrea entered the fourth room, she whooped in excitement.

"Now, this is what I'm talking about!" Andrea skipped over to a wall covered with swords, bows, knives, and many weapons Gemma couldn't identify. Andrea picked up a huge battle-axe. "Oh, where have you been my whole life?"

Gemma watched her sister swing the axe from side to side. "Drea, none of this is ours. We shouldn't take anything. Besides, that thing is much too large for you to haul around."

Andrea set the axe down with only a hint of reluctance. "You're right. Not at all practical." She picked up a set of throwing knives. "Ah, now these will do quite nicely."

Theo nodded in agreement as he bounded from Andrea's shoulder and searched around the room.

Andrea packed the throwing knives into her boots before grabbing more knives, methodically slipping them into her sleeves and under her belt. "Come on, Gemma. If her story is to be believed, Baiya stumbled on this place just as we did. She doesn't have any claim on any of this."

Gemma bit her lip, but her sister had a point. An intricate silver bow with a matching quiver caught her eye, and she gingerly picked it up, rubbing her hand along the cold metal.

"Serania would love that, as long as she doesn't think it's stolen," Andrea said over Gemma's shoulder. "You should hang onto it for now."

A pang of guilt settled in Gemma's stomach as she filled the quiver with arrows and took both it and the bow to her room. The guilt continued to nag after she set them on the loveseat and sat next to them. *It's not stealing if no one owns it, right?* With the thought giving her courage, she snatched up a green stone that had caught her eye the night before. It was about the size of Theo, and the dark green sparkled in the light of the chandelier. She tucked it into her pouch. At least she'd have one souvenir from this crazy place. Sitting down on the edge of the bed, she fought the urge to replace the stone and bow. It wasn't right to steal. Her mother ingrained that in her from the time she could talk. After another minute of wrestling with the guilt, she finally pushed it away. *Baiya doesn't own any of this. I'm not actually stealing.*

As evening approached, Brayden and Gemma were in the couch room. He insisted they needed to leave, whether it was dark or not.

"It's useless to start traveling at night, and you said one day; so we should leave in the morning. Besides, my leg can bear some weight. A bit more time and I'll be able to walk without help. Just one more night."

He glared at her. "Gemma, you're being a fool."

Gemma drew back, his words hurting like a slap to the face. "I don't need your permission to stay. I'm an adult and can make my own decisions."

"Oh, you're an adult? I'll believe it when I see it."

"Excuse me? Why do you have to be such a jerk?"

He stepped closer to her, forcing her to take a step back. "I'm trying to keep *you* safe, in case you forgot!" He balled his hands into fists. "Which you don't make easy to do."

"And how are you supposed to keep me 'safe' when you're trying to force me out into the dark of an unknown forest with a still-injured leg?"

"Need I remind you that our enemies have already found you more than once? The longer we stay in one place, the more we tempt fate."

"I'm tired, Brayden. I need a break!"

"You don't think I'm tired, too? I wish our enemies would stop and let us breathe, but wake up! We can't call a truce! They *will* find us, and when, not if, but *when* they do, I might not be able to save you this time!"

"Maybe I don't want or need you to save me!" Gemma held his gaze, crossing her arms. She may have been more willing to relent if he hadn't been so cruel with his words.

Serania had silently watched the argument, her book left forgotten in her lap. "I think you both should take a step back and calm down. This arguing isn't going to help anyone."

"Tell that to him, not me." Gemma paced to the far side of the room.

"I'm telling it to *both* of you." Serania's voice was tight, and she arched a brow. "Both of you, take a step away and calm down before you talk to each other again."

"No problem," Brayden spat as he turned and left.

The burning anger in Gemma's chest deflated to a harsh sadness as Brayden stomped away. She brushed a tear from her cheek. "He's being unreasonable."

Serania held up a hand. "I don't want to hear any more. Go to your room and cool down."

Gemma bit back a response and quickly made her way to her room, shutting the door firmly behind her. Plopping down on the bed, she grabbed a pillow and hugged it to her stomach. Theo wasn't there to comfort her; he was probably still exploring with Andrea. For the first time since leaving home, she felt completely alone. She laid down on the bed, tucking her knees around the pillow. *I wish I were home.* Her tears flowed freely until she finally drifted off to sleep.

CHAPTER SIXTEEN

By morning, Gemma could walk on her damaged leg with only mild tenderness. If the healing kept up this pace, her leg would feel brand new by the end of the day. She turned to tell Theo the good news, but he wasn't in the room. Her stomach soured as she stared at the closed bedroom door. He couldn't have entered the room; she hadn't left the door ajar for him or even thought to do so. *He probably scratched at the door wanting in, and I didn't even hear him.*

Making her way down the hall was excruciating. Not because of the ache in her leg, but because of the images of Theo sitting outside her room, scratching at the door and squeaking for her. Never in her life had she forgotten Theo. She wasn't sure what to expect from him when she saw him.

In the bookroom, she found everyone else already up and finished eating—Baiya was nowhere to be seen. Theo eyed her and hopped over with a scolding squeak.

"I know, bud. I'm so sorry." Gemma held her hand out for him. He scowled, but soon jumped onto her offered hand. "I really am sorry. My mind was elsewhere, and I didn't think about the door."

Theo crossed his forelegs as he harumphed.

Her eyes burned, and she hoped she wouldn't break into tears again. "Forgive me?"

He rolled his eyes and scolded her for another minute. Then he kissed her on the cheek and took his usual place on her shoulder.

Gemma's stomach eased as Theo smiled at her. "I promise I won't ever do that again." She sat next to Serania on the couch, taking a biscuit from a plate on the tea table. Gemma nibbled on it while she snuck a furtive glance at Brayden, who was planted in one of the reading chairs holding an open book. "So, I was thinking. Maybe we could spend one more night here..."

Brayden shut the book with a loud slap. "Absolutely not."

Gemma leaned forward, holding a hand up. "Just hear me out. My leg is almost fully healed—"

"Which means you'll be fine to travel," Brayden interrupted.

Gemma narrowed her eyes. "One more night, and I'll be able to run without any problems."

"One more night, and our enemies might be too close to run from," Brayden countered.

"Come on, Brayden. There hasn't been any sign of pursuit. One more night won't hurt," Gemma persisted.

Andrea scoffed. "One more night might be the thing that gets us all killed."

Brayden stood, dropping the book onto the tea table. "We leave within the hour. No negotiations."

Gemma crossed her arms, leaning back into the couch. "I'm staying one more night."

Theo growled before abandoning her shoulder for Brayden's and shooting a disappointed look in her direction.

Brayden's face turned two shades darker as he held Gemma's stare. "Are you determined to get yourself killed?"

"I'm not going to get myself killed." Gemma averted her gaze. She knew she was being stubborn, but for once, she wasn't going to let anyone decide for her. "I promise we can leave tomorrow."

Serania quickly moved to Brayden, placing a hand on his arm. "It's okay. We could all use one more day to rest and prepare for the journey."

Brayden's neck muscles tightened, and a muscle in his jaw twitched as he glared at Serania. He shook her hand off before jabbing a finger in Gemma's direction. "We leave tomorrow morning even if I have to tie you up and drag you out of here." He grabbed the book off the tea table and stomped through the door down the hall—Theo remaining firmly on his shoulder.

The moment the door shut behind him, Gemma wished she could take the entire conversation back. The temptation to run down the hall and apologize made her feet shuffle restlessly under her.

Andrea arched a brow at Gemma. "You're being dumb, sis. For one thing, Baiya keeps disappearing for hours at a time. Which is quite convenient if you want to avoid being questioned. And for another, Brayden and I tried opening the doors in the entryway in case we needed to make a quick escape, and none of them would budge. We're locked in a magical house with someone who hasn't offered anything substantial about her past."

Gemma sank deeper into the couch as Andrea's words struck a warning bell in the back of her mind. But as quickly as the warning came, it was replaced with indignation. "She probably keeps the doors locked for safety reasons. If the lizards in the cave were any indication of the wildlife in these parts, it would be safe to keep the doors locked. Besides, I can't blame her for not wanting to answer questions."

Andrea shook her head and left without another word.

Serania plopped down hard on the couch. "Well, that could have gone better."

Gemma nodded as hot tears stung her eyes. She buried her face in her hands. "I'm sorry. I know I should listen to them. The last thing I want is for everyone to be mad at me. I'm just so tired of running."

Serania pulled Gemma into a tight hug and rubbed her back. "I know. Tensions are strained right now, but it will pass."

"Not before Brayden hates me more than he did before."

Serania pulled back, wiping tears and mucus from Gemma's face. "He doesn't hate you—"

"Yes, he does." Gemma closed her eyes. "He's hated me a long time."

"Gemma, look at me." Serania's voice remained calm and gentle. "Sometimes we can't see things clearly if we're too close to them, and in this instance, you are too close to the situation." She cupped Gemma's chin with one hand. "Brayden does not, nor will he ever hate you. I know hate when I see it, and that isn't anywhere near the way he looks at you."

Gemma took a shuddering breath as she held Serania's gaze. "Are you sure?"

"One hundred percent."

Gemma fell into her sister's arms, taking comfort from her big sister's words. Her relationship with Brayden might be strained at the moment, but she wouldn't give up hope that it would mend, and maybe become stronger from the straining. *I won't argue anymore. From here on out, I'll trust what he has to say. Even if I don't agree with it.*

Serania removed Gemma's stitches shortly after, noting how faint the scar would be. The morning went by quietly as everyone found ways to occupy themselves. Andrea and Theo continued their exploration of the house. Serania remained in the bookroom, curled up on the couch with a stack of books by her side. Gemma didn't see Brayden except when he came to switch out books. She tried to catch his eye, but he refused to look at her.

Baiya made an entrance at noon, wearing a silky, red dress and carrying a basket overflowing with fruits and vegetables. Gemma helped her unload the items in the kitchen and took the opportunity to find out more about their host. "Baiya? Do you mind me asking about your childhood? What were your parents like?"

Baiya smiled as her eyes glazed with a far-off look. "I loved my childhood. My parents were antiquarians; some of the best in Elefrisia. We traveled to some of the most remote and dangerous places. Nothing scared them; their love of history overpowered any fear." She finished unloading the basket and led Gemma to the bookroom. The two sat in the reading chairs as she continued. "My parents outwitted pirates, searched ancient tombs, and sailed through fierce storms. My life was one adventure after another." Leaning in, she whispered, "I even found a petrified dragon egg. Or at least, I'm almost positive it was a dragon egg."

Gemma didn't try to hide the wonder on her face. Compared to Baiya's childhood, Gemma's was a bore. "What about this house? How long have you lived here?"

"Oh, a few years or so. I've never kept track."

"Have you explored much? I looked around a little with Andrea, and this place is entirely odd."

Baiya waved a dismissive hand. "I was never much for exploring indoors. I much prefer to be outside."

When she didn't offer anything more, Serania, who sat on the couch with a book in her lap, jumped in. "What about the doors leading out? Andrea said they're all locked. So how do you get in and out?"

"When my parents and I came here, the door we came through—the same one you entered—had the key resting in it." She shrugged. "All the other doors were already locked when we came."

Serania pursed her lips. "But the house was unoccupied when you found it?"

Baiya nodded. "Yes. And no one showed up claiming ownership."

Serania returned to her reading, but as Gemma and Baiya continued their conversation, Serania snuck glances at Baiya every few minutes. A nagging worry lit in the back of Gemma's mind as her big sister's mannerisms changed, but Baiya's stories soon drew her in again, and the worry faded into the background.

As nighttime drew close, Baiya held a hand to her throat. "Well then, I am quite parched from all that storytelling. Would you like some tea?"

Gemma smiled. "Tea would be great, thank you."

"And how is your leg feeling?"

Gemma stood and bounced on her toes a few times. "Like it was never broken at all."

"Perfect!" Baiya clapped her hands together as she beamed at Gemma. "Then I'll make a special tea to celebrate."

As Baiya swept into the kitchen, Gemma sank back with a small sigh. If she didn't miss her parents so much, it would be tempting to stay in Baiya's house indefinitely. She was safe, healed, and rested. Baiya was kind and entertaining. If Brayden, Andrea, and Theo weren't mad at her for choosing to stay, she'd beg them to remain here for a while longer. But she couldn't mention the idea of staying. If she tried, Brayden might follow through on his threat to tie her up and drag her out against her will.

The door to the hallway cracked open, and Andrea stepped through. Brayden followed behind, but a shrill scream resounded from the kitchen before he'd taken more than a step.

The group ran into the kitchen, bumping into each other as they piled through the archway.

Baiya's face was set in an ugly scowl, and she brandished a pot toward Theo. Theo stood on the counter growling at her, a few strands of Baiya's hair clutched in his forefoot.

Gemma rushed forward, scooping Theo up while he squeaked at Baiya and shook his balled-up forefoot at her. "What do you mean she was going to try to kill us?"

Brayden unsheathed his battered sword while he took a few cautious steps forward. "What exactly is going on in here?"

Theo squeaked again, and Gemma interpreted. "He says Baiya was going to poison us." She clamped her hands tighter while Theo tried to wriggle free.

Andrea leaned toward Brayden as the room filled with the high pitch ringing of her swords leaving their sheaths. "So, do you get to say, 'I told you so', or do I?"

Baiya smiled, lowering the pot. "I would never do such a thing. I was brewing some tea from the purple fruits native to these woods. They have relaxing qualities, not harmful in the least. I think you'll like it even more than the healing tea you've been drinking already."

"I'm with the squirrel on this one," Andrea said.

Theo growled low in his throat. Whether the growl was directed at Andrea for calling him a squirrel again or at Baiya, Gemma didn't know. He finally managed to wriggle free and hurried over to the counter. Narrowing his eyes at Baiya, he hunched his head and shoulders while his growl grew louder.

"Look," Baiya said, "why would I try to poison you now? It makes no sense. I've done nothing but help heal you. I wanted to share another gift, that's all."

Usually, Gemma would take Theo's side and brandish a weapon, but when she looked at Baiya, she couldn't see an enemy. Baiya had healed her, entertained her, and kept her safe. Baiya was a friend, not a foe. Even as those thoughts passed through her mind, a small ringing of warning echoed through them, but trying to pull the warning to the forefront was like trying to uproot a tree stump with nothing but her hands. She took a step back. *What's wrong with me?*

"*...Gemma...*" Dream Thalia's voice whispered to Gemma's mind, but it was faint and too far away.

"That's it. We're leaving. Everyone, gather your things. I want to be out of here within the hour, even if we have to break the door down." Brayden started out of the room but stopped short as Baiya burst into tears.

Baiya's shoulders drooped low, and she leaned heavily against the counter. "I enjoyed having the company, but I see you no longer trust me." She sniffled and wiped her nose with a handkerchief. "I get so little company here. Sometimes years pass before anyone stumbles upon this place. I was hoping for a little more time."

Andrea curled her lip. "Right...I'm with Brayden. Let's get going."

Serania's face remained unreadable as she watched Baiya's crying fit. "I'm so sorry, but I think it's best we leave."

Baiya sniffled with a disheartened nod. "I understand. Perhaps one last cup of tea?"

"I...I think we...need to go...or maybe...I don't know." Gemma struggled to make her feet move. The warning still rang in the back of her mind, but she couldn't look away from Baiya's wet eyes and sad frown.

Brayden tilted his head as he eyed Gemma with a furrowed brow. "It's settled; let's go."

Baiya's crying ceased. Her eyes hardened, and she stood up taller. She chanted in a low, droning tone as she weaved her hands and fingers in a complicated pattern.

Andrea shouted as she rushed toward Baiya, but before she took more than a step, ropes, the same color as the wall, snaked around her waist and pinned her to the wall.

In the same breath, Gemma found herself slamming painfully against the wall. More wall-colored ropes wrapped around her wrists and ankles, pulling tight so she was spread-eagle on the wall. Each of her companions soon found themselves in the same precarious position. Her gaze skittered around the room, looking for Theo, but there was no sign of him anywhere.

A couple of thuds resounded through the kitchen as Andrea lost her grip on her swords. "Fint! You've got to be kidding me! I knew there was something up with this freaky house!"

Baiya doubled over as her laughter filled the small room. "I wish you could see your faces. Priceless." She wiped beneath her eyes. "Oh, I haven't had this much fun in so long."

"You better enjoy it. I promise it won't last long," Andrea growled between her teeth as she pulled against her restraints.

Brayden struggled next to Gemma. "I knew we shouldn't have stayed. I told you something bad would happen!"

"Now is not the time to start throwing around blame," Serania said as she, too, struggled to free herself.

Baiya waved a hand in a dismissing gesture. "You can give up trying to free yourselves. The walls won't release you unless I choose to let them." She made her way to the counter, pouring a deep purple tea into a clay cup. "Sorry for the discomfort. This all could have been much more pleasant for you if you'd remained ignorant and trusting."

"What are you talking about?" Gemma didn't try to pull free of her restraints. Nothing that was happening made sense. Why would her friend be attacking her? Was Baiya trying to protect her somehow? *That must be it. She knew leaving would be dangerous. She's doing this to save me.*

Baiya turned bright eyes to Gemma. "I told you that I used a glamer to appear as an old woman outside this house, but the opposite is true. I use the glamer in here. It's served me well for a long time. Show them a batty old woman in need of help to lure them in. Present a beautiful young woman to comfort them and keep them enthralled once inside. It especially works wonders on men..." She scoffed at Brayden. "Well, most men."

Baiya carried the full cup toward Gemma. "I knew someone powerful had entered the forest. I felt it the moment you passed through the veil." She paused and brushed some stray hairs from Gemma's face. A small part of Gemma cringed, yet at the same time, she took comfort in Baiya's touch.

Baiya continued in a low tone. "You, dear girl, have a power about you that rivals the sun. That's why I spelled you."

"What did you do to her?" Brayden demanded, his voice coming out in a low growl.

"Oh, nothing harmful. I simply made sure she would see things a bit differently. It's a clever spell that's taken me a long time to perfect." She caressed Gemma's face.

"Get your hands off her!" Brayden struggled harder against his bonds.

Baiya chuckled, moving to stand in front of Brayden. "It was amusing to watch your anger grow toward her. I thought about spelling you as well. We could have had a lot of fun together, but it was much more enjoyable to watch you attack poor little Gemma." She gave Brayden a quick kiss on the lips before pulling back with a low laugh. "Little Gemma didn't know her choices weren't hers. The spell is subtle enough; she believed she was acting and thinking of her own free will." She placed the cup to Gemma's lips. "You must be thirsty. Drink as much as you like."

Brayden struggled against his restraints to the point where he drew blood. "I will kill you if you harm her."

Gemma watched Brayden struggle and knew the words he spoke meant he was furious, but she didn't understand why he was so bothered. Baiya was offering another sweet tea; she wasn't threatening Gemma in any way. Gemma breathed in the sweet scent of the purple liquid before drinking deeply from the cup. She gagged as the liquid soured in her stomach and the back of her throat. An invisible thread that had linked her to Baiya snapped. *Baiya's not saving me; she's trying to kill me!* It all made sense now, but she was powerless to do anything about it.

"There." Baiya returned the cup to the counter and leaned back as she studied her captives. "It won't take too long, and I promise it's not painful. In a few hours, you'll fall asleep. It's quite peaceful."

Andrea sent a string of curses in Baiya's direction. Serania's face blanched. Brayden's entire body shook as his nostrils flared. Gemma couldn't imagine how angry he was to know he'd failed his promise.

Tears escaped Gemma's eyes, and her chin trembled as memories of the past couple of days ran through her mind. All the times she should have listened to Brayden, Theo, and Andrea, but she didn't. Looking at them now, she could see how stupid she must have sounded. But at the time, her desire to stay made complete sense. *Where is Theo? Why isn't he doing something? Did she hurt him somehow?* She hung her head low. "Brayden, I'm so sorry."

"No, I'm sorry." Brayden hit the back of his head against the wall in frustration. "I should have known."

Andrea spoke between gritted teeth. "Now would be a great time to make something explode, Gemma."

Gemma briefly closed her eyes, searching for the feel of the jewel, but nothing came. She didn't know how to make the jewel work. So far, it seemed to have a mind of its own. She shook her head at Andrea, and her sister growled in frustration.

The blood returned to Serania's face as a scowl hardened her features. "Why poison us now? Why bother to heal us just to kill us?"

"Oh, it's not poison, dear." Baiya took her time refilling the cup. "No. I'm not some psychotic murderer who kills on a whim. This is made from the fruits of the trees here. It will drain your life and give it to me. Why else would I take the time to heal you first? The healthier the person, the more life to be taken."

"How old are you?" Serania asked.

Baiya squinted her eyes as she glanced at the ceiling. "That's not an easy question for me to answer. However, I can tell you I was born in the third age on the fifteenth of Iberthu in the year 3995."

Serania's eyes went as wide as saucers. "That would make you over five hundred years old."

"Is that all?" Baiya shrugged. "I thought it would've been much more than that."

A cast-iron pan inched forward on the shelf a couple of feet above Baiya's head, making a faint scraping sound as it moved. Gemma could just make out Theo's tail twitching behind the pan. She cleared her throat and drew her gaze away from Theo's work. "So, everything you told me about your life, your parents, they were all a lie?"

"It wasn't all a lie," Baiya answered. "I did grow up the way I told you. All those adventures were real. My parents and grandfather did stumble upon this house, and my grandfather died from his wounds, just as I said. But my parents didn't die from any wounds, and the house wasn't empty." She set the cup on the counter and crossed her arms. "You see, the previous occupant was kind to my parents and me. He consoled us after losing my grandfather and nursed us back to health. He became especially close to me.

"Even though this form,"—She waved her hand down the length of her body— "is an illusion, this is how I look when age hasn't ravished me. Mr. Nell was quite overcome by my beauty. That's what saved me, you know. My exquisite looks." The skin around her eyes tightened, and her voice took on a bitter tone. "So, in his lust, he chose to save me. He gave this same drink to my parents, but he gave me something else. By morning, he was young and vibrant, and my parents were nothing more than a couple of skeletons still lying on their bed."

The shame that ate at Gemma's insides took a backseat to the onslaught of compassion that welled up inside. No matter how evil Baiya might be, no one deserved such a thing.

Baiya stood up taller. "It doesn't matter. I made sure he paid for what he did. After that, I stayed here." She scrunched her eyebrows. "I never planned to follow in his footsteps, but the life I received the day I killed Nell was something I had never felt before. The power that coursed through my veins was beyond anything I could describe. I almost let the first poor traveler go, but I needed to taste that power again. Each one since has become much easier. Though fewer and fewer travelers have found this place over the last couple of decades. I was beginning to fear no more would come." Her eyes lit as the corners of her lips turned up. "I couldn't believe my luck when not one, but four people stumbled through the veil. It was like the Creator Himself gave me a gift just as I thought all hope was lost."

"You won't be so grateful for us when I get out of these bonds," Andrea said, her voice icy.

"Oh, Drea; so feisty and full of life. You won't have the chance to kill me; you'll be dead with everyone else. It will be much more pleasant for you if you—"

The cast-iron pan fell from the shelf and slammed into Baiya's head before clattering to the ground. She transformed back into the old woman wearing a tattered, tan dress as she crumpled like a doll. The cup fell to the floor, splashing its purple contents across the tile.

The bonds holding Gemma and the others vanished.

Theo squeaked as he hopped down to the counter and pushed the teapot off, so it shattered on the floor.

Gemma rushed to the counter and scooped Theo up, pulling him into a tight squeeze while Andrea and Brayden worked at tying Baiya's hands behind her back.

Theo squeaked in urgent tones, and Gemma translated, "He says we should get out of here."

"You think?" Andrea growled before giving Baiya a swift kick to the midsection. Baiya remained unresponsive on the floor.

"Is she dead?" Gemma asked.

Andrea wrinkled her nose as she stared at Baiya. "Unfortunately, no."

Brayden heaved Baiya's body up and over his shoulder. "Let's get out of this place before she wakes up."

"Why are you bringing her along?" Andrea asked.

Brayden tromped out of the kitchen, heading toward the room with the doors. "She gave Gemma that tea. We have to find out if there's an antidote or any way to reverse the effects. Each of you, get your things."

Serania followed on his heels. "But what if she refuses to tell us? Or what if the antidote is here in this house? We have to think this through."

Andrea glanced over her shoulder as she rushed toward the hall to gather her things. "I think we need to get as far away from this crazy place as possible. That is, if we can even open the door."

Serania fidgeted with her hands as she shifted her weight from foot to foot.

Gemma didn't know what they should do and didn't trust herself to decide. She rushed to her room and gathered the bow and quiver full of arrows, taking a quick glance to make sure she didn't forget anything.

Theo wrapped his tail around her neck as he squeaked in worry.

"I know, bud. I'm worried, too." Gemma rubbed between his ears as she made her way back down the hall. If they couldn't find an antidote, or if one didn't exist, this might be her last few hours alive. The thought caused a painful fist of sadness to lodge in her chest. She'd never see her parents again. Never get to tell them one last time that she loved them. She didn't even know if they were alive or not. It was mildly consoling to know she would see her parents again in Mistria—the realm of the Creator—but the longing to see them alive once more broke the dam holding back her tears. *I'd give anything to hug them one last time.*

Gemma arrived back at the entryway shortly before Andrea, who had a backpack on her back that towered over her head and a belt with a sheathed sword in her hand. Gemma handed the bow and quiver to Serania. "These are for you."

Serania hesitantly took them. "Where did these—"

"Just take them and be grateful," Andrea said, handing the sword belt to Brayden.

Brayden appraised the new sword before quickly tossing his battered one, belt and all, aside. "Let's go." He tried the nearest door handle, and it swung open to reveal a curtain of white fog.

"Fint!" Andrea stood in front of a different door that held the same foggy view.

Serania chose a door at random and opened it as well. Once again, all that greeted them was a dense, white fog. "At least they aren't locked anymore."

"But how do we know which one to choose?" Brayden continued to open doors until the group stood in front of a dozen curtains of white fog.

"Let's just pick one and go," Andrea offered.

Brayden kicked the wall. "That wouldn't be wise. For all we know, one of these could lead us back into the caves again."

Andrea rolled her eyes. "I'll take caves over walls that hold me prisoner any day."

Serania grabbed Andrea's wrist. "No, he's right. If we choose the wrong door, we might end up in an even worse situation."

"Anything's better than standing around and staring at them all night," Andrea spat.

An argument ensued as Serania, Andrea, and Brayden couldn't agree on which door to try. Gemma remained silent. *If it weren't for me, we wouldn't even be in this situation.*

Theo sighed heavily in Gemma's ear. He slowly pulled his forefeet down his face before turning to her. He pointed at an arched door near the center of the wall directly in front of the group.

Gemma gave him a small smile. "Theo knows which doorway."

Her quiet voice was drowned out by Andrea's near shout. "I'm telling you; we should try that one!"

"You're just guessing. We can't make this decision on a guess," Serania countered.

Gemma tried again in a slightly louder voice. "It's the one with the gold arch."

The others continued to argue.

Gemma put her thumb and middle finger between her lips and blew a shrill whistle that startled the others into silence. "Theo says it's that one." She gestured to the golden arched door.

Andrea trudged through the door without a backward glance. Brayden stalked through, followed by Serania, who tugged Gemma's hand before stepping through. Gemma watched them all disappear into the fog. She bit her lip as Theo leaned into her. "I'm sorry for everything, bud."

Theo purred as he rubbed his head against her cheek.

He didn't hold anything against her. She'd been spelled. She had no control over that, but guilt and shame made her want to vanish into the fog, never to face anyone again. She sighed as someone called her name. Balling her fists, she strode through the doorway.

CHAPTER SEVENTEEN

Brayden sucked in a sharp breath as his nose smacked hard against the low doorframe. Serania grunted behind him as the top of her head met the same fate as his nose.

Andrea grinned. "Sometimes it pays to be short." She chuckled as Serania glared at her while rubbing the top of her head. "Come on, Gemma! We don't have all night!"

Serania leaned closer to the door. "Just watch out—"

A loud thud followed by Gemma's sharp intake of air cut off Serania's warning. Gemma held both hands to her forehead. "I completely forgot about that."

Andrea snickered. "Don't worry. They did, too."

If the situation hadn't been so dire, Brayden might have laughed. But Baiya's unconscious weight over his shoulder remained a constant reminder that Gemma's life might be hanging by a thread.

"Well, now that we're out of the freaky house, might I be the first to officially say—I told you so?" Andrea gave a small bow with her arms stretched wide.

"Now is not the time, Drea," Serania scolded. "Gemma is in danger right now. We need to wake Baiya, and figure out how to save our sister."

Andrea smirked. "Yeah, I'm sticking to it; I told you so."

"Let's move." Brayden trudged forward while he adjusted his hold on Baiya. "I want to put some distance between us and this magical house before we wake our hostess. Who knows what else she might throw at us?"

The evening light grew grey as Brayden led the group deeper into the forest. There was no telling what Baiya would do once she woke. From what he observed in the house, her magic was Trualech—a degraded form of magic that required the use of hand gestures and incantations. Only the lowliest of magic users stooped to using it. But if he were correct, then it would work in their favor. As long as they kept her hands bound, she would be powerless. Assuming she didn't have anything else up her sleeve. Brayden swept the thought away. There was nothing to do but face one problem at a time, and the biggest problem was figuring out how to save Gemma.

He entered a small clearing and nodded. "This is as good a place as any." He dropped Baiya to the ground. When that didn't wake her, he splashed her with water from his canteen.

Baiya's eyes snapped open. "What happened?" She struggled to sit up with her hands bound behind her. "Oh, my head." She blinked slowly and grimaced. "How did you best me?"

Andrea grabbed Baiya by the shoulders while she leaned in close. "No. You don't get to ask any questions. You're going to tell us how to stop your tea from killing Gemma. Nothing more, nothing less."

Baiya set her jaw. "And why would I do that? The moment I do, you'll kill me. The only insurance I have right now is the secret to saving your precious Gemma."

Brayden nudged Andrea aside. "You'll tell us because it's your only chance to survive. Something tells me survival is something you'll do anything for."

Baiya sighed heavily and slowly worked her way into a kneeling position. "How about we compromise? You tell me how you bested me, and I tell you what you want to know."

Gemma chimed in. "Theo pushed a cast-iron pan on your head."

A loud laugh burst from Baiya. It took her a few moments before she was able to speak. "All these years, and I get done in by a stupid rat. I've outsmarted some of the brightest minds and most powerful wizards, and it was all undone by someone so small."

Theo growled and jumped at Baiya, but Gemma caught him mid-flight and held on tight. Brayden debated telling her to let Theo go. Let him terrorize Baiya as much as he liked. But every moment they wasted was another risk to Gemma's life.

As Gemma struggled to keep a furious Theo in her hands, her eyes glazed, and she swayed on her feet.

Brayden grabbed her elbow before she could fall. He glared at Baiya. "Tell us how to save her, and I promise we'll let you go."

Baiya studied him. She opened her mouth but snapped it shut before glancing around. "Was I unconscious all night? I can't tell by the light. Is it morning or evening?"

It took Baiya's sudden shift in demeanor for Brayden to notice the change in the forest around him. The evening sounds, which had been steady as they trudged along, were gone. The air was still and eerily silent. He gripped the hilt of his sword. "It's evening. You've been out less than an hour."

Baiya's eyes grew wide, and her breathing quickened. "You must take me back to the house!" She shuffled closer to Brayden. "Please. I'll tell you everything you want to know. Just take me back to the house first."

Brayden stepped back, narrowing his eyes at Baiya. The sudden quiet spoke of danger, but he didn't think the house would be any safer for anyone but Baiya. "No. I think we'll stay right here."

"Please!" Baiya nearly shouted the word. She shook like a leaf as her gaze skittered around the trees. "You can save Gemma! All you need to do is get her as far away from me as you can." Her wide eyes turned to Brayden. "Preferably out of this forest altogether. That's how you save her. Distance."

Andrea scoffed. "Right. And we're supposed to believe you? Do you think we're going to fall for that? You know we'll have to leave you to follow through on this 'antidote.' You know we won't be splitting up, which means we have to let you go free. The next thing we know, Gemma will die, and you'll be dancing free with your youth again!"

"I'm telling the truth!" Baiya's voice shook. "Just let me go back to the house. You can all go. I won't harm you."

Brayden tilted his head, studying Baiya. The old woman's wrinkled skin was as white as cotton. Small beads of sweat rose on her forehead and upper lip. The woman was terrified—unless she was an excellent actress.

"Baiya..."

The hair on Brayden's arms stood alert as a voice whispered Baiya's name from deep in the forest. He drew his sword as more whispering voices filtered through the darkness. The voices didn't sound natural, more like wind whispering through leaves than sound from human vocal cords.

"Baiya, Baiya, Baiya..."

Baiya stood and rushed away from the voices, but Brayden caught her and held her fast. Baiya struggled against his hold. "I'll do anything! You can have anything you want. I have treasure in the house that will make you wealthier than a king. Just take me back!"

Brayden held onto Baiya as she tried to pull free from him. For the first time, he wondered if staying in the forest might be a mistake. The voices grew closer. A constant stream of them whispering Baiya's name. He turned to the others. "What do you think?"

Serania scanned the trees with an arrow nocked and ready. "I think I don't like the sounds of whatever is heading our way."

Andrea's backpack thumped to the ground, and she withdrew a huge battle-axe. "Whatever it is, we can take it."

Brayden furrowed his brow as Andrea lifted the axe to shoulder height. *Where in Elefrisia did she find that thing? And how did she fit it in the backpack?* There was no feasible way Andrea could fight long with such a large axe. He shook his head. *One problem at a time.* He glanced at Gemma, but she remained unarmed and quiet as she stared at Baiya.

Human-shaped shadows detached from the darkness beneath the trees, and made their way toward the group as they continued to whisper.

Baiya screamed as she thrashed against Brayden's hold. Her scream ripped louder as she was jerked from his arms. The shadows gathered around her ankles and dragged her away as her screams escalated.

Gemma dropped Theo and lunged for Baiya, grabbing under one of the old woman's arms. "No!" Gemma squeezed tighter as she was dragged along the ground. "You can't have her!"

Brayden threw himself toward Gemma and wrapped his arms around her waist. "Let her go, Gemma! She's not worth the risk!"

Gemma's gaze remained fixed on Baiya. "No one deserves this!"

Brayden searched for a hook to anchor his foot, but the shadows increased their pull, and he shot across the ground until someone grabbed his ankle and jolted him to a stop.

"Gemma! Drop the wratch!" Andrea shouted.

Gemma clenched her jaw in response.

The shadows continued to pull, their whispers growing louder and more urgent.

Theo squeaked incessantly as he tried to pry Gemma's hands apart with his tiny forefeet.

Brayden's hands slipped as sweat gathered on his palms. "Gemma, please! I can't hold on much longer, and I'm not losing you!" When she didn't respond, he softened his voice. "I know you want to save her, but not everyone can be saved. I don't know what the shadows are, but I can bet they're a product of her choices. She made this mess; she has to face it."

A harsh sob tore from Gemma's throat before she released Baiya's arm.

"No!" Baiya screamed as the shadows pulled her away. The moment she disappeared into the dark, her screams cut off.

A few seconds passed before crickets started chirping, and a light breeze rustled the trees. Gemma cried as she stared into the darkness. Serania rushed to her little sister and engulfed her in a tight hug.

Brayden sat heavily on his heels as he stared at the two sisters. Gemma's body shook as she sobbed into her sister's shoulder. He swallowed hard as he watched Gemma weep for the woman who would have killed her. He stood and cleared his throat. "We should get out of this forest. I don't know if those shadows killed Baiya or not, but we should get as far away as we can, just in case."

Serania whispered gently to Gemma, brushing tears from her little sister's cheeks. "Brayden's right. We should get moving." She helped Gemma stand, keeping an arm wrapped protectively around her.

Brayden walked on, the others trailing behind him.

Andrea's loud voice filled the evening air. "How much do you want to bet she somehow lives through that?"

Theo squeaked what Brayden guessed was an agreement. Brayden didn't know what those shadows were or what they had in mind for Baiya, but with her use of the warped Trualech magic, whatever it was didn't bode well for her. Of the many books Brayden read throughout his life, one thing they all agreed on: most who used Trualech eventually met with a horrific end. He hoped Baiya would spend a long time on Mathana's fiery shores.

Gemma plodded along with Theo's warm tail wrapped around her neck. The night grew deeper as the group traveled farther away from the magical house. Her head buzzed. Not from the tea—any draining vanished the moment Baiya disappeared—but from the mountain of sadness that remained rooted in her chest. Baiya deserved what came to her. That's what most would say. But Gemma couldn't erase the look of sheer terror that had warped Baiya's old, wrinkled face. Gemma said a silent prayer to the Creator for Baiya—that she would pass through the fires of Mathana quickly and be welcomed into Mistria's shores as a new creation.

Serania walked ahead of Gemma, sending worried glances over her shoulder every few steps.

Gemma sighed. "Serania, I'm fine."

"Are you sure? You don't feel anything off?" Serania asked.

"As far as I can tell, there aren't any effects of the tea left."

Serania gave her a small smile. "Good. I like having two sisters and want to keep it that way."

Warmth melted away some of Gemma's sadness. "Me too."

Brayden led the group at his usual grueling pace. Gemma studied his stiff shoulders and jerky movements. *He must be furious at me for everything, especially for trying to save Baiya's life.* She bit her lip as tears obstructed her vision. All the ground they had covered toward friendship was thrown away. It might take twice as long to recover, if it could be recovered at all. She wouldn't blame him if he chose to give up on his promise and drop her at the first town they came to.

She wrung her hands together as she debated starting a conversation with Brayden. His silence hung in the air like a giant weight about to crush her. Images of the verbal barrage she would endure, once they found a safe place to stop, made her hug her arms to her chest. Everything was her fault. They wouldn't have needed a place to recover if she hadn't broken her leg. Baiya probably wouldn't have been able to spell her if she'd listened to Brayden when they entered the house. All of them could have left any time if Gemma hadn't been spelled. She should have known something was up with Baiya before they entered that crazy house. *Brayden wouldn't even be in this mess if he didn't promise my dad he would take care of me.*

A popping sensation followed by a thrum in her bones snapped her out of her dark thoughts. In the next step, she snapped her eyes shut as sunlight streamed through nearly bare tree branches above. She blinked rapidly and held a hand above her eyes as she glanced around. The air was noticeably cooler, cold enough that each breath was visible. A blanket of fallen, brown leaves covered the forest floor.

"Fint!" Andrea skidded to a stop with her mouth open. "What the drim just happened?"

Behind the group was no evidence of the forest with the purple fruit, but the air shimmered as though they were looking through a thin sheet of water.

Andrea hopped through the shimmer and disappeared, reappearing a second later. "It's still night in there."

Serania slowly dipped her hand through the shimmer. "Huh. It must be the veil Baiya talked about."

Gemma copied her big sister, dipping her hand into the veil. As her hand entered, it disappeared, and the low thrum worked its way up to her elbow.

"At least that explains why it was night when we wandered into the caves and morning when we came out," Brayden said in a soft voice.

Andrea shivered. "This whole place gives me the creeps."

"Agreed," Serania said in a whisper at the same time Theo squeaked in agreement.

Brayden squared his shoulders. "Then let's keep moving."

Gemma tightened her arms around herself as they moved away from the veil. She wouldn't miss all the terrifying things beyond the shimmering wall, but she wouldn't mind avoiding the feel of winter that hung in the air. It wouldn't be long before the first snowfall would make travel much harder.

Near nightfall, it surprised Gemma when Brayden announced they could stop for the night. She expected him to drive them on through the dark hours. Breathing a sigh of relief, Gemma busied herself helping Serania to gather materials for lean-tos while keeping herself as far from Brayden as she could. He worked in silence, hardly looking up from his various tasks. Gemma's stomach clenched as she prepared for the inevitable scolding she would receive when the work was done. When they finished the lean-tos, Andrea provided bags of food from her enormous backpack. Gemma accepted her portion with a mumbled thank you, but she set the bag down for Theo, having no desire to eat. She chewed on her lip as Theo came up with a large cookie in his mouth and a biscuit in each forefoot. Serania pulled her knees closer and rubbed her arms. "It feels like winter is finally here."

Andrea clapped her hands as she shot to her feet. "Well, I'm getting a fire going."

Serania grabbed Andrea's leg. "It's not safe to start a fire in the open."

"It's not safe to freeze to death either," Andrea shot back.

Serania looked to Brayden. "What do you think? Should we risk it?"

Brayden shrugged. "Andrea has a point—"

Andrea gasped in mock surprise. "He's still agreeing with me. He must be spelled." She narrowed her eyes as she leaned closer to Brayden. "Maybe you're Baiya wearing a Brayden glamer."

Brayden rolled his eyes and slapped Andrea's hand away as she tried to poke him. "We'll keep the fire small and bury the coals under the lean-tos to help keep us warm. It's a risk, but everything is risky these days."

Andrea narrowed her eyes and leaned closer to Brayden. "I'll keep an eye on you for the next couple of days." She pointed two fingers at her eyes, then at Brayden before leaving to look for firewood.

Serania glanced from Brayden to Gemma before standing up and brushing off her pants. "Come on, Theo. Drea is likely to pick a fight with a group of badgers or something if we don't keep an eye on her."

Theo paused as he was about to pull another biscuit out of the bag.

Serania lifted her eyebrows. "She really needs some supervision."

Theo looked from Brayden to Gemma before his ears drooped. With a resigned squeak, he made his way up to Serania's shoulder, and the two disappeared after Andrea.

Gemma hugged her knees to her chest as silence stretched like a chasm between her and Brayden.

Brayden exhaled sharply through his nose before moving to sit next to Gemma. "I'm sorry, Gemma. Everything that happened was all my fault. I—"

"What?" Gemma blinked and shook her head. "None of it was your fault; it was mine. I'm the one who broke my leg. I'm the one Baiya spelled. I'm the reason you're in this mess at all."

Brayden clasped one of Gemma's hands. "It wasn't your fault you broke your leg. And I should have stopped us from following Baiya into that house in the first place. I knew something wasn't right, but I didn't know what to do. You were hurt, and it wasn't something I could immediately fix. Later, I should have known you weren't acting like yourself. I was so cruel with the way I talked to you...I messed up..."

Gemma wrapped her arms around his neck and was pleased when he accepted her hug without hesitation. "We both made mistakes, but we survived. That's what counts, right? You didn't break your promise to my dad."

He pulled back so they were face to face. "I'm not keeping you safe just to please your dad, Gemma. I care about you." He stared intently into her eyes. "You have to know; *nothing* has been your fault."

Gemma held his gaze as his words sank in. The way he'd said them, and the look in his eyes told her those words were about more than what had happened with Baiya. Her vision blurred, but she swallowed back the tears.

Brayden gave her a half-smile and nudged her shoulder with his. "I'll forgive you if you forgive me."

Gemma's heart fluttered in a way she'd never felt before, but she pulled her shoulders back and held out an arm. "Deal."

Brayden chuckled, grasping her forearm. "Deal."

The others arrived shortly with armloads of sticks. Serania caught Gemma's eye and gave a quick wink. Gemma's cheeks burned, and she busied herself with helping Andrea prepare a place for the fire.

Gemma breathed in the crisp air as Theo scuttled to her shoulder and rubbed against her neck. She stroked Theo's back, and he purred into her ear. A calm replaced the sadness and unease that had followed her since Baiya's spell broke. She nibbled on a cookie as Andrea's fire leaped to life. The warm light danced merrily, dispersing the gloom of the night as its heat warmed Gemma's fingers and toes. Closing her eyes, a small smile lifted the corners of her lips. They were far from being safe, but she chose to enjoy the moment and not dwell on the many unknowns trying to steal her calm.

CHAPTER EIGHTEEN

Kalami kept her back to the men while she breathed in the fresh warm air. She grimaced at her shaking sword hand before kneeling to clean her blade. They had wasted so much time. From the grumble in her stomach and the weight of her eyelids, she guessed they lost at least two days stumbling through the labyrinth of caves and tunnels. One of those days had been spent searching for the entrance to the tunnels. She'd almost given up and started the arduous trip over the mountain when they finally discovered the enchanted entrance. The enchantment could only be breached if it wasn't seen. They only discovered it when one of the men fell asleep on his feet and fell right through. Her prey had pranced through because they'd fled in the dark.

She sheathed her sword with a harsh jerk. Her hand betrayed her again as tremors overtook it. A low, angry growl escaped her lips as she dug her fingers into her palm. Between the constant barrage of distant memories and the waves of ravenous lizards, their travels had been painfully slow.

A flash of her mother and father teaching her to sharpen a blade made her grind her teeth. Her head pounded from fighting the memories. She clenched her jaw tighter. *You're stronger than this, Kalami! Pull it together!* The longer the memories attacked, the closer she came to completely losing it. She held a trembling hand to her temple. What if they didn't stop? What if her mind finally broke after so many years of staying strong?

A loud snore behind her drew her attention. The three men sprawled on the ground, each deep in slumber. Had they been Henathians, she would have given them a lashing for falling asleep before the job was done. However, it was a miracle they had lasted this long, especially with the number of injuries they had incurred. And it did her a service; they wouldn't witness how rattled she was. Leaning her back against a tree, she opened her mind and allowed a memory to flow freely.

Her father smiled at her as she sat on his lap. "We do not let fear master us, now do we?"

Kalami lifted her chin. "No."

"And why is that?"

"Because fear is a tool, and we wield tools; they don't wield us."

He chucked her chin with his knuckle. "That's right, my little desert flower. We never run when we're afraid. We stand. We fight."

Kalami jumped off his lap. "And we face death head-on!" She mimicked slashing a sword at a foe.

Her father picked her up and tossed her in the air. "To the last!"

"To the last!" She giggled as he threw her higher.

The pounding in her head eased. Letting the memories flow was the only relief she found, and allowing that one through should give her a few hours of peace. As the pain lessened, the glow of the Cornerstone once again burned brightly in the back of her mind. They weren't far off now. It was all she could do not to wake the men and run after the jewel. But if the men were to be of any use, they needed some rest. She would give them an hour or two; then, they would move on. The hunt would be easy now that the jewel shone and they were out in the open. As long as she could keep herself from having a mental breakdown before her prey was found.

Brayden sat with his back against a fallen tree while he stared into the dancing flames of their campfire. Birdsong rang through the trees as they woke for the day. A wet earthy scent permeated the crisp early winter air. The crunch of leaves announced Serania's return from her perimeter check. She offered Brayden a soft smile before sitting beside him. Her smile widened as she watched her two sisters sleep on the fire's other side.

She shook her head. "Those two couldn't be more opposite."

Brayden followed her stare and chuckled. Gemma slept quietly on her side—her hand draped protectively over Theo, who was wrapped in a small ball at her stomach. Andrea slept on her back, arms and legs splayed and snoring loudly. "Sometimes, it's hard to believe you're all related."

Serania laughed before growing more serious. "I'm glad you and Gemma talked things out."

Brayden twirled a small twig between his fingers. "If nothing else, we're getting pretty good at apologizing to each other." At Serania's questioning gaze, he brushed a hand through the air. "It's just been a long journey." He pulled his knees up and rested his arms on them. "She's different than most people I've known. She's genuine. I'm not used to people being so open about everything."

Serania's eyes settled fondly on her little sister. "She's innocent and pure. I think anyone could read her like a book. I haven't known anyone like that before either."

"I imagine it would be hard to find genuine people amongst bounty hunters."

Serania's back stiffened. "How did you—"

"Drea told us."

"Of course, she did." She narrowed her eyes at Andrea. "I'll have to have words with her when she wakes up. What did she tell you?"

Brayden shrugged. "Just that you both were bounty hunters, nothing more. In her defense, she was answering my question. I recognized the name of the town, Farensvir."

Serania turned her face away. "Right."

"Why keep it such a secret? I know it's not the most conventional way to live, but why didn't you want us to know? Gemma would have found out sooner or later. And it's not that big a deal."

Serania silently watched Gemma for a few heartbeats before answering. "It's as I said; she's so pure and innocent. I guess I feared she wouldn't want to stay around us if she knew." She tucked her feet to the side and fiddled with a loose string on her tunic. "I couldn't risk losing her, not again."

"If it helps, she didn't care when Drea told us. She looked slightly afraid of Drea, but who can blame her?" They both chuckled, and Brayden nudged her with his shoulder. "Seriously, I think she's happy to get to know you, no matter your past."

Serania's eyes misted as she bit her lip. "I've lost so many people in my life, and I pictured her walking away the moment she found out."

Her words resonated deep in Brayden's soul. "I understand that better than you could possibly know." He eased back. "I'd like to know your story. How in Elefrisia did you two become bounty hunters?"

Serania sighed. "I want to tell you and Gemma our entire story, but I need some time. I hope you understand."

Brayden held her gaze. "Fair enough."

Serania drummed her fingers on her thigh. "Brayden, can I ask you a favor?"

"Of course."

"Can you try to be gentle with Gemma from here on out?"

He narrowed his eyes. "I'm not sure what you mean by that."

She held up a hand. "I don't mean anything bad by it. It's just...I don't know her well yet, but I can already tell she has a gentle spirit. In my experience, those with a gentle spirit tend to break more easily than others."

"I think you'll find she's much stronger than you give her credit for."

Serania smirked. "Is that admiration I sense?"

Brayden stood to put another log on the fire, hoping the distance would hide the warmth that crept into his face. "She and I have been traveling together for some time. She has a lot more to offer than you know."

"I'm sure you're right, but please, be careful. I may not have been a part of her life for long, but I'm still her big sister." Serania's gaze returned to Gemma. "Drea doesn't remember Gemma. She was too young when we were split up. But I do. I used to hold her until she fell asleep. Mom would often have me watch Gemma while she cooked. I promised both my sisters that I would always protect them from harm. Including emotional harm."

The bitter bite of annoyance brushed against Brayden's chest at the implication in Serania's tone. He returned to his seat. "I made my own promise. I promised to protect her, and that's what I plan to do."

Serania placed a hand on his arm. "I'm glad she has you in her life. I don't know your story or how you came to know my sister, but I thank the Creator you're here."

At Serania's soft touch Brayden swept his annoyance away. She was only doing what a good big sister would do. He gave her a half smile before staring into the flames once more. He struggled to swallow through the dryness in his throat. Serania had so much faith in her eyes when she looked at him. But Gemma had already come close to death on more than one occasion, and he had no doubt their journey would get harder as they went. It would take a miracle for them all to make it through alive.

He fisted both hands. Slowly, these women were worming their way through his defenses. For years he kept everyone at arm's length, but now they were forcing their way in. A part of him wanted this; wanted the friendships they had to offer, though a more prominent part feared they would be killed the moment he did. He rubbed a hand down his face. *When did life get so complicated?*

Gemma knew she was sleeping. She wasn't actually standing in a vast darkness staring at her jewel floating in mid-air and glowing like a star. Even so, her feet refused to carry her forward. A sweet melody resonated from the jewel, ebbing and flowing in time with the light that poured from it. Every muscle in her body trembled, and she didn't trust them to hold her up if she moved.

"Gemma, don't be afraid. Come."

She lifted a hand to her throat as the trembling worsened. The voice reverberated through her entire being. "Who are you?"

"Come..."

She bit her lip as she took a few hesitant steps. The melody and the light intensified as she neared the jewel. With shaking fingers, Gemma reached out and touched the jewel. The light enveloped her and the melody cut short. She lifted a hand in front of her eyes and squinted until the light dimmed. Now seven jewels hung in the air. The jewels floated out until they formed a circle around her before shooting away and disappearing in the distance.

A bed appeared before Gemma. Mariah sat on the edge of the bed, stroking four-year-old Gemma's hair. "You have to close your eyes now. Close your eyes, and let your mind drift."

The bed disappeared, replaced by the owner of the Anvil, who was drying a plate in his hands. "Go on, girl. Just head on through the curtain. It won't bite." He vanished and, in his place, a wooden pole formed. Colored strings attached to the pole and ran as far as her eyes could see. Gemma stepped up to the pole and reached for a string. Before her finger touched it, the string shot forward and buried itself in her stomach. She stumbled back with a startled cry, but the string remained fixed and tugged against her. Grabbing the string with both hands, she tried to pull it out, but it refused to budge. After another minute of struggle, she calmed. The string wasn't hurting her. It felt comfortable. The string hummed and spread warmth through her midsection and up her hands where she held onto it. As she calmed, she noticed the gentle pull of the string, and as she surrendered to it, she was pulled faster and faster.

Gemma awoke with a startled cry.

Theo made a disgruntled squeak and held a forefoot to his chest.

Andrea shot to her feet while brandishing her swords. "What is it? Where are they? I'll make them sorry they were born!"

Serania held a hand up toward her sister. "Put those away, Drea. We're not under attack. Gemma must have had a bad dream."

Gemma slowly stood. "It wasn't a bad dream. I know what we need to do next." She pulled her necklace from her pouch. "I think I know how to find the other jewels."

Theo scurried up to Gemma's shoulder and gave her a questioning look.

Brayden joined her and held her gaze. "What are you talking about?"

Gemma cleared her throat. "This is going to sound crazy, but I think the jewel talked to me while I was sleeping. It showed me how to find the others."

Serania slowly edged toward them. "The jewel talked to you?"

Gemma pulled her braid over her shoulder and played with the end of it. "I know how that must sound."

"It wouldn't be the craziest thing to happen in the past month." Brayden rubbed his hand behind his neck. "You think you can find the other jewels?"

Gemma hesitated. *What if it was just a dream? Something my overtaxed mind made up?* She sighed. There was only one way to find out. "I think so."

Brayden studied her before nodding. "Okay. What do you need to do?"

Serania grabbed Gemma's arm. "Hold on. Isn't this dangerous? Won't searching for the other jewels just put a bigger target on your back?"

Gemma shrugged. "Probably. But I have to. I'm the only one who can, and we need to ensure Skotadi never gets his hands on the rest of the jewels."

"I get trying to keep them away from Skotadi," Serania said. "But we could take this to King Travis. He could bring the entire army to find the jewels."

Gemma placed her hands on Serania's shoulders. "Even if we took this to King Travis, I would still be the one searching for the jewels. I know you want to protect me, but I'm in this no matter what. This is something I have to do."

Serania lowered her head. "I know. I don't like having my family involved. That's what got Mom and Dad killed. I don't want the same to happen to you."

Gemma gave her a small smile. "None of us are guaranteed tomorrow, no matter how safe a life we lead. If this journey takes my life, we'll meet again on Mistria's shores."

Andrea loudly clapped her hands together. "Right. Let's do this thing!"

CHAPTER NINETEEN

Kalami's heart sped in her chest like a ravenous lion moving in on its prey. It took everything she had to keep her movements slow enough for the men to stay with her. She was close. Finally, so close to her goal. Her prey wouldn't escape this time. This was it. This would be her chance to get the one thing she needed to free herself from the people who haunted her nightmares and every waking moment. So many years had led up to this, and now she could taste it. Nothing would stand in her way. She would either get the jewel or die trying.

Her lips curled up in a cold smile. Today, everything would change.

Gemma sat with entwined fingers to hide their shaking. But it was a wonder her companions didn't hear the steady pounding of her heart. In the face of what she had to do, she wasn't sure if she dared to follow through. What if something evil was waiting for her? Could her mind be captured while she searched for the jewels? What if this was precisely what Skotadi wanted her to do? She closed her eyes. *I wish my parents were here.* A hand on her shoulder made her jump.

"I'm sorry. I didn't mean to startle you," Brayden said.

Gemma pulled her knees to her chest and wrapped her arms around them. "It's okay. I think anything would startle me right now."

"I can see that." He gave her shoulder a gentle squeeze as he sat next to her. "Breathe deep; that will help calm your nerves." He paused. "I hate to put more pressure on you, but we need to get moving soon…"

"Right." She cleared her throat and closed her eyes. "Here goes nothing." *Or everything.*

She breathed in slow through her nose, working to calm her tumultuous mind. Thoughts raced like stampeding animals. In her mind's eye, she stared into a bleak and unknown future where everyone she ever loved was in danger or already dead. Memories of peaceful days filled with her parents' laughter brought a hot poker of pain to her chest. She wriggled on her seat and forced air harshly out her nose. The dream told her to let her mind drift, but how could she accomplish that? The more she tried to let her mind go blank, the more questions, memories, and fears crowded in. She pursed her lips at the onset of a headache.

The urge to give up crept into the back of her mind. Who did she think she was? She didn't know what she was doing. She was nothing more than a young girl playing pretend. Brayden's strong hand gently settled on her arm while Theo's soft tail wrapped around her neck. It was like finding a steady rock in a raging ocean. Their touch was an anchor allowing calm to pierce through, and the stampede ceased with a suddenness that made her head buzz. A ball of warmth in her chest grew as her face relaxed.

With eyes still closed, the world around her dissipated like a morning fog burned away by the sun. What looked like layers of dark curtains stood before her. Her mind-self's hands lifted, parting the curtains, and she stood out of her physical body and walked through. Slowly, the now-familiar tug began in her gut.

As she walked farther, a pinprick of light shone ahead. She moved toward it. Her muscles shook as the light grew stronger with each step. Before she reached it, a flash of movement made her freeze. A young woman, not much older than Gemma, wandered around. Her clothes were unlike anything Gemma had ever seen. The red shirt was too bright, and the black jacket may have been leather, but it would take a master to work leather so thin. Her blue pants were tight to her ankles, where they tucked into a pair of black boots with no laces. Locks of dark curls hid the woman's face. Gemma scrunched her eyebrows, her mission momentarily forgotten. "Who are you?"

The woman's dark eyes snapped to Gemma's and she took a step as she said something in a foreign language before the ground beneath the woman opened up, and she fell through. Gemma took a step forward. A small pop resounded through her mind, and she emerged through the light. The mystery woman vanished from her thoughts as she stood before her physical body sitting with her eyes closed and surrounded by her companions. Raising her hands, they appeared fuzzy, like she was looking at them through a dense veil. "This is so strange."

Thalia's voice came from behind her. *"No time to be distracted, dear."*

Gemma's heart skipped, and she whipped around, but a lead weight pulled on her heart as her eyes met nothing but a wall of dark clouds. She didn't have long to waver before a spark of light flared to life in the distance like someone lit a signal fire. The tug in her gut pulled in the direction of the spark. With one last calming breath, she slowly headed toward the light. The clouds drifted away silently as she walked through them, keeping her eyes fixed on the light ahead. As she drew closer, the light became stronger and sharper. A small warning rang at the back of her mind. She paused, but the call of the light intensified, and her feet moved of their own accord.

With every heartbeat, the light brightened. Slowly, the whisper of a melody began. The black clouds slowly took on dark, blurred shapes after a few more steps. Another step, and some of the shapes shifted into trees and bushes. With her next step, she threw a hand over her mouth to keep herself from screaming.

The Henathian huntress, Kalami, and her entourage tramped through the forest. The jewel around Kalami's neck pulsed with brilliant, red light, beckoning Gemma to come closer.

Kalami tensed and threw up a fist. The men stopped and lifted their swords while they glanced around.

Gemma froze. *Can she sense I'm here?* She took shallow breaths through her mouth. Her feet remained rooted in place while Kalami's eyes scanned around, moving closer to where Gemma stood.

Gemma snapped to attention before Kalami's eyes reached her, and reeled backward. Kalami, her men, the trees, and everything else misted back into formless black shapes. Gemma turned and ran. She didn't know how far she ran. There was no way to sense distance with nothing but dark clouds all around. A second tug slowly started and pulled relentlessly at her gut, but she ignored it, wanting nothing more than to put as much distance between herself and the Henathian as possible. She slammed into an invisible wall and fell onto her butt. Something she couldn't see wrapped around her waist and snatched her away at breakneck speed. She screamed as she shot through the air. She was sure she would have broken something if she'd been in her physical body.

Gemma struggled against the force, but it merely carried her faster. Her stomach somersaulted as dark clouds whipped by. The awful thought that her mind would be dragged so far from her body that she would be lost forever made tears prick the backs of her eyes. What if this was how she died? Her mind thrown somewhere in this abyss, left to wander while her body withered away?

She hyperventilated, and her vision darkened before the dark clouds vanished, replaced by a white beach and a shimmering ocean. The force came to a jarring stop, leaving her suspended in mid-air as she gasped for breath and took in the sights around her.

Chills ran up and down her arms as she stared at the beauty before her. She'd never seen the ocean. Many travelers had told stories about the sea, but she never imagined it would be this enchanting. The water was crystal clear, the most beautiful color of teal she had ever seen. It sparkled in the sunlight, sending diamonds dancing across the tops of the gentle waves. To her left stood a tremendous cliff shaped like an eagle standing guard. A small town sat behind her, nestled in a circle of palm trees.

Without warning, the force sped up again, pulling her down. She found it hard to breathe as the water came crashing toward her. She held her breath, closed her eyes, and threw her arms in front of her face, bracing for the impact of the water. Nothing happened. No resounding smack of water. No warm or cold temperatures. Nothing but the continuing sensation of being pulled by the same force.

She slowly opened her eyes, lowered her arms, and took a small breath. Her muscles relaxed as she glanced around. Coral dotted the ocean floor in small clumps while seaweed swayed gently. Vibrantly colored fish swam lazily between the seaweed and coral. She wanted to stay here. To take time to watch the beautiful fish sparkling like gems swimming to and fro, but the force didn't stop. The water was clear enough that she could see her shadow on the ocean floor as she was pulled farther down. Her brow furrowed as she wondered why she even had a shadow.

The light faded as she went deeper until it was so black, she couldn't see her hand in front of her face. A few moments passed before a green glow emanated ahead. The glow brightened to reveal tall cylindrical structures. Soon a grand city spread out before her.

As she approached, pillars and walls made from a mixture of rock, coral, and seashells drew into view before she flew past them. Human shapes flitted past, but she moved too fast to take in any details about them. The force pulled her down coral streets into the center of the city. A giant statue of a man on some sort of sea creature stood in the middle, but she flew past, down the street, up a couple of stories, and through an open window into a large bedroom.

The force released her with one final push, and she took a few steps to steady herself. Her head spun as it tried to orient itself with the sudden lack of movement. She rested her hands on her legs as she caught her breath and took stock of where she was. The bedroom looked mostly normal. It held a vanity, a wardrobe, and a small couch, all of which were made from the same combination of rock, coral, and shells. A hammock hung in a far corner, swaying with the movements of the water. A large mirror covered one wall, and a young woman danced in front of it.

Gemma had heard stories of mermaids. Ghastly creatures that were half human, half fish. The stories told of sailors being lured to their deaths and drowned by the fearsome creatures. One man said he had seen one up close and swore they had red eyes, sharp teeth, and claws. He had shown severe scars on his arm, claiming a mermaid had tried to pull him to his death. But the woman dancing in front of the mirror was neither ugly nor scary. She danced with her eyes closed on two perfectly normal legs. A white dress floated around her, standing out in stark contrast to her ebony skin. Soft white hair, long enough to reach the tips of her fingers, fanned out around her in swirling circles. Her full lips turned up in a contented smile.

A faint melody drew Gemma's attention to the vanity where an intricate necklace glowed. The silver chain shone as if it was braided with light. A single jewel adorned the end of the chain. The jewel appeared at first to be blue, then green, then red, fading between every shade of color and sometimes holding more than one color at once.

"Heiveir etü?"

Gemma jumped. The woman glared at Gemma with her hands on her hips. Gemma opened her mouth to speak, but no words came as she stared into the woman's eyes. Her irises were a deep amethyst that glowed like living embers.

"Svaroo mair. Hvad ertü ad hera heir?" The woman's voice held a note of command.

"I-I'm sorry, I can't understand you...wait, you can see me?"

The woman squinted and took a step closer to Gemma. She tilted her head and spoke with a strong, lilting accent. "If I could not see you, I would not be talking to you, would I? Who are you, and what are you doing here?"

Gemma swallowed hard. "I'm sorry to intrude. Believe me when I tell you, I didn't have much choice. I'm looking for something."

"My jewel."

Gemma scrunched her eyebrows. *Can she read my thoughts?*

The woman rolled her eyes with an exasperated exhale. "You are not in your corporeal form. You are here in a dream state, so you must be searching for the only thing that could have drawn you to this place."

Gemma chewed on her lip. The idea of lying played across her thoughts. There was a chance this woman had magic that could harm Gemma's mind self. Her dad's voice whispered to her soul. *The truth always finds its way to the surface.* She squared her shoulders. "Yes, I'm searching for your jewel."

The woman appraised Gemma from head to foot before going to her vanity and retrieving the necklace. "I have known for years that someone evil was looking for my jewel. I never worried about it. It would be impossible for anyone to get here to steal it."

"Someone evil is looking for the jewels. And I'm sure he'll find a way here somehow. I'm trying to get to them first."

"How am I to know that you are not working for this evil individual?"

Gemma blinked. "I hadn't thought of that. I'm not." She knew it was a stupid answer, but it was all she could think of to say.

The woman studied Gemma before lifting her chin. "I believe you."

Gemma was taken aback. She'd been racking her brain for the right words to convince the woman. She shook her head. "You do?"

The corner of the woman's mouth lifted. "Maybe you are unaware, but you are an easy person to read."

Gemma played with the end of her braid. "Yes, I've been told I'm not good at hiding things."

"Do not be ashamed. It is refreshing." She rubbed the jewel with her thumb. "The evil that has been searching for this jewel has been resilient. It refuses to give up the search. I have not dared travel near the surface. I have felt their prying essence invading my home more times than I can count." She stepped toward Gemma. "What are your plans? You say you are trying to find the jewels first, then what?"

Gemma sighed, and her shoulders sagged. "Um...well, honestly, I haven't thought that far ahead. I'm pretty much making this up as I go."

"You have no idea how to hide anything, do you?" The woman smiled like Gemma was an intriguing curiosity.

Gemma rolled her eyes. "I know. I wear every emotion on my face."

The woman chuckled. "Of all the people to be the Keeper of the Cornerstone, I never expected it to be someone so transparent." Her eyes softened. "Maybe it will help put you at ease if I show some transparency myself?" She put her right hand over her heart and bowed at the waist. "My name is Narida, daughter of Abdiel, niece of Kelil—ruler of the Hophenil people."

Gemma awkwardly mimicked Narida's stance. "Gemma Carpenter, daughter of Thomas and Mariah Carpenter, who happen to be farmers."

A musical laugh escaped Narida's lips. "Are all surface dwellers like you?"

Gemma's cheeks burned, and she hugged her arms to herself. "I'm pretty sure I'm unique. I don't fit in most places."

The sides of Narida's eyes crinkled. "That is a shame. I like you, Gemma Carpenter, daughter of farmers. I think I know why you were entrusted with the Cornerstone, even if you cannot see it yet yourself." Narida's gaze flitted across Gemma's face. "A voice warned me a long time ago that my jewel would be coveted by evil, and that I must do everything I could to keep this evil from getting it. But I have a good feeling about you. I will help you, Gemma."

Gemma lowered her arms as her mouth fell open. "Just like that?"

Narida arched an eyebrow. "Would you prefer I make you go through a series of trials first? If so, that can be arranged."

Gemma held her hands up. "No, no! You surprised me, is all. I'm thankful you trust me." Her face fell. "But how in Elefrisia will you help me from the bottom of the ocean?"

"Come to the shore. I will meet you there—"

Gemma tensed when she felt the pressure return around her midsection before she was jerked out of the window. The underwater city flew by, then shrank as she zoomed away. The darkness came, then the sunlight as she resurfaced from the water. She had one last glimpse of the cliff shaped like an eagle before everything faded into the dark clouds once more.

Her speed didn't slow until the clouds dissipated to reveal the forest where she first started. She flew down, weaving through the trees. A small group of people made their way swiftly through the underbrush. Goosebumps rose on Gemma's arms as her gaze locked with Kalami's. The warrior woman tilted her chin down, her eyes narrowing, and her lips turned up in a smile that sent a shiver down Gemma's back.

In the next breath, Gemma slammed into her physical body.

CHAPTER TWENTY

Theo let out a high-pitched squeal as Gemma shot to her feet. "She's here!" Her ears rang as she fought to steady her breathing. Serania and Andrea stared at her, confused.

Brayden took hold of Gemma's elbow, lowering his face to hers. "Who's here?"

"The tall huntress woman, Kalami. I don't know how far away, but she's here in these woods!" Despite her best efforts, Gemma couldn't keep the quiver out of her voice as adrenaline shot through her veins.

Andrea sprang to her feet, pulling her swords free as her lips tugged up in a sly smile. "So, she's back for another round, huh? This should be fun."

Theo growled as his claws extended, pricking Gemma's skin.

Brayden grabbed Gemma's hand and ran, tugging her along before letting her hand go.

"Hey!" Andrea dashed to catch up, fumbling as she threw on her backpack. "Why are we running? We can totally take her."

Brayden answered, his eyes remaining focused ahead. "Have you forgotten the enchantment last time? Who knows what they'll have going on this time? I'd rather not find out if we can help it."

Serania huffed out her agreement while she ran at Gemma's heels.

Gemma's head swam as she tried to time her breathing to accommodate the frantic pace. Every nerve ending tingled, making her skin itch. She wasn't sure how close the Henathian woman was, but it couldn't be far. Branches scraped her arms as she crashed through the dense underbrush, but she hardly felt them. She shuddered as a spiderweb plastered itself to her face. At any other time, she'd be dancing around like an idiot while frantically swiping the invisible web away, but all she could do was hope that the spider wasn't making a new home in her hair as she matched Brayden's pounding steps.

A thought slammed hard enough into Gemma's mind that she stumbled. *What if we're running toward the danger rather than away?* Surging ahead, she struggled to remember which direction her dream self had traveled from.

To Gemma's right, branches snapped with loud cracks a fraction before a figure slammed into her, sending her flying to the left. She yelled as she rolled down a hill, bashing her shoulder into something hard before coming to a jarring stop. Gasping and coughing, she struggled to get her feet under her as a tall form loomed over her.

Kalami scoffed as she plucked a leaf from her shoulder and flicked it away. "Well, well. Looks like it's finally down to you and me."

Up the hill, shouts and the clash of steel against steel filtered through the trees, growing fainter as it moved farther away. Brayden's voice rose above the rest as he called for Gemma before his shout was cut short.

Gemma's chest squeezed painfully as she imagined the worst possible reason for his sudden silence.

Kalami smiled smugly. "Did you misplace your rat?"

Gemma's hand shot to her shoulder, and her eyes went wide when her fingers brushed empty air where Theo should have been. "Theo!" she screamed his name at the top of her lungs and strained her ears, but there was no answering squeak. Tears blurred her vision. *He's only out of earshot; that's all.* Her gaze flitted around, searching for any sign of her best friend.

"Are you going to cry, little girl? You weren't fond of that rat, were you?" Kalami clicked her tongue. "Too bad. I'm pretty sure I sliced through him as we fell."

Gemma leaned a hand on her leg as the ground tilted beneath her. *Theo can't be dead!* That's something that couldn't happen. It would defy the laws of the world, because there was no world without Theo in it. A small huff of air escaped Kalami's lips, and her mouth twitched like she hid a smile.

Gemma narrowed her eyes. "You're lying. You're saying that to hurt me; throw me off."

Kalami shrugged. "Huh? I guess you're smarter than you look."

The vise around Gemma's chest eased, and she straightened. Theo was alive somewhere, simply unable to come to her. She furtively glanced up the hill and tensed as she debated making a run for it.

However, one look at Kalami's long legs and Gemma knew she'd never be able to outrun her. With no other options, she withdrew her dagger, raising it in front of her. Her hand shook, and she clasped her other hand around it, trying to hide how foolish she felt.

Kalami raised her eyebrows as she chuckled. "I take it back. You *are* as dumb as you look." She pointed with the tip of her massive sword. "You're going to fight me with that thing?"

Gemma's lip quivered, and her mouth went dry. "I don't want to fight you." *I can't fight you. I'd never win.*

Kalami smirked and shook her head. "No one is coming to help you this time." She raised her hands, circling to show the empty clearing. "See? We're completely alone, you and I." She sighed. "I feel a little bad. It's going to be so easy for me to kill you. You're trying so hard to put on a brave face. You're failing miserably, but I can see that you're trying, and I'll give you points for that." She ran her thumb along her sword, slowing down as it reached the sharp hook at the top. "Skotadi ordered me to bring you back alive, but I have plans, you see? You have what I need to finally be free. It's nothing against you. You just happen to be in my way." She leaned in like she was telling a friend a secret. "That pesky 'wrong place, wrong time' thing."

Gemma lowered her dagger a couple of inches. "You don't have to kill me. Whatever your plans are, maybe I can help."

The mirth vanished from Kalami's face. "You would be nothing but dead weight, and we would inevitably end up being caught." She swallowed and briefly looked at the ground. "I don't *want* to kill you. Despite what you might think. I'm not a monster. But if I don't kill you and we get caught, it would be signing my own death warrant. I can't do that. I've fought too long and hard to get to this moment, and I can't let anything stop me."

Gemma's mind spun. She had to find a way to buy herself some time for the others to find her. Assuming they survived their fight. If they were dead…she couldn't allow herself to think about that. "Why would he kill you? Aren't you the best warrior he has?"

Kalami laughed without humor. "You know nothing. Skotadi doesn't need warriors. It's the bond you have with your jewel that he needs. Once he has you, the rest will be easy to find, and he won't need me."

Gemma frowned. "We could work something out. We could be allies."

Kalami hesitated, searching Gemma's face. Doubt flickered through Kalami's eyes for a moment, but her lips turned down in a scowl. "You're wasting my time. Let's get this over with." She raised her sword as she plowed forward.

Gemma dodged backward and gasped as the sword edge grazed across her chest, just below her collar bones, burning a slight cut across her skin. "We can help each other!" She ducked and rolled clumsily to the side as Kalami continued to advance.

"Defend yourself!" Kalami ground out through clenched teeth.

Gemma stumbled to her feet and jumped back, narrowly missing another scrape of the sword. Kalami's eyes burned with anger as she surged forward, but her movements were slower, almost hesitant. An idea formed in Gemma's mind, and she groaned. *This is such a dumb idea.* Before she could talk herself out of it, she threw her dagger down and held both hands in front of her. "Wait!"

Kalami's eyes went wide, and she pulled back mid-swing. "What are you doing? Pick up your weapon!"

Gemma lowered her hands and pulled herself up to her full height. "It's obvious I can't win. I have no training, and I can't even tap into the jewel when I want to. You'll get your way no matter what. So, if I'm about to die, would you allow me to get some questions answered first?"

Kalami growled deep in her throat and shoved her sword into its sheath. "I don't have time for these silly games!" She surged forward, throwing a punch with her right arm. "Fight me!"

Gemma dodged, but not fast enough. Kalami's knuckles grazed Gemma's ear and she yelped as she threw herself behind a tree.

Kalami didn't slow. Reaching around the tree, she grabbed Gemma's shirt and threw her to the ground.

Gemma rolled out of reach. "Skotadi might not kill you!" she croaked out as she scrambled around a boulder. "Wouldn't he be better off with two bonded Keepers?"

Kalami growled again sounding much like an angered mountain lion. "If he gets you, I'm useless to him. With the Cornerstone, you can find any jewel whether they're worn or not."

Gemma ran around the boulder then yelled as Kalami grabbed her braid and pulled her to a stop. Gemma fell to her knees and grasped a handful of dirt. Turning, she threw the dirt in Kalami's face. Kalami screamed and coughed as she swiped at her eyes, giving Gemma the chance to duck around another tree. *I'll never outrun her.* With all the tossing and dodging, her bearings were thrown off. Quick glances around didn't help. She had no idea which direction the others were.

An arm wrapped around Gemma's shoulders while another one pinned her arms to her sides. Kalami's voice hissed directly into Gemma's ear. "You fight without honor."

Gemma struggled against Kalami's hold, but she might as well have been a small puppy for all the good it did. "Unlike you, I wasn't trained to fight, so I do what I have to."

Kalami tightened her hold, making Gemma gasp. "If I wasn't Henathian I would have killed you in your sleep, but to do so would be to betray everything that I am. Now. You'll pick up your dagger and fight."

Gemma ground her teeth as Kalami's grip squeezed the air from her lungs. "You think there's honor in fighting someone as defenseless as me?"

Kalami threw Gemma to the ground and shouted at the sky. She paced as she pulled in quick, hard breaths. "I can't believe you were the one to become Keeper of the Cornerstone! If I had the power of that jewel, Skotadi and all those who willingly follow him would've already been dead. You're like a child playing with her father's sword." She pulled her sword free, her eyes like flint as she glared at Gemma. "I can't risk Skotadi taking you alive. I swore on my father's grave that Skotadi's life would be mine, and I won't let anything stand in my way. I've tried to remain honorable, but I'm done talking. Now pick up your dagger."

Gemma pulled herself to her knees and clenched her hands into fists. "No. If you're going to kill me, you'll have to do so while I'm defenseless."

Kalami lowered the tip of her sword before she shook her head sadly. "Have it your way." She swung her sword in an arc toward Gemma's neck.

Gemma tensed and held her breath. This was the end. The sword would slice through her as easily as an arrow slices through the air. The thought of the end should have been enough to cause her to weep in fear, but for the first time, she wasn't afraid. Instead, there was nothing but a cold certainty that she was about to die. Time slowed as the sword inched closer. She watched, expressionless, as the light glinted off the razor-sharp edge.

"*Let go.*" Thalia's voice whispered.

Gemma closed her eyes as her mother's warm voice wrapped around her like a warm blanket. She lifted her face to the sky, releasing the tension from her muscles. A silent wave of power pulsed from the direction of her pouch where her necklace lay. Something hard and cold wrapped around her waist. She opened her eyes wide and gasped as she was flung into the air.

Brayden parried a blow before dodging to the side. Sweat dripped down his back despite the chill in the air. Clashing and shouts behind him resounded as Serania and Andrea fought the other two soldiers. The soldier attacking Brayden pressed forward with unnatural strength, eyes glossed over, and his face expressionless.

Brayden blocked another blow, then countered with a low swing. His sword tugged as it tore through the man's tunic and ripped into his abdomen, but the man didn't slow. Brayden growled. "They're enchanted again!"

"I know! Just don't stop!" Serania hissed, her voice tight with exertion.

Andrea grunted out a curse. "No, duh!" She growled in frustration. "Would you hold still so I can kill you?"

Brayden fought on, his mind only half on the fight. Gemma and Theo hadn't reappeared. Theo would put up a good fight, but there was only so much a small Scruff could do. Gemma wouldn't stand a chance against the Henathian. He wanted to search for her, but the soldier attacked so strongly, Brayden barely had time to block each blow. A sharp, burning pain in Brayden's side forced him to push his worry for Gemma away. He pressed his hand against the wound as he jumped out of reach of another strike. There was barely enough time to steady his feet before the next blow came, and he threw up his sword to block. The clash of his sword against the soldier's caused a painful shudder to travel up Brayden's arms.

Brayden spun away, dodging behind a tree a fraction of a second before the soldier's sword thudded into the wood where Brayden's neck had been. In one swift move, Brayden rounded the other side of the tree and sliced through the man's wrist. The soldier's hand—still gripping the sword—fell useless to the ground. The soldier rushed toward Brayden, continuing as Brayden's sword thrust through his gut and out his back. The soldier turned, ripping Brayden's grip from his sword hilt. Brayden dropped and swept the man's legs out from under him before jumping on top of him and striking with his fists. The man's nose snapped, and blood poured from his nostrils, but he clawed at Brayden's hands, his face remaining deadpan. The soldier threw Brayden off, sending him flying with a loud crash into a tree. Brayden groaned and clutched his side as he struggled to orient himself. The soldier made to stand when an axe swung from the side, cleanly severing the man's head from his shoulders. His body and head landed at different times with dull thumps.

Andrea swung her axe into his dead body a few more times, yelling obscenities while Serania offered Brayden a hand up.

Brayden huffed out a thank you as he stood on shaking legs. He concentrated on his breathing as he scanned for any more danger. All three soldiers' heads lay separated from their bodies. Brayden turned away from the grim sight. "Let's find Gemma."

Muffled squeaks emitted from the forest shortly before Theo shot across the ground and scrambled up to Brayden's shoulder while continuing his incessant squeaks.

Brayden plucked Theo off his shoulder, holding him out so he could look him in the eye. "Slow down, Theo."

Theo huffed out impatiently, then squeaked slowly, waving his forefeet in large frantic gestures.

Serania joined Brayden and tapped his arm. "Can you tell what he's saying?"

Brayden shook his head. "I'm only catching a few words. I recognize Gemma's name and something about a tree, but I'm not getting much else." He pulled Theo closer. "Do you know where Gemma is?"

Theo shook his head emphatically.

Brayden nodded and placed Theo back on his shoulder. "Don't worry, bud. We'll find her."

Serania nodded in response. Andrea shoved her axe into the backpack she'd tossed to the side then slung it over her shoulders as the three of them ran forward.

The burning in Brayden's side numbed as fresh adrenaline coursed through his veins. The fight hadn't lasted long, but it was long enough that Gemma could be dead or captured by now. *Don't be dead, don't be dead, don't be dead.* The thought became a cadence in rhythm with his footfalls as he dashed ahead.

The wind whipped strands of Gemma's hair across her face as she was thrown through the air. By the third throw, she'd figured out what the cold, hard thing was. The trees tossed her like they were playing a game of catch. Her throat was raw from the screams that tore from it, and her stomach churned as she was tossed up, then dropped, passed from tree to tree.

Even though the trees grabbed her gently, twigs scraped her exposed arms, and tenderness encircling her midsection warned of the forming of a deep bruise. Finally, after what felt like an eternity, the last tree gently lowered her to the ground. She sank to her hands and knees and disgorged the contents of her stomach.

When she was finished, she crawled away from her mess with shaking limbs and sat back on her heels.

The chill in the air made her shiver and hug her arms to herself. She had no idea where she was. Birds sang happily as they went about their day. A couple of squirrels chittered as they fought over a nut. The gentle breeze sent stray hairs tickling across her face, but no other sounds drifted through the air. No cries, no signs of a continuing fight, nothing. She was utterly alone. "Breathe, Gemma. You've been in worse places than this."

She swallowed hard as she scanned around her. *I should move. Try to find the others...something.* But she couldn't make herself move. This was the first time she'd ever truly been alone. Someone had always been there, be it Theo, friends, or parents. Her shoulders slumped as the world around her blurred with tears. Even if she chose to find her friends, she didn't know which way to go. *What if I choose the wrong direction? What if I come across Kalami or more bandits?* She could try to use the jewel to find Serania, but she didn't want to alert Kalami of her presence.

Pulling her arms close, she closed her eyes and lowered her chin to her chest, letting the tears fall. As sobs shook her body, she lay on the ground, curled up on her side, and hugged her knees. Not for the first time, she longed for her parents' loving arms. If her mom was here, she'd wrap Gemma up and tell her everything would be fine. Her dad would look at her with his strong stare and give her his wise advice. She would sit taller because she knew how much her father loved her.

After a few minutes, the sobs slowed, and silent tears trickled across her nose before dropping to the ground. Leaves crunched behind her, and she gasped as she jerked up to her knees.

An older man with grey around his temples looked at her with concern. "I'm sorry; I didn't mean to startle you." He held a hand up and gave a gentle smile. "I just thought you might need some help."

Gemma wiped her wet eyes and nose as she stared at the newcomer. His dark hair was cropped short. Grey peppered his full, black mustache and goatee. Laugh lines etched deeply on either side of his dark, brown eyes. He was dressed in simple travel clothes, holding a walking stick, and a large satchel hung across his body.

He offered a hand to Gemma. "Allow me to introduce myself. My name is Gairwulf Labanaynda. But you can simply call me Gairwulf, of course."

Gemma hesitantly took his hand, brushing herself off as she rose to her feet.

Gairwulf's smile widened to show teeth darkened with age. "It's a fine day for a walk in the woods, is it not?"

Gemma rubbed her arms, grimacing as her hands brushed across the many scrapes. "I guess so." She studied his face more intently. His skin held a yellow undertone, and his eyes slanted down at the outer corners. "You're Efevrie."

The sides of his eyes crinkled. "Have you met many Efevrie before?"

She shook her head. "Only a few. None of them smiled as much as you."

His smile dimmed. "Ah, yes. That doesn't surprise me. So many of my people tend to think too highly of themselves." He exhaled sadly. "Such a shame. They miss out on so many incredible relationships." After leaning his walking stick against a tree, he rubbed his hands together. "You must wonder why an old man like me is alone so deep in the forest?"

The thought had crossed Gemma's mind. *Is he another servant of the enemy?*

Gairwulf glanced around at the trees as he continued. "I've been searching for something precious I lost many years ago, but alas, there doesn't seem to be any sign of it. You haven't seen anything depicting a picture of me lying around, have you?"

Gemma shook her head before peeking over her shoulder. The man seemed kind enough, but it could be a tactic to make her trust him. If his appearance was authentic, outrunning him wouldn't be a problem, but what if he had a magic of some kind and running caused him to use it? She needed to find her friends but still didn't know which way to start looking. *Assuming they're still alive.* Her eyes burned, but she blinked back the tears. She'd had enough of crying to last a lifetime.

Gairwulf sighed and nodded. "No matter. It's good to learn to let go of things, is it not?" He sat down on a nearby rock and pulled a blanket from his satchel, snapping it in the air before spreading it on the ground. He pulled out a bowl of fruit, followed by a basket of steaming rolls.

Gemma's jaw slowly dropped as he pulled item after item out of his satchel. A rack of meat, a jar of jam, plates and cutlery for two, cups, and a pitcher of water. As each item was placed on the blanket, Gemma grew more and more uneasy. Nothing good could come from magical food.

He glanced up at Gemma with a twinkle in his eye. "I have plenty here if you would like to join me."

Gemma crossed her arms over her chest and stepped back. "How did you do that?"

He patted his satchel fondly. "It's a clever invention of my people. I have much more than I need. I would be honored if you'd join me." At her hesitation, he raised his brows. "Are you not hungry, friend?"

Her stomach growled loudly in response. After all the tension and losing what little had been in her stomach, she was so hungry her throat ached, but the last time she'd trusted someone with magic, she'd nearly died. "I'm a bit wary of strangers with magical powers that involve food."

He took a bite of meat, calmly chewed and swallowed before answering. "There is no magic involved here, simply a knowledge of the rules of this world. I can't stand enchantments and the like."

"It looks like magic to me."

"Ah, yes. Our eyes are such tricky things, are they not? They see something and tell us what it is. Sometimes they're right, sometimes they're wrong. You can't always trust what your eyes tell you. Though, you can tell a lot about someone when you look into their eyes. They truly are the window into the soul."

He slathered a roll with jam and bit into it, looking deep into Gemma's face. "I can see you've been through a trial. It won't offend me if you choose not to eat. Feel free to rest with me if you would like."

Gemma pulled her braid forward and tugged on it as she quickly looked around once more. Still no sign of pursuit, either friend or foe. She bit her lip before slowly sitting on the edge of the blanket and tucking her feet to the side. Her stomach betrayed her yet again with another loud protest as a yeasty scent wafted from the rolls, mixing with the smell of spiced meat. Cautiously, she picked up a small roll and turned it over in her hand as she examined it. It looked normal. If Theo were there, he would know if she should eat or not. He would knock it out of her hands if he thought it was unsafe. She nibbled on it, chewing slowly. Her mouth flooded with moisture as the roll melted in her mouth. A small moan escaped her throat as her eyes closed briefly before she devoured the rest of the roll in a fashion that would have made Theo proud. She grabbed a portion of meat and wolfed it before snatching another roll.

Gairwulf's eyes crinkled again, and one side of his mouth tipped up as he watched her eat. "It isn't made of magic; therefore, it won't magically disappear. You can take your time, friend."

Gemma put a hand in front of her mouth while she quickly chewed and swallowed. "I'm sorry. I didn't know how hungry I was."

"No need for apology. I don't want you to choke." He offered her a cup of water which she took with a mumbled thanks. "So. What brings a young woman like yourself into these woods all alone?"

The trees decided to play a game of 'catch the Gemma.' Gemma opened her mouth to speak, then froze. *Is his question mere curiosity or a way to find out if I have help coming?* She schooled her face into a neutral expression—at least she hoped it was neutral—as she dropped her hands to her lap. "I'm not alone. My friends are on their way." A twinge of guilt made her avert her gaze. It wasn't like she was lying, not really. If her friends were alive, they would be searching for her. Nonetheless, she inwardly grimaced as the white lie left a bitter taste at the back of her throat.

"Lovely!" He swept his arms wide. "Life is better experienced with others, is it not?"

Gemma mumbled in agreement as she swung her legs in front and wrapped her arms around them. *How can I get him to go? Should I leave and hope I pick the right direction?*

They ate in silence until Gairwulf washed down his last bite and then sighed in contentment. "This was a lovely meal, made lovelier by the company." He braced a hand on his leg as he slowly rose to his feet before returning items to his satchel. Gemma helped, grateful he would be moving on soon and awed once again as the items disappeared into the much-too-small satchel.

Gairwulf smiled and placed his hands on his hips. "I must be on my way. I have a dear friend in a town nearby who needs some encouragement." He offered a hand to Gemma, cupping her hand between both of his when she gave it to him. "I know things seem overwhelming. Especially with the burden you carry."

Gemma snatched her hand back. *Does he know about the jewel?*

He took up his walking stick, seemingly undisturbed by her sudden stiffness. "Yes, my friend. I know what you carry in your pouch."

The blood fled from Gemma's face so fast she almost fell. "H-how did you know—"

Gairwulf held up a hand. "After you live as long as I have, you learn to sense certain things. But fear not, friend, I have no need or desire to take the jewel from you."

Gemma's heart hammered in her chest despite his assurances. "You don't want to take it for yourself?"

He sighed. "You are wise to be cautious. Many would do anything to have the power you hold, but I assure you—I'm not one of them."

"How did you know I have it?"

"I studied many years under a Keeper of History." He smiled with a far-off look. "I learned much from him and am now a Keeper myself, though not yet as learned as he was." He chuckled.

"I didn't know there were people who did that. Didn't most history books and scrolls get destroyed in the uprising?"

A shadow crossed his face. "Yes, they did. But no matter how hard evil tries, it can never eradicate the truth."

"How does history help you know how to sense a jewel?"

"The answer to that question would take many hours to properly explain. But, suffice it to say, the jewels are as ancient as the foundations of this world, and because of that, they have an essence few things do."

Gemma didn't know what to make of the information. *Were the jewels here from the beginning of time?* She'd never really thought about where they came from. She shuddered as her hand brushed her pouch. *Just how much power am I carrying?*

Gairwulf smiled kindly. "No worries, friend. You'll find that many truths in life are best learned through much digging and seeking and often take years for us to comprehend. Perhaps all you need to know is sometimes, to move in the right direction, we need to let go of our insistence on controlling which way is right for us. Now, it's time for me to be on my way. And I'm sure your friends must be close." He dipped his head. "Thank you for sharing a meal with me, Gemma. I look forward to our next interaction, should the Creator deem it right to lead us back together."

Gemma gave him a small smile, but it fell as she watched him round a tree. "Wait, how did you know my name?" She rushed forward, but as she rounded the tree, the space was empty; there was no sign of Gairwulf anywhere. She spun in a circle, but there was no flash of movement or rustle of leaves. *He couldn't have just disappeared!*

"Gemma!" Serania's voice called out from the forest.

Brayden and Andrea's voices filtered through the trees soon after. "Gemma!"

"I'm over here!" she called out as she started running toward the voices. "I'm here!" The wind was knocked out of her as she collided with someone, and they both fell to the ground. Hands grabbed her arm, pulling her to her feet and into a bone-crushing hug.

Serania whispered into Gemma's ear, her voice thick with emotion. "You're safe. I was so scared when we couldn't find you!"

Theo's warm fur pressed against Gemma's neck, and she leaned her head into him.

Andrea came to her feet, brushing off her butt. "I'm all right. Thanks for asking."

Gemma turned to her other sister and wrapped her in a hug. "I'm sorry I crashed into you, but I'm so glad you're here." Andrea remained tense, her arms frozen to her sides, but Gemma didn't care. Over Andrea's shoulder, Brayden caught Gemma's eye, and they shared a small smile.

Andrea squirmed in Gemma's embrace. "Okay, yep, can't breathe!"

Gemma released her sister, holding back a laugh at the awkward look on Andrea's face.

Brayden placed a hand on Gemma's shoulder and gave it a gentle squeeze. "It's good to see you in one piece."

Gemma threw her arms around his neck, tucking her head into his shoulder. He tightened his arms around her and whispered low enough that only she could hear. "You had me worried."

"You had me worried, too," she whispered back. "For a moment there, I thought I'd lost you." She squeezed him tighter as she let tears of joy slip quietly down her cheeks.

CHAPTER TWENTY-ONE

Kalami stared blankly at the bodies of the three soldiers. Any other time she would bury them. It didn't matter how she felt about them; no one deserved the disrespect of being left for the animals, but there wasn't time left for honor. Her father would be disappointed in her. Giving them a proper burial would have been worth it to him, even at the risk of his own life. He'd been like that. Honor, duty, loyalty—those things above anything else.

She wondered what her life would have been if Skotadi hadn't killed her people and taken her. By now, she'd be preparing to take over as High Chieftain. Henathians didn't wait for a firstborn son. Male or female, the firstborn would lead. Her father would have remained close, offering wisdom while she made mistakes.

"Stop being sentimental, Kalami," she growled and marched away.

Obtaining the jewel was turning out to be a lot harder than she'd planned. It should have been easy. Find the Keeper, kill her, take the jewel and run. Killing an untrained civilian didn't sit well—it made the back of her throat turn bitter—but there wasn't any way around it. The Keeper said they could work together. Kalami would be lying to herself if she didn't say the thought was appealing. However, it was far too risky.

Kalami snarled into the open air. "Pull yourself together." Squaring her shoulders, she lowered her chin and focused ahead. It was time to readjust. She needed a new plan.

"**A**re you positive it was a cliff shaped like an eagle?" Serania asked for the third time, her face growing tighter with each repetition.

Gemma nodded once again. "I'm positive. It must have been at least two hundred feet high and looked like an eagle standing guard."

Andrea dropped from a tree, brushed off her hands, snatched up her backpack, and made her way to her sisters. She slowed as she took in Serania's agitated face and turned to Gemma. "What did I miss?"

Serania answered before Gemma could open her mouth. "Gemma was just informing us where to find the next jewel." After another long sigh, she crossed her arms and continued in a low tone. "We have to go to Taicala."

Andrea's brows slowly rose as her mouth fell open before she doubled over in laughter.

Serania let out an exasperated groan. "It's not funny, Drea."

Andrea wiped her eyes as she continued to laugh. "Oh, but it is." She bent over again as another bout of laughter took her.

Brayden looked from one sister to the other. "What are you not telling us?"

Serania ground her teeth and looked away before her shoulders slumped. "Taicala is the one place in Elefrisia I swore I'd never return to."

"What are the odds?" Andrea said between huffs of laughter. "Oh, the look on your face, Serania."

Serania punched her sister's arm. "Would you stop that? You'll draw every bandit within fifty miles with your braying."

Andrea rubbed her shoulder as she clamped her mouth shut, but she only managed to remain serious for a second before another laugh burst from her throat. She continued to chuckle as she pulled the backpack over her shoulders.

Brayden's face slowly darkened as he watched the two sisters, but he pursed his lips. "We should move. We've already been standing around too long." He took the lead and spoke over his shoulder. "But I expect an explanation soon."

Andrea sped up to travel next to Brayden while she wiped the rest of the tears from her eyes. "I saw a clearing off that way." She pointed to the right. "It shouldn't take long to get to, and it would be the perfect place to stop for the night."

"What else did you see?" Gemma asked as she skirted around a giant spiderweb. She shuddered, remembering the one she ran through not long ago. If they made it to a town any time soon, she'd soak in a bath for hours. "Any sign of Kalami?"

Andrea shook her head, her lips turning down into a frown. "No sign of the giant."

Theo squeaked in Gemma's ear as his eyes scanned around.

"I know. I don't like wondering. I'd almost rather have her attacking us outright." She stroked his head, being extra gentle. Her stomach clenched every time she looked at the small splotch of red on Theo's gleaming, white head. He'd been knocked unconscious when Kalami shoved Gemma down the hill. He woke up just in time to see the trees come to life and snatch Gemma away. The experience had shaken him enough that he kept himself pressed against Gemma as if the contact reassured him that everything was all right.

Gemma sped up to walk on Brayden's other side. "Shouldn't we push on through the night? Kalami can't be that far away."

Brayden tilted his head from side to side. "On one hand, that might be good. Even if she's alone, I don't desire another fight with her. On the other hand, none of us are in shape to press on through the night. Everyone's beat up and tired—"

"I'm fine. I don't even have a scratch," Andrea interrupted.

Brayden rolled his eyes at the interruption. Gemma suppressed a smile as they remained silent for a few paces. She wished she could say the same as her sister, but she had so many cuts and scrapes she looked like she'd picked a fight with a hundred roosters. And she felt drained after all the adrenaline highs and lows. The last thing she wanted was another mad dash through the night, but it didn't seem safe to stop either. "How is stopping in the open a good thing? Doesn't that make us an easy target?"

"It could, but it also prevents anyone from sneaking up on us," Brayden answered.

A loud snap behind them caused the group to freeze. They waited, but all remained quiet.

"Let's pick up the pace." Brayden tugged Gemma's arm as he fell into a light jog.

Gemma scolded herself as she kept pace with Brayden. The small snap nearly made her jump out of her skin. For all they knew, the snap was a squirrel or a deer. Even if it was Kalami, they were now five against one. Though, Gemma didn't really count. She was as useful as a child in a fight. "What if someone other than Kalami sees us in the clearing? These woods could be crawling with bandits."

"It's not the bandits you should worry about," Andrea said as she ran, making the exertion look easy despite her short stature and the large backpack slapping her back with every step. "This part of Elefrisia is known for the Binthrell Lions. They hunt at night. Their kills increase as winter draws close because they hibernate like bears."

A tremor coursed through Gemma's body. "I thought you and Serania spent most of your time on the west side of the Cattaway. How do you know so much about this area?"

Andrea scoffed as she weaved around a large tree. "We research before a hunt. It would be pretty stupid to charge into a foreign region without knowing what dangers await."

Gemma pursed her lips at Andrea's snarky tone. The most dangerous creatures around Dano were the large black bears. At least, that she knew of. Wolves roamed in the area as well, but unless diseased, they wouldn't attack unprovoked. Again, she was reminded of how little she knew.

Brayden seemed to sense her melancholy and shot her a small smile. "I've never heard of Binthrell Lions either. We'll just add them to the list of things to watch out for." He winked at her before forging ahead.

Gemma's heart sped again, but this time not because of fear. Not too long ago, Brayden was the one making Gemma feel inadequate. Now he was the reason a smile returned to her face, and she held her head a little higher. *We've come so far.*

Theo squealed a warning, and Gemma threw herself to the side as an arrow whistled past.

Brayden cursed as he pulled Gemma to her feet while he scanned for the source of the arrow.

Hoots and hollers echoed behind them, followed by an enthusiastic shout. "We've got ourselves some lively ones, boys!"

Serania sent an arrow flying. "What were you saying about not worrying about bandits?"

The group surged ahead. "How many?" Brayden shouted as he tugged Gemma along.

"The trees are too dense to tell," Serania replied as she shot another arrow.

Andrea let her backpack drop to the ground and grinned as she pulled her swords free and melted into the forest.

Gemma pulled against Brayden. "Where's she going? Shouldn't we help her?"

Serania grabbed Gemma's free arm and hauled her ahead. "Trust me, the best help you can give is to get to safety."

Gemma ground her teeth but ran ahead as another arrow bounced off a tree near her head.

Serania kept a steady pace of arrows flying behind them as she ran, and yelps of pain filtered through the trees. Whether from Serania's shots or something Andrea was doing, Gemma didn't know, but she cringed every time a new scream ripped through the air.

They shot from the tree line and kept running as the number of returning arrows slowly decreased. Frightened shouts cut short echoed through the trees before silence followed.

Gemma gasped for air as she watched the tree line. A few pounding heartbeats later, Andrea sauntered from the forest, a satisfied grin plastered on her face. She had one thumb hooked under a strap of her backpack and tossed a small bag up and down in her other hand.

Gemma grimaced at the blood splatter across her sister's face and clothes.

As Andrea neared the others, she tossed the bag high and caught it, making the coins inside clink together. "There were only eight of them." She snorted. "And just this one coin bag between the lot of them. Hardly worth the effort. I was hoping for a better fight."

Serania rolled her eyes. "Honestly, Drea."

Andrea turned her face to her sister, her eyes twinkling with mischief. "If you don't use it, you lose it. I need to keep up my skills, especially with the giant stalking us."

Serania crossed her arms and narrowed her eyes. "You shouldn't take so much joy in killing people."

"They were bandits, Serania. They kill people all the time."

Serania dropped her arms and balled her fists. "That isn't the point. Bad or not, they were people."

Andrea leaned in. "Oh, so I should just let them live to keep robbing and murdering—"

"You know that's not what I mean."

Brayden tugged Gemma's arm and nodded his head away from the arguing sisters. "Want to help me pick a spot for the night?"

Gemma gave him a grateful smile. "Absolutely. Anything to get away from all the tension."

Theo wriggled indecisively before squeaking into Gemma's ear.

Gemma laughed. "Yes, you can stay here and watch. Though I don't think anything exciting will happen."

He cracked a cheeky smile and made a happy squeak as he scampered to the ground and planted himself in front of Serania and Andrea.

Gemma watched Theo's ears perk up as his head whipped from side to side, enjoying the entertainment of a good argument. "It doesn't take him long to return to his happy self."

Brayden smiled as he strolled ahead. "Not much bothers him. It's kind of nice having that constant joy in the group."

"Yeah. He's always been great at lifting others' spirits."

Brayden chuckled, then winced as his hand shot to his side.

The warmth of Theo's antics vanished from Gemma's mind as a grimace played across Brayden's face. She grabbed his arm and pulled him to a stop. "You're hurt! Why didn't you say anything?"

He tried to brush her hands away. "One, because we didn't have time, and two, because it's not big enough to worry about."

Gemma swatted his hand as he continued to ward her off. "I'll be the judge of that." She looked around before pulling Brayden toward a large rock. When they arrived, she placed her hands on Brayden's shoulders. "Sit."

Brayden raised his brows at the stern command but complied. "Yes, ma'am."

Gemma scowled at him before gently tugging up his shirt. He sucked in a breath as parts of the shirt stuck where the blood had already dried. Gemma frowned as she peeled the shirt off as gently as she could. As the last of his shirt pulled up, she gasped. "Brayden, this is awful!"

He glanced down and shrugged. "It looks worse than it is."

Gemma shot him a glare before grabbing her canteen. She searched for something to use to wipe away the blood and noticed a tear on the end of her shirt. It took only a moment to decide it would have to do before she ripped a large strip off the bottom of her shirt and doused it with water.

"You're overreacting." Brayden's lips twitched like he barely contained a smile. "This is far from the worst I've ever—" He hissed as Gemma pressed the wet cloth to his side.

She arched a brow. "You were saying?"

His mouth pulled into a tight smile. "If I say I'm sorry, will you be more gentle?"

Gemma scowled, but her face softened, and she eased the pressure. "Can you blame me for being worried? How many times have we both almost died already?" She swallowed as she focused on her task. "I couldn't do this without you."

Brayden kept his eyes fixed on Gemma's hands while she worked. "I think you're capable of much more than you think."

Gemma blinked back sudden tears. "Even if that's true, I don't *want* to do this without you." She kept her gaze down as she rinsed off the cloth before continuing to work on his side. At the beginning of this journey, Gemma would have gladly parted ways with Brayden. But somewhere along the line, she found it impossible to imagine the future without him. A strange flutter danced in her stomach, and she bit her lip.

"I don't want to do this without you either." Brayden's voice came out almost as a whisper.

Gemma froze, and locked eyes with him. His face was much closer than she realized, and his warm brown eyes were like deep pools, calling her closer.

Andrea's loud voice startled Gemma out of her trance, and she jerked back, coming to her feet and stepping back.

"Are you two just going to sit around all evening?" Andrea demanded as she stomped over.

Brayden coughed as he tugged his shirt back down. He winced as he stood and sidestepped away from Gemma. "Are you two finally finished arguing?"

Serania remained tense, leaving a distance between herself and her sister. "Sorry, Brayden. I know how much you hate our fights." Her eyes widened as she saw the blood staining his side. "I didn't know you were hurt!"

Brayden held one hand up and covered his side with the other. "Gemma already took care of it. Let's just focus on bedding down for the night." With that, he quickly strode away.

"What's up with him?" Andrea asked as she shuffled behind him.

"He's just anxious about Kalami," Gemma mumbled, only half-bothered by her lie.

Theo climbed up to Gemma's shoulder and squeaked in her ear, but she hardly heard him as she stared at Brayden's back. She placed a hand over her heart, which refused to stop racing. *What just happened?*

They found a place far enough away from the trees to make camp for the night, which consisted of building a fire and moving any hard or sharp objects out of the way. Theo kept busy while he scrounged around for anything edible. Gemma hugged her bare arms to her chest to fight the chill in the air. She missed the warm blanket her dad had attached to her pack. The night would be long and uncomfortable.

Brayden grumbled about their need to keep the fire going through the night, but without winter supplies, they couldn't go without a source of warmth. He pressed Serania about Taicala, but she remained vague with her answers.

"There are some people in that area I'd rather avoid," Serania said in a tone that made it clear that she wouldn't discuss it any further.

Andrea snickered. "I'm looking forward to it. Tavid still owes me fifty fin."

The shadow over Brayden's face deepened, and Gemma knew he wouldn't let it go. She stepped in front of him and placed a hand on his arm. "If it was a risk to us, she'd say. She wants to protect me as much as you do."

Brayden's nostrils flared as he exhaled sharply. He leaned closer and dropped his voice low. "I know she's your sister, but I don't like how little we know about her history."

"She's just private. Not unlike someone else I know." Gemma gave him a pointed look.

Brayden rubbed a hand down his face. "My secrets don't endanger you. I don't know if the same can be said of your sisters' secrets."

Gemma nodded. She didn't blame him for his caution. Serania had imparted little about her life—a few fun stories, but nothing more. Gemma had so many things she wanted to know. How did they end up as bounty hunters? Who raised them? And the question that screamed loudest in Gemma's mind: what did they remember of their parents?

She sighed, capturing Brayden's gaze. "I want to know their story as much as you. But we can't force them to tell us. We'll have to hope

Serania will trust us enough to tell us some day. Until then, we have to trust them."

Brayden ground his teeth and looked away. Gemma used a finger to turn his face to hers. "I trust them, Brayden. If you can't trust them, trust me."

Silence spanned between them for a few breaths before he spoke. "I trust you."

Gemma leaned back, trying to hide the shock his words created. He'd never said that before. He'd shown his trust in actions, but the words had never escaped his lips. Her ridiculous heart picked up speed once again, and she pulled away. "It looks like Drea's getting dinner ready." She tucked a hair behind her ear. "I should go help. You know how she tends to burn things."

Brayden averted his gaze, drawing a hand across his chin, and nodded in response.

Gemma hurried away, desperate to put distance between them. She silently scolded her heart as she made her way toward her sister. *I don't know what your problem is, but you better cut it out.*

CHAPTER TWENTY-TWO

Kalami squatted at the edge of the woods, hidden behind dense branches. Smoke from the Keeper's campfire drifted lazily to the sky. Her prey was sitting out in the open with a blazing fire. Were they stupid or unafraid? Did they think she'd turn and run now that she was alone?

She pursed her lips, unsure of what to do. She couldn't help but remember the look of sheer peace that had washed over the Keeper's face just before the trees snatched her away. How could the Keeper find such peace when she knew she was about to die? Over the years, Kalami had witnessed hundreds of deaths, each preceded by fear, pleading, or even crying. Never had she seen such acceptance. There was something different about the young Keeper. Something that pulled on the thread of doubt that slowly grew in Kalami's mind.

The light greyed as the sun dipped behind a hill. Clouds blocked the moon; the night would be dark. It would be the perfect setting for an ambush, but somehow that didn't seem like the right course of action. Each time she thought up a plan to attack, her stomach soured. No. For now, she'd watch and wait. They were expecting an attack. She'd wait until they were unprepared. Years of planning had brought Kalami to this place. Another couple of nights wouldn't hurt anything.

Gemma forced a harsh breath through her nose and opened her eyes, giving up on sleep. When she had lain down, she was so tired she figured she'd be out the moment her head hit the ground, but her mind had buzzed and refused to let her relax. Hours had passed with only a few short spurts of slumber. She'd watched as Andrea returned from her rounds of the perimeter and threw a stone at Brayden to wake him. Brayden's eyes had been hard, and he had stared daggers at Andrea before stomping away. Gemma had gazed into the dark long after he disappeared. His words kept repeating in her mind over and over. *"I don't want to do this without you either...I trust you."*

Gemma closed her eyes and rubbed them with her thumb and middle finger, trying to remain still so she wouldn't wake Theo, who slept soundly, tucked in a ball against her side. *Why did Brayden's words affect me so much? Why am I even worried about it? Kalami could attack any time. More bandits are surely scouring the forest for unsuspecting souls, and Binthrell Lions could be stalking us for all I know.*

The hours passed, and Brayden returned. He knelt next to Serania and gently shook her arm. The two had a quick, whispered conversation. Serania's quiet laughter drifted to Gemma, and it bothered her. And *that* bothered her. *I should be happy they get along so well. What is wrong with me?* Finally, Serania walked away with a grace Gemma knew she'd never be able to attain. Brayden glanced Gemma's way as he laid down, and Gemma snapped her eyes closed, hoping he hadn't seen her staring. A while later, soft snores drifted from his direction, and Gemma stared at the dark cloud-filled sky.

After another hour of attempted sleep, Gemma slowly sat up, leaning her back against a large rock and tucking her knees to her chest. Her gaze remained fixed into the darkness, listening to the dying fire's quiet cracks and pops, and she let her mind wander. Her conversation with Gairwulf played through her mind, but it made as little sense now as it did before. She pulled her necklace from her pouch and held it up, rubbing her fingers so it spun around. It still amazed her that something so small and simple held so much power. Again, she wondered why, of all the people in Elefrisia, the jewel was entrusted to her. *I'm nothing more than a simple girl from a dying town.*

Another heavy sigh escaped her lungs as she returned the jewel to her pouch and rested her chin on her knees. She remained like that, staring unseeing at the glowing embers before her, until a soft rustling heralded Serania's return.

Serania smiled warmly as she approached. "You couldn't sleep?" She kept her voice to a whisper.

Gemma shook her head and matched her sister's volume. "Anything of note out there?"

"Not a thing. All is entirely quiet," Serania said. "Not even the wind stirs tonight. Almost as if the world itself holds its breath." Then, after a moment of silence, she laughed softly. "Sorry. That came out more ominous than I thought. I think my mind is a bit taxed."

Gemma smiled up at her sister. "Could you do me a favor? Would you take this spot? Theo's sleeping so soundly; I don't want to wake him."

"Of course."

The two swapped places, and Serania curled up next to Theo. Her eyes were already closed, but she spoke in a low voice. "Don't hesitate to wake me if you need anything..." The last word ended in a mumble as Serania's breathing deepened.

Gemma inhaled deeply, allowing the cold air to clear away her heavy thoughts. She stretched her neck from side to side and shook her arms and legs to get the blood flowing. A red glimmer flashed from the forest as she stretched her arms above her head. Her arms dropped, and she stared in that direction. Again, another glimmer, but it was faint enough she could have been imagining it.

She bit her lip as she gazed at her sleeping companions. *Should I wake them?*

The glimmer appeared again, but this time it was accompanied by a soft tug on Gemma's gut. She placed one hand on her stomach and the other over her mouth. She knew that feeling. A jewel was calling to her, and the only jewel that could be that close was Kalami's.

Gemma chewed on her lower lip as she looked from the red pulse to her companions. Brayden would insist on running. Andrea would be looking for a fight. Serania...well, she didn't know what Serania would do, but she wouldn't want Gemma in danger either way.

The tug pulled harder, beckoning Gemma to follow. She swallowed before shuffling forward. "Oh, this is a really, really dumb idea," she whispered as she inched slowly away from her companions.

With excruciatingly slow steps, she snuck across the clearing, wincing at every loud rustle she made. Her movement remained at a snail's pace as every small noise made her jump and wait and listen. Andrea's telling of the Binthrell Lions made every boulder and oddly shaped tree seem like a monster about to pounce. *Why didn't I bring Theo with me? At least with him, I'd have a warning if something was about to attack.* But she pressed on. She couldn't turn back now. An idea had been gnawing at Gemma's mind for a while now, and she had to see it through. It began after her second encounter with the Henathian. The way Kalami had hesitated, the regret in her eyes as she swung the sword toward Gemma's neck. There was something there, something that Gemma couldn't shake, and she had to take this risk.

Halfway to the jewel, she veered to the right, working her way in a wide circle. Yes, she was probably walking to her death, but if she could approach unnoticed, it might give her an extra minute to talk. She stopped mid-step. *If I feel Kalami's jewel, does it mean she feels mine? If she does, she'll know I'm coming. She shouldn't be able to sense me, since I'm not wearing mine, but she's found us more than once already.* Indecision held her in place for a few painful minutes. If she turned back now, she could still make it to the others and wake them before Kalami could catch up.

The memory of Kalami's sad eyes flashed through Gemma's mind. *"Despite what you might think, I'm not a monster."*

Gripping her hands into fists, Gemma took a steadying breath before inching forward again. She was the Keeper of the Cornerstone. If anyone could reach Kalami, she could. At least that's what she told herself as her heart started slamming in her chest. But she couldn't shake the memory of the red jewel and the sadness that had poured from it. *Does the jewel want to be saved? Or is it all Kalami's sadness crying out from it?*

The sky was beginning to grey by the time Gemma drew close to the source of the tug. The walk was long enough for her to convince herself just how stupid this was, but she had to try—she'd never forgive herself if she didn't. Her hands shook, and her breathing quickened to gasps. *Brayden's going to be so angry when I die. Serania will be heartbroken. Theo's going to be devastated, and Andrea...I think she'll be sad.*

As she rounded a large tree, she drew to a stop.

Kalami stood with shoulders pulled back, her sword in hand. She glanced over her shoulder before turning a sneer to Gemma. "What's your plan? Distract me so the others can sneak up on me from behind?"

So, she didn't see that it's just me. Gemma rubbed her palms on her hips. She could try bluffing Kalami. Tell her the others were waiting for her signal. But she was terrible at lying. Kalami would see the deceit written all over her face. "No one else is coming. It's just me." She inwardly cringed as her voice broke on the last word. *Way to sound brave, Gemma.*

Kalami pulled her head back an inch and narrowed her eyes. "Why would you come alone? Do you want to die?"

A voice in the back of Gemma's mind joined the pounding of her heart, begging for her to run. She'd tried talking to Kalami before, and it didn't do any good. So, what made her think this time would be any different? "I came to talk to you."

Kalami rolled her eyes. "I thought I made myself clear; you're not going to talk me into teaming up with you."

"Why are you so insistent I'd make things harder for you?" Gemma took a hesitant step forward. "Twice now, you've tried to kill me, and twice now, I've escaped. My friends killed all your men. We could be an asset to you, not a hindrance."

Kalami took a deep breath, letting it out slowly. "I'll admit; you've been more of a challenge than I expected. But it's still a huge risk if I let you live. You don't know Skotadi like I do. If he captures us, I'll be dead in a heartbeat. I'm not afraid to die, but I have to see him destroyed first."

Gemma held up her hands in a non-threatening gesture. "I get that. I do. But we're working toward the same goal. We both want to see Skotadi's reign end. We both want to find the jewels and be free of him. It's not just you and me. We have my friends. There's strength in numbers."

Kalami's sword lowered a fraction, and Gemma stepped closer, hoping she was finally getting through. "Think about it, Kalami. I have the Cornerstone. You have your jewel. If I've been so hard to capture already, just imagine how hard it will be with us working together."

Kalami scoffed. "Everything you've done with the jewel so far was nothing more than dumb luck. You don't even know how to wield it."

"Then you can teach me." Gemma edged closer. She was close enough now that Kalami could run her through if she wanted to. "Please, Kalami. You don't have to kill me, and you said yourself you don't want to. We *can* do this. I don't know why I was chosen to keep the Cornerstone jewel, but I know, deep down, you can see the benefit of us working together. No one else has to die here." A thought came to her, and she spoke before she could talk herself out of it. "I already know where to find the next jewel. If you join us, soon we'll have more than half the jewels." Brayden would be furious if he knew the risk Gemma was taking. Kalami was smart. She'd work out that Gemma's group already had another jewel. But there wasn't another obvious course of action. It was all out there now. One way or another, everything would change today. She would either gain a powerful ally or die. A warm peace melted into her soul at the thought. It was out of her hands; she only had to wait and see.

Kalami's arms relaxed, so her sword hung limply at her side. Her eyes bored into Gemma's as silence stretched between them. Slowly she sheathed her sword. Her hands went to her hips, dropped, then returned. Gemma could plainly see the struggle playing across Kalami's face. Finally, Kalami balled her fist and forced a harsh breath out of her nose. "I can't believe I'm saying this...but fine. Against my better judgment, I'll work with you." She took a step, closing the distance between them, and leaned down so her face was directly in front of Gemma's. "But if it looks like we're going to be caught, I will kill you without a second thought."

Prickling cold ran up and down Gemma's spine, but she forced her shoulders back and held Kalami's gaze. "I wouldn't expect anything else. I'm glad you chose to join us."

Kalami pulled back and crossed her arms. "I'm sure I'm going to regret this." She waved a hand in the direction of the clearing. "What about your companions? I have a feeling the small one isn't going to be too fond of this arrangement."

A long sigh escaped Gemma's lungs. "She won't be, but I'll talk to her." For some reason, trying to convince Andrea sounded ten times harder than convincing Kalami.

Kalami eyed Gemma sideways. "You certainly do love to talk. Though I'm not convinced the midget will listen."

Gemma chewed on her bottom lip. She couldn't argue with that.

"You didn't think this through, did you?"

Gemma's shoulders slumped, and she tossed her hands up, then let them fall and slap against her legs. "I'm figuring everything out as I go. You wouldn't happen to have any suggestions, would you?"

Kalami's face hardened, and her shoulders tensed. "You're already looking a lot like dead weight."

Gemma held up a hand. "Just wait here while I talk to the others." She strode ahead before Kalami could answer. She wasn't worried about Serania, Theo, or Brayden. They would hear her out. Brayden would be hesitant. He didn't trust new people, but he trusted Gemma. Andrea would be nearly impossible to convince. Gemma breathed a small prayer for help to the Creator as she closed the distance to the others.

Everyone was awake and milling about. Theo perched on Brayden's shoulder and stared in Gemma's direction, having already spotted her. She was a few paces away when Andrea stiffened, then, in a blurring movement, threw a knife past Gemma's face, close enough to move her hair as it went by. Gemma gasped as she turned to see what had caused Andrea's attack. Kalami caught the knife and flipped it in her hand, preparing to throw it back.

Gemma groaned. "I told you to stay back!"

Kalami's eyes lit with anger. "I don't take orders from you."

Gemma whipped around. Andrea already held another throwing knife. Serania stood, bow at the ready, and Brayden held his sword in front of him.

Gemma threw her hands up. "Wait! Stop! She's not here to hurt us!"

"Gemma, get out of the way!" Andrea shouted.

"No, Drea! Listen! She's on our side now."

Andrea scowled and kept her eyes fixed on Kalami. "I don't know what trick you're playing, but you won't catch the next one so easily."

Kalami's voice held a hint of humor as she responded. "You think you can throw yours faster than I throw mine? I'd love to see you try."

Brayden slowly edged closer to Gemma. "Drea, stand down. You can't risk hitting Gemma."

"I won't hit her." Andrea lowered her chin. "But you might want to step aside, sis, just in case."

Gemma planted her feet. "Please, Drea. You have to listen to me. She just wants Skotadi dead. We need her."

Andrea relaxed her arm as her brows furrowed. She studied Gemma's face, for the first time looking uncertain.

Gemma lowered her hands, turning to Kalami, who rolled her eyes and tucked the knife away.

"Okay," Gemma said as she turned back to Andrea. "Maybe now we can have an actual co—"

The rest of her sentence died on her lips as Andrea grinned. Her arm blurred as she threw the second knife. Gemma shouted and threw herself in the path of the blade. She cried out as a searing pain sliced through her shoulder, throwing her hard to the ground. Her hand shot up and grasped the knife hilt protruding from her shoulder.

Brayden skidded to her side. "Gemma! What were you thinking?"

"I wasn't thinking; I just reacted," she gasped between gritted teeth.

Theo scurried around Gemma's head, wringing his forefeet as he assessed the damage.

Steel against steel rang through the air as Andrea attacked Kalami while Serania shouted at her sister to stop.

Gemma clutched at her shoulder and moaned as warm blood seeped through her fingers. "Brayden, you have to stop them. We need to fight together, not against each other."

Brayden's jaw clenched, but he nodded and stood. "Serania! Come help Gemma." With that, he ran toward the fight.

Serania dropped down next to Gemma, her face tight as her gaze flitted between the fight and her wounded sister. "I can't believe you did that. She probably would've just caught the knife like she did the first one." Her hands shook as she helped Gemma stand.

The world around Gemma tilted, and she sagged against Serania's side as they stumbled toward the smoldering firepit. "I know. It was stupid." She pinched her eyes shut and groaned as Serania lowered her to the ground, propping her up against a large boulder.

"You could have gotten yourself killed." Serania sniffed as tears streamed from her eyes. She searched through her small bag. "I don't have any of the items I need to help you! I don't have my suture kit. My bottle of Sifa oil was in my other bag. If she hit the artery—"

Gemma grabbed Serania's hand and held her still. "It'll be okay. You can figure it out."

Serania nodded as she swiped the tears from her eyes. "Right. We'll need to cauterize the wound after we take out the knife. Just hang on." She rushed to the firepit and threw kindling onto the embers.

Shouts and cursing drew Gemma's attention. Brayden stood between Kalami and Andrea, holding his arms out between them. Both women bled from multiple cuts, and Kalami snarled as she swiped blood from her blade before shoving it back into its sheath. Andrea's face remained stony as she gripped her short swords in front of her. Gemma couldn't hear what they were saying, but Brayden appeared to be talking Andrea down. Soon Andrea cleaned her blades, shoved them into their sheaths, and crossed her arms as she stared at Kalami.

Theo squeaked and nudged his head under Gemma's good hand. She gave him a shaky smile. "I'll be okay. I'm in good hands."

He whimpered and pressed his head into her stomach.

"I know." She rubbed his neck with her thumb, frowning as her blood smeared across his soft, white fur. "I wanted to bring you with me, but you were sleeping so soundly."

He crossed his forefeet and growled.

Gemma chuckled, but it ended in a grimace as the movement sent burning pain slicing through her shoulder. "I promise I'll take you with me the next time I go to recruit an enemy."

He rolled his eyes, but his face softened as Gemma clenched her teeth and groaned. With a soft squeak, he curled up on her lap and waited.

A small fire crackled to life as Brayden and the others made their way toward it. Andrea marched; every muscle held tight. Kalami sauntered, slipping once again back into the self-confident warrior. She sat nearby on a small boulder and crossed one leg over the other, her face a perfect picture of calm.

At least that's done for now. Gemma pursed her lips. The new alliance was as fragile as a spiderweb, but she hoped the worst part was over.

Brayden planted himself next to Gemma. "Give me a little warning the next time you're going to try and kill yourself."

Gemma laughed, regretting it immediately. "Don't make me laugh. It hurts."

Brayden smiled a tight smile before it fell. He called over his shoulder. "Serania. How can I help?"

"Toss me a knife. I need to get one heating up."

Andrea beat Brayden to it, jogging over and handing her sister what she needed. She caught Gemma's eye and opened her mouth to speak but closed it and shook her head, lowering her eyes to the ground before plopping to her seat and pulling her knees to her chest.

"Brayden," Serania called over her shoulder. "You need to cut Gemma's clothes away from the wound. When we pull the knife free, I need to press the hot knife against it right away. We don't want to be fumbling around her clothes."

Brayden nodded and worked as cautiously as he could, ripping the sleeve of Gemma's shirt and pulling it up and away from the knife. He tied the torn ends close to Gemma's neck so her shirt would stay in place. "Ready," he called to Serania.

"Okay," Serania replied. "When I get over there, pull the knife out as straight as you can, then move out of the way."

Brayden pressed a hand against Gemma's cheek, turning her face to his. "Brace yourself."

Gemma breathed in quick, short gasps as she tensed for the awful process ahead.

Theo pushed harder against Gemma's stomach, his tiny whimpers pulling at Gemma's heart.

Serania strode their way. Gemma cried out as Brayden swiftly pulled the knife from her shoulder. Her cry turned into an all-out scream through her teeth as Serania pressed the hot knife against the wound. The pain of the hot knife searing into her flesh trumped the memory of her broken leg. The smell of burnt flesh made Gemma's stomach roil before the edges of her world dimmed. She fought to remain awake, but soon her head fell limp as darkness took her.

Brayden helped Serania clean around the wound, then ripped a portion of his shirt to tie around it. Gemma moaned in her sleep but didn't wake.

"She's going to be the death of me." Brayden inwardly cringed at the instability of his voice.

Serania sniffled, fighting back tears. "She certainly has a knack for getting hurt." Her hands continued to tremble as she checked the impromptu bandage.

Brayden took her hands, steadying them with his own. "She's tough. She'll make it through this."

Serania gave his hands a gentle squeeze before letting go. "I know she's tough, but I'm worried about infection. Or what if there's more damage on the inside than we know? She could be bleeding internally and without equipment, I can't do anything about it." She gently stroked Gemma's forehead, moving stray hairs away from her face. "I can't lose her, Brayden. Not again."

Brayden gave Serania a quick sideways hug. "You won't." He didn't know who he was reassuring more, Serania or himself.

"I should go talk to Drea." Serania took a shuddering breath as she stood. She stared down at Gemma for a moment before pulling away.

Brayden watched her go. He understood Serania's fear; he was no stranger to loss. And to have someone returned, only to lose them again, was almost worse than losing them in the first place. He turned his attention to Kalami and sighed. The Henathian sat on her boulder, dabbing at a cut on her arm, her face expressionless. He clenched his teeth. He didn't know how in Elefrisia Gemma managed to win her over. He shook his head and whispered to Gemma. "You truly are one of a kind. No one else would've gone near the Henathian, let alone manage to recruit her." He stroked Theo's head. "Keep an eye on her."

Theo solemnly nodded as Brayden stood and made his way to Kalami. The Henathian's gaze flicked up once, but she gave no other reaction. Brayden stopped in front of her, crossed his arms, and waited.

She continued to sop up her blood before huffing out a sigh and turning her face to his. "What? You here to threaten me? Tell me I better stay in line, or else I'm dead?"

Brayden fought the sudden rage that boiled inside him, begging to be released. He balled his fists, then forcefully relaxed his hands as he exhaled. "No. Don't get me wrong. I don't trust you as far as I can throw you...but I trust her." He nodded his head in Gemma's direction. "I want to know what your goal is. Why did you decide to join us?"

Kalami's eyes skittered to Gemma and then back to Brayden. "She made the point that we both want the same thing; Skotadi's death. She has the Cornerstone. With some training, she'll be a powerful ally. Joining you is a means to an end." She scowled as she glanced in Andrea's direction. "Though I make no promises if the midget attacks me again." Dry rubbing her hands together, she continued. "The Keeper said she knows where to find the next jewel?"

Brayden hid his jolt of surprise. It was one thing to have Kalami join them—another thing entirely to trust her with that much information. "Her name is Gemma. As for the next jewel...we're working on it. We haven't hammered out all the details."

Kalami arched a brow. "Meaning you don't have a clue what you're doing."

"Meaning you'll know when we tell you." He rubbed his chin, his fingers scratching against the rough stubble. Yet another reminder just how much his structured life was turned on end.

Gemma moaned loudly behind him. Her face pinched as she grabbed at her shoulder while Theo squeaked in protest on her lap.

"Just stay within sight for now," Brayden told Kalami, ignoring her exaggerated eye-roll as he hurried to Gemma. "Hey, hey. No. Don't mess with that." He clutched her hand in one of his and cupped her face with the other. "Look at me, Gemma." When her eyes snapped to his, he smiled. "You're okay. You need to rest."

She blinked a long, slow blink. "Sorry. It's just, the inside is throbbing, and the outside is burning."

"I know." He tucked some hair behind her ear. "You really did a number on yourself this time."

Her eyes searched around. "Where are Kalami and Andrea? I should—"

Brayden moved aside and pointed. "They're both fine, see."

She relaxed, resting her head back. Theo climbed up to her good shoulder and rubbed his head against her neck. She gave him a strained smile and stroked him as she spoke to Brayden. "This went a lot better in my head."

Brayden laughed. "I'm sure it did."

Gemma's face scrunched, and she moaned. "I need something to distract me from this."

He nodded, understanding all too well how much pain she'd endure over the next couple of weeks. "Serania, Drea, we need you over here!" When Andrea hung back, Brayden shouted, putting more authority into his voice. "Both of you!" He hesitated, then turned to Kalami. Even though he didn't like it, Kalami was a part of this now. She deserved to hear what they had to discuss. "You too."

Kalami huffed before strolling over.

Serania joined them, Andrea shuffling behind her with her eyes to the ground.

"All right," he said as he aligned his thoughts. "Serania. You know where we have to go to find the next jewel. How far is it?"

"Taicala's on the west coast. About a week's travel north of Farensvir," she answered.

Brayden grimaced. "I was afraid of that."

Gemma looked between Serania and Brayden. "What? Why is that bad?"

Brayden rubbed the back of his neck. "In case you've forgotten, we're on the east side of the Cattaway. The west coast must be close to three thousand miles from here. And we'll have to cross the Cattaway. There aren't many safe crossings, and most of the bridges were destroyed in the uprising. Not to mention, Skotadi will most likely have the safe crossings and bridges watched."

"Add to that the months it will take us to get there," Serania added. "With winter coming, it will take us even longer. If we could find some horses, we could cut the time in half, but even if we find horses for sale, none of us can afford them. On foot, I wouldn't be surprised if it takes us the entire winter to get there."

"And we still have to resupply." Brayden looked at the sky as the weight of it all felt like the sky itself pressed down on his shoulders. They had to travel halfway across Elefrisia while avoiding Skotadi's followers and battling the ravages of winter. All that with the tension of the Henathian thrown into the mix. *This is impossible. And it's just the first jewel. We still have to find three more.*

Andrea knelt next to Gemma and kept her gaze on the ground as she spoke in a timid voice that sounded nothing like her. "I'm sorry, Gemma. I should have trusted you. I'll listen from here on out."

Brayden had to bite his tongue to hold back his retort. *The day Drea finally starts listening is the day I'll be crowned king.*

Gemma gave her sister a sweet smile. "It's all good, Drea. I love you no matter what."

Andrea's eyes snapped up and widened before she relaxed her face and gave a half-smile. "Love you too, sis."

Brayden chuckled to himself. *Leave it to Gemma to forgive without a thought.* He leaned back on his heels and pondered the long journey ahead. They weren't off to a great start. In just over a month, he and Gemma had nearly died several times. They had narrowly stayed ahead of the enemy and had a knack for finding extra trouble along the way. *It'll take a miracle for all of us to make it through this alive. For that matter, it'll take a miracle for us to succeed at all.* He caught Gemma's eye; she lifted her chin and smiled like she knew what he was thinking and wanted to encourage him. Brayden slowly shook his head. *Yes, this will be the most challenging journey of my life, but at least I can face it with a friend by my side.*

Gairwulf sipped water from a cup while he watched the clouds drift lazily across the sky. He breathed in the cool air and smiled as a ray of sun broke from behind a cloud and warmed his face. *This is a beautiful day you have given me. You bless this old man far more than he deserves.*

A tiny squeak announced the arrival of one of Gairwulf's longtime friends. He smiled broadly as he held out a hand. "Ah, Waythenell. It has been a while, my friend. What brings you to me on this glorious day?"

The Scruff's black fur warmed Gairwulf's hand as he stroked it. A light, grey mask of fur surrounded ice-blue eyes that held a look of solemnity as he squeaked in answer.

Gairwulf's smile slowly flattened into a grim line. "The Keeper of Südaila has joined with the Keeper of the Cornerstone." He closed his eyes and let out a long, slow breath. "So, it begins."

EPILOGUE

Fovos flexed his hands as he paced back and forth, staring into the distance. Trees as wide as a house stood sentry across the rolling hills. Massive boulders—some large enough to be a small cliff—were strewn about haphazardly. The sun glinted through the trees, just above the horizon. Already the temperature of the air dropped like the sun had recalled all its warmth, snatching it away. He rolled his shoulders as he stretched his neck. It didn't come as a surprise that he'd been demoted to errand boy. He couldn't expect much more after his many failures. But this was an errand he was loath to do.

Even from here, the sharp clicks of the creatures talking to each other reached his ears, and the foreign presence knocked unending against his mind. Flashes of movement could be seen as the giant, black and green creatures skittered to and fro.

Not for the first time, Fovos entertained the idea of fleeing. The sea wasn't far, and he had enough coin to buy his way onto a ship. He could find an island and live out his days in peace. He sucked his teeth and spat to the side. Peace. The word alone was enough to make his skin crawl. No. He was built for battle, for constant movement.

Instead, he could sail across the waters. There were rumors of strange people claiming to be from a land across the vast ocean, though he didn't waste much thought on rumors. Even if he chose to leave, he would never be free of Skotadi. Eventually, even Fovos' strong mind would wear down, and Skotadi would destroy him. Most likely in the most painful way possible.

No. There was no retreat. A war was brewing, and he had to ensure he stayed on the winning side. If the tides should turn against Skotadi...well, his loyalties were easily swayed. But it would take an army—the size of which he'd never seen—to take down Skotadi and his followers.

A giant face with bulging beady eyes peeked out from behind a boulder, clicking loudly as it watched Fovos in the hope of a meal.

Fovos lowered his chin, drew his shoulders back, and spoke into the dusk. "Come, you foul creatures. Your lord summons you."

ACKNOWLEDGMENTS

First, I would like to give a huge shout-out to my amazing family. I'm beyond blessed to be a Saunders.

Thanks to the best sisters in the world, Sarah Hummer, and Ashley Grove. You both have been on this wild ride for over a decade now. You were the first ones to hear the inception of this story, and you've stuck with me ever since. You've seen this story grow from a goofy idea to a fully formed world, and you never made it feel impossible. Your reassurances kept me going when I felt like quitting and pulled me out of so many doubts.

Joshua and Caleb Saunders, you guys are the kind of brothers everyone wishes they had. Thank you for listening through all my wild thoughts. Thank you Caleb for stoking the fire for me to dream big.

Natasha Nicole, I cannot stress enough just how amazing you are! You not only put up with all my crazy requests, but you set aside time from your own dreams to help me with mine. You are my fellow dreamer, and I'm so thankful to have you.

Thank you, Terry Rickards, for wading through a marsh of grammatical mistakes. I know I don't make it easy on you.

A big ole thanks to my critique group, the Drossburners. Ya'll are amazing! You helped grind away all the unnecessary gunk.

And last, but not even close to least, thank you to my proofreader, Kathleen Phillips-Hellman—your notes polished this story to a beautiful shine. And a huge thanks to my early readers. Your excitement for the story gave me the oomph needed to press across the finish line.

ABOUT THE AUTHOR

J. A. Saunders grew up homeschooled, and the staff kid of full-time summer camp workers. Instead of sports and school lockers, her childhood consisted of horseback riding, rock wall climbing, ziplining, archery, and riflery. A love of reading, storytelling, travel, and adventure was set ablaze from a young age. She has lived in and visited multiple places, including Hawaii, China, and Haiti. Her current home is in Tennessee with her faithful, fluffy Husky, Chloe who has traveled across the waters with J. A. on more than one occasion.

THE SPARK IGNITES IN

BOOK TWO *of the* GEMMA CHRONICLES

Coming Soon!